THE LIZARD'S BITE

David Hewson was born in Yorkshire in 1953. He was a journalist from the age of seventeen working most recently for the *Sunday Times*. He has also written several novels, as well as a number of travel books. Following *A Season for the Dead*, *The Villa of Mysteries* and *The Sacred Cut*, *The Lizard's Bite* is the fourth in his Italian crime series featuring Detective Nic Costa. The author lives in Kent.

Also by David Hewson

A SEASON FOR THE DEAD

THE VILLA OF MYSTERIES

THE SACRED CUT

DAVID
HEWSON

THE LIZARD'S BITE

MACMILLAN

First published 2006 by Macmillan
an imprint of Pan Macmillan Ltd
Pan Macmillan, 20 New Wharf Road, London N1 9RR
Basingstoke and Oxford
Associated companies throughout the world
www.panmacmillan.com

ISBN-13: 978-1-4050-5514-7
ISBN-10: 1-4050-5514-6

1 3 5 7 9 8 6 4 2

A CIP catalogue record for this book is available from
the British Library.

Typeset by Intype London Ltd
Printed and bound in Great Britain by
Mackays of Chatham plc, Chatham, Kent

THE LIZARD'S BITE

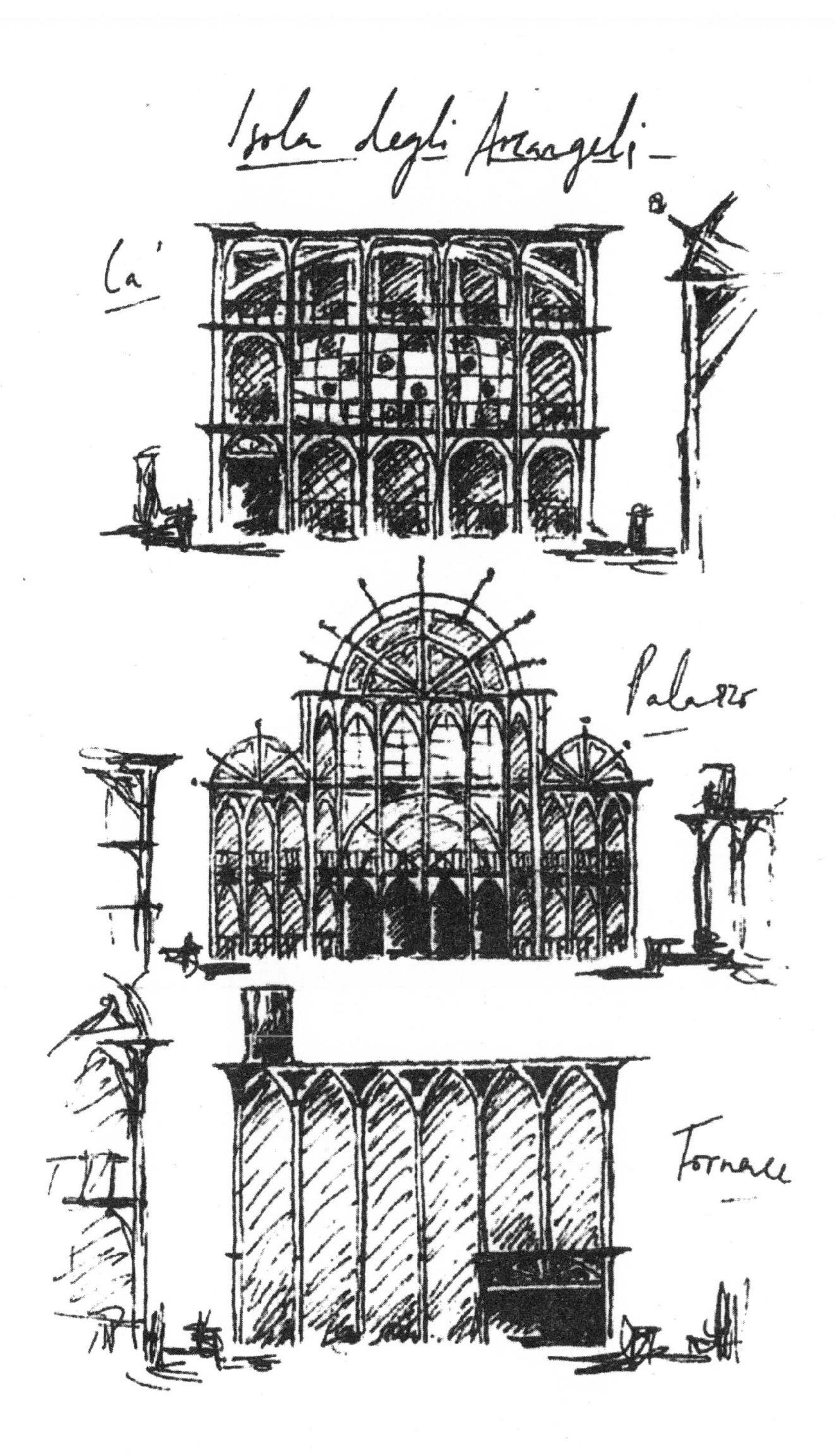
Isola degli Arcangeli
Ca'
Palazzo
Fornace

Part 1

THE INFERNO

1

In the shifting darkness of the vessel's bowels, low over the undulating black water, the dog waited, trembling. The man, the much-loved man, his master, worked around him, puzzled by the creature's fear, clucking sounds of consolation, not noticing events on the quayside above. Men possessed, the animal understood, a weaker, coarser form of consciousness. Sometimes it seemed they scarcely noticed the presence of blood at all . . .

For a moment the black breath of the sirocco eased. The Isola degli Arcangeli, small, solitary, shining in the brief glimpse of moonlight, was still. Then the night wind returned, more fierce and relentless than before. The fragile frame of the grandiose palazzo shook beneath the onslaught. Shards of brittle glass tumbled from shutters half-finished by the restoration men only the day before. Close by, clouds of sandy dust raked the golden stone of the Arcangeli's mansion, hammering at the ornate windows of the exaggerated first-floor viewpoint arching out over the lagoon. On the other side of the palazzo in the foundry, once the mother lode of the clan's fortunes, the blast chased down the single-funnel chimney, emerging to find every last corner, probing for some weakness, like a giant from the world beyond breathing into a fragile paper bag, rattling the high rickety doors, bending the misshapen glass roof with its brittle span of supporting ancient timbers.

The summer gale from the Sahara had been over the city for three days, rarely pausing in its relentless progress north. Dry choking dust lurked in its belly, working its way into the crevices of the *fornace*, disturbing the precious processes working inside, looking for something clean and bright and perfect to despoil. The daily yield of good glass, which had never been on target of late, was as low as it had ever been. Disturbance was everywhere. Dust devils swirled over the canals and chased each other in and out of the island's constricted alleys. Beyond Murano, across the lagoon, in Venice proper, churning black water lapped insistently over the stonework at the edge of the Piazza San Marco.

The August storm had taken away the month's familiar enervating humid heat and put something alien in its place. Even now, at just after two in the morning, under the frank gaze of a full moon stained rust-coloured by the storm, the lagoon seemed breathless, starved of oxygen. Beyond the Isola degli Arcangeli lay an entire city choking on the sirocco's sand-filled wheezings. He listened to the storm's anger as it threw itself upon the fragile shell of the foundry. The wind's sighs seemed to vibrate to the rhythm of the deep, smoky gasps of the hulking primitive furnace in front of him.

Half loved, half hated, the leviathan stood at the heart of the solitary room, roaring as the wind's blasts fought their way down the crumbling brick chimney and raked their scorching breath across the embers. He didn't need to look at the temperature gauge to see the fire was too intense. The hemisphere of the interior was approaching a white, incandescent heat too painfully bright to look at. In its maw the costly crock of nascent slow-mix glass – ground *cogoli* pebbles from Istria and the soda ash of burnt seaweed, just what a Murano maestro would have demanded five hundred years before – was churning uncertainly, part of a mystery he directed but never quite controlled.

An hour earlier nothing had been out of the ordinary. Then, when he'd gone back to the empty office for a while and sunk a couple of glasses of grappa, trying to make the night go more quickly, she'd called, demanding he examine the fiery beast before his time, though her work here was done. She had given no reason for the summons to the *fornace*. And she wasn't there when he arrived either, after he'd splashed his face half clean in the office washroom, gargled some water around his mouth to disguise the stink of alcohol. He'd found one of the double doors ajar, walked in, closed it behind him and met nothing.

He shook his head, wishing the effects of the drink would disappear. The furnace was always awkward; the archaic use of both wood and gas, part of the Arcangeli's secret process, made sure of that. But nothing now made sense. As he watched, the grunting, groaning monster roared again beneath the shifting bulk of the fenestrated roof then exhaled in concert with the wind.

Uriel.

One – or both – seemed to whisper his name, taunting him. His father had called him that for a reason. The Arcangeli were always different even when, before his father's time, they were just a bunch of bourgeois boat builders maintaining the last worthwhile *squero* in Chioggia. Growing up as a child in Murano, Uriel had been aware of the distance between the Arcangeli and their peers, always. You never met a Bracci or a Bullo who had to bear such a burden. They'd have been teased, without mercy, every single day in the plain, hard school by the church. Uriel Arcangelo was never mocked. Never befriended either, not even when he took one of them for a wife.

Maybe, the grappa said, laughing at the back of his head, they knew what the name meant.

Fire of God. Angel of terror.

It was just another of his father's cruel little jokes, to make every one of his four children an angel twice over each with their set role. Michele to succeed him as *capo*, 'like God'. Gabriele to be the strong man by the furnace, the maestro with the pipe, seeing that the clan prospered. Or not. Raffaela to intercede when matters went too far, to bring a woman's sense to their deliberations, to heal. And Uriel. The hardest, the loneliest of vocations. Uriel the magician, the alchemist, the family's *omo de note*, the Venetians' whispered, almost fearful name for a man of the night, keeper of the secrets, which had been passed on from the small black book that used to live in his father Angelo's jacket pocket, kept from the curious gaze of outsiders.

Uriel closed his eyes, felt the heat of the furnace travel the room and scorch his skin and recalled those last days with Angelo fading towards death in the master bedroom of the mansion next to the damned palazzo – the money pit that had consumed them over the years. The image of that final night would never leave him: how the old man had ordered the rest of them out, made him – little more than a boy just out of his teens – read the pocket book, study its ancient recipes, commit those secrets to memory. Uriel had obeyed, as always. So well that Angelo Arcangelo had called a servant and had the book burned in front of their eyes, until it was just ash in an ancient pisspot. His father had laughed, not kindly either, for this was a test. The Arcangeli would be tested, always.

By midnight, his family at his side, Angelo Arcangelo was dead, a pale, stiff cadaver on the white sheets of the antique four-poster where each of the children had been conceived. In Uriel's head the scene was as real, as cruelly vivid now, thirty years later, as it had been that night. The recipes lay secure in his head still, living shifting potions of arsenic and lead, antimony and feldspar, each betokening a shape or a colour that would form within the substance of the raw crude *fritta* growing in the belly of the furnace and metamorphose into something beautiful when the next magician, Gabriele the maestro, with his steely arms, his bellows for lungs, his pincers and his pipe, worked the sinuous, writhing form in the morning. This was how the Arcangeli tried to put food on the table, not by building *bragozzi* barques for Chioggia fishing clans. Magic made them money, kept them alive. But magic was a harsh and temperamental mistress, demanding, sometimes reluctant to perform. Now more than ever.

Angelo had passed on those secrets with a cunning, certain deliberation. The memory of his father's skull-like face in those last moments – grinning, knowing – stayed with Uriel always, taunting, awaiting the time when the son would fail, as every *omo de note* did because theirs was an imprecise art, one which could be destroyed by an extra milligram of soda or a slight shift in the searing 1400-degree heat of flaming wood and gas. Even so Uriel had memorized the formulae, repeating them constantly, burning them into his synapses, swearing that a day would come when he would find the courage to defeat the demon of his father's last admonition: 'Never write them down, or the foreigners will steal from you.' He was still waiting. Even now, just the thought of doing so, long after his father had turned to dust, made him sweat all the more heavily beneath the tan furnace apron he wore over an old, tattered cotton suit.

That time *would* come. But until it did the litany of recipes would race through his head automatically, unbidden, unwanted: when he woke up, head throbbing from drink, in the blazing light of their apartment in the mansion; on those rare occasions he wrestled with Bella on the old, creaky brass bed, trying to find some other kind of secret in her hot, taut body, wondering why this was now the only way they could converse.

'Bella,' he murmured to himself, and was shocked how aged and dry his own voice sounded. Uriel Arcangelo was forty-nine. A lifetime of working nights in the furnace, the cursed, beloved furnace, feeling the fire break the veins of his hardening cheeks, had given him the complexion and the dull, depressed outlook of an old man.

'What is this?' he yelled angrily to no one, hearing only the furnace's animal roar in return.

He understood this fiery beast better than any man. He'd grown up with it, fought for hours to control its tantrums and its sulks. He knew its many moods: none better than those long, torpid hours in which it refused to come to temperature. It had never overheated before. The fabric of decrepit iron and brick was too insubstantial, leaked out too much expensive energy through its cracked pores.

A thought entered Uriel Arcangelo's head. He'd been burned many times in the furnace. Once he had nearly lost an eye. His hearing was bad, his sense of smell ruined by another close call. But there'd never been a blaze, a real blaze, the kind that had put rival furnaces out of business from time to time. That meant the Arcangeli were lax when it came to precautions. They'd never followed the fire department's orders to the letter. It was always cheaper to send round the bribe than carry out the work.

The hose was outside, attached to the exterior wall of the foundry, a curling snake of dusty pipe. There wasn't even so much as an extinguisher close by.

Uriel coughed. There was smoke in the miasma issuing from the furnace, a foreign smell too. Not thinking, doing this because it was, simply, what came naturally, he took out the flask of grappa clumsily and knocked back a swig, aware that a dribble of the harsh liquid had spilled down his front, staining the bib of his brown apron.

She'd know. She'd sniff and she'd look at him, that Bracci look, the cruel grimace of hatred and despair that spoiled her features so often these days.

A noise emerged from the heart of the furnace. It was a sound he'd never heard before, not from gas or wood or glass. A soft, organic explosion sent a shower of sparks flying out of structure's angry, orange mouth. The lights danced in dusty reflections across the ceiling. The sirocco roared and shook the foundry as if it were a dried seed head shaking in the wind.

Uriel Arcangelo took out his set of keys, walked back to the door and placed one in the old mortise, just in case he had to make a quick exit.

The furnace needed help. Perhaps it was more than one man could manage. If that were the case, he had, at least, a swift route of escape, out to the quay and the house beyond the palazzo, where the rest of them now slept, unaware of this strange event shaping just a few metres away on their private island.

2

They called Piero Scacchi the *garzone de note*, but in truth he was no boy at all. Scacchi was forty-three, a hulk of a man with the build and demeanour of the peasant farmer he was during the day, out on the low, green pastures of Sant' Erasmo, the farming island of the lagoon that provided Venice with fresh vegetables throughout the year. His hard-won crops of artichokes, Treviso radicchio, and bright red bunches of *peperoncini* were insufficient to keep even a single man alive these days. So, some months before, reluctantly accepting there was no alternative, he had approached the Arcangeli, spoken to the boss of the clan, Michele, and offered his labour at a rate he knew would be hard to refuse.

It was common knowledge the Arcangeli were short of money. The pittance they bargained him down to was insignificant, even paid in cash to circumvent the taxmen. It was simple work, with flexible hours: picking up wood and ash from farmers and small suppliers dotted around the lagoon, transporting it to the family's private island that hung off the southern edge of Murano like a tear about to fall. It entailed a little shifting, a little cleaning, and the occasional illegal disposal of rubbish. The work kept Scacchi on the water, a place both he and his dog liked, far away from Venice with its dark alleys and darker human beings. He'd grown up in the lagoon, on the solitary farm his mother had bequeathed him a decade before. When Scacchi was there, or in his boat, he felt he was home, safe from the city and its dangers.

Like him, the Arcangeli were different, but this bond never seemed to bring them closer. The family was insular, silent, in a way which Scacchi found sad and, at times, almost sinister. In spite of his solitary life, or, perhaps, because of it, he was a talkative man, outgoing, fond of a drink and a joke with his peers. He never sailed home from the early morning market trips to the Rialto entirely sober. Piero Scacchi knew how to be sociable when it suited him. These talents were entirely wasted once the *Sophia* navigated its way beneath the narrow iron bridge that linked the private island the clan called the Isola degli Arcangeli – an artificial name he found pretentious – and moored at the small jetty between the palazzo and the house, Ca' degli Arcangeli, where they lived, rattling around like pebbles in its echoing, dusty corridors.

The family's story was well known. They'd come from Chioggia at the insistence of their late father, taken over the glass business, tried to turn back the clock and persuade a dubious world that it was worth paying double – or more – for a mix of traditional and experimental work that seemed out of place alongside the rest of Murano's predictable gaudy offerings. The early years of novelty and success, under Angelo Arcangelo, were long past. Rumour had it the family would go bankrupt soon or be bought out by someone with half a business brain. Then Piero Scacchi would be looking for other work on the side again. Unless there was a sudden rise in the market price of *peperoncini*. Or some other kind of miracle.

He pulled his collar tighter around his neck to keep out the dusty wind then groaned at the sight of the dog. It was lying flat to the planks of the motor launch, face buried beneath its soft, long black ears, quivering.

'Don't look so miserable. We'll be home soon.'

The dog hated the foundry. Scacchi had called the animal Xerxes because it was the master of the lone and desolate places they hunted together. The stink of the furnace, the smoke, the roar of the flames above . . . everything seemed designed to instil foreboding into its keen, incisive black head. Out on the island, or in the marshland of the lagoon, hunting for ducks downed by Scacchi's ever-accurate shotgun, the dog was in its element, fearlessly launching itself into chill brown sludge to retrieve the still-warm body of some wildfowl lost to view in the marram grass and tamarisk trees of the littoral islets. Here it cowered constantly. Scacchi would have left it at the farm if only the dog would have allowed it. Just the sound of the boat's asthmatic engine was enough to send it into raptures. Animals had little understanding of consequences. For Xerxes, every action was a prelude to possible delight, whatever past experience dictated to the contrary. Scacchi envied the spaniel that.

'Xerxes . . .' he said, then heard a sound, a strange, febrile hissing, followed by what appeared to be a human cry, and found, for a brief moment, he shared the creature's fears.

He turned to look at the iron footbridge, one of Angelo Arcangelo's most profligate follies, a grand design in miniature, crossing no more than thirty metres of water using a single pier, reached on each side by identical, ornate cantilevers. The short central span was built artificially high on the southern side, close to the lighthouse by the vaporetto stop and the jetty where Scacchi was moored. Here it was surmounted by a skeletal extended angel with rusting upright wings a good five metres high, the entire sculpture constructed of wrought iron. It looked like a tortured spirit trapped in metal. Electric fairy lights outlined the figure. Its right arm was extended and held a torch which stabbed high into the air, a real gas flame burning vividly at its head, fed constantly from the foundry's own methane system, day in, day out, in memory of the old man.

Piero Scacchi hated the thing as much as the dog did.

He listened again. There'd been a human sound floating down from the island. Now it was gone. All he could hear was the iron angel wheezing over the blast of the wind, choking and popping as the fiery torch flared erratically.

He knew nothing about gas. He was the night boy, the lackey, someone who carried and cleaned, tapped gauges to make sure they weren't hitting the red and called on Uriel, poor, sad Uriel, locked in his office with a grappa bottle for the night, should something appear wrong. Piero Scacchi understood little about the various contraptions inside the foundry, only what he'd seen from watching Uriel work them, flying at the wheels and switches without a word, throwing kindling into the *fornace*, adjusting the all-important fires to his will.

But Scacchi was wise enough to understand when something was wrong. The wind could, perhaps, extinguish the flame of the angel's stupid torch, sending raw inflammable gas out into the Murano night. Except that the problem seemed to be a lack of gas, not an excess of it. As he watched, wondering, the torch died suddenly, expiring into itself, with a sudden, explosive blowback.

The dog whined, looked up at him and wagged its feathery tail.

He'd every reason to go. He wasn't even supposed to be there. Scacchi had stopped by only to save himself some work the following night. The Arcangeli got their money's worth, always.

Then the hunter in him caught another sound. A human voice again, indistinguishable, whisked away by the sirocco before he could interpret it.

'Xerxes—' he said, and never finished the sentence.

Something roared into the night from the quay above him. A long fiery tongue of flame, like that of some angry dragon, extended into the black sky for one brief moment. The spaniel shrieked. Piero Scacchi threw his jacket over the small, trembling form, then fought his way up the slippery treacherous ladder next to the mooring, hearing the sound of a man's screams grow louder with every step.

3

The flames in the furnace looked wrong. So did the smoke, a sooty black swirl escaping from the kiln's mouth, then spiralling upwards towards the shaking roof. Uriel knew how the furnace was supposed to look. He could judge the state of the fire just from the intensity of its heat on the cracked veins in his cheeks.

There was something foreign in the maw of the beehive structure, behind the crock of forming glass, something burning with a bright, smoky anger. He racked his half-drunk head, searching for an explanation, wondering what to do. Uriel Arcangelo had worked in here since he was twelve. The process was so familiar he scarcely thought about it any more. Around five on a working afternoon he would load wood and raise the gas burner to 1250 degrees centigrade before placing the first crude load in position. Throughout the early evening, he or Bella would return from time to time to see the temperature rise steadily to 1400 degrees, adding wood according to his father's instructions, until the furnace was hot enough to allow any bubbles to escape from the glass. Then around three, Uriel, and he alone, as *omo de note*, would make his final visit and begin gradually to lower the temperature. By seven in the morning the glass he'd created would be sufficiently malleable for Gabriele to begin making the expensive and individual goblets and vases that bore the foundry's trademark, that of a skeletal angel, on the base.

Nothing in all his decades of attentive night-time activity helped explain the sight that lay before him now: a furnace racing inexplicably out of control.

'Bella?' he called out, over the roar of the kiln, half hoping she was there.

No one answered. There was only the call of the fire.

Uriel Arcangelo took a deep breath, knowing the decision that faced him: to close down the furnace would mean an entire day of lost production. The family was broke already. They couldn't afford the blow.

Except . . .

There was always a lone, bitter voice at the back of his head when he'd been drinking. Except they'd scarcely sold anything at all of late. All they'd be losing was another set of unwanted items to store in the warehouse, alongside boxes and boxes of identical pieces of expensive, beautiful glass; they *were* beautiful, he still believed that – works of art.

Uriel looked at his watch and wondered whether to call his brother. It was now approaching three. The loss of a run was bad, but not so terrible that it was worth risking Michele's wrath. Besides, Uriel was the *omo de note*. He was employed to make these decisions. It was his role, his responsibility.

He walked over to the tangle of old methane pipes and the single giant stopcock that controlled the gas supply to the burners. It was possible he could adjust the temperature manually. He ought to be doing this by now in any case.

Then he remembered what he had seemed to see when he stared inside the furnace's belly, and turned to look at the spiral of smoke still working its way to the stained moon visible through the roof. Something was out of place here and, without understanding what it was, he found it impossible to assess the full degree of the danger. He couldn't take risks with the furnace. If something damaged the beast itself, it would mean more than a day's lost production. An extended closure could spell the end of the business entirely.

He gripped the wheel with both hands, fingers tight on the familiar marks, and tried to turn it ninety degrees to shut off the gas supply completely. Michele could complain all he liked in the morning. This was a decision that couldn't wait.

Uriel Arcangelo heaved at the metal with increasing pressure for a minute or more. It was so hot it burned his desperate hands. It didn't move, not the slightest amount.

He coughed. The smoke was getting heavier, becoming so thick it was starting to drift back down from the ceiling. His head felt heavy, stupid. He tried to run through the options in his mind. The only working phone in the foundry was by the door. The Arcangeli didn't believe in mobiles. If matters took a turn for the worse – and he had to consider this now – he would have no choice but to call Michele and the fire station, get out of the building and wait.

Becoming desperate, he lunged at the wheel one more time. It was immovable. Something – the heat itself perhaps, or year after year of poor maintenance – had locked it into position.

He swore under his breath and, with one last, somewhat fearful look at the furnace, started to walk to the door.

He was halfway there when he felt something move on his apron, an odd, hot finger tickling his chest. He looked down and refused to believe his eyes. A fire was growing out of the fabric over his midriff. A healthy, palpable head of flame, like that of an oversized candle, was emerging from beneath the apron as if his own body possessed some kind of internal burner beneath the skin. And it was growing.

The flame flickered upwards, outwards. He stamped at it with his sleeve, only to see the fire catch the fabric there, dance along his arm, mocking him, like the furnace itself which was wheezing at his back, louder and louder . . .

Uriel. Uriel.

The air shook. Instinctively, he knew what had happened. One of the burners had crumbled into dust. The searing heat had worked its way back through the pipe, towards the dead stopcock, feeding on the flammable carbon gas, devouring it every inch of the way.

The explosion hit him full in the back, so hard he fell screeching to the unforgiving bone-hard timber floor. He felt his teeth bite on the fossilized wood, something shatter in his mouth, sending a pain running into his head where it met so many other messages: fear and agony and a dimming determination that he could survive all this if only he could reach the door and the key, the magic key he'd had the foresight to leave there only a few long minutes before.

4

Scacchi clambered up the rusty ladder, staggered onto land and found his own momentum sent him tumbling onto the hard, dusty stone of the island's tiny quay. He crawled on all fours, catching his breath against the force of the hot wind. His mobile phone was still in the boat. He'd no idea how to alert anyone nearby quickly. But someone, somewhere, would surely notice the fire, even in this backwater of Murano, on an island that kept its little footbridge to the outside world permanently locked now there was no public showroom for visitors to see. If the fire were to spread to the palazzo it would then threaten the house itself, where the rest of the Arcangeli tribe were sleeping in their separate bedrooms spread throughout the capacious mansion.

The burst of flame that had raged over the *Sophia* had died quickly. That, at least, was a mercy. But the cobbled stones of the broad jetty outside the foundry were strewn with shattered glass and hot, glowing embers of smouldering timber. Already he'd cut his hands stumbling into the shards and felt the burning stab of scorching splinters bite into his skin.

Cursing, he climbed to his feet and lumbered towards the half-shattered foundry windows, trying to locate the human sound he'd heard earlier. The windows went down to the ground to allow spectators outside to watch the process within. Now a miasmic storm of dust and smoke poured out of the chasm the blast had made in the centre. He shielded his eyes against the black, churning cloud and tried to imagine what force could have wrought such terrible damage.

Scacchi had no experience of fire. It rarely happened on Sant' Erasmo, was scarcely worth considering on the boat. With its scorching breath close in his face, he felt ignorant and powerless against the inferno's might.

The old hosepipe was where he remembered, against the brick wall next to the double doors, curled like a dead serpent slumped against a hydrant that looked as if it hadn't been used in years.

He heard the hiss of escaping gas, and behind it the sound from before, magnified, a pitch higher: a human being, screeching in agony.

Piero Scacchi swore angrily, ripped the hose from its fastenings, lugged it under one arm and tore at the huge industrial tap with his powerful right hand. After much effort, it gave. A stream of water, not a powerful one, probably nothing but the island's feeble mains under normal pressure, began to make an unenthusiastic exit from the nozzle.

He edged towards the shattered windows, directing the flow at the nearest flames as they ate into the tinder-like woodwork, watching them diminish reluctantly into a hissing, steamy mass, allowing just enough scope for him to get closer. Scacchi stole forward and edged in front of the glass and the bright, sun-like light streaming from the interior. The colossal heat of the building made each brief, laboured breath agony, made his skin shrink and become painful on his face. Then all thoughts of his personal predicament disappeared. Piero Scacchi found himself full of grief and sorrow for the human being he had known, all along, would be inside.

Scacchi raced to the old wooden double doors, tugged up the handle and heaved backwards with all his weight. Nothing moved. They were locked, from the inside in all probability. He could feel the force of the mechanism holding firm against his strength. Uriel must have the key, he thought, but he was too scared, too gripped by the flames, perhaps, to use it.

Scacchi held his head to the hot, dry wood of the door, trying to make himself heard.

'Uriel!' he shouted, not knowing how his voice would carry in this strange, fiery world beyond his vision. 'The door, man! The key!'

There was no human sound inside now, nothing but the triumphant roar of the inferno.

Scacchi threw aside the hose and looked around for something, an iron bar or a piece of timber, that he could use to lever open the entrance. The quayside was empty save for a few boxes of broken glass, ready to feed the new firings. Then he looked again at the windows and knew there really was no other way.

He'd saved a couple of lives on the lagoon before. Idiots from terra firma playing stupid games with boats, unaware of the dangers. If he'd been willing to risk his neck for them, there was really no excuse to stand back and allow a good man like Uriel Arcangelo to die in these flames.

'No choice,' he muttered, and grasped the hose beneath his arm. 'None . . .'

Scacchi's attention fell to the cobbled terrace. The dog had left the boat to find him. The animal now stared back from the edge of the quay, its terrified eyes reflecting the fire inside, black fur shiny and slicked back against its skinny body. Xerxes must have swum the short distance to the steps by the bridge, away from the ladder where the subterranean goods entrance lay with the *Sophia* moored next to it. In spite of his fear.

The spaniel put back its head and let loose a long, pained howl.

Scacchi looked at the dog. He'd brought it up since the day it was born. It did everything he asked. Usually.

'Bark,' he ordered. 'Bark, Xerxes. Wake the dead, for God's sake.'

Then, listening to the fevered yelping beginning to rise in volume as the animal started racing back and forth along the waterfront, he tucked the hose beneath his arm, and took a deep breath, wondering now long it would last him in the ordeal ahead.

Cuts and bruises. Smoke and flame. In the end they didn't matter much at all when a human life was at stake.

Piero Scacchi hammered out an entry route through the window with the iron nozzle of the decrepit hose, widened it with his elbow, trying to judge when it was large enough to take his frame. Then he launched himself through the remaining spikes and shards of glass, not feeling a thing because that would require a loss of concentration and, at that point, there was too much for one man to focus on. Everything – machines, walls, work tables, timber beams and pillars – seemed to be ablaze. He was entering a world that was not quite real, a universe of flame and agony where he felt like a dismal foot soldier fighting a lone battle against an army of bright fiery creatures.

One brighter, more animated than the rest.

'Uriel,' he said again, quietly this time, unsure whether the words were of any use to the half man, half fiery spirit rolling and screeching on the ground in front of him.

The creature paused for a moment and looked at him. He was, Scacchi understood, not quite human at that point, beyond rescue, and knew it too.

The authorities had arrived. Late as ever.

He watched in quiet dismay as two jets of water, thick, powerful streams – nothing like his own pathetic effort – burst through what remained of the windows, brutally taking out the last of the glass, then worked their way into the hall, so forcefully that they raked debris from the brickwork and the blackened, fragile timber trying to support the foundry roof.

A huge storm cloud of steam rose from the furnace to join the smoke; the flames hissed in fury at their impending end. Piero Scacchi looked again at what remained of the dark form, like human charcoal, lying in front of him, trying to remind himself this had once been a man. He had liked Uriel. He'd always felt touched by his sadness, and the strange sense of loss that seemed to hang around him.

One racing stream of water met the furnace itself, fell upon the beehive structure, fought with the baking hot bricks of the convex roof.

The fire was dead, killed by a flood tide of foam and water. Some kind of victory had been won, too late for Uriel Arcangelo, but soon enough to save his family, that insular clan who would now, Scacchi thought, be gathering to witness the strange, inexplicable tragedy that had burst out of the night, bringing a fiery death to their doorstep.

Unable to stop himself he walked forward and peered into the belly of the beast. An object lay there, crumbling in the moaning embers, an unmistakable shape that would, perhaps, explain everything, though not now because there was insufficient space in Piero

Scacchi's head to accommodate the stress of comprehending what it might mean.

A tumultuous crash at his back made him turn round. The fire fighters' axes were finally tackling the stupid wooden doors. If only the man inside had found the strength to turn the key.

If only . . .

Scacchi nodded at the white, fragile skull, sitting flat and jawless in the embers, shining back at him, and murmured a wordless benison.

A strong arm took him by the shoulder, barked at him to move. He removed the fireman's fingers and stared into the man's face with an expression that brooked no argument.

Then he went outside, through the shattered doors, coughing, feeling his eyes begin to sting from the smoke, his skin chafe with steam burns, cuts and splinters biting into his hands.

On the cobbled quayside the family was gathering among the firemen and a couple of local police. Two Arcangeli were missing, Uriel and his wife. Some wordless intuition, which he hoped was just stupid, anxiety-fraught speculation, whispered to Piero Scacchi a version of what might have happened that night, and why, perhaps, a man might die rather than turn the key to an ancient set of doors and save himself.

Almost immediately Michele was on him, eyes flaming, shaking a bony hand in his face, so close his fingers touched Scacchi's weary painful cheeks from time to time.

'Island moron,' this chief of the clan spat at him, shaking with fury. He was a short man, not far off sixty. And in a suit. The Arcangeli dressed for their own funerals, Scacchi thought to himself, and cursed his own impudence.

Michele wound his two puny fists into Scacchi's smoky, tattered jacket.

'What did you do, you idiot? *What?*'

Scacchi removed the man's hands from his clothes and pushed him away, making sure that Michele saw this was not a good idea, not an action to be repeated.

Gabriele stood away from his elder brother, in an old suit too, silent, dark, liquid eyes staring at the black shining water. Perhaps he was awaiting orders, as always. Raffaela was next to him, still in a nightdress, eyes bright with shock and anticipation, staring at Scacchi with some sympathy, he thought, and also a little fear.

An ambulance boat had arrived. A medic came up and looked at him. Scacchi shook his head and nodded towards the foundry.

'I tried to help,' he said quietly over his shoulder, half to Michele, half to anyone who cared to hear. He was aware of how old and hoarse and exhausted his voice sounded.

Part 2

A TASK FOR THE ROMANS

1

The two men stood outside Santa Lucia station, shielding their eyes against the bright sun, watching the constant commotion on the crammed and busy channel close to the head of the Grand Canal. It was close to eight in the morning and Venice's brief rush hour was under way. Commuters poured in on the buses from Mestre and beyond discharging their loads across the water in Piazzale Roma. Vaporetti challenged one another for the next available landing jetty. Water taxis revved their engines trying to impress the foreigners they were about to fleece. An endless flow of lesser vessels, private dinghies, commercial barges, skiffs carrying flowers and vegetables, the low slender shape of the occasional gondola, fought to weave their way through the flotilla of traffic. Behind them a train clattered across the bridge from the mainland, terra firma, its rattle carrying across to the canal with a resonant, unnatural force.

Light and noise. Those, Nic Costa thought, would be the overriding impressions he'd take home with him to Rome once this tour of duty was done. Both seemed amplified in this city on the water, where everything was brighter than on land and every sound seemed to make some distant echo among the warrens of tightly packed buildings crowded together over the constant wash of the lagoon.

The sirocco had expired overnight. Even at this early hour high summer was upon the city, airless, humid and dank with the sweat of puzzled tourists trying to work out how to navigate the foreign metropolis in which they found themselves.

Gianni Peroni finished his small *panino*, stuffed with soft, raw prosciutto, and was about to jettison the paper bag it came in towards the canal until Costa's disapproving frown stopped him. Instead, he thrust it into his pocket and cast a backwards glance at the steps of the forecourt where a couple of shady-looking characters were exchanging money.

'Why do you think stations always attract dirtbags?' he wondered. 'I mean, half these people wouldn't look out of place around Termini. In Rome it makes sense. Almost. But here?'

Nic Costa thought his partner was right, up to a point. They'd spent almost nine months in Venice. It had been exile of a kind, a form of punishment for an act of internal disobedience too subtle for conventional discipline. In truth it had almost been a holiday. Venice was so unlike Rome. Everyday crime here meant minor pickpockets, drunks and petty drugs. Even the layabouts around Santa Lucia bore only a passing resemblance to the hard-core hoods who made a crooked living around Rome's main station, and Gianni Peroni knew it. Still, Costa couldn't throw off his natural sense of caution. In spite of appearances, Venice wasn't some backwater paradise where a couple of cops, now in uniform because that was part of their sentence, could allow their minds to wander for too long. They'd been treated with too much suspicion and resentment in the little neighbourhood station in Castello for any of them to be comfortable. There was more too. The melancholy torpor of the lagoon was deceptive. Costa had heard snippets of the gossip going round the station. There were no big crimes filling the columns of the papers, but that didn't mean there were no big criminals. Life was never black and white in Italy but, in the lagoon light, water, sky and buildings sometimes resembled the conjoined universe of doubt Turner depicted in the canvases of the city Costa had admired, awestruck, at the temporary Accademia exhibition earlier in the summer. Something about Venice both disturbed and interested him. It reminded him of a bad yet familiar relative, dangerous to know, difficult to let go.

He looked his partner up and down. Peroni and uniforms didn't fit. The blue trousers and shirt hung baggily on the older man's big frame, one size too large in all probability. And, as always, Peroni was bending the rules just to make a point. On his hefty flat feet were a pair of trainers, black leather trainers, true, and ones that were, on this occasion, shiny from a rare application of polish. Costa had taken to wearing the uniform without a thought. It wasn't so long since he'd been a rookie Rome street cop who had donned one every day. But Gianni Peroni hadn't pulled on the blue for almost three decades; he wasn't going to go back in rank and time without a protest.

Costa considered those huge feet again, squeezed tightly into a couple of expensive-looking Reeboks.

'It's a health thing,' Peroni complained. 'Don't start. I've done more damn walking in this place than I managed in an entire lifetime back home. It's downright cruel.'

'We don't have squad cars . . .'

'They could've let us drive a boat!'

This had been a source of grievance for Peroni ever since they arrived. Gianfranco Randazzo, the surly Castello commissario, had, perhaps with some justification, reasoned there was no point in putting a couple of fleeting visitors through the complex and intensive training course needed for a lagoon licence. That had condemned both of them to the streets, public transport or begging a lift from one of the local cops.

'The argument's lost, Gianni. We're almost through here. What use would a boat licence be back home? Also, I don't think "drive" is quite the right word.'

'That,' Peroni insisted, waving a big, fat finger in Costa's face, 'is not the point. We should have been on an equal footing. Not treated like outsiders. Foreigners even.'

Foreigners. Yet, in a sense, that was what they were. Venice was *so* different. It was a place that constantly went out of its way to make them feel like strangers flitting through a bright, two-dimensional landscape that was never quite real. The locals even dropped into the lagoon dialect, a strange, glottal tongue largely impenetrable to ordinary Italians, whenever they felt like a little privacy. Costa had learned a little of the language. Sometimes it was easy to guess – *mèrkore* for *mercoledì*, Wednesday. Sometimes it sounded like a Balkan tongue, Croat perhaps. Today, for the Venetians, was *xòbia*, a day that began with a letter utterly foreign to true Italian.

This hadn't been the exile they expected. Leo Falcone, the inspector who joined them in their subtle disgrace, had been seconded to some art-theft squad in Verona not long after they arrived. On the street, a couple of arrests for robbery apart, their time in Venice had been without much incident, for which both men were grateful. Yet they had never been quite comfortable, and there were two excellent reasons for this, two omissions from their lives which would shortly be rectified.

There was a louder clatter from the tracks beyond the station. Costa looked at his watch. The fast train from Rome was on time. Emily Deacon and Teresa Lupo would be sitting on it, expecting a two-week holiday beginning that very night. It had all been planned. Earlier in the month, as a surprise, he'd paid a small fortune for a couple of tickets for La Fenice the following evening. Tonight Peroni had booked a quiet table for the four of them at his favourite restaurant, a place the big man loved, and where he was loved in return by the two sisters behind the bar, who fed him extra *cicchetti* as if he were a stray canine which had wandered in through the door. Emily and Teresa had planned to be regular visitors during the men's temporary banishment. It hadn't worked out like that. Teresa's workload in the Rome morgue never seemed to diminish. Emily had found herself immersed in academic life the moment she started working on her master's degree in architecture at the school in Trastevere. Matching their free time with that of two street cops who always seemed to get the worst shifts hadn't proved easy. Costa had seen Emily just three times in the past six months, even though she was living in his own farmhouse off the Appian Way. But now they were all free. Two weeks' leave beginning at the end of the day, and two police apartments in the narrow working-class back streets of Castello, far from tourist-land, to use as a base.

Peroni was eyeing him and Costa knew he was reading his thoughts. The two of them had been partners for eighteen months. More than partners, friends.

The big man looked down at his black trainers, shuffled his shoulders as a sign he was about to move, then laughed.

'It's a good feeling, huh?' he asked.

Before Costa could answer he found he was facing Peroni's back.

The big man was heading towards the station doors with that sudden burst of speed that always took people by surprise.

'You know,' Costa said, catching up, 'perhaps I could get another two tickets for La Fenice tomorrow. Teresa might like it.'

Peroni glanced back at him, appalled. The long, modern train was drawing up at the final platform.

'*Opera?*'

Costa scanned the platform. They were there, just visible in a sea of bodies, half running in spite of their hefty shoulder bags like a couple of schoolgirls on a trip to somewhere new. He wished to God he wasn't working just then. He wished he wasn't wearing a stupid uniform, doggedly prepared to spend one last day trudging the streets of Venice, helping lost tourists find their way back to the waterfront, glancing at his watch to see how long until the end of his shift.

Some dumb commuter in a shiny suit bumped into him and muttered a curse. The Venetians were even worse in a crowd than the Romans. There was a steady stream of them coming off the busy platforms. He'd followed Peroni's bulky form and stumbled straight into their path. The big man didn't care who got pushed and shoved out of the way. By the time Costa fought through, Peroni had his arms around Teresa Lupo in a bear hug, was slapping wet kisses on her full, pink cheeks, ignoring the flap of her arms on his back, a gesture that didn't really convince as a protest at all.

Costa watched the pair of them and shook his head, wondering, as he often did these days, who exactly was the junior partner in his and Peroni's relationship.

His mind was still on them when Emily arrived, breaking into his line of vision, peering at him, amusement and pleasure in her smart, inquisitive face. Her hair was longer, a lively natural shade of gold. Her eyes shone with that brightness that seemed to look straight through him. She was so unlike the serious, single-minded FBI agent he'd first met, a lifetime before.

Emily smiled: lovely white teeth, perfect pink lips, a face that was burned in his memory, unforgettable, a part of him. She wore jeans and a simple cream shirt, the V-neck displaying a new tan. Hugging the bag to her shoulder she looked like a student embarking on her first long trip abroad.

'I was looking for directions, officer,' she said quietly, almost meekly, not a touch of her native American audible through the measured, easy Italian.

'Where do you want to go?' he asked, a little awkward in the unfamiliar blue costume, wishing he had Gianni Peroni's lack of self-awareness, and that he could forget he was a cop standing in a crowded railway station, slap in the middle of rush hour.

Emily Deacon ran one slim index finger down the front of his jacket.

'You're the man in the uniform. You tell me.'

Costa glanced at the photo machine by the platform, took a deep breath, wondering if anyone would notice, then led her inside and pulled the curtain. The booth was tiny and smelled of cigarette smoke. Emily's eyes glittered at him in the faint light.

'Such discretion,' she whispered, clutching him. 'I think this calls for evidence.'

Her coins fell into the slot as he wrapped his arms around her slim, soft body. The flashes started firing the instant they kissed.

'Nic!'

The bursts of bright light stopped. Costa found his breath again. He wondered what was wrong. Emily looked flushed, embarrassed.

'What is it?' he asked, half wondering if there wasn't some way he could bunk off duty for the day.

'Company,' she murmured and flashed a glance at the curtains.

Leo Falcone stood there, holding the grimy fabric open. A slightly sardonic smile ran across his thin-lipped mouth, denoting some amusement that had never been there a couple of years ago, when he'd just been another hard-bitten boss in Rome.

'I was under the impression you were in Verona,' Costa said quickly, remembering to add, 'sir.'

'I was under the impression you were out looking for criminals,' Falcone replied, not unpleasantly.

Costa stepped outside the booth. Peroni was there, Teresa by his side, a look of suspicious bewilderment on his face. Commissario

Randazzo stood by the platform, rocking back and forth on his shiny shoes, looking every inch the businessman in a smart grey suit. Next to him was a curious-looking individual in his fifties. He was of medium build, quite fit and strong, and had an aristocratic northern face, very clean shaven, with cheeks that were red from sunburn or bad habits. Handsome once, Costa thought, but in that forced, artificial way that movie stars possessed, the kind of beauty that looked better from a distance. The man wore bright blue slacks and a perfectly pressed white silk shirt with a bright red scarf at the neck. He was balding, and trying to cover it up by brushing the remaining wisps of fine, fair hair across his tanned scalp. A foreigner, Costa thought immediately. English perhaps. With money and a story behind him.

'Is there something wrong?' Costa asked no one in particular.

It was Randazzo who answered, and Costa found himself unable to shake off the impression that the commissario was, somehow, measuring each word to make sure the individual next to him approved.

'Not at all,' Randazzo said, in the dry, dour tone of voice that belonged to a certain type of Venetian. 'You've been chosen. All three of you. Congratulations.'

'For what?' Peroni demanded.

'A very important task,' the stranger interjected, in good Italian though with an obvious English accent. 'I think,' he added, turning to Randazzo, 'the uniforms . . .?'

He stabbed a long index finger at the two men in blue.

'Best they go, Gianfranco.'

Randazzo nodded obediently.

Nic Costa turned to Emily. She was slipping the photos from the machine into her bag discreetly, as if they were somehow objects of shame.

'My name is Hugo Massiter,' the Englishman declared, and extended a long pale hand to each of them in turn, pausing to imbue his smile with a little extra warmth when he took Emily's outstretched fingers. 'Let me offer you a lift.'

2

It was more than a boat. It was a floating limousine, a compact, lithe waterborne Ferrari that sped through the lagoon traffic with an arrogant disregard for the law. The deck was of polished walnut, gleaming under the sun, with a helmsman in a white uniform at the open wheel. The five of them sat in the covered cabin, on plush antique brown leather seats, Randazzo and Massiter on one side, both smoking. The three Romans opposite remained silent, each of them, Costa thought, more than a touch apprehensive, and in Peroni's case downright furious.

'I'm sorry if we interrupted something,' Massiter said as the vessel eased out from the waterfront towards the dockyards and Murano. It had taken just over fifteen minutes to get from the station to the jetty close to the Giardini vaporetto stop. From there Costa and Peroni had led the women to the police apartments, in a narrow street of cottages hung with washing and painted in bright, peeling shades of blue and ochre. There'd been scant time to change or explain the household arrangements. Randazzo had been outside, glancing constantly at his watch, waiting to hurry back to the waterfront.

'We have two weeks' leave booked,' Peroni grumbled. 'Signed for. On the line. As of tonight.'

'You're still on duty now, aren't you?' Randazzo snapped back.

Costa reflected on the fact that he'd heard the commissario utter more words that morning than at any time in the past nine months. Nothing the stiff, sour-faced man had said so far, though, explained why Falcone had been recalled from Verona, and why they'd been dragged from normal street duties and pulled out of uniform, all for the apparent benefit of this odd foreigner, who was staring at Randazzo with a look that spoke of disapproval and a kind of ownership.

'That's no way to talk if we're to get these chaps on our side,' Massiter complained. 'Look. I'm sorry about this. If there were an alternative, we'd be taking it. Also, I owe you all something by way of compensation. It's best we get to know one another a little. Tomorrow night there's a reception at what I trust will one day be my gallery. Meet and greet. Keep some potential backers sweet. You get the idea. The place is still undergoing restoration, but what isn't in Venice? You will come, I hope, all three of you – with your partners.'

Peroni and Falcone looked at each other, said nothing, then looked at him. Costa sighed. He got the message.

'I've seats for La Fenice,' he said. 'But thanks anyway.'

Massiter's eyebrows rose.

'You have the tickets with you?'

Costa pulled the envelope from La Fenice out of his jacket pocket. They were the most expensive tickets he'd ever bought.

'Hmmm.' Massiter frowned at the pair of *biglietti*, topped by the house's phoenix crest. 'I can't say I know that part of the house, but I suspect you'd need binoculars. That is if there isn't a pillar in the way. I've a company box. One of the best there is. It seats eight people. Bring along some friends. Any time you like.'

Peroni coughed hard into his fist and gave Costa a terrified glance.

'Just let me know the dates.'

'I'm not sure . . .' Costa objected.

Massiter scarcely listened.

'This week's sold out entirely, you know. I've a contact who can get you twice what you paid for these. Here . . .'

He reached into the pocket of his slacks, took out a fold of money set inside a silver clasp, withdrew a couple of €200 notes, reached over and let them fall in Costa's lap, then took the tickets for himself.

'I don't mind running the risk. If they fetch more, I'll pass it on.'

Costa said nothing, waiting for one of the two men next to him to intervene.

'Good,' Massiter went on. 'Tomorrow it is. Seven p.m. Nothing fancy. Just some decent food and drink. A little music. It'll be pleasant to have some real human beings there instead of the usual hangers-on. And—'

Leo Falcone leaned forward and stared into Massiter's face. The Englishmen looked affronted. He wasn't accustomed to being interrupted.

'Why are we here?' Falcone demanded. 'Why are we in some fancy private boat, going God knows where? And who the hell are you anyway?'

Randazzo glowered at the three men opposite him.

'Falcone . . .' he said brusquely. 'You're not in Rome now. I want some respect here.'

'They're reasonable questions,' Massiter objected. 'I'd be surprised if he didn't want to know. Disappointed frankly. We don't want idiots for this job now, do we?'

Peroni issued a low grunt of disapproval, then asked, 'So what *do* you want?'

Massiter leaned back on the old brown leather, let his arm wander over to the tiny fridge built into the cabinet at the end of the seats, and withdrew a small bottle of Pellegrino, misty with ice.

'Help yourself,' he said.

'We're waiting,' Falcone insisted.

The Englishman took a long gulp, then wiped his mouth with the sleeve of his silk shirt. They rounded the corner of the island, past the giant boatyards and docks, the football stadium and the odd collection of workers' houses that no one, not even the police, paid much attention to. Murano now stood on the low, bright horizon, a spiky forest of chimneys and cranes rising up from the grey-blue of the lagoon, beyond the cemetery island of San Michele, with its pale brick exterior wall, like that of a private castle, topped by a green fringe of cedar points.

'What we want,' Hugo Massiter said, 'is to stop this poor old city sinking any further into its own shit. If we can.'

He leaned back, closed his eyes, then tossed the empty water bottle out of the open window, into the grey, foaming wake of the speeding vessel.

'And that, gentlemen, very much depends on you.'

3

Angelo Arcangelo had created the island himself, designed every last detail, intent on raising an everlasting masterpiece from the rubble he'd bought for a pittance. Everything was new, everything unique, cast in shapes that seemed impossible. The island was a testament to the power and beauty of glass and, by implication, the Arcangeli themselves. On three separate plots, Angelo had set out his stall for an admiring world to see. The palazzo was ninety per cent leaded crystal, ten per cent black iron and timber, a towering, organic beacon of light, with three curving roofs, the centre higher than the rest, rising more than twenty metres above the quayside. Behind the entrance doors the skeleton of a gigantic palm tree Angelo had imported from Sicily still lurked, its corpse now awaiting Hugo Massiter's restorers, who had their own ideas, ones that Angelo would never have countenanced. To the right, seen from the water, stood the foundry, a four-square elegant artisans' workplace, fronted by six of the longest windows in Venice. They reached from the ground to the low, sloping roof, large enough to accommodate the crowds who would press their noses against the glass, wondering at the marvels being wrought by the Arcangeli's *maestri* inside. And in the final third of the frontage, on the other side of the palazzo, stood Ca' degli Arcangeli, the family home, ten apartments on three floors, with kitchens and bathrooms, offices and space to house meetings, receptions, banquets . . . Angelo had begun his life's project as a testament to the dynasty he was creating. By the time he died he knew the truth: that the island was an impossibility. It was too expensive to maintain in the face of a public whose taste for glass was fickle and shifting;

too complex and unwieldy to be managed by the children who followed him.

Some of the beauty remained, though. Most of all in the Arcangeli temple, the shrine to the clan that was the focus of the family home: an airy, cavernous dining room that occupied much of the first-floor frontage, filled by the constant light of the lagoon, with uninterrupted views past the Murano lighthouse, out to San Michele and the Fondamente Nove waterfront. Angelo had made the glass with his own hands, labouring for almost a year to produce an astonishing, multi-windowed eyelid over the waterfront, some panes clear, some distorting bullseyes with myriad stains, all pulled together into a massive, curving viewpoint that dominated the facade of the building.

Angelo told everyone he wanted to emulate the captain's cabin of some medieval Venetian war galley, a nod back towards the Arcangeli's boat-building past, though the *squero* in Chioggia had turned out nothing fancier than fishing barques that never went beyond the Adriatic. His face, stern, demanding, with some hard, unrelenting love inside it too, still stared down at the family from the large portrait that hung over the marble Doric fireplace opposite what all of them knew simply as the *occhio*, the eye. In the sixties, when the Isola degli Arcangeli was in its heyday, artists would gather here. Raffaela still recalled some: Igor Stravinsky patting her head fondly, then patiently listening to her run through the scale of C on the old Steinway; Ezra Pound, a dark, morose man, sitting in the corner of the room, saying nothing, clutching a glass. Both now lay beneath the earth on San Michele across the water, among the privileged handful who were allowed to stay beyond the strict decade allotted any who now wished to follow them there.

For all the fame of their visitors, it was her father's presence that continued to haunt the place. This was where the clan would gather three times each day, to eat, to talk, to plot the future. Over the long years – forty-seven since Raffaela came into the world – they'd headed off rifts here, organized liaisons and alliances, planned marriages and, on one painful occasion, a divorce. And held some kind of board meeting too, from time to time. Not that the foundry ran along conventional lines, or was ever a business open to the voice of more than one man. There was always a *capo*. First Angelo, then Michele, the eldest, whose name meant 'like God', as he knew only too well.

Raffaela had researched a little history in her spare time, after she'd been recalled home from her too-brief studies in Paris to work in the family business when its finances began to falter. The room's supposed antecedents were, like so much to do with the Arcangeli, a myth. The republic's galleys never had that kind of ornate, impractical windowed platform at the stern. Venice was Venice, single-minded, sensible always. Warships were made to carry cannon, not a complex panoply of hand-crafted windows, tessellated like the bulging, multicoloured eye of a fly. Angelo Arcangelo had exaggerated, invented, as he always did. Beauty forgave everything, in his view, and the curious, bulbous addition to the house was extraordinarily beautiful. His daughter now sat in the embrace of the long bend of the cushioned bench built into the window's base, her fingers touching the familiar fading red velvet, her eyes wandering around the room.

Outside she could hear the firemen working by the quay, grumbling, shifting their machines and their heavy hoses, loading what they no longer needed back onto their boats. The bright morning air seeped in through the shuttered windows. It stank of smothered smoke. She knew that, if she looked, there would be a handful of policemen shuffling their feet by the foundry entrance, bored behind the yellow tape they'd erected.

Raffaela wondered when she would pluck up the courage to leave this room and face the world outside. Among the many myths they'd propagated within the clan these last few years was the idea that this room, with its eye over the lagoon, was a place where the power of the Arcangeli remained intact, untouched by the troubles gathering around their small island home. While the rest of the Isola crumbled and gathered dust, this place remained pristine, swept daily by her own hand now the servants were gone. Polished, cared for, it remained a symbol of what they once were, perhaps could be again. This was where she served breakfast, lunch and dinner, good plain Murano food, *cornetti* from the bakery a short walk away across the bridge, fat *bigoli* pasta with thick red sauce made from anchovies and Sant' Erasmo tomatoes. Meat for supper, though not necessarily the best. And fish sometimes, if she could find it at the right price. This was where, she had come to believe, they could retreat forever.

Staring out over the grey lagoon, her vision blurred by tears, she found her mind wrestling with so many strands of thought. Memories and regrets mingled with practicalities, funeral details, people who had to be told. The family had been spared death for so long. Not a single close member had left them since their father had passed away. And even he hadn't really departed. The room where he took his last breath was still empty. She swept it every day, making the bed, changing the pressed white sheets once a week, because that was what Michele wanted, how the *capo* said matters should stand. A photograph of their mother, an attractive, worn-looking woman, stood over the head of the bed by a small crucifix. She had died when Raffaela was tiny. For her daughter she had always remained somehow unreal, a person who had never quite existed, except, perhaps, as a comment on those who survived her, a question mark asking why they were enjoying the gift of life when the woman who gave them it was gone.

They hadn't thought about the family grave, not in a long time. There'd been so many other dark, pressing issues to worry about. Now death had arrived on the back of the night sirocco and taken two souls with sudden brutal cruelty.

There was a sound at the door. Michele bustled in, followed, as always, by Gabriele, and she found, to her surprise, that she saw both of them differently. Michele was twelve years older than her. In a way, he'd always been an adult and now he looked his age, more so than she'd ever noticed before. Uriel's death had made her conscious of the Arcangeli's shared mortality, something they'd all sought to hide over the years. It was as if the event had drawn away a veil that had stood between them, and in doing so revealed distance, not the closeness she would have hoped for.

A minor stroke had creased the right side of Michele's face. With his greying hair slicked back and pomaded, leaving a silver widow's peak in the middle, he looked like a man entering the final part of the journey of existence sooner than he should. He was of less than medium height with a slight build, an unimpressive man to look at, she thought, until he spoke, and in that voice, a powerful monotone switching from Veneto to Italian, French to English or German, lay an authority none could mistake. And now he was old. Old and bewildered and angry.

He sat down at the polished table, banged a fist on the surface, hard enough to send the old china briefly flying, then, without another word, gulped at the coffee she'd provided before tearing at a *cornetto*.

Gabriele joined him and reached for some coffee and pastries too.

Raffaela wiped her face with the sleeve of her old cotton shirt, took one last look at the lagoon then made her way to the seat opposite them, facing both across the bright, gleaming wood. The Arcangeli ate together. They always would.

She waited. After he'd done with the coffee and the pastries Michele fixed her with his one good eye.

'More police will be here soon. They'll want to talk to everyone again. Same damn questions. Poking their long, sharp noses in where no one wants them.'

'Michele . . .' she said softly, hoping her voice did not sound as if she wished to contradict him. 'The police have to be involved. What do you expect? Uriel. Poor Bella—'

'Poor Bella!' he barked back at her, spitting flakes of *cornetto* from the corners of his mouth. 'That woman's been nothing but trouble since she came here. One more mouth to feed and nothing in return. *Poor Bella!* What about us?'

Gabriele, two years younger than Michele, though the gap seemed larger, stared at his plate and gently tore his food into strips, silent, unwilling to become involved.

'They're dead,' Raffaela said quietly. 'Both of them. Whatever happened they deserve some respect.'

Michele put down his coffee cup and glared at her. She was unable to stop herself stealing a glance at the portrait above them. He was their father sometimes. It was hard to separate the two of them.

'We all *know* what happened,' he said plainly. 'The sooner it's put down in black and white on paper, the sooner we return to what matters. The business.'

'Michele . . .'

Just the look on his face silenced her. There'd never been physical contact within the Arcangeli. Not even when Angelo was alive. This was not through choice. Force had simply never been needed, not when the fierceness of a cold, heartless eye could stun any of them into submission.

'We *will* not fail, Raffaela. I will not allow that to happen.'

He brushed the crumbs off his lap with a brisk hand then stood up. Gabriele, to her disgust, was rushing down his food and coffee in order to do the same.

'Where on earth are you going?' she asked.

'To test the fires,' Michele answered. 'To connect the gas. To see how soon we can get the foundry up and running. I'll bring in others from the outside if need be. The insurance money will surely pay for it.'

'Do you know that?' she demanded.

'Nothing's insurmountable. We'll hire some furnace space elsewhere if it's necessary. What's a fire in this business? It used to happen all the time.'

He was so single-minded. He really believed this was all there was to consider.

Gabriele finally found the strength to speak.

'We'll lose a day or two, Michele. That at least. Don't fool yourself.'

'A day, a day.' The older man sniffed, waving an arm. 'What's a day?'

'It's a day in which we fail to make something no one wishes to buy,' she said sourly, hating the bitter tone in her voice the moment she heard it. This was a kind of heresy. The one taboo subject barred from discussion beneath the eye that gazed constantly out onto the lagoon.

Both men turned to regard her with undisguised aversion.

'It's true,' she insisted, determined not to be bullied into silence. 'The longer you two fools stay away from that place, the longer the money lasts. If you make nothing, Michele, we don't have to pay anyone for raw materials, do we?'

'We don't pay anyone as it is,' he retorted unpleasantly. 'Leave business to men. It's not for you.'

She felt the red heat of anger rise in her head, a foreign emotion, one that had been placed there by tragedy and refused to go away.

'So what's a woman to do in this position? To bury our brother and his wife? Where? And with what?'

Michele nodded at the window.

'You know where Uriel belongs. The island. For now anyway. The Braccis can deal with the other one. She's their problem. She should have stayed that way all along.'

Her voice rose to a screech. She couldn't help it.

'We can't afford San Michele!' she yelled at him, unable to control her emotions. 'Undertakers want money. Not promises. We're not good for credit any more. Don't you understand?'

He had the demeanour of the patriarch; at that moment he might have been his father. Michele Arcangelo walked over to one of the cabinets and took out the most precious item left there. It was a sixteenth-century water bowl in the form of a galley, a beautiful piece, the hull of the vessel in clear glass, the rigging in blue. On the side was the seal of the Tre Mori furnace, a guarantee that it would fetch a good price anywhere. They'd owned it forever, or so it seemed to her. Angelo, in particular, had adored the work, which was why it had remained unsold thus far.

Michele turned the precious object in his hand, admiring it with one sharp, professional eye.

'Then bury him with that,' he said with not a trace of emotion.

4

It only took a couple of minutes to hear Randazzo's story. After that, the three men from Rome looked at each other and wondered what they'd done to deserve this one. Venice had police aplenty. Any of the locals could have taken on the case, done what the miserable commissario wanted, signed off the report, then returned to guiding tourists back to their cruise ships. There was, Costa knew, some reason why Randazzo had picked three temporary strangers in the little Questura in Castello for the job. He wondered whether they were going to hear it. And one more thing bothered him. Hugo Massiter's name was somehow familiar. He just couldn't put a finger on how he knew it.

Falcone nodded when the narrative was done, then asked, 'So you're sure this is what happened? There can't be any other explanation?'

Randazzo waved a hand at the approaching jetty. Costa could smell the smoke from the island. The fire fighters' vessels clustered around the blackened quayside, near the still-smouldering outline of what looked like a large, once elegant industrial building, a small, stocky chimney emerging from its shattered and smoke-stained glass roof. To its left stood an extraordinary glass structure, like a gigantic hothouse designed by a madman, patched with scaffolding and ladders. On the other side was a stone palace, not unlike the Doge's, but with an extraordinary eye-like bubble of glass protruding from an upper floor. These odd architect's fantasies sat alone on a small island, next to a squat lighthouse by a vaporetto stop marked 'Murano Faro'. Only a narrow metal bridge joined the property to Murano proper. It was surmounted by the iron figure of an angel, like an icon beckoning to visitors. A silver-haired man was working at its base, his face red with anger as he fought with a writhing serpent's nest of cables.

'See for yourself,' the commissario said. 'The Arcangeli are the only people who live here. It's locked at night.'

He gazed into their faces, trying to make sure they understood that what he said next was pivotal to the argument.

'The room where they were found was locked from the inside. There's no other access except through the windows, and the labourer said they were intact until the fire blew them out.'

'How do you know he's telling the truth?' Peroni wondered.

Randazzo snorted, amused.

'So what's the alternative? This character somehow let himself in, killed both Uriel Arcangelo and his wife, then locked the door, went out through the fire, went back in and made out he was trying to rescue the man he'd just killed. Why?'

'And the one who's dead? He's supposed to have a motive for killing his wife?' Costa asked.

'It's there somewhere. You'll find it. We all know the statistics. Families kill one another. That would be your instinct anyway, wouldn't it?'

'You can't convict someone on statistics,' Falcone said carefully, 'or instinct. I don't mean any disrespect, sir, but I think we've more experience of murder inquiries than you. Rome's that kind of place.'

'I don't doubt it!' the commissario snapped. 'But I didn't bring you back from Verona for a tutorial in criminology. I want a piece of paperwork done and I'm cancelling your leave so you can do it. Uriel Arcangelo murdered his wife and placed her corpse in the furnace. Then, deliberately or by accident, he was burned to death himself. There's no other possible explanation. We'll know more later. They're working on the post mortems now.'

Falcone was speechless for a moment. Then he asked, 'You mean the victims are no longer in place?'

'No! Why should they be?'

'I'm not used to investigating crimes where the evidence has been removed before we arrive.'

Randazzo paused, furious.

'And I'm not used to having to explain myself when I give orders. You can see the bodies in the morgue if that's what turns you on.'

'Why us?' Costa asked.

'Because I want it.'

That wasn't good enough.

'But you've had men here already,' Costa objected. 'Local men. Why can't they follow through on the case?'

'They've better things to do. Besides, you said it yourself. You've a track record.'

Peroni's eyes widened.

'Not for sweeping up we haven't,' he objected. 'You don't want an investigation. You want clerical work. You—'

'I want you to do as you're damn well told,' Randazzo interrupted. 'I never asked for you people to be here in the first place. It's time you earned your pay. You've just been a burden so far, something I had to watch every time my back was turned. Why do you think I packed *him* off to Verona?'

Falcone smiled, which infuriated the commissario.

'That seems a little harsh, sir,' the inspector commented brightly. 'By our standards we've been exceptionally well behaved.'

'By your standards.' Randazzo let loose the ghost of a smile. 'Which is why I'll release you the moment you finish this inquiry. That could give you an extra three weeks' paid vacation if you add it up. You can go back to Rome where you belong. You can do what the hell you like. Provided . . .'

He reached down to the walnut cigarette box that sat on the table between them. Randazzo knew this boat, Costa thought. He was familiar with the Englishman, who had sat in silence throughout this entire interlude, an amused expression on his striking features.

'. . . you deliver what I want. A report, a *thorough* report from a team that's experienced in murder. One that says what we know to be true: that Uriel Arcangelo killed his wife and then died, possibly by his own hand. You've got a week. That's plenty of time. Don't rush it either. I don't want anyone saying this was slipshod. I don't expect you to be working your balls off. You two might even get some extra time with your girlfriends.'

Peroni punched his partner lightly on the shoulder.

'See! So that's why it's us. Get it? We've credibility.'

'We get it,' Falcone grumbled. He looked at Hugo Massiter. 'And you?'

The Englishman opened his arms in a gesture of innocence. They were at the quay now. For all the damage and mess left by the firemen, it was an impressive sight. From the first floor of the house, which was more in keeping with the Grand Canal than the backwater of Murano, the feature Costa had noticed earlier was revealing itself to be something like the stern of a medieval galley, a great glass eye curving out over the lagoon.

'What the hell is this place?' Peroni asked, amazed.

'Fairyland gone wrong, I fear,' Massiter said quietly. 'This is all a great tragedy, gentlemen. But do understand, I'm simply the concerned benefactor in these proceedings, as Commissario Randazzo will readily confirm. Without me, the island is lost. And if the island is lost, so are several million euros of city money that could have been better spent.'

'Meaning . . .?' Falcone insisted.

Massiter sighed and glanced at the blackened foundry.

'The Isola degli Arcangeli is bankrupt. It's been bankrupt for some time and only two things have been keeping it float. Some considerable, and in my view unwise, *investment*, shall we say, on the part of the city and the regional authorities. They need the tourists, you see. In theory anyway, this is a prime leisure location. Plus there has been some weekly generosity from me in renting the palazzo, that glass exhibition hall. If all this works out, I plan to turn it into a gallery. If I can finally fix the thing. It was designed by a lunatic, but you can probably see that for yourselves.'

Costa thought about the man, with his old-fashioned film star looks, his fancy boat and something lurking in his past too. Costa was sure of that. On the way from the station to Castello, Massiter had pointed out his 'home' as they passed, partly to impress Emily, he thought. It was a large, palatial motor yacht big enough to swallow their present vessel ten times ever, moored conspicuously on the waterfront near the Arsenale.

'Why are the city involved? ' he said. 'You look like someone who can afford it.'

'Appearances can be deceptive,' Massiter replied. 'Wealth and debt go hand in hand. None of this is without self-interest, naturally. Six months ago certain people in the city and the regional authority approached me to help. There'd been potential buyers before, but none of them met the Arcangeli's approval. There is a limit to how much good public money can be thrown after bad. The Arcangeli aren't the easiest of people to deal with, but eventually I managed to strike a deal to buy the island lock, stock and barrel, provided I rent the foundry and part of the palazzo back to them on a peppercorn rent to get them back on their feet. After which, I open the gallery, perhaps, build a few apartments in the rest of the place to pay for it all, and add another tourist attraction to bring in more hordes for the Venetians to fleece. It's not *just* money though, not from my point of view. I hate seeing traditions founder simply because they're badly run. The glass is exquisite, if a little unfashionable. With a little help they could make a go of it, once they free themselves of debt. And we take over the running of the island. Which is where—'

'They don't need the details,' Randazzo interrupted. 'It's none of their damn business.'

Massiter flashed the man a sharp look, one that silenced him. 'What does it matter, Gianfranco? If they don't do their job all this goes public anyway. And God alone knows what happens then.'

The speedboat docked at the jetty. Massiter barked at the helmsman to tie up, allow Falcone and his men to disembark, then return to the city. Costa glanced up at the extraordinary glass structure fronting the mansion. There was a figure at the windows. A woman, tall, erect, with long dark hair and a pale face, was watching their arrival intently.

'I am,' continued Massiter, 'at an awkward juncture in this negotiation. The lawyers have been bleeding us dry. The deal is still unsigned. The public purse is empty. It's only my rental of the hall that keeps the family afloat. This damned island's covered by all manner of trusts and covenants. It's taken us months just to go through the fine print. Now' – a morose frown briefly broke the handsome cast of his face – 'we have to close or walk away. I have until the end of next week to bring this negotiation to a conclusion or my backers will look to place their money elsewhere. Nor can I blame them.'

Falcone stared at Randazzo.

'So we're doing this in order to expedite some private financial transaction of his?'

It was Massiter who answered.

'In a sense, but with good reason. If you can just write up that report to say Uriel killed his wife – which we're all assured is the only possibility – then the contract can go ahead. Since you're experienced detectives, and from Rome too, not hereabouts, no one will question it. Alternatively . . .'

'I don't care about your business affairs, Mr Massiter,' Falcone declared. 'They're nothing to do with us.'

Randazzo stabbed out his cigarette in the silver ashtray between them. The smell of dead tobacco mingled with the fire smoke from the jetty above.

'They're everything to do with us,' the commissario declared. 'If this case is still open by the end of next week, then it can only say to the outside world that we consider one of the other Arcangeli to be a suspect. No one else was on the island after all. However ridiculous that is – and hear me, Falcone, it *is* ridiculous – it kills Signor Massiter's contract stone dead. In order for that to proceed, all three living Arcangeli must sign. If they do, and one is then charged with the murder of Uriel Arcangelo, all manner of civil proceedings could follow that might throw the entire contract into jeopardy. These people are drowning in debt. There's any number of shark lawyers out there who'd leap on a criminal charge as an excuse to try to void the contract and seize the property direct, or blackmail Signor Massiter for more money he doesn't have in return for keeping quiet. The negotiations are fragile enough as it is. Any doubt about future litigation would end them for good. No investor would take that risk. The case has to be closed or the Arcangeli go into liquidation next week and . . .'

He didn't want to go any further. Falcone leaned back in his seat and shook his head.

'I repeat,' the inspector said, 'I don't care.'

Massiter nodded at the man beside him.

'You have to tell them, Gianfranco. What's there to lose?'

The commissario swore bitterly then lit another cigarette before continuing.

'This isn't about business. It's about politics. You three of all people should know that's not a place to make enemies. *More* enemies in your case.'

They were on probation. Costa understood that as well as Falcone and Peroni. It didn't make them anybody's fools.

'We're listening,' Costa said.

'Jesus,' Randazzo grunted, flashing Falcone a grimace. 'You smug bastards really think you're a team, don't you? All for one, one for all. Wise up. Do you think you're untouchable because of that? Listen to me. The Arcangeli have been bankrupt for years. Five at least. Probably more. They've managed to stay afloat because they've been working their way through some influential friends. If you know the right people here you'd be amazed how easy it is to dip your beak into the public purse. They owe millions in taxes going back a decade. They've been quietly getting subsidies from everywhere to keep that stupid place running, even though it's just a museum that's no longer even fit to open its doors to the public. The cultural people have paid. The historical commissioners have paid. The city, the region. They've all been sweet-talked by the Arcangeli into stumping up cash on the promise that some time soon it would all come right.'

'And I guess a little went back into some private pockets?' Peroni suggested. 'Is that what we're talking about here?'

'Maybe,' Randazzo snapped. 'Maybe not. Nothing comes for free anywhere, does it? Or don't you have kickbacks in Rome? Are you people all just too high-minded for that?'

Falcone scowled. '*We* are.'

'Well, that's your privilege. But let me say this. If the Arcangeli go down, this city suddenly has a hole in its books the size of the lagoon. They won't be able to keep it quiet any longer. There's just too much money at stake. If it goes to some kind of judicial inquiry – and it would – then all manner of decent people are going to find themselves standing in the dock, or worse.'

Peroni raised a battered eyebrow. 'Decent?'

'Don't preach to me!' Randazzo yelled. 'You don't belong here. You don't know how we work.'

Massiter leaned forward and tapped the commissario lightly on the knee.

'No need to lose your temper,' he cautioned. 'These are practical men. They know which side their bread's buttered.' The Englishman eyed them. 'Don't you?'

Falcone took out his notepad, scribbled something on it, tore off the sheet and threw it into Randazzo's lap.

'There's my signature,' he said. 'Write the report and stick that at the end. Then we can all go home.'

'No!' the commissario bellowed. 'I need you to do this. You're outsiders. You've got background. No one's going to argue with what you say. Uriel Arcangelo killed his wife. We *know* that. I'm not asking you to bend the evidence or sign off anything you don't believe. The facts are there. I just want them put down on paper. You've got a week. Then . . .' He gestured towards the lagoon and the cloudless blue sky. 'You're gone. Do we have a deal?'

Falcone shook his head.

'You can't put a time limit on an investigation.'

Massiter opened another bottle of water for himself and shrugged.

'A week's all I've got. After that the whole business goes tits up, and me with it. At least I just lose money. Some of the other people hereabouts . . .'

'What if we find out he didn't do it?' Peroni asked.

'That's not going to happen,' Randazzo said wearily. 'It's impossible. Listen, we're just trying to keep a lid on an awkward situation that would hurt a lot of people if it got out of hand.'

He glowered at Falcone.

'Hurt them *unnecessarily*,' the commissario insisted. 'Uriel Arcangelo killed his wife. There is no other possible explanation. Prove otherwise, Falcone, and you can have my job. God knows there's times I'd happily do without it.'

Falcone looked tempted by the offer. Costa could understand why. The idea of a leisurely investigation that guaranteed them all an early ticket home was attractive, even in these extraordinary circumstances.

'What exactly did you have in mind?' Falcone asked.

Randazzo suddenly turned hopeful.

'Go through the statements we already have. Take a look at the scene. Interview the Arcangeli again if you want. Together. One by one. It's up to you. This nightwatchman character is probably worth talking to again, too, and anyone else you want. I should warn you that you're going to have to talk to the dead woman's family – the Braccis. They're regular customers of ours: petty crime – you name it. A bunch of assholes. My, are they going to be pissed off right now.'

'What about the morgue?' Costa asked.

'Go in and ask for what you want. We've got a good pathologist. Tosi's been here for years. I'm not asking you to cover anything up. I just want a compact, efficient establishment of the facts, then a report I can wave everywhere and say this matter is dead and buried. Understood?'

Commissario Randazzo waited, a little fearful. Then, when he heard no objections, not even from Peroni, he looked at his watch and raised half a smile.

'Don't rush. That would look bad. When it's done, disappear on vacation. You'll have earned it.'

He waited, nervous.

Peroni leaned forward, paused, just to give the commissario a nasty turn.

'We're going to need a boat,' he insisted. 'Our own boat. With a driver too.'

'Of course,' Randazzo said quietly. 'Except you don't call it—'

The small 'paff' of an explosion interrupted the commissario, loud enough to make them all jump. There was the sound of a man's excited shouts. Nic Costa strained his neck trying to see what was happening.

A flame had emerged from the torch at the end of the iron angel's extended hand. The silver-haired individual who'd been working at the cables watched it.

'Michele Arcangelo,' Randazzo said by way of explanation. 'He's the *capo* around here.'

A smiling *capo*, Costa noted. With a crooked face. A man who couldn't take his eyes off the beacon of fire he'd just revived.

5

Nic Costa surveyed the blackened interior of the foundry and wondered how much the flames and the smoke had managed to destroy. A blaze of this nature and magnitude was outside his realm of experience. What evidence might also have disappeared in the blasts from the fire fighters' hoses and the tramp of feet by the unseen cops and others who'd entered the building long before Randazzo had invited them onto the scene?

All three had quietly acquiesced in the face of the commissario's demands. There was precious little point in arguing anyway. Besides, each of them was, Costa knew, tempted by what was on offer, in spite of the immediate loss of leave. Conduct a thorough investigation, produce a sound, predictable report into a crime which seemed a closed case from the outset, then enjoy some extra holiday before returning to Rome. The circumstances were unusual but not, perhaps, unknown, particularly in Venice. Besides, Emily was free of college work for the next month. They could visit Sicily first, perhaps, or make a lazy progress back to Lazio through Tuscany and Umbria.

Provided they gave Gianfranco Randazzo and the Englishman to whom the commissario seemed somehow beholden exactly what they wanted.

Costa and Falcone had walked carefully around the foundry, first examining the furnace where the woman's remains had been recovered, then looking at the chalk outline around the stained and partially missing portion of planked flooring where Uriel Arcangelo had fallen. They examined the peripheral details too. The shattered windows were being covered by wooden shutters hammered into place by a couple of carpenters – against all conventional police routine. The tall wooden doors, almost turned to charcoal by the heat, had been smashed from their hinges by the axes of the entry team. Falcone fussed over the hatchet marks then took out a handkerchief and bent over the door which now lay on the floor. The key was still in the lock, on a ring with a bunch of others. It was an old-fashioned mortised mechanism, which meant that, once a key was inserted from one side, it was impossible for anyone to open the door from the other. Falcone juggled at the key in the mechanism then withdrew it and placed the item in a plastic evidence pouch which he pocketed. Costa watched him, thinking.

'The door is locked, isn't it?' he asked.

'Definitely,' Falcone replied. 'They told us that already. You don't imagine they lied, do you?'

He tried to read Falcone's demeanour. Was he being sarcastic? It was difficult to tell exactly what the distant, expressionless inspector was thinking at the best of times. Just then, Costa really had no idea.

'In that case he must surely have shut himself in here.'

The icy, judgmental eyes bored into him. Falcone looked disappointed.

'That's one possibility,' he conceded.

'What else? His key's in the door . . .' Costa stuttered, trying to understand how many other possibilities there could be.

'Quite. Don't read ahead of yourself, Nic. It's a bad habit. Start from ignorance and let the facts inform you, not your own guesswork. Randazzo's doubtless right and this case is as simple as he says. But you can't expect me to throw away a lifetime's habits now, can you? Go and take a look around on your own. I'm not quite finished here. I can't believe I'm working a location without scene of crime people. Please . . . Unless you have something else to add.'

'Hugo Massiter has a history,' Nic said curtly.

Falcone looked interested.

'What kind of history?'

'I can't remember. But I know the name. He was in the papers. Something to do with music. And a death. Perhaps more than one. I can find out.'

'I think someone like Massiter's best left to me,' Falcone replied.

Feeling more than a little like an unwanted and chastised small child, Costa walked back towards the shattered remains of the windows and watched the men in overalls hammering in their cheap wooden shutters.

'Do you work here?' he asked the first, a squat, middle-aged individual in grimy clothes.

The two of them looked at each other and laughed.

'Nice joke,' the man said. 'You think they've got money to pay staff? News to me. News to the whole of Murano. Insurance, mister. They sent us, they pay us. They want these windows boarded because if they're not the bill just gets bigger. Surprised me the Arcangeli still got insurance, mind. Probably the only bill they've paid this last year.'

'Thanks,' Costa muttered, and moved a little away from the beat of their hammers and the stink of their cigarettes.

Peroni was attempting to start a conversation with the two Arcangelo brothers, both of whom seemed more interested in attacking the furnace with hacksaws and blowlamps, working on the spider's web of gas pipes that led to it, removing the areas that had been mangled beyond repair by the heat. There was little point in joining his partner in the effort. Randazzo had obviously given the family carte blanche to destroy any evidence remaining in the place.

Improvise. That was Falcone's guiding advice in circumstances like these: cases which seemed to be blank pages needing evidence to fill them. Costa knew his inspector well enough by now to understand what it meant. Poke around, get a feel for the crime scene. In this instance, try to imagine yourself in the shoes of Uriel Arcangelo, waiting for the flames to consume him, his dead wife turning to ash and smoke in the furnace which his two brothers were now treating with an everyday disdain, as if it were simply another piece of malfunctioning machinery.

He couldn't do what Falcone wanted, though. Something was wrong here and, from Falcone's diffident yet taut manner, he wondered if the inspector knew it as well. No two families reacted to tragedy in the same way: sometimes there was anger and hatred; sometimes simple disbelief and a mute refusal to accept plain fact.

Michele and Gabriele Arcangelo, on the other hand, seemed almost indifferent to what had occurred. Or, more accurately, they felt the resuscitation of the foundry – and the flame of the giant angel's beacon outside – came first, ranked higher on their inflexible set of priorities than the idea that their youngest brother had murdered his wife just a few hours before, in this very place.

Nic Costa felt lost for a moment, then was aware he wasn't alone. He turned and found himself looking at a woman who had come to stand by his side without making a sound. She seemed to be in her mid-forties. Her long dark hair was very clean and straight, with a touch of silver to it, as if the true colour was grey but disguised by dye. She was wearing an old red cotton shirt, good quality once, made shapeless over the years, and dark cheap slacks. The poor clothes didn't match her unlined face, which was aristocratic and striking, dominated by inquisitive brown eyes. This was the person he'd seen at the strange window jutting out over the lagoon, staring out at them, seeming lost.

That impression was immediately dispelled by her manner.

'I thought there might be more of you,' she said in a warm, well-spoken, northern voice. 'I'm Raffaela Arcangelo. I must apologize for my brothers. They're . . . single-minded sometimes.'

'Nic Costa,' he replied, aware that Falcone was bearing down on them, eagle-eyed, curious. 'This is Inspector Falcone.'

'Signor Costa,' she said, a little warily. 'Inspector.'

He waited for Falcone to take the lead. It wasn't happening. Some small, puzzled inner voice told him Falcone felt a little awed by this fetching woman who returned his open gaze with an equal frankness.

'It would be best if we spoke upstairs,' she said. 'I'll ask my brothers to join us once they're ready.' She glanced at Peroni, who'd almost given up trying to get a word out of the Arcangeli. 'It's no use. We've been through this once already with the men who preceded you. My brothers will talk when they want to talk. Not before.'

Falcone found his voice.

'That's understandable, Signora Arcangelo,' he said, giving her his personal card. 'You have our condolences, naturally. And my apologies for the fact we must be here now. To lose two family members simultaneously must be terrible. I can understand why we're the last people you want to see.'

The woman's eyes fell on the card he'd supplied, then swept over Falcone.

'You're the first person who's had the good grace to say anything like that today,' Raffaela Arcangelo replied, somewhat surprised. 'Thank you. May we get out of this place? Please? It's not . . . somewhere I care to be right now.'

'Of course,' Falcone agreed. 'This is quite the wrong time. These officers who spoke to you earlier. They took statements?'

She was bemused.

'They did. I thought you might have known.'

'The system is a little slow to catch up sometimes. It's inexcusable.'

He couldn't take his eyes off the keys on her belt. Falcone extended a hand towards them.

'May I see those, please?'

The request caught her off guard. Nevertheless, without any hesitation, Raffaela unhooked the bunch and handed them over. Falcone examined each in turn, spending most time on the long, old shaft of metal which was, Costa thought, a match for the one in the door. Then he quickly brought the bunch up to his nose, sniffed, and handed them back.

'I'm sorry,' he said. 'That was stupid of me. Everything smells of smoke around here at the moment.'

She wasn't put out by his actions, or offended either.

'It does,' she agreed. 'Were you . . . looking for something, Inspector?'

He smiled, an expression Nic Costa rarely saw, one that, at that moment, seemed remarkably genuine.

'Just a bad habit, I'm afraid. Who else would have keys to this building? I'm sorry, I imagine you've been asked all this before.'

'No,' she replied, thinking. 'I haven't been asked that question at all. Only the family keep keys. Myself. Michele, Gabriele. And Uriel and Bella, of course.'

'Hugo Massiter?' Costa asked.

A brief cloud of distaste crossed her face.

'Why should he have keys?'

'I thought he was working on the palazzo next door.'

'His men are working on the palazzo. Massiter visits from time to time. They are allowed in only during the day. Michele opens the gates for them. There's no need for anything else. Not yet anyway. Signor Massiter' – there was an unmistakable note of bitterness in her voice – 'has not acquired us. Not yet.'

Falcone considered this.

'You and your brothers. You're not married.'

'Michele is divorced. Gabriele and I never married.'

'And no one else lives on the island?'

She gave him a cautious look.

'It's been a while since we could afford servants, Inspector. I thought they might have told you that too.'

'We're not local. But I'm sure you noticed. And this nightwatchman? He had no keys?'

'Piero? No. There was no need. He just brings material to the lower warehouse by boat. We don't even bother to lock that. There's nothing of great value in it and it doesn't allow access to any other part of the buildings.'

'And,' Falcone persisted, 'Uriel and Bella? They would have had a set each.'

'Yes,' she answered, a small note of testiness starting to appear in her voice. 'Bella worked in here a little too. Is all this important?'

'Probably not,' he replied, shaking his head, smiling. 'You must understand – these days we're tied in regulations from head to toe. In cases like this we have to account for every last piece of evidence, however unimportant. It's just paperwork really. Oh . . .'

He withdrew the evidence pouch from his pocket and held the transparent bag in front of her.

'I do need you to identify this set for me, please. Yours has a green sash on it, I see. This has a crimson one, mostly burned by the heat but recognizable nonetheless. These were Uriel's?'

She gazed miserably at the object in the bag.

'That's correct,' she replied.

'And Bella's? They had a sash too?'

'Yellow.' She was thinking. 'And before you ask, Michele's is black and Gabriele's blue. We're an organized family. Michele likes to know who to blame if there's carelessness about.'

'It would be useful for the records if we knew where Bella's keys are,' he said, as if it were a matter of small importance.

Raffaela's eyes wandered towards the furnace.

'Surely . . . She was found there. Wouldn't that be the place to look?'

Falcone nodded.

'Probably. I gather there's an abundance of material back at the Questura. This is an awkward time, signora. I really believe the police should intrude on a family's grief as little as possible. You've been pestered enough already. We may not know why this tragedy occurred but it seems clear it is . . . self-contained, shall I say?'

Raffaela Arcangelo's strong, handsome face became stern and determined.

'It's inexplicable, Inspector. Uriel was my brother. He had a temper. All the Arcangelo men have. But to kill someone. His wife . . . No. I don't believe it. All I can think of is that there was a terrible accident of some kind.'

Falcone's eyes sparkled.

'Possibly. And Bella? What was she like? Had they been married long. Were they a . . . loving couple?'

Raffaela grimaced.

'They'd been married for twelve years or so. I don't recall exactly. They'd been cold with one another for some time. These things occur a marriage, I believe. She wanted children. It never happened.'

He paused, then asked, 'Bella told you this?'

There was a rush of anger in her eyes that both men understood. Raffaela Arcangelo was at the very limit of her patience with them.

'Uriel,' she replied curtly. 'What's that about blood being thicker than water? It was an accident, Inspector. There's no other possible explanation.'

'An accident he could have avoided,' Falcone replied quietly. 'You see the problem for me there? Whatever happened in this room, he could have walked to the door, opened it and gone for help. Instead . . .'

Falcone left the matter there. Raffaela Arcangelo's deep, attractive eyes had welled with tears, suddenly, and it was as much a shock to her as it was to them.

She dashed a bitter look at her two brothers, who worked on the furnace oblivious to the world.

'I can't cope with this,' she said finally, once she'd recovered some composure. 'There are arrangements to be made, and just me to make them.'

'If there's any way we can help,' Costa offered.

Raffaela Arcangelo gave him a dark look.

'This family buries its own. It's not police work. When do you wish to interview us again, Inspector?'

'Tomorrow,' Falcone replied. 'I'll be in touch about a convenient time. If you need me beforehand, you have my mobile number on the card.'

'Tomorrow.'

Then she walked off, stepping over the fallen doors, out into the bright blue day.

Falcone's eyes followed her departure avidly. There was an unhealthy amount of interest in his sharp, ascetic face.

'Is there something I should know, sir?' Costa asked.

'Presently,' Falcone replied cheerily, then looked at his watch. 'Now, listen to me carefully. I'm going back to town to see what passes for a morgue in this place. You poke around in here for a little while, just to let them know we're interested. Then take an hour for lunch. More if you like. Visit a few cafés. Peroni's good at that. Be nosy. Be obvious. After that, talk to this Bracci family. I want people to understand we're asking lots of questions. That'll get back to Randazzo which should do us some good. Tomorrow, first thing, I want to see this casual worker they had out on Sant' Erasmo. We've got the boat after all. Best use it. When you're through here it'll be close to five o'clock anyway. That's when your shift ends. You've got your women in tow. Leave early if you're finished.'

Costa didn't know what to say. Falcone was a man who never let go once a case began. They were all used to working every hour of the day to get a result. Shifts, lunch, dinner, family . . . everything went out of the window to get him what he wanted.

'Why are you looking at me in that curious way?' the inspector asked.

'I just . . .' Costa stuttered. '*Lunch?* We never take lunch. This is a murder inquiry.'

'Ten out of ten for observation!' Falcone replied chirpily. 'But you heard Randazzo. He's the commissario. He just wants a painstaking inquiry, and that is what I intend to deliver. Besides, you've seen this for yourself. What happened here happened in this room. I don't think there's a guilty party trying to escape us now, is there? In fact, I don't see anyone hereabouts keen to make much of a move at all. Even for a funeral.'

Costa was silent. The man had the scent of something, and it was useless trying to probe. He would say what he wanted, when he wanted, and nothing would bring it out into the light of day any earlier.

Falcone rattled the keys in his jacket pocket.

'Oh,' he added. 'You'll be eating together tonight, presumably? The four of you? I imagine it's that little restaurant that Peroni found? The one with the peasant food?'

'"Family cooking" is how it's described, I think.'

'Not in my family it wasn't. Still I'm willing to slum it once in a while. You don't mind if I string along, do you? It's been ages since I saw the ladies. I won't intrude, I promise. The time?'

'Eight thirty,' Costa muttered, half rebellious. He hadn't wanted to share a meal with Peroni and Teresa. He and Emily had spent too little time together as it was. Now with another chair at the table . . .

'Good.'

Falcone took one last, self-satisfied look around the room. Then he caught Costa's eye.

'Two deaths usually mean *two* murders, Nic. Remember that. Always start off from the obvious. Let the unlikely prove itself later. I'll make a detective of you yet.'

'*Two* murders?'

'Exactly,' Falcone said. The keys rattled in his pocket again. 'But at least we've one of them in the bag.'

6

At four that afternoon Teresa and Emily sat on the waterfront a little way down from San Marco, escaping the crowds and the heat. After the phone calls from the men, breaking the bad news, they'd gorged on pasta in a little restaurant under the shadow of the Greci church's crooked tower, then bought a couple of *gelati*, a boozy confection of vanilla and brandy-soaked raisins for Teresa Lupo, a lemon water ice for Emily Deacon. Now they slumped, half dozing, a little bored, in the shade made by the prow of a gigantic cruise ship, with just enough room past the white metal for a view of the beautiful and busy lagoon beyond.

'Venice in August,' Teresa moaned. 'We must be mad. I mean, the place even *smells*. I thought that was supposed to be a myth.'

'Italians complain too much,' Emily declared. 'Most of the time it is a myth. Sit back, ignore your nose and enjoy yourself.'

'In this heat!'

Teresa Lupo felt as though she could squeeze a bucket of water out of her limp cotton shirt. The humidity was astonishing. It made every step she took an effort, a drain on what reserves of energy she had after the night train. She wasn't even sure how annoyed she was that Peroni wouldn't be on vacation with her after all at the end of the day. The city instilled lethargy in her. If he really could take extra time once the case was over, she could rework her own vacation schedule and possibly find another two weeks. Emily was in the same position. They had been livid initially – that went without saying. But it could still work out in the end.

And, she was out of Rome. Away from the morgue for the first time in months. It was the quiet season there anyway. Silvio Di

Capua, her assistant, could surely cope. Silvio was becoming the coping kind more and more each day. Some time soon she could cast off from the whole show if she liked, and never have to worry – much – about what was left behind. She'd talked the idea over with Peroni, usually when the grappa bottle had materialized after dinner. The two of them quitting the city, moving out to Tuscany. She could work as a rural doctor, stitching up farmers, caring for their fat, pregnant wives. And he could go and try out what he had really wanted all along, from when he was a country kid: raising pigs on some rural smallholding, selling gorgeous roast *porchetta* at the weekend markets in and around Siena. Dreams . . . They were ridiculous, impossible. They teased her too, if only because, until Gianni Peroni came along, she'd never really had any.

Emily finished her *gelato* then threw her napkin into the nearby bin with an accuracy Teresa wished she could teach Peroni.

She stared out at the flat expanse of grey water, with its ever-active flotilla of vessels, the ferries and the vaporetti, the speedboats and the transport barges, then sighed.

'I'm going to have to tell him, Emily. I can't just not say a thing.'

They'd discussed this on the train, huddled close together in a second-class carriage as it rattled through the black airless night. Teresa's shift hadn't finished till two a.m. There really hadn't been an alternative to the early morning departure. And it was typical of Emily that she had gone along with the awkward timing. Teresa had known her for little more than eight months. Even so, she'd found she was a good person to talk to. On this subject the best. It was all so much easier than trying to explain the matter to Gianni Peroni's face.

Emily frowned, took the spent cone of the *gelato* from Teresa's fingers, and disposed of it in an oddly maternal fashion.

'You don't know for sure,' she said, gazing steadily into her face. 'Don't rush things.'

'Oh, for Christ's sake!' Teresa snapped. 'I'm a doctor, remember? I can cut through all that bullshit with a knife. I used to dispense it myself once upon a time. That's how it is, Emily. Nothing's going to change.'

You never let a patient lose all hope. Not unless there really was no alternative. All those specialists she'd seen without Peroni's knowledge had done their best to hide the truth. But it was impossible in the circumstances. She wasn't phased by talk of severe tubal occlusion. She knew how to unpick what they told her. When she did, she was amazed to discover that there could be something so fundamentally, if benignly, wrong with her reproductive system without her knowing. And she could read the look in all their eyes too, when she fixed them with every last unavoidable question she could dream up. Nothing – not surgery, not even in vitro fertilization – would make a difference. Teresa Lupo was – she loathed the word but it summed up the situation with an apt finality – barren, and would remain so for the rest of her diminishing supposedly child-bearing years.

Emily looked downcast. Teresa hated herself for that brief outburst. It was unlike her, and undeserved too.

'Sorry, sorry, sorry,' she said, and squeezed the American woman's hands. Nic had done well with her, Teresa thought. She was kind and pretty and straight as a die. Intelligent too. One day she'd make a tidy living as an architect in her own right. Teresa didn't doubt that, though she couldn't help but wonder whether it was a profession that would sit well alongside a cop for a partner. 'I hereby renounce my bad temper and undertake to be the epitome of sweet and happy innocence for the remainder of this holiday.'

'Let's not get too ambitious,' Emily cautioned.

'Why not? The idea was ridiculous in the first place. Gianni and I having kids. Him pushing fifty, with two of his own already. Me a spinster of thirty . . . whatever . . . who, up till the point he came along, thought children belonged in a pet shop.'

Emily's sparky face clouded with shrewd, measured scepticism. Teresa envied her her looks so much. She was slim, she was blonde, she had fine straight hair that never appeared heavy. She was the sort of woman other women hated. No, not *hated* exactly. Just looked at and thought: *why you, why not me?* Because it all seemed to come so easily, though perhaps that was deceptive. There'd been times recently when Teresa had thought so. When she came to believe she saw a shadow cross Emily's face if the subject of Rome and Nic and that big old house off the Via Appia Antica, where she now lived and studied alone, came into the discussion.

This was in danger of turning into one of those conversations Teresa hated. The kind she normally disrupted with a kiss, a tantrum or a sudden demand for a coffee, none of which was available or appropriate in the circumstances.

'The trouble is Gianni,' she confessed. 'He'll take it in his stride. I never met anyone who copes, straight out of the box, with whatever crap gets thrown in his direction. I'm not like that. I dwell on it. If I get the chance I throw myself into my work and try to forget what's running round my head. Doesn't take long either. Except I can't now. Not here. Not . . .' she waved her hand in the direction of the campanile of San Giorgio Maggiore, like a mirror image of that in San Marco, reflecting in the dappled water. '. . . with all this.'

'Art,' Emily declared, with a stern glance, one with that disturbing maternal touch about it again.

'I don't know a single thing about art!'

'I'll teach you.'

Teresa was pouting like a schoolgirl, and she knew it. She was lost for words too, a touch ashamed. A woman in her mid-thirties shouldn't be leaning on a slim, pretty American, the young girlfriend of a man she liked and admired. She shouldn't be hoping some twenty-six-year-old could lend a little balance to a life that had spent so many years out on the far edge of normality.

'Do they have anything gory here?' Teresa asked. 'It's just so I can keep my hand in.'

Emily Deacon frowned.

'Not really. Venice is different. More . . . subtle. I imagine that's the right word. But I'll do my best.'

'Thanks,' Teresa said. 'You make an old woman very happy. And . . .'

Emily Deacon laughed at that last one. Maybe that was why Teresa felt able to say what she said next, to let slip the dumb thought that should have remained unsaid, hidden at the back of her head.

'. . . when you two come round to having kids I can be the Mad Aunt. The soft touch for presents. Babysitter. What have you . . .'

She swore at herself then looked at Emily Deacon, who was staring at the lagoon in silence. It was a beautiful view, Teresa thought, even with that faint, antiseptic stink behind everything.

'I'm sorry, Emily,' she said. 'That was really thoughtless of me. Presumptuous too. I just meant . . .'

Those long, young fingers squeezed her hand. Emily's pale, smiling face turned to look at her. Teresa hoped she was mistaken, but it seemed there was just the hint of moisture at the corner of those sharp blue eyes.

'It doesn't matter,' Emily remarked, with a quiet insistence.

7

Aldo Bracci was a squat, sour-faced man around fifty, with a bald head and narrow, beady eyes. He worked in a tiny office on the ground floor of the family foundry almost a kilometre from the Isola degli Arcangeli, down a dark narrow *ramo* near the museum. It was a world away from the Murano the tourists saw. Dismal, malodorous passages ran up from the canal, high-walled on both sides, too slender to take more than a couple of pedestrians at a time. The rank aroma of foundry smoke and spent gas hung in the air. There was no artifice, no pretension in the workaday premises around the Bracci furnace. These were people desperate to earn a living out of that daily dance with molten glass and blazing fire. Bracci, in his dusty blue overalls, looked more hungry than most. The chaos in the little office – invoices and bills everywhere – and the meagreness of the works told their own story. These were minnows, a class beneath the grand names found close to the vaporetti stops. Individuals who lived in the margins left by the big players, hoping to find some crumbs falling between the cracks.

Bracci cast a weary eye over a dated-looking vase newly out of the workshop, cursed in impenetrable Venetian, then walked over to the office and placed it in a pile marked 'Seconds'. The two cops waited in their seats, wondering, Costa feeling a little edgy after downing three coffees in succession as they trawled the bars for gossip before approaching Aldo Bracci. They had followed Falcone's orders to the letter. They'd eaten a couple of plates of pasta in a small, unimpressive restaurant. To Costa's surprise it had been a smart move. People hereabouts weren't naturally talkative, until you mentioned the magic name, Arcangelo. Then a picture began to emerge, both of the family and of Murano itself, somewhere with little time for incomers who failed to appreciate their place.

'You've got workers,' Peroni noted. 'One up on your late brother-in-law.'

Bracci's cold eyes glowered at them.

'Men like to be paid from time to time. Don't you?'

'Sure,' Costa replied. 'Is this a convenient time to talk, sir? We don't wish to intrude on your grief.'

Not that there seemed much of that, Costa thought. Bracci was as brisk and unmoved as the Arcangeli, though in a different way. There was a sign on the door of the foundry which announced 'Closed for Mourning'. It was only when they persisted that they realized the place was working behind shuttered windows, perhaps not wanting the world outside to know.

'Grief,' Bracci repeated. 'Bella got a morning of grief. When you people allow us to bury her she'll get some more. Not that it makes much difference to her now, does it? We don't overdo the ceremonies. You're outsiders. You won't understand.'

Costa and Peroni looked at one another. Neither was sure how to conduct this interview. Bracci didn't look like the bereaved brother. Nor did he seem entirely detached either.

'Are the Arcangeli outsiders?' Costa asked.

Bracci stifled a grim laugh.

'What do you think? You've met them?'

Peroni nodded. 'They've been here fifty, sixty years or something? How long does it take?'

'It was 1952,' Bracci corrected him. 'That arrogant old bastard sold his boatyard in Chioggia and took on that wreck of an island thinking he could teach us all a lesson or two.'

'Did he?' Costa asked.

The man wriggled on the old, battered leather chair at the desk.

'For a while. Angelo Arcangelo was a different breed. Not like those kids of his at all. He treated them so hard they never learned how to stand on their own two feet. Stupid. Angelo knew how to make money, though. He knew how to sweet-talk all those rich foreigners, to say to them, "Look, see this! It's how they made it three centuries ago! Burnt seaweed and pebbles. A furnace burning wood. It's perfect! Think what it'll be worth twenty years from now!" Or to get some so-called modern artist to come up with some designs he could pretend were some kind of masterpiece or something. Except . . .'

He reached down into the desk drawers and pulled out a small box that rattled as he moved it.

'Fashions change. You change with them or one day no one rings the bell.'

He scattered the contents of the box on the table. They were tiny trinkets, gaudily coloured. Cartoon characters: Mickey Mouse; Homer Simpson; Donald Duck. Only just recognizable. They were junk, and Bracci knew it.

'I can get some school kid in here turning out fifty of those an hour. I pay him four euros. I sell them for fifty to some huckster near the station. He passes them on for four euros, maybe five a pop to the idiot tourists who want to take home some genuine Murano glass. Which is what they get too. No arguments there. Do you think the Arcangeli are going to stoop that low?'

That wasn't their business, Costa thought, and said so.

'So what is their business, smart guy?' Bracci asked. 'Let me tell you. They work in a museum. That stupid old furnace, ten times bigger than they need. They got no modern equipment, nothing that saves time or money. They use all these old recipes and designs. It takes them four times longer than the rest of us to make something that, for most of the world out there, looks exactly the same. You think they're going to get four times the price? No. Not even twice. Not even the same price sometimes, because this is old stuff they're selling. Designs that went out years ago. With flaws, because the old ways give you flaws and no one buys the fact they're really features, not any more. You know what their business is? Going bust, that's what. And if it wasn't for Bella I wouldn't care a damn. Except that now she's gone, so as far as I'm concerned they can go screw themselves. Sell the whole damn place to that Englishman and turn it into an amusement park or something. Who gives a shit?'

'The Englishman?' Costa asked blithely.

'Oh, come on!' Bracci spat back. 'It's an open secret they've been trying to screw a deal out of him. It'd be done by now if the old man hadn't set up so many covenants the lawyers are getting rich trying to deal with them all. Mind you' – Bracci raised a finger to make his point – 'what the Englishman wants, the Englishman gets. I wouldn't want to jerk him around for a moment. Too many important friends. And if he buys that island . . .'

'What?' Peroni demanded.

Bracci scowled. 'Then he's made. You could put anything up there. A hotel. Some kind of shopping mall like they have on terra firma. If the Arcangeli had any sense they'd just put the whole plot out to tender on the open market. They'd make a fortune. Except they want to keep on making glass. Stupid.'

Costa found this information about Massiter interesting. He was a man of substance already. With the island in his grasp, he would become even more important.

'How do you feel about the idea of an English neighbour?' he asked.

'Wonderful. But at least we'd have just the one asshole to contend with. Is there something serious you want to ask me? Because if there isn't . . .'

He looked at the pile of glass cartoon characters on the desk, then gently scooped them back into the box.

Costa wasn't about to let go.

'Tell me about the Bracci family. Parents. Brothers. Sisters.'

'I'm the brother.' He kicked open the door to the furnace room. Two men in their twenties, thick-set and surly, glared back at them from the side of an oven a tenth the size of the Arcangeli's. One had close-cropped hair. His sleeves were rolled up, revealing a set of old deep blue tattoos on each arm. The other was a touch slimmer, with longer hair, a little less aggressive-looking, but not much.

'Enzo.'

Tattoos nodded.

'Fredo. These are my sons. The staff here too, most of the time. Their mother pissed off to Padova with some insurance clerk years back. Better off without the bitch.'

'Yeah.' Enzo Bracci nodded, then glowered at his brother, waited for him to go back to work before closing the door on them.

'Nobody else?' Peroni wondered.

'It was just me and Bella. I think my dad kind of stretched some of the rules about being a Catholic if you get my meaning. Not that there's anyone around to ask any more. There's been Braccis here for five hundred years. Go and take a look in the church if you don't believe me. The old man spawned the two of us and that was enough to make sure we won't disappear. My boys will do the same. As for Bella . . . She was the one who decided to marry into that bunch of jumped-up peasants. That was her problem. Besides . . .'

Aldo Bracci suddenly looked displeased with himself, a rare event Costa guessed. It was as if he'd gone too far.

'Yes?' Peroni prodded.

'It was a bad idea all along,' Bracci said with a dismissive wave of his hand. 'I never really got it. Uriel wasn't the greatest catch in the sea. Bella was pretty. A looker. She could have done better. It was almost as if . . .'

He grimaced, wondering about what he was going to say.

'This was after my dad was gone. He'd never have allowed it. I almost thought it was an arranged marriage, somehow. Bella and Uriel just sprung it on us and I wasn't going to get into some vendetta to stop them. Besides, it was Michele who kept pushing. To begin with I thought he was the one who was really after her. But he was just too damned old. It was all money anyway. I guess he thought maybe we could save him. Bella was from a glass family. She knew things. Production techniques. Little secrets we don't share outside the island. I used to think that what Michele really wanted was to get his hands on those. But she never let them see her working. She did it at dead of night when no one was around. At least, that's what she said. Good job too. If they'd been found stealing, they'd have been dead in Murano. Finished. What we've got is ours. It doesn't go elsewhere. Least of all to a bunch of boatmen.'

Bracci's comments rang a bell in Costa's head. He'd read several histories of Venice during all those long empty evenings on his own. One of them went into detail about the glass industry on the island, which had been placed there from the thirteenth century, moved on the Doge's orders because of the constant fires it caused in Venice itself. There was a brotherhood on the island, a closed, almost Masonic organization that swore its members to secrecy, and threatened dire consequences to any who gave away its techniques to those outside.

'Bella knew about glass?' Costa asked.

Bracci nodded vigorously. 'She was as good with a furnace as any man out there. Not that a woman was supposed to do that work. The Arcangeli thought different. She never used to talk about it much, but they let her in there a lot. She had her own clothes. Her own apron. Bella made Uriel a better *omo de note* than he deserved to be. And look what she got in return.'

Thrust into the Arcangeli's vast anachronism of a furnace, Costa thought. For no apparent reason.

'Did it ever occur to you that your sister could be in danger?' Peroni wondered.

'Bella?' Bracci laughed. 'You never knew her. Bella was in fear of no one. Certainly not that husband of hers.'

'Someone killed her,' Costa said severely, and instantly regretted it. There was thunder in Bracci's face, an ugly, rapid response that perhaps said more about the man than he intended.

'Don't fucking patronize me, sonny!' Bracci bellowed. 'It's your job to work out what went on there, isn't it? If I knew Uriel was going to kill her *he'd* have been the one in that furnace. But I didn't.'

The man's dead, tired face turned thoughtful for a brief moment.

'You want the truth?' he asked. 'I still can't believe he'd do that to her. Not really. It seems crazy. But that's Bella's bad luck and my bad judgement. Now do you have any more stupid questions? Or can a man get on with his work around here?'

Work. That was all Murano seemed interested in. Not two strange, inexplicable deaths. Just money, the daily spectacle of fires and mutable gobbets of glass visible through so many workshop doorways, beacons trying to attract the diminishing numbers of passers-by, lure them into the darkness and loosen their purses.

'You could tell us whether you have a set of keys to the Arcangeli's place,' Costa asked, undeterred. 'And where you were around two this morning.'

Bracci stood up, stormed across the room and held open the door into the alley outside.

'Get out!' he barked.

Neither man moved.

'They're simple questions,' Peroni observed. 'I don't think they should interfere with your grief.'

Bracci's furious glance fell on both of them. The door to the workshop opened. His two sons stood there, big and menacing, both eyeing Gianni Peroni, recognizing him as the greatest threat. There was violence inside this particular clan, Costa thought. Something he hadn't detected within the Arcangeli at all.

The cops didn't move. Peroni gave the sons his best, battered grin and said, 'Just two questions, Bracci. Then we're gone.'

The older man shot a vicious, bitter look at his offspring, mad their presence hadn't done the job.

'No! I don't have a set of keys. Why the hell should I? And last night? Ask them. We were all here. I was the *omo de note*. They were helping. Or' – he shot a bitter glance at the box of seconds – 'trying to anyway. We do what's necessary around here. We work. We earn.'

'All night?' Costa wondered.

Enzo stepped forward. He had his father's sour face; it was covered in soot and sweat. A big, strong man, Costa thought. The tattoos were something to do with music. Heavy metal. Thrash. Images of swords and skulls, thick strokes, the kind that must have hurt.

'All night,' Fredo said half-heartedly, glancing at the other two to see if he was doing the right thing. 'The three of us. We can vouch for each other.'

'That's what families do best,' Peroni said gently.

Enzo picked up a rag and wiped the soot and grease from his over-large hands. Then he looked them over and asked, 'You're not from around here, are you?'

Peroni smiled again.

'You noticed?'

'Yeah,' Enzo grunted, walked over to the seconds box, withdrew the flawed vase, and crashed it on the side of the table, exposing a line of jagged sharp glassy teeth.

He didn't wave the thing in their direction. He didn't need to.

'A word of advice,' he said. 'Go careful out there. It gets dark sooner than you think.'

8

Enzo Bracci was wrong. Night fell slowly on Venice, the way it did at the end of every clear, fine day, with a sunset so lovely it seemed unreal, a lasting hour of golden glory that trapped the city on the water in radiant amber. Leo Falcone watched it from the busy vaporetto terminus at Piazzale Roma, wondering about what he'd just seen in the city morgue and what he'd heard from a pathologist who was so unlike Teresa Lupo it was difficult to imagine the man was in the same profession. Alberto Tosi was seventy if he was a day, a tall, stiff individual of the old school, more meticulous in his manners than his work, if Falcone had read him correctly. A man of ideas, too. He didn't possess Teresa Lupo's down-to-earth practicality, though he was well enough read to have mentioned some of her cases when Falcone revealed he was on attachment from Rome. And that, with the formal news Tosi had imparted, raised possibilities along with the meagre report on Hugo Massiter that Falcone had read in the central Questura. An act which had, he noted, been watched with a degree of curiosity by the archives officer in charge of the place.

The inspector glanced at his watch, wondered, with some foreboding, what kind of restaurant Gianni Peroni would find so compelling he ate there four or five times a week, then walked down the jetty, out to the boat stop, and waited for the fast service, straight to San Zaccaria.

Raffaela Arcangelo watched the dying golden light too, acknowledging the familiar sight at the window of the kitchen in the dusty, crumbling mansion by the water. She was untouched by any sense of wonder. This was one more unexpected side effect of sudden loss. She was thinking of herself, of her life on this little island, home for nearly half a century apart from that brief period at college in Paris when, foolishly, she had briefly believed she might escape Murano and the hard, unrelenting grip of her family. But they had been dreams, and the Arcangeli never put much store in anything they couldn't see and touch, buy and sell. Which was why she was about to do what she always did at this time of night: make a meal, on this occasion simple *penne* pasta and tomato sauce. Some salad too. And fruit. She didn't have the time or money for better.

Raffaela had visited the city briefly, walked into a few of the antique shops scattered close to Fondamente Nove, negotiated the best price she could for her father's crystal, then used the cash to pay for a burial on San Michele, when the police allowed, with one of the undertakers situated by the vaporetto stop across from the island. He'd given a good discount when she offered to pay in full. It was an odd thing for a Venetian to do, stumping up money early. But at least that way Uriel's burial was settled. No one, not even Michele, could use the money once it was locked in the safe of a funeral service across the water.

After that, she'd made a perfunctory stop at the small grocery store near the lighthouse, paid cash for two fewer portions than normal, accepting their quiet, muted sympathies with a nod, nothing more. It was her opinion that the island did not dislike the Arcangeli anything like as much as the family imagined. Even the residents of Murano lacked the unhealthy enthusiasm needed to maintain a vendetta over the years. Ordinary people simply weren't made that way.

Then, before starting on the meal, she sat down with a glass of weak spritz and began to turn over the day's events in her mind. The dead were buried twice, she thought. Once in the earth. A second, more important time, in the memory. Neither event seemed as close as the family deserved.

The card was still in the pocket of her bag. She took it out and stared at the name there: Inspector Leo Falcone. With the address of a questura in Rome and two phone numbers, one, the land line, scribbled out and, in a legible, firm hand, replaced with a number for Verona. She walked to the window and watched the fire dying on the lagoon, tapping the card on her lips, wondering. The pasta was boiling: eight minutes to al dente. A decision had to be made. The Arcangeli had rarely dealt with the police over the years. They shared the conviction of the community around them that it was best to avoid all contact, unless absolutely necessary. Problems were there to be solved in the old ways, by negotiation and bargaining, alliances and trysts.

'In normal times,' she whispered to herself.

Raffaela Arcangelo turned down the flame under the pasta then called Falcone's mobile from the kitchen phone, speaking quietly, praying she would not be overheard.

'*Pronto*,' said a firm voice on the other end of the line.

'Inspector . . .'

There was the sound of a vaporetto, the chatter of people close to the man. Police inspectors led ordinary lives too, she reminded herself. They were merely mortal.

'Signora Arcangelo?'

He was surprised. Flattered perhaps.

'I was wondering . . .' she began, and found it difficult to phrase such a simple question.

'Wondering?' he asked.

There was the hint of amusement in his voice, which was quite warm it seemed to her.

'I didn't find the keys,' he said pleasantly. 'They weren't in the furnace. That was the question, I believe?'

'You're a very perceptive man, Inspector. Are you sure?'

'Absolutely. The only metal they found . . .'

His voice disappeared. She wondered if the line had gone dead.

'Yes?'

'The only metal they found was gold,' he said flatly. 'A small amount. Melted. Bella had a wedding ring?'

'Yes,' she replied in a quiet yet untroubled voice. These were practical matters. An Arcangelo knew how to address such things.

His voice sounded dejected.

'I'm sorry. These aren't pleasant details. Perhaps you would prefer it if I discussed them with your brothers.'

'I can speak for myself, thank you. And this *is* my business. More than yours in some ways.'

There was a pause on the line again.

'You didn't find anything either then?' he asked.

An intelligent man, she thought. One who didn't miss much.

'I've looked everywhere. Not a sign. To be honest with you I never saw Bella and Uriel's apartment looking so tidy. She was never one for housework.'

There was the sound of voices, an attendant calling the stop. San Zaccaria.

'Signora . . .'

'My name is Raffaela,' she interjected with a sudden determination. 'From listening to your men speaking when you're not around, I believe yours is Leo, which is interesting in itself. Do they normally call their superiors by their first name? No matter. We should. I want the truth now. You don't believe this is as simple as it seems. Nor do I. You have professional reasons. I have personal ones. Are we going to work together? Or are you going to be some stiff and pompous policeman who does everything by the book?'

He laughed then. She could hear him clearly over the crowd and the sound made her feel bold, more confident than ever that this was a man she could trust.

'I'm not from round here,' he answered. 'I don't know what passes for a book in Venice.'

'Leave that to me. I must make it clear, Leo. No one must know about this. Not my brothers. Not your officers either. This city has a very poor record of keeping secrets. I want to make an exception.'

'Of course. So what do you want me to do?'

She hesitated.

'Tell me what you think.'

There was caution in his voice.

'I have to have some limits,' he warned her.

'I understand that.'

'When?' he wondered.

'Not with my brothers tomorrow, Leo. We'll act as if this conversation has never taken place.'

A small rush of excitement and pleasure ran through her veins. Raffaela Arcangelo was aware she was blushing, and the thought made her feel deeply guilty.

'After that . . .' she continued.

'Massiter has this party in your exhibition hall tomorrow.'

'He does?'

Another detail kept from her. Michele must surely have known.

'I thought you would have been invited.'

'We're not the sociable kind. Not normally. A party?' It was inconceivable. Should she wear black? Or what? 'That wouldn't be right, Leo. Not in the circumstances.'

'Right or not,' he said, 'I think you should go. I *want* you to go. This is important. Besides . . .'

His voice was firm. But not like Michele's. There was no coercion, no threat there. Leo Falcone had a reason to ask this, she believed.

She waited before answering, trying to imagine what he was doing now, on that busy portion of waterfront close to La Pietà, where the fast boat to Murano departed every hour.

'There's something else,' Falcone added, rapidly changing the direction of the conversation. 'Did Bella or anyone else in the family own a mobile phone?'

'No,' she answered. 'Why do you ask?'

'No reason.'

A policeman never asked questions without some point.

'I don't believe you, Leo. We've never needed a mobile phone. None of us. *Why?*'

'I'm fishing in the dark, I'm afraid,' the voice on the line confessed, and sounded a little weary. 'Do you have any suggestions?'

'No.' It was a family matter, she thought. Not something to be shared with strangers.

The inspector would keep pressing, though. In the end . . .

'There is one thing you ought to know, Leo,' she said eventually. 'You'd doubtless find out in any case. The police never forget anything.'

'If only . . .'

She could sense his anticipation.

'There was trouble. Many, many years ago with Bella and her brother. I'm not saying any more. I'd never have told you this if I didn't think it would come out anyway. I believe you'll find the Questura knows Aldo Bracci. I'm pleased to say I don't, not well anyway.'

'I'll make some inquiries.'

'Do that. Is there anything else I can tell you?'

'You can tell me what you know about Hugo Massiter.'

The question surprised her.

'You mean you haven't heard of him?' she asked.

'Not till today. Now I know he's very rich. Very influential. And that, for a few years anyway, he was very much persona non grata in Italy.'

'It was in all the papers, Leo!' she objected. 'Surely you must remember. There was a terrible scandal. A piece of music – a wonderful piece of music by the way; I've heard it – was peddled as something it wasn't. First Massiter was responsible. Then he wasn't. Some Englishman and his girlfriend hoodwinked him apparently.'

'So I understand,' said the voice on the line. 'And people died.'

She'd forgotten that part somehow. It was the music that had stayed in her head. Small professional orchestras playing for the tourists now made it a centrepiece of their repertoire, one that was almost as popular as the *Seasons*. Just as memorable, and fresher somehow.

'People died. It was nothing to do with Hugo Massiter. The papers all said that in the end. Why would he have returned to Venice otherwise? You're a police officer. You should surely know more about this than me.'

'I should,' Leo Falcone conceded. 'And tomorrow?'

She looked at the pasta pot and the cloud of steam finding the window, working its way out towards the iron angel, whose flame burned once more, flickering in the wind, devouring gas they could ill afford. Raffaela Arcangelo wondered how many meals she'd cooked over the years, how much of her life had been spent working in this kitchen.

'Tomorrow they can feed themselves for a change,' she said.

9

Arms gingerly interlocked, Nic Costa and Emily Deacon walked the short distance from the small apartment in Castello to the waterfront by Giardini. It was just ten minutes from here to Peroni's restaurant in the back streets, beyond the Arsenale. They needed some time to themselves. More than the evening's dinner with Peroni and Teresa – and Leo Falcone as self-invited guest – would allow.

Emily freed herself and took a table outside a small café. They ordered a couple of over-priced coffees, the cost enhanced by the unencumbered view of the lagoon. The deep yellow stain of the sun was flooding down from the mountains that rippled the distant horizon of terra firma and everything – the lagoon, the city, the reflections of buildings in the dappled water – took on its warm, rich hue. Sometimes, when he was alone with nothing better to do, Costa would catch the slow vaporetto, number one, up the Grand Canal just to witness this moment, and watch the quiet wonder it created in the eyes of his fellow travellers, even of a few Venetians from time to time.

'Tell me about the case, Nic,' she suggested. 'As much as you can. It must be important if they're cancelling your leave.'

Costa couldn't forget that Emily was making a fundamental shift in her life: trying to put away her lost career as an FBI agent kicked out of the Bureau for insubordination, and replace it with a future as an architect in a foreign country. All the same, her past lived with her still. She was always curious, always interested in a challenge. It was one of the aspects of her complex, multi-faceted personality that intrigued him.

'It's . . .' he paused, wondering if he were really on the right track '. . . the usual story. A family affair. A man kills his wife, then either kills himself, or dies accidentally. We don't know yet.'

'It sounds straightforward.'

But this was Venice, he thought. Or, more accurately, Murano, a place that welcomed the prying eyes of investigators even less.

'I think so. By the way, we have an invitation to a party tomorrow night. Hugo Massiter. The Englishman with the boat. Does the name ring a bell?'

She looked baffled.

'No. Should it?'

'Five years ago. There was a scandal.'

'Five years ago I was in Washington trying to be someone else,' she said quickly. 'And when aren't there scandals?'

He must have looked downcast.

'I'm sorry, Nic. Do you really think I should have heard of him?'

'I have,' he replied. 'And I want to know the details before I meet him again. He sees himself as a player in the city. He's buying the Arcangeli's island on Murano, where those people died. Tomorrow night we're invited to a party there. He's renovating it apparently; it's going to be a gallery.'

Emily's forehead grew even more furrowed.

'This is the Isola degli Arcangeli you're talking about?'

'You've heard of it?'

'Anyone who's studied modern Italian architecture has heard of it. It's one of the great follies of the twentieth century.'

Her blue eyes were wide with anticipation.

'That place is supposed to be amazing. They've kept the public out for years. I thought it was unsafe.'

'Not with the work Hugo Massiter's having done.'

'He's buying it? I would have thought a site like that would end up being the property of the city. It's a kind of local monument. An odd one, a forgotten one, but all the same . . .'

Costa recalled Massiter's quiet complaints of penury, and his obvious closeness to local officials.

'Perhaps there was a small arrangement. I don't know. He certainly hopes to own it now. He seems a little short of cash too. Does that add up?'

'If he's trying to restore a failed project like that, you bet. I've read up on the Isola degli Arcangeli. Everyone who hopes to get an architecture degree in Italy does. It's mandatory, an object lesson in what happens when you're more interested in design than structure. Much of it was judged to be fundamentally unsound from the outset. The man who came up with most of the plans wasn't even a professional architect if I recall correctly. A couple of people got badly hurt when a roof collapsed twenty years or so ago. It's been closed to the public ever since. You have to be talking about a big, big project to get it back to something close to usable.'

Massiter had seemed desperate, perhaps in more ways than he was admitting. And he wasn't bluffing about the deadline to conclude the deal with the Arcangeli either.

'Rich men's toys,' he murmured.

'Some toy,' she said, eyes glittering. 'I'd give anything to see inside. And we're going to a party there?'

But it was just another old building, he wanted to say. In a city full of them. Nic Costa was no boor. He appreciated Venice. He loved many of the sights. There was still something about the place that disturbed him. Nothing moved. Nothing changed in the lethargic melancholy of the lagoon. Even the people seemed to think their small, mundane lives would run on forever, trapped in the bright wash of the sky that flooded over them.

'I must be coming up in the world,' he murmured.

'*We* must coming up in the world,' she corrected him quietly.

He brushed the soft hair aside from her cheek, and kissed her again, more slowly this time, pleased to feel her responding.

'We . . .' he whispered '. . . must eat.'

'Do we have to?' she murmured.

There was no choice. Falcone had ordered a chair at the table for a reason. Besides, something told Nic Costa he needed to be on his guard. Perhaps for all of them. Peroni was winding down into holiday mode. Falcone seemed to believe everything, while more complex than it appeared at first, would be a piece of cake. To him, Venice was a backwater, a place where a city cop could wipe the floor with the locals. Costa wasn't so certain.

'We do,' he said. 'Just for a while.'

10

The restaurant was down a back alley between Arsenale and the main drag of Castello, the Via Garibaldi, a quarter of low working-class houses not far from the police apartments. Peroni had found it within a week of their arrival in the city. He had an uncanny sense about where to eat, and a way of buttering up the staff too. Two sisters, big, friendly women, ran the place. Their daughters, pretty young teenagers, worked the ten cramped tables, each with four settings, that filled the dark interior. Most nights Costa and Peroni had to queue – though not for long, his partner's quick wit had soon seen to that. But this was August, when hordes of locals abandoned the city for somewhere cooler. There was only one other group in the place, so Peroni pulled together a couple of tables at the far end of the room to give the five of them plenty of space and privacy, listened, beaming with pleasure, to the brief list of evening specials, then sat back to enjoy the meal, a man in gastronomic heaven.

Nic Costa knew good eating when he saw it and this was good, seriously good in a way rarely found in Venice because it was all utterly authentic, as close to home cooking as they were likely to get outside a private house. Costa's vegetarianism had now relaxed to the extent that he ate fish, principally because it was so good there. A plate of pasta with tiny brown shrimps was the first course for each of them, some crisp, fresh rocket on the side. Peroni had insisted on *stinchi* for the meat-eaters, ham hocks slowly roasted in garlic and oil. Costa had decided to stick with the gorgeous *sarde in saor*, fresh sardines slowly marinated with vinegar, oil, onions, pine nuts and sultanas, a Venetian speciality the two sisters prepared themselves, day in and day out, and one which couldn't be bettered anywhere in the city. Even Leo Falcone looked content once he'd pulled a bad-tempered face at the house red, a weedy Veneto makeweight pumped straight from the barrel, and replaced it with a couple of bottles of fancy Amarone from behind the counter.

Then Falcone pushed away his plate with that wily expression on his face that always made Costa feel uneasy, smiled at Teresa Lupo and said, 'Spontaneous combustion. You're a pathologist. Have you ever met a case? Is it rare?'

She gagged on her ham joint and stared at him, dumbfounded. 'Spontaneous combustion?'

Falcone pulled a sheet of paper out of his pocket and placed it on the table. Teresa picked it up, began reading, looked at the official crest on the top then choked again.

'He's quite an old pathologist they have here,' Falcone said. 'Seems knowledgeable. According to him Uriel Arcangelo died of spontan—'

'What next?' she interrupted. 'Are we going to have people expiring of witchcraft or something? Did you find any wax dolls with pins in them lying around, Leo? Are you going to give up forensic and use a Ouija board instead? Good God . . .' She put down her knife and fork, a sign that she was surely taking the matter seriously. 'You cannot allow this to be recorded as a stated cause of death. I won't allow it. You'll be a laughing stock. Every nut magazine and TV programme on the planet will be after you.'

Falcone beamed back at her, unruffled.

'The pathologist here, Tosi, said it's a documented phenomenon. There was even a case in Dickens. *Bleak House*, I believe . . .'

Teresa's voice rose to an angry howl.

'Dickens wrote fiction, for Christ's sake! I'm a pathologist. I deal in science, not mumbo-jumbo. Listen to what I am saying. Regardless of some ancient British author's opinions to the contrary, there is no such thing as spontaneous combustion. It is physically impossible. A myth. A fantasy. The kind of thing that should be filed alongside alien abductions, telepathy and stigmata.'

'All matters which some people believe in. With documented cases—' he repeated.

'No, no, no! Look. This is just part of the fashion for irrational bullshit that poor bastards like me have to put up with these days. People hate a world that's logical, rational and largely capable of explanation. So they fill it with this crap because it makes them feel safe at night somehow, thinking that there really are ghosts and flying saucers out there, and we're not just what we appear: a collection of atoms wandering through the world waiting for the day we start to fall apart. You cannot—'

'He's adamant he's going to put that on the death certificate,' Falcone pressed.

'Stop him! Please! It's not possible. The man must be gaga or something.'

Peroni put down his knife and fork and pointed a finger at Falcone.

'If Teresa says it's not possible, Leo . . .'

'You heard Randazzo!' Falcone objected. 'We just do as we're told. Sign off the papers. Then go home early. Besides, we've got a witness statement from this *garzone* who saw Uriel Arcangelo die. He was on fire.'

Falcone's incisive, bird-like eyes peered out at them from that familiar, walnut face. His bald scalp was glowing under the yellow restaurant lights. He was engrossed by this case, Costa saw, and would surely refuse to let go until he got to the bottom of what happened on the Isola degli Arcangeli.

'Fire, the witness said, that came from inside him,' the inspector continued. 'Fire's combustion, isn't it? It sounds spontaneous to me.'

'Oh no!' Teresa wagged a finger in Falcone's impassive brown face. 'I know what you're trying to do. I'm off duty here. You're not stealing my holiday the way you stole theirs. This is down to you, Leo. If the pathologist you've got believes in fairies that's your problem. Go take an aromatherapy course and deal with it.'

'He seems a rational man,' Falcone replied mildly. 'A little traditional. A little set in his ways, perhaps. You have to remember he doesn't have your kind of experience. Murder and Venice rarely meet. He knows that too. He was very flattering about you when I mentioned we'd worked together.'

He poured some more wine and left it at that with Teresa gagging for the rest of the compliment.

'He's heard of me?'

Falcone held the glass up to the light, admiring the deep red stain it cast on the white tablecloth.

'First thing he said when I told him I came from Rome. "Do you know Dr Lupo? Did you read about the wonderful work she did on the body from the bog?" And the rest.'

'Leo . . .' Peroni growled.

'All I'm saying,' he continued, 'is that if Teresa here would like to take a look at this case of spontaneous combustion—'

'Don't use that phrase,' she cautioned menacingly. 'Don't even utter the words.'

'If you wished to take a peek at the body, I don't think it would be a problem.'

Teresa Lupo reached over, snatched the expensive bottle from his grasp, then tried to pour herself a glass. It was empty.

'Hard to make a decision without a drink,' she announced.

Falcone sniffed and stared at the label on the Amarone. Costa had found it so good he'd checked the label: Dal Forno Romano. His late father had had a taste for that one. It was, he said, like Barolo, a fighting wine.

'At forty euros a bottle that's an expensive decision. So will you just cast your eyes over what I've got here? Give me a second opinion. Just me, you understand. I don't want you getting into a catfight with Tosi. He doesn't look as if his heart could stand it.'

'I don't give second opinions,' she snapped. 'I dish out facts.'

'Facts then,' Falcone agreed, waving at the pretty teenage waitress for more wine. Then, ruefully, 'That's all we need. Consider these . . .'

'This doesn't concern anyone but us three,' Costa warned him. 'We didn't invite you to dinner to share the case around.'

'Come, come, Nic!' Falcone was loving this. He'd had more wine than anyone else. He was different too somehow. Off the leash, in new territory. 'I invited myself here. And where are we going to find a better table in Venice to knock around a few ideas? We all know

Teresa wishes she wore a badge instead of carrying that leather bag around.'

He watched her, eyebrows raised, waiting for an objection.

'Quite,' Falcone continued when none came. 'Emily's ex-FBI. One colleague. One ex-colleague. Discreet ladies both. Think of all the expertise we have here. And what are we ranged against? You saw it for yourselves today. A bunch of provincials.'

'Provincials who happen to be in charge,' Peroni grumbled.

Ignoring the remark, Falcone reached into his jacket pocket and pulled out the plastic bag with Uriel Arcangelo's keys inside.

'So let's consider this.'

'Oh great,' Peroni sighed. 'Now we're taking evidence out of the Questura. Here it begins, gentlemen. Behold, another nosedive in our faltering careers.'

'Don't be so stuffy,' Falcone moaned, waving down his complaints. 'The people here think criminal procedure begins and ends with a screaming match in an interview room. They won't even notice it's gone. Consider this. A man dies, consumed by fire, inside a locked glass foundry, with his own wife's body – clearly predeceased since the one witness we have was unaware of it to begin with – in the furnace in the same room. There is only one door into the place, and no other easy way of entry and exit. The man's key is in that door, on his side. What are we meant to assume?'

Costa noticed the gleam in the women's eyes. Falcone knew what he was doing.

'That he killed his wife then perhaps killed himself?' Emily suggested.

Teresa was already shaking her head.

'Self-immolation is a very rare form of suicide,' she noted. 'Men who kill their wives are invariably the cowardly sort – this is a practical observation, not a personal judgement. They take pills. They drive a car off a cliff. More often they nick themselves with a knife and don't have the guts or the decency to take it any further.'

'An accident then?' Peroni asked.

Teresa nudged his elbow. Hard.

Falcone looked delighted.

'See,' he said to Costa and Peroni. 'Just a few small facts and already we discover something we didn't know. What would we do without these two?'

Teresa Lupo screwed up her pale, round face.

'Please don't praise me, Leo. It feels so *wrong*. This Uriel man must have died for some reason. How badly was he burned? What tests have forensic run on his clothing?'

'I'm a detective.' He shrugged. 'I can't give you a meaningful answer. He was terribly burned from the waist up. The rest of his clothing seems pretty much intact. Everything was covered by foam from the fire officers, which hampers forensic, or so they told me. But we're not talking your calibre of people here. Or . . .' This next point appeared to have only just occurred to him. 'Or people who would be quite as diligent as you, I suspect. You should look for yourself.'

'There you go again,' Teresa complained. 'If I'm to help, you need to cut out the praise.'

'If you wish. So what else do we know?'

Falcone's comments about the key had been bugging Costa all day. The inspector had made him feel like an idiot when he drew the obvious conclusions. Now Costa could see why.

'That perhaps the key doesn't signify what it appears to signify,' Costa observed.

Peroni nodded. 'Meaning?'

'The door could have been locked from the outside. Uriel *could* have been locked in there by someone else and simply placed his own key in the door from the inside. Except . . .'

Falcone picked up the plastic bag and shook it.

'Except . . . why didn't he just unlock it himself and walk free?'

'I seem to recall,' Teresa said, 'a little lecture from a Roman inspector not a million miles away from here. One we used to hear a lot back home. One that said, look for the simple solution. Usually it's the right one.'

Falcone sipped his wine and closed his eyes briefly, appreciating it.

'In Rome usually it is. But this is a different place. We mustn't forget that. Here's one more thing. The dead woman had a mobile phone.'

The four of them waited. Finally, Peroni asked, 'Is that such a surprise, Leo? Most people do.'

'Not the Arcangeli. I checked with Raffaela. As far as she was aware none of them owned one. Yet it was there. In the corner of the foundry. I found it when you two were supposed to be looking around today. It was underneath a portable table they used for moving glass. Something that could just as easily have been used for dumping a body into the furnace. Clearly our Venetian colleagues don't believe in such a thing as a thorough search. I checked with the phone company. The phone was registered under the name of Bella *Bracci*. Her maiden name. Her old family address too. There've been no outgoing calls for weeks, which is useful of course because that doubtless means it was used mainly for receiving them, where we can't trace the incoming number if it's been blocked. But ninety minutes before we had the first report of the fire someone did phone out on it. To the direct line in the Arcangeli's office at the back of the foundry. The very place where, as far as we understand it, Uriel would have been before he went to work.'

Teresa was scribbling some notes on a napkin.

'I can see where you're going with this. But as you said yourself, you've still got one big problem. Uriel had a key. He could have walked out, at any point, if he'd wanted to. The fact he didn't means as sure as hell he wasn't entirely innocent here.'

Falcone pushed the plastic bag over to her and indicated the long shaft of the mortise key.

'What do you think?'

Teresa threw up her hands in despair.

'It's a key! I'm a pathologist. Not forensic. I don't do keys!'

She couldn't stop staring at it.

'Take it out if you like,' Falcone suggested.

'Oh Jesus,' Peroni sighed. 'Listen to the sound of distant shit meeting a distant fan.'

By the time his miserable face was looking up from the table Teresa Lupo had the key in her hand and was turning it round in her large, powerful fingers, staring at it close up, pulling a serious frown.

'It's been altered,' she said, placing the bunch back on the table, leaving the big key uppermost, pointing to the inside edge, which gleamed, just faintly, through the grime and smoke of the blaze. 'As I said, I'm not a key person but it looks to me as if someone's filed off a tooth or something.' She looked at Falcone. 'Does it still work?'

'That depends how you define "work",' he answered. 'I tried it in the lock. It goes in. It turns. And turns. And turns. It's useless. It doesn't lock. It doesn't unlock. Which is how it's meant to be.'

'And Bella's keys are missing,' Costa noted.

The five of them absorbed this information. The young waitress came over and asked about dessert. Falcone cheerily ordered tiramisu and was amazed by their silence.

'Make that five,' he said to the girl. 'They'll get their appetites back.'

They still hadn't said a word by the time the girl got back to the kitchen, laughing and joking with the women there.

'Excellent food here,' Falcone said. 'I wish you'd told me about it earlier.'

Peroni cast him an angry glance.

'And I wish I'd never mentioned it in the first place. Why can't you leave these things in the Questura, Leo?'

Falcone seemed surprised by the question.

'Because the Questura, Gianni, is probably the last place we should be discussing them, don't you think? They're working on behalf of Hugo Massiter, no one else. Someone who clearly inspires terror in the likes of Randazzo, and will doubtless do so even more once the island is his. The Questura simply wants us to sign off two deaths as something we know, for a fact, they cannot be. All to crown this Englishman the saviour of Murano, and save a few city officials some awkward questions about the healthy state of their bank accounts.'

He left it at that.

'We're just supposed to deliver what they want,' Peroni pointed out. 'If we jerk them around, they could make life pretty difficult for us. Randazzo's an asshole. That Massiter individual looks as if he could pull strings all the way up to the Quirinale Palace if he wanted.'

'That's the most apposite comment you've made all evening,' Falcone replied, smiling that infuriating smile again, in Costa's direction this time. 'You were right, Nic. Massiter's name should have rung a bell. He owns an important auction house. Offices in New York and London. There *was* a scandal too. Five years ago he would have been arrested on the spot, if we could have found him.'

'But now,' Costa asked, 'we think he's in the clear?'

'Absolutely in the clear,' Falcone insisted. 'Otherwise he'd never be fool enough to come back here, would he? It's an interesting tale, though. Here . . .'

He reached down into the briefcase he'd brought and took out two folders.

'I photocopied what little there is. Not much, I'm afraid. I suspect Mr Massiter's records have been thinned somewhat over the years.'

Falcone gave Costa and Peroni a searching glance.

'Why clog up the filing cabinets with information on innocent people after all? Nevertheless, you will need to read them before we talk to this nightwatchman tomorrow. It'll soon be clear why.'

Peroni eyed the folder in front of him.

'A week they said. That's all we have. After that it turns nasty for us. Again.'

Falcone sniffed at the grappa that had just arrived, tasted it with an approving lick of his thin lips, then thanked the waitress. Costa watched him, concerned. Spirits never used to be a part of his routine.

'A week should be ample. I don't think this is complicated, Gianni. It's just . . . not as straightforward as it might appear. They want a result which leaves the Arcangeli clear to sell their little island and then places Hugo Massiter on a pedestal from which he can lord it over the crooked pen-pushers who put him there. This is their city, not ours. I'm indifferent to both prospects. There's no reason why we can't deliver. We need to get to the bottom of this spontaneous combustion idea, naturally. We need to think about the question of keys, too, and I'm not sure I fully understand that yet either. And we need to know more about Bella Arcangelo.'

'What does the autopsy say about her?' Teresa asked with a marked professional concern.

'About as much as you can expect from a pile of dust. She was in the furnace. If she'd been there much longer . . .'

'You need to see her medical file,' Teresa advised him. 'In the absence of real forensic, look for someone who'll have some actual records. And that phone. I don't need to tell you what it probably means.'

'An affair?' Emily wondered.

'Something she wanted to keep quiet, certainly. Let's not run ahead of ourselves,' Falcone cautioned.

Emily gazed around the table, dismayed.

'This is a vacation?' she wondered.

Falcone picked up the report on Massiter, weighed it in his hand, then let the thing fall on the table.

'This is a free ticket into the Isola degli Arcangeli. It's made for you, Emily. Talk to Hugo Massiter. Take a look at what he's doing there. See if it's really the charitable act he's making out. I'd value your professional opinion.'

She wasn't mollified by that idea.

'I didn't come to Venice to give professional opinions.'

Falcone raised his glass.

'Of course not! You came here for the sights. And the company. And you'll have it. Once we've put this little domestic drama to bed and freed ourselves to return to civilization. *Salute!*'

None of them moved an inch.

'Leo?' Teresa asked. 'What the hell were these art police in Verona like? You've come back different somehow.'

'Improved, I hope.'

'I said different.'

Falcone toasted them all again.

'They weren't police, actually. They were Carabinieri. Some of the nicest and most interesting people I've met in a long time.'

Even Teresa Lupo was lost for words at that. Leo Falcone, the original version, wouldn't have been seen dead with the Carabinieri.

'*Salute!*' this odd, half-familiar stranger in their midst said again.

Five bright clear vials of grappa chinked around the table, not all with the same degree of vigour.

Costa discreetly poured his glass into the coffee cup and caught Emily's eye. She was intrigued, in spite of herself. There were consolations too. This wasn't Rome. There were no murderous hoods or lunatics on the prowl. It was, as Falcone said, a self-contained tragedy awaiting resolution. The answers lay somewhere out on the lagoon, in Murano's dark alleyways and on the Isola degli Arcangeli.

'So, Nic,' Falcone asked, 'tell me. I have a duty to train you now. One day you will want to be more than a mere *agente*.'

'Tell you what?' Costa asked, a little uncomfortable that Falcone should take such a direct interest in him at that moment.

'What's changed after our discussion here tonight?'

He thought about that, thought about the keys and the door, Bella Arcangelo and the tragic figure her dying husband must have cut on that odd island across the water.

'What's changed,' Costa said, 'is the question. We're no longer trying to understand the means by which Uriel Arcangelo killed his wife. But why, how and with whom, the late Bella appears to have conspired to kill him.'

'Bravo!' Falcone declared, laughing, toasting him with his glass. 'An inspector in the making!'

Part 3

AN ALCHEMICAL PROBLEM

1

In the dazzling light of the lagoon morning the police launch sped across the shining expanse of water that separated Venice from Sant' Erasmo. Nic Costa sat up front, enjoying the breeze, trying to extract some local information out of Goldoni, the Venetian cop who was their boatman for the day, and thinking about the avid, enthusiastic way Emily had read the report on Hugo Massiter over breakfast, wondering if it was right for her to become involved. Her enthusiasm was, in part, fired by his own interest in the Englishman, which might well be misplaced. Dragging her into his fixation made him uneasy.

Even so, hindsight was pointless. Almost as pointless as trying to get Goldoni talking. The man seemed to know the unseen channels of this inland sea by heart, never referring to a chart or a dial, just pointing the vessel in the direction of the Adriatic, setting the speed to cruise, changing tack when necessary, and picking at a pack of cigarettes throughout. Costa didn't even know how he understood where to head in the wide expanse of low countryside now looming ahead of them. Sant' Erasmo, in spite of its size, had no resident police presence, Goldoni said. Most of the locals – the *matti*, the crazies – rarely used their cars to go elsewhere so there were few traffic issues. There was just one bar and a couple of restaurants. Tourists were tolerated but never fleeced. There was nothing to occupy a cop on the vast, flat green farmland, though it covered a larger surface area than Venice itself. Just fields and fields of vegetables, artichokes and peppers, rocket and grapes, and a small flotilla of battered craft to ferry them to the Rialto markets each day.

They were close enough now to allow Costa to make out a few

rusting vehicles, clearly unfit for the road, lumbering along the bright margin between land and sky. He cast a glance back into the cabin. Falcone was there, leaning back in his seat, eyes closed, looking asleep. It was that kind of morning: hot, hazy and airless, a time for lassitude. Peroni was quietly scanning the report he should have read the night before. Costa looked at Goldoni, a man not much older than him, chewing on a fast-expiring cigarette in the face of the sea breeze.

'Have you heard of Hugo Massiter?' he asked. 'He's an Englishman.'

Goldoni sucked hard then launched the butt of his cigarette overboard and gave Costa a jaundiced stare.

'Heard of him,' he said simply.

This was the battle they always faced with the locals. Extracting information was like pulling teeth, even with men who were supposed to be part of the same team.

'Good or bad?' Costa asked.

Goldoni smiled, a quick, fetching smile, with precious little sincerity inside. He reminded Costa of the gondoliers who chatted up the teenage girls back in the city, knowing they would never have the money to pay the fare, hoping there'd be a different kind of reward if the pursuit went on long enough. He looked more like that than a cop if Costa was being honest with himself.

'Good guy,' Goldoni replied. 'Knows all the right people. What else is there to say?'

Maybe nothing, Costa thought. That was what the report claimed, and he was inclined to believe it for two reasons. First, if it was wrong, Venice had acquiesced to more than a simple bending of the rules. It had allowed murder, callous, cold bloodshed, which included the deaths of two police officers too, to go unpunished. And second, because of Emily's objections. She had an American insistence on precision and certainty and applied it instinctively to the web of half facts and rumours that the report repeated. There was, he knew, nothing concrete there, certainly nothing that could begin to justify any further police investigation. Just shapes in an old, dusty mirror. Idle talk which probably drifted in the wake of any rich and successful man who made enemies, and mistakes, during his career.

The file was the summary of the curious case that had occurred five years earlier. Among Massiter's many charitable interventions in the city was a biennial summer music school at La Pietà, the church connected with Vivaldi on the Riva degli Schiavoni not far from the Doge's Palace. During the last event – he ceased them after this particular incident, on understandable grounds – he'd paid for the debut of a work by an unknown English composer, a student from Oxford, Daniel Forster. This was, Massiter later told officers, an unwise adventure into new territory. His own expertise lay in antiques – sculpture, painting, objets d'art. He knew nothing about music, but had been taken in by the apparently guileless and gifted Forster. What transpired was tragedy. Forster was no composer but a fraud who had stolen an unknown historical manuscript from the house of the retired antiquarian where he was staying. Anxious to keep the deception quiet, the young Englishman had conspired with the old man's housekeeper, one Laura Conti, to murder the collector and his American companion. As the police began to see through their deceit, the pair had then killed two officers from the main Questura at Piazzale Roma, one of them a woman leading the investigation.

What made the headlines even bigger, though, was Massiter's involvement. If the report was to be believed, Daniel Forster was so subtle in his engineering of the fraud that he succeeded in making Massiter appear a party to it. After the death of the two police officers, Forster was taken into custody and managed to convince the police that he was guilty of the deception, not the murders. He served a short sentence and was released, only to take up with Laura Conti, living as man and wife on the profits of the music he'd never written, and a book he produced about the affair.

Massiter, meanwhile, retired – *fled* seemed a more apposite word to Costa – to America and consulted his lawyers at length. After more than two years in exile he'd acted, filing a wealth of evidence to counter the claims in Forster's book, which he was able to remove from sale on the grounds of libel. A protracted series of legal cases followed, with Massiter's lawyers winning victory after victory in the courts, paving the way for his return, and finally winning a reopening of the original investigation into Forster and his lover. Before that could be concluded, the couple disappeared. Massiter was able to return to Venice a vindicated man. Two warrants for the fugitives' arrest remained on file, not that anyone in the Questura seemed much interested in pursuing them. The closing piece in the report was some unsourced piece of police intelligence indicating the pair had gone on the run first to Asia, then possibly to South America, and a note, signed by Commissario Randazzo no less, who must have been working at the main Questura at the time, stating that it would be a waste of police money to expend resources chasing them.

Hugo Massiter was, in the eyes of the Venetian police, an innocent man who'd been badly wronged by false accusations, and spent heavily to refute them. Could this explain the city's desire to placate him? Some innate sense of guilt? Costa thought this unconvincing. All the same, it was an interesting story. He found himself wishing he could read more about this particular case. Or better, spend a few hours in the company of the missing Daniel Forster and Laura Conti. The couple had a substantial talent, it seemed to him, to create such a successful alternative version of the crimes, one that fooled a good few people before collapsing under the weight of Massiter's legal team. But all that would be a luxury. It was difficult to see how what happened five years before had any bearing whatsoever on the problems of the Arcangeli. Apart from one curious, doubtless coincidental fact. The dead antiquarian, murdered by Daniel Forster who then tried to pin the blame on Massiter, was called Scacchi, cousin to the same Sant' Erasmo farmer they were now about to visit, the last man to see Uriel Arcangelo alive.

Venice was a small place, Costa reminded himself. Families interlocked in many different ways over the years. This was, surely, nothing but coincidence, though one worthy of scrutiny before they set it aside.

He climbed back down into the boat and watched Peroni finishing the last of the report. Falcone still appeared to be slumbering.

'What do you make of it?' Costa asked softly as his partner turned the final page.

Peroni frowned.

'I was brought up to believe there was never smoke without fire. This Englishman moves in some queer circles, Nic. Although he seemed quite pleasant to me, I must admit.'

'The company you keep doesn't make you a murderer,' Falcone interjected without moving so much as an eyelid. 'It just tells us he's very well connected.'

'Four people died,' Costa objected. 'Two of them were police officers.'

Falcone opened his eyes and gave him an icy glance.

'It's not our case. Not unless it has some relevance to the Arcangeli, which I doubt.'

'Then why give us the report to read?' Peroni wondered.

Falcone seemed disappointed by the question.

'Because I like my men to be informed! And to know with whom they're dealing. Massiter is a man of substance who has very successfully dismissed a series of very severe allegations. As far as the authorities are concerned – as far as *we're* concerned – he's spotlessly clean and always has been. He's also probably a little short of ready cash at the moment after years of paying out for lawyers.'

'He said that himself,' Peroni pointed out.

'Exactly,' Falcone agreed. 'Which is one reason to believe he's telling us the truth. Now we know what he is, let's just concentrate on the case we *do* have. I ran Piero Scacchi's name through the station records. Not a thing, except for some noncommittal interview when his cousin got killed. About all that reveals is the fact the two of them apparently weren't close enough for the old man to leave Piero anything in his will. Everything went to Forster. It was probably forged. Is there an officer on the island we could pump or anything?'

Costa shook his head.

'Not a soul. Apparently Sant' Erasmo doesn't merit a police presence.'

Peroni laughed. 'You're kidding me? This place is huge.'

'Yes,' Costa agreed. 'But the population's just a couple of hundred people. I guess there's no point.'

'My kind of town,' Peroni said.

Falcone looked disappointed.

'We'll have to make up our own minds then. Here's one other piece of information I got out of records this morning, while you two were taking breakfast in bed. Bella's brother has history.'

Costa thought of Aldo Bracci, miserable as sin, getting eaten up by poverty and resentment in his grubby little factory.

'I would be lying if I said I was surprised,' Peroni observed.

'So what's your guess?' Falcone asked. 'Thieving? Violence?'

'Either,' the big man answered. 'Or both.'

Falcone pulled himself upright. It was a struggle. He looked old under the bright lagoon sun, somehow. Nic Costa couldn't help but wonder whether the cunning inspector, a man who'd taught him more about police work than anyone he knew, was his customary self.

'Both,' Falcone declared. 'And one more. A long time ago, so long ago it may be quite irrelevant.'

The two men waited. Peroni was puzzled too. A semblance of doubt was buzzing around Falcone's head, like some unwanted, unrecognized insect wondering whether to bite.

'Aldo Bracci got interviewed for sexually assaulting his sister when he was nineteen – she was four years younger. It never went anywhere. Cases like that rarely did in those days. But the file suggests it was the real thing with at least some acquiescence on Bella's part. It was a neighbour who filed the report, not someone from the family.'

'Nice story,' Peroni grumbled.

'But is it anything more than that?' Costa asked.

'We don't know,' Falcone admitted. 'But think about this. Bracci would surely have had access to Bella's keys. He'd have known that island. His only alibi is in the family. The opportunity's there. He and Bella could have conspired to kill Uriel. Then Aldo turned on her. But why?'

He frowned and stared towards the island. The launch was heading for a rickety old jetty fronting a dusty path that led to a small farmhouse. They were still on the Venice side of Sant' Erasmo, but far from any other sign of habitation. Costa could just make out the familiar yellow sign of a vaporetto jetty near a low church and some houses a good kilometre or more north. Then there was the sound of a dog's bark, a lively, amusing sound, not the aggressive tone one might have expected out in this backwater.

Peroni leapt off the boat first with surprising agility, given his bulk. Costa followed him. Falcone ordered Goldoni to wait with the vessel until they returned.

A black spaniel was bounding down the path wagging its tail. Peroni, always a sucker for animals, bent down and chucked the creature under the chin, beaming into its dark, watery eyes.

'What a dog,' he sighed, admiration written all over his ugly face. 'They've got ones like this back home. Not pets, mind. Working dogs. *Hunting* dogs. They could find anything, anywhere.'

'Shame it doesn't do police work,' Falcone sniffed, keeping a safe distance between himself and the animal.

A man was walking down the path, someone just a little less heavy than Peroni, a few years younger too. He wore a torn white shirt and grubby black trousers. He had a full head of black, slightly greasy hair, a round, expressionless face, and, in his left hand, a shotgun, broken, held loose and low as if it were a familiar item, one as happy in his grip as a household tool.

'Piero Scacchi?' Costa asked.

Peroni was still clucking over the dog, stroking its sleek black head with a gigantic, gentle hand.

'That's me,' the man said. He could see they were looking at the gun. 'It's duck season soon. I was cleaning it.'

He nodded at Peroni, surprised by the dog's warm welcome.

'He likes you.'

Costa flashed the card. 'Police.'

Piero Scacchi scowled at the animal.

'And I thought I'd taught you well.'

2

The city morgue was a low, one-storey extension to the main Questura behind Piazzale Roma, a grey, unmemorable building that made Teresa Lupo pine for her own offices in the *centro storico*. Alberto Tosi also had a view. The double windows of his room gave onto the factories and refineries of Mestre bristling across the channel of water separating Venice from the mainland, ugly, out-of-place accretions that constantly pumped dirt and smoke into the atmosphere. Cars and buses crawled up the nearby ramp leading to the terminus of the road system once it worked its way over the bridge next to the railway line. The vista was uniformly glum, even in the bright summer sun. On balance, Teresa Lupo thought, recalling the simple expanse of plain courtyard outside her own office, she had the better deal.

Tosi had greeted her as if she were some visiting academic, an honoured guest in his humble premises. It was all a little – and Teresa was shocked to find this word entering her head – creepy. Not because it was a morgue. They were places she could walk into any day without a second thought. The problem lay with Tosi, a stiff, erect pensioner-type with half-moon glasses and a white nylon coat so bright it must have been changed every day, and the waif-like girl, no more than twenty-one, surely, and similarly dressed, though with John Lennon spectacles, who acted as his assistant. The two of them were inseparable. More than that, they seemed almost to operate as one, exchanging thoughts and ideas in a random, open way, answering questions in turn like identical twins testing out their telepathic powers.

Then, in response to her questioning, Tosi revealed the secret. Anna was his granddaughter. This small operation – most of the work went to a bigger place on terra firma, Tosi said – was a family affair. Its big brother in Mestre was, naturally, run by his son, Anna's father. Teresa was, briefly, speechless. The Tosis seemed to be running their own pathologists' guild, taking upon themselves the role of sorting and categorizing the region's dead, then passing the task on to their offspring. She had to ask the old man, even though she knew the answer. His father had been a pathologist too, and his grandfather a city surgeon who specialized in post mortems before the job of pathologist became official.

Venice, she thought, then forced her mind to focus on the task in hand.

'I don't wish to intrude,' she insisted, sitting in an uncomfortable plastic chair opposite the two of them, both perched bird-like next to each other behind a large shiny desk.

'You're not intruding,' Tosi replied with a smile.

'Not a bit,' added the granddaughter. 'It's a pleasure.'

'An *honour*,' Tosi added.

Teresa silently cursed Leo Falcone for talking her into this.

'It's just that spontaneous combustion . . .' it was hard even to say the words '. . . seems such an *unusual* finding.'

'Unheard of,' agreed Tosi the elder.

'Hereabouts,' junior corrected him. 'There are plenty of antecedents.'

'Anna . . .?' he wondered. 'Could you possibly show Dr Lupo the "computer".'

He spoke the word with near-religious veneration.

The girl got up and walked across the office to the single old and very dusty PC that sat on a tiny, cheap desk.

'That contraption is quite astonishing,' Tosi revealed. 'I expect you have more than the one. Here . . . it's not necessary. Wasted expense and we *never* spend more than is absolutely necessary. Mind you, I don't know what we'd do without it. Did you know that in Milwaukee in 1843 there was a documented case of spontaneous combustion in an iron foundry? Very like our own.'

'People catching fire in foundries . . .' She didn't want to annoy the old man. He'd surely clam up if that happened. 'It's not that hard to fathom really, is it?'

'These cases are,' Anna interjected, tapping slowly at the keys with one short, slender finger. 'For instance, in Arras, northern France. October 1953. A private house, body on the floor, no sign of fire elsewhere. Same in London, six years later—'

'Whoa, whoa, whoa,' Teresa said, fighting back her temper. 'Details I can read for myself any time. Can you just zip those files and e-mail them to me?'

Two very young, very innocent eyes blinked at her from behind the anachronistic round glasses.

'Zip?' Anna asked.

'Watch me.'

Teresa pulled her chair up to the desk, elbowed the girl out of the way, hacked manically at the keys with her stubby fingers, bundled the pile of documents the girl had there into an attachment then forwarded the lot to her own private e-mail address, one she could access later through Nic's computer, Peroni being as allergic to the things as Tosi elder apparently was.

The Tosis glanced at each other in awe, as if a creature from the future had walked into the room.

'Bodies,' Teresa declared firmly, wishing she'd never given up smoking as part of the if-it-hurts-it's-bound-to-make-you-pregnant routine. 'I can't think without seeing one. Can we start there please?'

'Whatever we have is yours to behold,' Tosi elder declared, and got up after he'd finished scrawling a single word on his notepad: *Zip!*

They walked along the corridor, into a tiny white room with a single shining table and a collection of equipment so old most of it belonged in a museum. Teresa wondered if she couldn't get rid of the Tosis for a while, maybe by entering them for a game show called *Name that Century*. She didn't want to try to think straight under the gaze of the pair.

'What about forensic?' she asked.

Tosi smiled.

'Let me guess,' she sighed. 'Mestre.'

'They have things there . . .' he said, wide-eyed.

'What did those things tell you?'

Anna went to a tiny wooden desk and took out two reports which were, if Teresa's eyesight wasn't playing tricks, *typed*.

'Nothing much about Bella Arcangelo,' the girl declared, spreading three pages on the table top. 'There wasn't a lot to look at really.'

'Remains,' Tosi senior mouthed gloomily, walking to one of the refrigerated compartments, then pulling it open to reveal a box – a cardboard box no less – marked 'Arcangelo, Bella'. 'What can you do with remains?'

Usually lots, Teresa thought to herself, then stared at the skull, with its tapering stump of spinal cord. It sat on a bed of surgical cotton wool, surrounded by a few unidentifiable objects. She ran through the report. Plenty of traces of bone fragments, shattered by the heat, incapable of analysis to show how the woman died. A small amount of gold. No other metal. Nothing else at all. Maybe Tosi was right.

'How hot does a glass furnace run?' she asked, unable to take her eyes off the familiar shape, burnt a bleached-out white.

'At that time of the morning . . .' Tosi mused. 'Say 1400, 1500 degrees centigrade. About what you'd find in a modern crematorium. It's a fascinating process. I've studied it a little. You should see a glass furnace for yourself some time. I could arrange that. A modern one, though, not the ridiculous antiques the Arcangeli insist on using. Gas *and* wood for pity's sake—'

'Why was just the skull left, not—' she began to ask.

'It was in a cooler part of the chamber,' Tosi replied quickly, proud he could second-guess the question. 'If the woman was placed in the furnace head first . . .' He held up his hands, mimicking the movement of sliding an object off a trolley or the mobile table Falcone had said was there. 'That's what would happen. The hottest part is in the centre. The head would surely fetch up at the edge, where the temperature would be lower in a furnace of that age and nature. I spoke to our local crematorium. They think a woman of this size would reach such a state of dissolution in an hour, possibly less, at this temperature. Am I doing all right so far?'

She gave him a smile that was meant to say: *impressed.*

'Exactly the conclusion I would draw,' she admitted, and meant it too. Calling the crematorium to get some practical knowledge was precisely what she'd have done herself. 'But lacking your knowledge of glass-making I imagine it would have taken me longer.'

Tosi waved a hand in her direction, smiling.

'Romans,' he said. 'See, Anna. So self-deprecating. Whatever people say . . .'

Teresa looked around the room. There was no sign of any other work. The Tosis had all day to chat about their wonderful discovery. Presumably everything else was getting shipped off to Mestre.

'You're too kind. Now the man.'

Anna went to a second compartment and slid out the drawer. Teresa Lupo took a very good look at what lay there and wondered if, perhaps, she wasn't going crazy.

Uriel Arcangelo was half cadaver, half charcoal stump. From the waist down the man looked like someone who'd been dumped in a giant inkwell then left to dry. The fabric of his clothing – suit trousers and what looked like the remains of a work apron – was charred by the heat and flames. Most of the flesh beneath, revealed by some of the Tosis' exploratory incisions, seemed unexceptional, not that it would have much to tell. But above the belt the man had been transformed. The entire upper half of his body had been consumed by fire, incinerated into a black mass, shrunken in on itself, composed principally of bones and a few remaining carbonized pieces of flesh. His skull was now turned to one side, the mouth open in that familiar expression of agony which, on this occasion, had doubtless been warranted. Teresa Lupo was familiar with fire victims. Either half of Uriel's body fitted the picture she recognized. People were consumed, or they died asphyxiated, little marked by the fire itself. It was unheard of for a corpse to share both characteristics.

'Now let me get this straight,' she demanded. 'You're saying there was no direct combustion on the body? Everything from the chest up somehow happened without the application of any external flame whatsoever?'

'That's what we understand from the fire department,' Tosi confirmed. 'He was a good five metres from the furnace.'

'Photos?' Teresa asked.

The girl walked over to a filing cabinet and withdrew a file. There were just five, Teresa was astonished to learn, pretty poor quality too, as if they came from an instant camera. The prints depicted Uriel Arcangelo's corpse surrounded by what appeared to be a black pool of charred material. Teresa looked more closely. The heat around the upper torso had been so strong it had actually burned through the wooden flooring beneath the man.

'What's this hole?' she wondered. 'How big was it? What kind of condition was the floor in?'

Tosi appeared bemused.

'I didn't actually go to the scene. The police took notes and those photos. Then we sent an attendant for the body.'

She bit her tongue. The lack of care, of any kind of formal procedure, was astonishing. It was, she guessed, a question of supply and demand. Venice was a small place, more a receptacle for passing tourists than a real, living city. Tosi clearly had little experience of dealing with violent death. And, she reminded herself, there had been the assumption all along that they were dealing with an open and shut case.

'There *has* to be more,' Teresa insisted. 'What about the autopsy?'

Tosi sighed.

'What you see is what we have.'

'Analysis . . . don't tell me. It's in Mestre. Is there nothing else?'

'Such as what?' Anna asked.

'Such as how a man can die like this! Even in a furnace, it's not – possible.'

'Spontaneous combustion,' Tosi declared resolutely. 'As we said.'

'But *how*?'

Tosi smiled and nodded at his granddaughter.

'There are various theories,' she said. 'The most promising seems to be that, at a certain temperature, perhaps under prolonged external heat, the abdominal fat may ignite. The deceased was somewhat overweight. Not much. But perhaps it was enough.'

Teresa shook her head, unable to accept they could believe this. 'Enough to consume half his body? Then burn a hole in a timber floor?'

'Apparently,' Tosi observed, and displayed, for the first time, a little impatience with her doubts. 'Do you have an alternative explanation? I would, naturally, like to hear it.'

'His clothing,' she suggested. 'What did forensic make of that? Was there something flammable there? Gasoline perhaps? Alcohol?'

Tosi glanced at the lower half of the corpse. 'The fire crew used an astonishing amount of foam. It was everywhere. It's not easy trying to extract material in those circumstances. Besides . . .'

His old creased face wrinkled even further with displeasure.

'I hate trying to do the work of the police, as I'm sure do you, Dr Lupo. One would have to ask oneself, though. What kind of a man would walk into an overheating foundry with gasoline on his clothes?'

An idiot. A drunk. Someone suicidal because he'd murdered his wife an hour before, shoved her in the furnace, and started to get maudlin. There were plenty of alternatives. It was just that this pair didn't want to look for them.

'It is,' Tosi added, 'difficult to accept that a human body may burn of its own accord. But consider the idea that we may, in fact, be candles inside out. A candle has the wick in its centre and draws the fuel to it as it burns. A body such as Arcangelo's may be considered to have sufficient fat to act as fuel, and clothing as an external wick. Once the clothing catches fire, the fat is drawn to it and continues to feed the flames. This is not strange science, I feel. Rare, but not implausible.'

So one fine day you drop a match on your shirt and burn up from the inside. It was a theory, she thought. Along with alien abduction and the idea some poor bastards got reborn as aardvarks.

'Unless, of course,' he finished, 'you have other ideas.'

'Not really,' she said. 'I don't have problems with the combustion. It's that spontaneous part I'm struggling with. But I would like to think about it. I'm sorry. I should have asked. Does this bother you?'

Tosi's thin mouth creased in a modest smile.

'To have a famous Roman pathologist sit in on our work? Of course not. But I'm under some pressure. The police don't wish to sit on this case forever. I must wrap everything up by Tuesday. One way or another. I'm under no illusions there.' For a moment he looked troubled. 'None at all.'

Maybe Alberto Tosi wasn't as batty as he looked. He knew it was a strange incident. It was just that, in the circumstances, he hadn't got much else to say. And, it occurred to her, he was being strong-armed to close down the case too. Just like the rest of them.

'Medical records?'

The Tosis glanced at each other, a mutual measure of concern on their faces.

'I'm not sure we're authorized . . .' Anna murmured. 'They only arrived this morning. There are issues of confidentiality.'

'Understood,' she said. 'So Inspector Falcone hasn't seen them either? Perhaps I should mention them to him. I'm sure he'd like to know what's there. He is of course entitled to see them.'

The prospect of a return visit by Falcone tipped the balance. One minute later Teresa Lupo was going through two sets of comprehensive hand-written records from the family doctor who looked after both Uriel Arcangelo and his wife.

She made a few notes, then placed her pad in the bag, sniffed, and knew it was time to go. Tosi was eyeing her from across the desk, looking decidedly shifty.

'I would have told your inspector,' he said finally. 'As Anna said, we only received the reports this morning.'

'Of course.'

It wasn't the kind of detail any pathologist could keep hidden. And it had a certain personal resonance for Teresa Lupo too, one that reminded her of the conversation she'd never had with Gianni Peroni the night before.

'It's always shocking to make such a discovery,' Tosi said. 'One would have thought the family . . .'

But the family didn't know either, or so Teresa was guessing. And that, perhaps, could give Falcone his motive after all. At the age of forty-four, Bella Arcangelo was six weeks pregnant. All the comprehensive tests that had been carried out on her husband over the years made it absolutely clear he could not be the father. Uriel was, and always would have been, firing blank bullets, with a certainty Teresa understood completely, on both a medical and personal basis. He also had another interesting medical condition, the result of an accident while working in the furnace. Uriel had suffered a fracture of the skull in a small gas explosion. As a result he had diminished hearing and complained of an impaired sense of smell.

She filed away these facts then thought of the bones inside that scorching oven. Nothing that remained of Bella could be used to prove the paternity of the child that died with her. It was the fire, the all-consuming inferno that had removed from the scene everything that could be of conventional use. That was one reason a decent old man like Alberto Tosi was reaching out for bizarre theories on spontaneous combustion. So much real evidence disappeared in those vicious, transforming flames. Its loss left everyone, Falcone, Tosi, Teresa herself, clutching at straws, trying to rebuild some kind of truth from all those deconstructed atoms.

'Would you like me to pass this on to Inspector Falcone myself?' she asked, noting, with some satisfaction, the sudden relief in the old man's face.

'That would be kind. This isn't our sort of work,' Alberto Tosi said with an expression of marked distaste. 'Not the kind of case we see in Venice at all. And your inspector is such a . . . persistent man. To be honest, Dr Lupo, a part of me wishes I could pass everything over to you and go back to signing off a few expired tourists. For a Roman this may be normal . . .'

Actually, she ruminated, for a Roman it was still pretty damn weird too.

'You're doing just fine,' she answered, then rustled the medical reports in front of her. 'Family tragedies are sometimes—'

'Best swiftly buried,' Tosi interrupted. 'I couldn't agree more.'

3

There was a picnic area at Piero Scacchi's farm. They sat outside at one of the three tables, listening to the man tell his tale, slowly, with conviction and plenty of detail, as if he'd practised everything beforehand. There was little here that was new to them. Scacchi's recollections matched pretty much everything he was reported to have told the officers who first interviewed him. If anything, Costa thought, Scacchi had it all off a little too pat, as if he were trying to second-guess what they wanted to hear in the hope they'd nod, say thanks, and then be gone, leaving him to go back to his fields and the dog which sat, alert between Scacchi and Peroni, throughout their discussion.

Scacchi had arrived at the island fifteen minutes before the fire broke out. It was an unscheduled visit. He was dropping off some material the Arcangeli had ordered on his way back from an early morning delivery to the markets. He'd done his best to try to rescue Uriel, unaware that the man's wife was also in the foundry. That the attempt failed seemed a matter of deep regret for the farmer, who was close to tears when he described trying to force an entry into the building with what tools he could find. Costa couldn't help but notice the scores of cuts and burn marks on his hands and arms. If anyone could have dragged a man alive from that inferno, it was probably Piero Scacchi.

Yet there was something evasive about him too. He didn't like talking to the police, though it struck Nic Costa that he really had no good reason to feel that way. Scacchi seemed as straight as a die: a hard-working farmer, struggling to keep a large estate going single-handedly, unable to afford extra help. There seemed no reason why he couldn't wait to get them out of there.

Falcone checked the details about the door, which Scacchi confirmed was locked, apparently from the inside. Then he asked about the state of Uriel when Scacchi first came upon him.

'I told you. I told the ones I spoke to before. He was on fire. From his chest. Like it came from inside somehow. Then later . . .'

Scacchi kicked at some pebbles on the sandy ground.

'What a waste,' he murmured. 'I thought it was just one life. Then two. Why?'

'We don't know,' Costa replied. 'We don't even understand how Uriel died.'

Scacchi cast an eye at his fields. A healthy crop of purple artichokes waved in unison in the breeze next to a patch of bright red *peperoncini*, the fruits like tiny scarlet flower heads. These crops were waypoints in the man's life, Costa thought, beacons around which he could navigate with certainty.

'He wasn't human,' he continued. 'He was on the floor and there was so much fire. I knew I couldn't save him then. Not even if the stupid hose had been working properly. He was fire, just fire, his chest . . .'

He stared at each of them.

'I saw his eyes, though. He saw me too. He just wanted to die. What do you expect?'

'You could smell gas?'

Scacchi shook his head.

'It was all so fast. Smoke. Fire. I don't know what I could smell. Yes, there was gas everywhere. That ridiculous angel of theirs went out because it was leaking from the foundry so much. It's a miracle the house wasn't . . .'

He gave up. Peroni patted the man on his knee, a forward gesture, one only he could have got away with.

'You were brave, Piero,' Peroni declared. 'A sight braver than most of us would have been in the circumstances.'

It didn't make much difference.

'But for what reason?' Scacchi asked. 'They both died. I achieved nothing.'

'You did what you could,' Peroni insisted.

'Five minutes earlier . . .' he murmured. 'To die like that. No one deserves it.'

'Did you know Uriel?' Falcone asked.

Scacchi shook his head.

'Not well. I saw him when I was working. I did what he wanted. He seemed a nice enough man. A little lonely. A little sad. But they're all like that. He drank too. Most nights he was stinking drunk by other people's standards. I shouldn't say that but it's true. It didn't stop him working though. I never saw him miss a night there. Six, seven days a week.'

'And Bella?' Falcone wondered.

'She worked there on her own before Uriel came in usually. They didn't work together often. The way she talked to him you'd have thought she was the boss. I kept clear. After Michele employed me I only ever dealt with Uriel and Raffaela. He told me what to do. She paid me. She's the only Arcangelo you'd ever get money out of. A good woman.' He leaned forward. 'A *fine* woman. Without her that family would have been bankrupt years ago. The only reason anyone extends them any favours is out of respect for her.'

Costa thought of the tall, dignified figure he'd seen at the curious glass eyrie projecting out over the lagoon. She did possess something her surviving brothers – and Uriel for all he knew – lacked. Perhaps Scacchi, a lonely man himself, had ideas in that regard too.

'Why do you need the money?' Falcone asked suddenly.

Scacchi laughed.

'Huh! Finally a question I couldn't see coming! Why?'

He cast an eye around the estate, then got up for a better look. They rose too.

'What do you see here?' he asked. 'Gold? Frankincense? Myrrh?'

'You've got those purple artichokes they say only taste right if they come from Sant' Erasmo,' Peroni replied immediately. 'You've got leeks and onions as good as any I've seen back home. Some beautiful *peperoncini*. I think I see rocket. Also a smoking shed. What do you smoke there, Piero?'

'Sometimes eels,' the farmer replied, a little taken aback.

'Where I come from in Tuscany we smoke,' Peroni said. 'Eel. Boar. Plus we shoot ducks and put them in there too. You've got a good gundog. What's he called?'

The animal brightened and wagged its tail at the mention of some word.

Scacchi was melting a little under Peroni's insistent good nature.

'Xerxes. It's a stupid name. It's supposed to mean he's the general of the marshes. He is too when he's out there. The rest of the time . . . please, don't use the g-word. He gets worked up. When it's not the duck season he's bored witless.'

Peroni laughed and stroked the dog's soft head.

'Plus you've got these picnic tables,' Peroni added. 'Now they interest me.'

'A man needs money, OK? I have debts on this place. My mamma never paid everything. Farming won't cover it all. I do odd jobs for the Arcangeli. I take people places by boat for a quarter of what those crooks in the speedboats charge. The city. The airport. Wherever. And this friend of mine in the city brings tourists cycling out here sometimes. I get to feed them at the tables. And no' – he waved a strong, scarred finger in their faces – 'I don't declare a penny of it for tax. You're going to tell them now, I guess.'

Falcone smiled.

'You don't have police on Sant' Erasmo. Why should you have taxmen instead? That seems a little unfair.'

Scacchi calmed down a little.

'You don't look bad guys. What the hell are you doing in Venice?'

'Long story,' Peroni groaned. 'For another day. I want to try some of those artichokes, Piero. A couple of kilos. How much?'

The man spat on the ground and swore under his breath.

'Take what you want,' he groaned. 'You never go home empty-handed, do you?'

Peroni came back with a better oath, spoken more loudly, then pulled out a twenty note from his wallet.

'Now *that*,' he said, 'just shows you really don't know us. Fill a couple of bags with the best you've got, please. Keep the change.'

Piero Scacchi eyed the note for a while then took it, nodded, said a short word of thanks, and walked off. The three men watched him go.

'We've got to ask him about Massiter,' Costa pointed out.

'Don't try and go too quickly with him,' Peroni cautioned. 'It just won't work.'

Falcone seemed surprised.

'You mean you *do* see there's reason to go further?'

Peroni cast him a vicious look.

'I'm not stupid, Leo. I've been around you long enough now to spot a few things. Piero's got something to say all right. Although I'm not sure he can quite work out what it is exactly. Or how it fits in either.'

'Out here?' Falcone waved a disdainful hand at the nodding heads of *carciofi*. 'I don't think so. It's a waste of time—'

'Massiter.' Costa interrupted.

'Massiter's irrelevant. The answers are in Murano somewhere. In the here and now. Not in some old fairytale.'

There was the sound of a bark. With the dog at his heels, Piero Scacchi was returning carrying two old carrier bags brimming with food. The three men watched as Scacchi placed the contents of the bags on the table for their inspection. Peroni sorted through them with obvious delight: artichokes, peppers, a bag of frozen smoked eel, fresh new potatoes, waxy and yellow, grapes, a bottle of wine, almost black in colour. And three bunches of tiny *peperoncini*, like miniature bouquets of exotic flowers.

The farmer nodded at the peppers.

'You can let them dry. They'll keep all winter. Put them in some oil. I guess you have the idea.'

The big man was beaming over every last item in the bags, looking as if he wanted to start cooking there and then.

'You make wine too?'

'It's called self-sufficiency,' Scacchi said. 'You learn it in a place like this.'

'I guess so,' Peroni said. 'Don't you ever take a day off?'

Scacchi fixed him straight in the eye.

'Do you?'

They could have left it there, Costa thought. They could have let Leo Falcone have his way, walking on, not bothering with all those little questions, the ones that seemed irrelevant, and usually were. Except that wasn't Falcone's routine. Not in Rome. Sometimes it was the job of a friend and colleague to issue reminders.

'What do you think happened to Laura Conti and Daniel Forster?' Costa asked, scrutinizing Scacchi's bland, bloodless face for emotion, and finding none, just hearing Leo Falcone utter a low, heartfelt curse under his breath.

Scacchi considered the question.

'Why ask me? I'm just some scruffy farmer from the lagoon.'

'It was your cousin they killed. You must have known them.'

The dog lay down on the hard, dry ground, burying its nose in its paws, aware of the sudden chill in the conversation.

'Must I?' Scacchi asked.

'You mean they didn't kill him?' Costa persisted.

'Nic . . .' Falcone warned him, ostentatiously looking at his watch.

'I mean a scruffy farmer from the lagoon doesn't have a clue about what goes on' – Scacchi nodded towards Venice – 'over there. Any more than you do.'

It was an answer, of a kind. Nic Costa didn't know what to make of it either, though he was glad he'd asked, in spite of Falcone's obvious annoyance.

Scacchi was thinking about something. He asked them to wait, then walked back to his house, a low, ramshackle single-storey collection of old wood and corrugated iron, made more cheerful by a line of tall sunflowers, nodding their yellow heads in the light sea breeze.

'The next time I say no,' Falcone declared, 'you will listen. Or hear about it afterwards.'

'Understood,' Costa replied, and lived with the icy chill that followed.

Scacchi was returning with something in his hand. He came and threw them on the table: four postcards, each picture up. Standard tourist stuff. Cape Town. Bangkok. Sydney. Buenos Aires. The last, from Argentina, was posted three months before. The others spanned the previous year, roughly four months apart.

Costa turned them over. On the back of each was a single scrawled name, printed in individual letters, each drawn in a tidy, almost child-like hand.

Daniel.

'I imagine he wants to tell me they're alive,' Scacchi said.

'It just says "Daniel",' Costa pointed out.

'True,' Scacchi nodded. 'So what do you want me to say? I don't know why he sends them to me. I scarcely knew either of them. Perhaps it's insurance in case you people come knocking. Perhaps – really I don't know. I don't care either.'

'Can I take them?' Costa asked.

'If it makes you happy.'

He was about to put the cards in his pocket when Leo Falcone placed a hand over them.

'That won't be necessary,' he said curtly. 'This isn't part of our investigation. I'm grateful for your time. Now . . .'

Piero Scacchi and his dog stood immobile, watching as the police launch left Sant' Erasmo, two dark, unbending figures, at home in the solitary verdant landscape which enclosed them.

They sat mutely in the cabin for a while. Then Falcone glanced at Costa.

'I don't wish to labour the point. But I am not going to complicate what we have any further by going round picking up signed postcards from people who decamped from this place years ago, even if they are wanted for other crimes.'

'I heard you,' he said.

Falcone glowered at him, unable to miss the edge in Costa's voice.

'But . . .?' he asked.

'But they weren't signed postcards. They were printed. Letter by letter.'

The inspector had been wrong on this decision. It was time to let him know.

'Daniel Forster was a student at Oxford. A good one too, by all accounts,' Costa went on. 'Could he fool everyone – Massiter, the media, us – and still be unable to sign his own name?'

4

Emily Deacon stood on the small bridge to the island, beneath the outstretched arm of the iron angel, listening to the beacon's sighs, nervous, uncertain of herself. This was a rare condition. Since she had left the service of the US government eight months before she had refused to allow herself moments of doubt. The move to Europe had seemed obvious. She wanted to study architecture, Italian architecture more than anything. The school in Rome was superb, and more than happy to accept her. And there was Nic. Kind Nic, shy Nic, a man who wanted to make her happy, give her everything he wanted. Except, it seemed to her, himself. Something held him back, an invisible barrier she couldn't penetrate. Work had forced them together. Once that bond disappeared – as it had to – a vacuum had taken its place. Nic had spent most of the time in exile in Venice, occupied almost every weekend. She'd moved into his gorgeous old farmhouse on the outskirts of Rome and found herself, almost immediately, alone, reliant on awkward phone calls instead of real, human contact. Some vital step in the process of building a relationship had failed to take place along the way. They needed to retrace their steps, to find what had drawn them together in the first place, return to that moment, and discover a way forward again, together. After reading the report on Hugo Massiter she understood what the catalyst, if such a thing existed, might be. The selfsame element that had thrown them together in the beginning. Work.

Now she found herself hesitating on the bridge of the Isola degli Arcangeli, surprised to discover a part of her still enjoyed the old game. Architecture was fine: it stimulated her intellect, it was a challenge, a mountain to climb. But she'd spent four years learning how to be an agent in the FBI, and a person didn't shrug off all that effort so easily. She wanted to be part of Falcone's case. There was a quicker, bigger buzz there than anything she could expect in a studio.

Hugo Massiter strode up to the black iron gate that kept the public out of the island. By his side was an older man with a damaged face, one side stricken dead by a stroke. He unlocked the heavy mechanism without a word of welcome, watched her enter then locked it again before marching off towards the foundry, on the far end of the island from the exhibition hall, with its scaffolding and workmen.

'Mr Massiter,' she said hesitantly, 'when I called I thought you'd have a secretary or something. I didn't want to interrupt your day.'

'Just me and the brickies.' Massiter sighed. 'I'm not a fan of domestics, apart from Michele there who lets people in and out. Apparently the rest of us aren't trusted yet, even though I pay the rent. Welcome to Venice. Can I help?'

'I was hoping for a quick look,' she confessed. 'I'm sorry. I didn't expect you to be the guide.'

'I remember you from the station,' Massiter said pleasantly. 'You and the young police officer are . . .?'

'Friends.'

'And now you're at a loose end?'

Only during the day, she explained. And that evening she would be on the island in any case, for the reception.

From behind him, through the tall, open doors into the hall, came the sound of workmen screaming oaths at each other. Massiter winced as if afflicted by a physical pain.

'Then . . .?' he wondered. 'It is rather busy here, my dear. Not that I wouldn't mind some appealing company.'

'I'm sorry. It's just that I've always wondered what this place was like close up. I'm studying architecture. This is one of the buildings I've read about.'

'A perfect example of how to get things wrong, eh?' he murmured.

'In some ways. That doesn't mean it can't be put right.'

Massiter looked sceptical.

'You're not the first to tell me that.' His alert, attentive eyes ran over her, then he said, 'Very well. Come in. I was feeling a touch bored and lonely anyway.'

Surprised by the ease with which she'd got through the gate, Emily let him lead her round to the quayside to stand in front of the palazzo in the shadow cast by its towering central section. The sight took her breath away. The Arcangeli's exhibition hall was unlike any other structure she'd seen in her life, a vast glass monolith, roof curved into the shape of three rising semicircles, vertical walls all glass and wrought iron, encompassing an enormous space some hundred metres wide or more, going back almost as far to the other side of the tiny island. It had folly written all over it. The place could have been a theatre or an auditorium – if the glass allowed for good acoustics. Or some kind of crazy horticultural attraction. But it was too large, surely, ever to succeed as an exhibition site for a glass foundry. The space was beyond anything on a modest scale. It needed grandeur, effect.

Close up she could see some of the problems too. The ironwork was warped in some places, as if it were insufficiently robust to take the strain of the windows. Some of the glass was broken, other areas dirty from pollution.

'It's an old wreck, isn't it?' Massiter suggested, running his eyes across the building, staring, finally, at some point close to the summit. 'Like me.'

She followed the line of his gaze. There was a terrace at the very peak of the structure, and opaque windows indicating some need for privacy.

'You've an apartment here?' she asked.

'I *will* have. They only let me use it during the day, until we've signed the paperwork. The Arcangeli never give away a thing.'

He licked his lips.

'I could make you a cup of tea,' he added. 'Afterwards.'

'Afterwards?'

'The tour, dear. That's what you came for, isn't it?'

She found herself both amazed and appalled by what followed. For thirty minutes Massiter led her through the ground and first floors of the palace, past rusting ironwork being hastily repainted, past gaudy wall hangings that had no place there at all and hastily painted temporary walls with cheap collapsible tables for that evening's party. Emily dabbed a finger on the ironwork by the door and wished she'd had a few rudimentary instruments with her. There was decay, no doubt about it.

'You don't like what's being done, do you?' Massiter stated.

She smiled.

'What do I know?'

'Quite a lot, I suspect. Is it that bad? I'm spending heavily here. Money I can ill afford. People need to be impressed tonight. Venice is a cruel judge. In a short time I'll either be acclaimed as her saviour or damned as a swindling crook. I deserve to be told the truth.'

'It's not what I'd recommend, Mr Massiter.'

'Hugo. Why?'

She glanced around the vast, airy hall where two large, fussy paintings were now being measured for a couple of dismal screens clothed in scarlet velour.

'This place should be about simplicity. Glass is an odd medium. I can understand why your man is at a loss what to do with it. This is a challenge. But it seems to me you have to work with the glass, not against it. He's trying to hide it somehow and that's a sin. This wasn't just meant to be a container for the exhibition, it should be part of the show itself.'

She pointed out some panels in the curved ceiling.

'If I remember the story correctly, this wasn't designed by an architect, not in the first instance, but by a glass maker. You can see that. He's making a point. Some of the glass is transparent, some opaque or reflective. He's got the colours of the world up there: sun, night, sea, sky. You need to fit in with that, not fight it. This is too much. It's like . . .'

She felt too polite to finish the sentence.

'A bad hotel created for a rich man with no taste?'

'Your words. Not mine.'

'Bugger!' Massiter declared, looking at his watch. It was now close to midday. The heat was intense. That was another problem, she thought. The ventilation was poor, and probably always had been. 'In that case I need a drink. Will you join me? The apartment's not too foul. I decided what went in there. *This*' – he waved a hasty hand at the workmen – 'was the price of getting some restoration money from the city. The idiot architect's someone's nephew. You understand Italy, Emily?'

'Oh yes,' she answered, following him as he strode rapidly up a winding set of iron steps to the third floor, and the apartment which sat out of sight beyond a black-painted floor at the summit of the uppermost section. They reached the heavy iron door. Massiter unlocked it and ushered her into an altogether different kind of room, one furnished with spartan good taste in a modern, minimalist fashion.

'One day soon, God willing,' Massiter said, 'I'll be able to abandon that damned yacht of mine and live here full time. Until then it's just my day residence and an office.'

He walked to the front of the long, rectangular room, and threw open two large, semi-opaque, smoke-coloured doors to reveal a small table on the narrow balcony. Then he returned and entered a small, airy modern kitchen, heading for the fridge. Emily walked to the large windows, stepped outside, caught her breath at the height, which was exaggerated by the open iron grating beneath her feet, falling some thirty metres or so straight onto the hard cobbles of the quay. The dizzying view faced east, out to Sant' Erasmo and the Lido, with the shining Adriatic beyond.

'This is why I want to buy the place really,' Massiter announced, arriving with two glasses of pale wine, a plate of olives and some cured cheese. 'The view and pure bloody-minded arrogance. The chance to make a little money too, of course. You can see Torcello if you stretch out.'

She looked over the edge of the precipice. It was a long way down, and straight onto hard stone.

'Here,' he said, extending his arms. 'I'll hold you. It scared me too, first time round.'

She let Massiter place his arms around her waist, then leaned over the edge of the metal balustrade, looking to her left, feeling how he gripped her: firmly, mechanically, out of a pure practical need, not with over-familiarity. All the same, it was a strange sensation, to be dangling out towards the lagoon in the arms of this odd Englishman. She wondered, for a moment, what Nic would have made of the sight, then reminded herself why she had come here.

The tall tower of the distant church at the northern end of the lagoon was just visible in the distance.

'Thanks,' she said, and leaned back, noting the way he relaxed his grip immediately.

Hugo Massiter sat down, a handsome man, not yet past his prime, Emily thought, though perhaps he had a different opinion.

'I think you'd need a degree of arrogance to want to own a place like this,' she observed. 'That and a lot of money.'

'Cheers!' He raised his glass. 'Plenty of one. Little of the other, I'm afraid. My idea was to put up a little competition for Dame Peggy, once I'd knocked the place into shape.'

He nodded towards the city, and, she assumed, the Guggenheim.

'You want to start a gallery?' she asked.

'Why not? I've sold enough paintings and the rest over the years. Seemed to me it was time to keep a few for myself. I just hate the idea of them being stuck in a box in storage, or in a room where no one gets to see them except me. It's such a waste. Also, it makes me sound like Howard Hughes or someone, which I'm not.'

The wine was perfect, so cold it made her throat hurt. Massiter had quite a way with him.

'I don't imagine anyone would figure you for a recluse,' Emily suggested.

He placed his glass on the table, leaned back in his chair, frowning, looking exhausted.

'You've no idea what people figure me for,' Massiter complained ruefully, before shooting her a sharp, incisive glance. 'Or have you?'

He was staring at her with an open, unavoidable concern at that moment. Hugo Massiter was trying to understand just how much she knew.

'You've had a lot of press in your time,' she answered carefully.

'I've been a very visible man. That's understandable. It's just the damned lies. You've heard the story I'm talking about? Please be honest with me, Emily. Everyone around here knows and thinks that, by not mentioning it, they're being polite. That's kind of them but, to be honest, I hate beating about the bush. I don't want you sitting there thinking you might be supping with the Devil.'

She nodded.

'I remember the story. It was about a piece of music, wasn't it?'

'No,' he sighed, 'not really. It was about me. My ego. My need to feel I was doing something worthwhile.'

He paused to watch the traffic on the water.

'I trusted someone who betrayed me,' he continued. 'Very nearly brought me down, to be honest with you. If I hadn't got the hell out of Italy damn quick and found myself some very good and very expensive lawyers, I could be sitting in a jail cell right now. All because I let my guard down. All because . . .'

His eyes wandered down to the water again. Then he looked intently at her again.

'Let me tell you something about Venice. Something I should have learned years ago. It's not the crooks you need worry about. They're ten a penny and easy to spot a mile off. It's the innocents. They're the ones who kill you in the end. And here we are. Years later. Me wondering if I'm about to do the same again.'

'I'm sorry?'

'Remember Swift,' Massiter murmured.

> '"A flea hath smaller fleas that on him prey,
> And these have smaller fleas to bite 'em.
> And so proceed *ad infinitum*."

'My fleas are gathering, young Emily. Unless I can pull off some rather clever tricks over the next few days everything, this place included, will go down with the ship. What the hell. Fleeing the police on some trumped-up murder charges is one thing. But going bankrupt. My God . . . Do I need another drink or what?'

'No,' she said firmly. 'I don't think you do.'

He touched his forehead with his index finger, a deft salute of obedience.

'I need this charade to look good tonight. There are influential people coming. Tell me the truth now. What will they think of me with all this *junk* my young friend downstairs has introduced?'

She shrugged.

'Depends who they are.'

'People with taste – some of them. People with money. Power. If they knew the state of my bank account they'd never step through the door. You won't tell them, will you?'

'I won't even tell my police friend.'

Massiter smiled.

'Oh that's fine. He knows. But I'm pleased you're both discreet. I'm not, as you see, which is why I depend so much on discretion in others.'

He couldn't take his eyes off her.

'I was thinking . . .'

'Thinking what?'

'Wondering really. If I turned this building over to you. As a project say. You might even get paid something in the end. What would you do?'

Emily Deacon laughed then sipped her wine.

'Panic.'

'I don't believe that,' Massiter replied, serious all of a sudden. 'Not for a moment. I mean this. What would you suggest?'

She'd been thinking about that all along, as a highly perceptive man like Massiter doubtless knew. The building was, in a sense, unfinished, waiting for the final touches of someone's imagination. The answer was so obvious. She was amazed he hadn't seen it for himself. Emily glanced back at the plain apartment behind them, a place brimming with reserved taste.

'Do what you did here. Live with what you have. Make it habitable. Make it real.'

Massiter was chortling.

'It's not finished! There are interior walls half built. There are parts that simply make no sense.'

'Any less than those velvet drapes and fake Titians they're putting in downstairs? A half-finished masterpiece is better than a completed monstrosity any day. Please . . .'

He put his hand over his mouth, thinking.

'How's your Italian?'

'Better than yours. I've lived here for most of my life.'

'So have I!' he objected. 'Well, a good part anyway.'

'You've spent your time talking. I spent mine listening.'

He was no fool, though, she thought. Perhaps it was the prospect of putting off creditors. Perhaps – she'd seen the glint in Hugo Massiter's eye, she knew a man who liked women – it was something else altogether.

'You'd need to talk now, my dear,' he insisted. 'You'd need to tell a bunch of thieving Venetian builders what to do, and spot when they're rooking me. Think you're up to it?'

She drained her glass and placed it firmly on the table. The air below was alive with the curses of workmen, doing what the hell they liked, she suspected.

'I haven't applied for the job.'

Massiter didn't even notice her objection.

'And we'd need to dream up some ruse to allow me to fire that idiot down there. I can't just get rid of him. He's too well connected for that.'

There she was one step ahead.

'Did you order real marble for those dreadful tables by the door? Or fake?'

Massiter bristled. 'I didn't order anything. They were his idea. And I do not *deal* in fakes.'

'They're veneer. Marble layered on wood. It's obvious if you look at the edges. I doubt it's the only problem.'

'It's enough,' Massiter said, suddenly furious, getting to his feet. 'Follow me, please.'

He stormed downstairs at high speed, yelling for the architect, 'Andrea! *Andrea!*'

They finally found the man lounging on a dire purple velvet sofa next to the dead palm tree. He was smoking a cigarette, watching a couple of sweating workers attempt to fix the phoney marble tops with tubes of cement.

'Massiter! Massiter! So much noise. I try to think. Please!'

He was a skeletal creature in his twenties, dressed in a black suit and white shirt open at the neck. A ridiculously ornate moustache was trying to establish itself on his top lip.

'Problems,' Massiter said, picking up a massive club hammer from the floor.

The architect splayed his hands.

'What problems? Are you mad?'

Massiter swung the implement in a rapid, powerful arc and brought it down hard on the shining black surface. The two men who'd been working on it took two steps back, yelling obscenities. The 'marble' split instantly in two, revealing the shattered edges of cheap pale ply between.

'I'm mad now,' Massiter declared. 'I'm *bloody* mad.'

Andrea got up and started slapping one of the workmen round the head, swearing at him in a vivid burst of Veneto.

'No games!' Massiter bellowed. 'I've had enough of that. You can clear out of here now and tell your uncle he can shove his bill up his ass.'

'Screw you!' Andrea yelled. 'You can't come here and do what you like.'

The Englishman passed the huge hammer from one hand to the other and gave it a good swing. Andrea thought better of things and began to slink off towards the door, his workers following on behind.

'Where the hell do you think you're going?' Massiter shouted at them.

The men stopped in their tracks, worried, a little scared.

'Emily? Tell them.'

It was ridiculous. It was also highly amusing. They were staring at her, mute aggression in their faces, daring her to speak. Italian builders didn't take instruction from women. Especially not foreign ones.

She gave her orders briskly, in the kind of language they would understand.

'You've got a choice. You can crawl off home now and whistle for your money. Or you can take every last piece of this crap out of here and find me some paint. White paint. *Good* white paint. Matt only. And lots of brushes. Plus some fabric for hangings. White again. This is the island of the archangels. Angels like white.'

They looked at each other and said nothing.

Massiter laughed discreetly then leaned over to whisper in her ear.

'A silent Venetian is a defeated Venetian, my dear,' he murmured, his breath warm and familiar, sweet with the aroma of wine. 'Well done.'

5

Costa was mulling over his partner's rhetorical question: why did they always get the bum deal? Because he'd defied Leo Falcone, that's why. Pushing Scacchi for what he knew about the missing Daniel Forster and Laura Conti had been an act of direct rebellion. Falcone was too preoccupied with the case to make much of it. But both Costa and Peroni knew there'd be a price, and when they got to the Isola degli Arcangeli they discovered what it was. Falcone was keeping the sweet part – the house and Raffaela Arcangelo – for himself.

All the same, Costa didn't feel a single pang of regret. It would have been remiss to have left Sant' Erasmo without tackling Scacchi about the missing couple. And those postcards Scacchi had shown them were, it seemed to him, distinctly odd. No one printed their own name. Certainly not a student from Oxford. Scacchi had said he worked as an illicit ferryman for people who didn't want to pay the price of official water taxis. The cards could have been posted by anyone. Some Alitalia steward he took to the airport from time to time and asked for a little souvenir of the man's travels, signed in a particular way. But why?

Ordinarily, he'd have mulled the idea over with Falcone and Peroni. Now, it seemed pointless. They were both fixated with the Arcangeli, keen to see this case closed, then engineer an escape from the lagoon. Costa felt the same way. In principle, anyway. Watching Falcone march off to the mansion, with its glistening eye looming out over the lagoon, leaving them to the smoke-stink of the foundry and the two surly brothers, he almost wished he'd kept his mouth shut.

Almost.

The same face was at the great glass window: calm, attractive, sensitive.

'I *am* going to get a look inside that place before we leave for good,' Costa swore.

Peroni huffed and puffed.

'In that case maybe you'd better do what Leo says. You know he hates being crossed.'

But Falcone *was* wrong; Venice wasn't some backwater unworthy of their metropolitan talents. Costa wondered whether they weren't the ones being duped by doing Randazzo's bidding. Being forced to see matters the way the Venetians liked.

Falcone was at the window with Raffaela now, listening, nodding. Interested, Costa thought, and that was new too. The two brothers were working away inside the foundry, close to the furnace, Gabriele welding, Michele cutting pipe, as if they hadn't even noticed his and Peroni's presence.

Costa watched Gabriele extinguishing the lance and waited for the sound of the gas to die down. He walked over to the man, took the long metal implement out of his hand and placed it on the floor.

'Enough,' he said with a deliberate gruffness. 'And you.' He turned to Michele who was grappling with some joint work, trying to wrestle some tangle of metal into submission. 'Put that thing down and talk to us. If we don't get some cooperation here I *will*, I swear, arrest the pair of you and continue this at the Questura.'

Michele kept on straining away at the job, giving him just a single, filthy glance with the ruined side of his face.

'One call, *garzone*,' the old man spat back at him. 'That's all it takes and you're out of here.'

Costa walked up close to him.

'I am not your boy. Understand something. If we move off this case and someone else has to pick up the pieces you lose time. That means no deal with this Englishman who's looking to save your skin. Screw around with us all you like but don't think it won't come at a price.'

That, finally, got both of them listening.

'What the hell do you know about our private business?' Michele demanded.

Peroni burst out laughing.

'Private? What's your definition of the word "private" around here? We walked up and down Murano yesterday, talking to people who can't wait to gossip about you and your problems. Your dirty linen gets washed in public on a daily basis. Do you really not know that?'

It struck Costa that they didn't, and that in itself was interesting. The Arcangeli really were still outsiders, even after all these years.

'You can talk here. Or you can talk in the Questura,' he repeated.

'We don't have time for this crap,' the elder brother snarled.

'You get even less time if we have to haul you over to Castello,' Peroni pointed out.

Michele grunted. Then he walked out into the sunshine, lit a cigarette, and perched on one of the bollards on the quay, watching the water stretching between the island and San Michele.

'Ten minutes,' he said, in the cold grating voice that was starting to get to Costa. 'Then you can go and bore the hell out of someone else.'

6

Leo Falcone stood with Raffaela Arcangelo at the glass window, both of them watching the scene developing below, two brothers, two cops, beginning to talk underneath the sputtering torch of the iron angel on the bridge, not that far from the pair of carpenters who were still slowly putting the foundry doors back together.

'I told you there'd be no problem in the end,' she said. 'They're not unhelpful. Just preoccupied. And they've nothing new to say. You do understand that, Leo, don't you?'

She was wearing better clothes today, he thought. A smartly pressed white silk shirt and black trousers. A little make-up and two small, delicate earrings, crystal naturally.

Falcone had taken the call from Teresa Lupo just after he'd left Costa and Peroni grumbling their way to the men downstairs, chastened by his reprimand for the way the younger detective had stepped out of line with Piero Scacchi. He was heartened to hear the interest and determination in Teresa's voice, though. Something would, he thought, get resolved as a result. Even so, the nature of Uriel's death remained puzzling. He was unable, too, to decide whether the news of Bella's condition clarified matters or simply made them more opaque. The answers to these problems lay in small details, snatches of conversation, tentative, private relationships. Falcone preferred dealing with crooks. He knew he was somewhat out of his territory in these waters, though he was determined the locals, and Randazzo in particular, wouldn't notice.

'You promised to tell me what you know,' Raffaela reminded him.

He sipped the weak Earl Grey tea she'd brought. It was an

affectation, a pleasant one. There were many in this overlarge, slightly pretentious home of which the Arcangeli filled barely a quarter.

'I said there would be limits.'

'I understand that, Leo. So tell me something within those limits.'

'Within those limits there's precious little to say. What possible motive could Uriel have? What happened to Bella's keys? You've still not found them?'

She hesitated, a fleeting look of reserve on her face.

'No. I've looked again. Everywhere.'

In another case, one properly resourced, with strong backing from above, Falcone knew he'd be doing all the searching himself. Under Randazzo's curious restrictions this was, if not impossible, difficult. Besides, he trusted Raffaela Arcangelo. She knew this rambling mansion better than they did. If there was anything to be uncovered, she would surely find it. All the same . . .

'I ought to look.'

'Certainly.'

She led him to Uriel and Bella's apartment, on the floor above. There was nothing to see. Nothing to take away except the ambience, which was a little tawdry: old furniture, the smell of musty damp.

'This is better than it normally was,' Raffaela said, seeing the expression on his face. 'I wouldn't clean for them. Even I have limits.'

'Where do the rest of you live?'

The answer didn't surprise him. As far apart as possible. Michele's apartment was on the ground floor. Gabriele occupied a sprawling hovel behind the dining room. Raffaela's own room, about the same size but immaculate, though still with dated furniture and few modern conveniences, was a little way along from Uriel and Bella's, almost within earshot. The rest of the mansion was empty: dusty, bare rooms, cleared of anything valuable they might once have contained. The short tour depressed him. He was glad to return to the dining room, the one place in the house, it seemed to him, that retained some memories of what the Arcangeli had once been.

'Why did Bella have that phone, Leo?' Raffaela asked. 'It doesn't make sense.'

He frowned.

'There would be one obvious reason if she kept it hidden from all of you. How many possibilities are there?'

She didn't look convinced.

'Affairs . . . happen,' he pointed out. 'Even in Murano. There must have been others. Before Uriel, surely.'

'I wasn't Bella's keeper,' she replied quietly, evading the question.

'But you were Uriel's, weren't you?'

The dead man was two years older than her but something in Raffaela's attitude told Falcone the relationship had, in a way, reversed. That Uriel had been under her care, somehow, the weakest of the brothers. Perhaps that was why she chose to live so close to the couple, when there were so many other rooms she could have used.

'What do you mean?' she asked, not offended by the question, more puzzled.

'I was simply being presumptuous,' Falcone replied with a shrug. 'This job makes you think you can read people. Sometimes I can. Sometimes . . .'

She was watching him, interested.

'And how do you read me?'

'I think you cared for Uriel more than the other two. Perhaps because he was the youngest. The least happy—'

'He *wasn't* unhappy! Not in the way you mean.'

'How then?'

'He was . . . unfinished,' she said carefully. 'Even I got out of here for a while. Studying, in Paris, when we still had money. Uriel never escaped. He never really knew what it was like beyond Murano. And this place can be so cold, so close. You won't understand that. Most people don't even notice. Michele, Gabriele – they never did. Uriel knew there was more to life, but he didn't get the chance. And now . . .'

She paused, a sudden mist in her eyes.

'You read people well, Leo. I'm not sure that's a compliment. It must be a difficult talent to possess. Do you know when to turn it off?'

His former wife had once said something very similar, not long before she'd left him. He'd rejected the accusation at the time. The faculty she was describing was a necessary part of his job. Now, after several solitary years of single life, he wondered whether it didn't, in truth, carry a heavy personal cost.

'I'm trying to learn,' he said with a smile. 'You will still accompany me this evening, won't you?'

A faint rush of pink appeared on Raffaela's cheeks.

'Of course. I said I would.'

'Good. I understand you want to get to the bottom of this. I hope it helps.'

'I would have gone anyway,' she answered, not looking directly into his face. 'We were invited, apparently. Not that I knew of it. Michele had thoughtfully rejected Mr Massiter's offer without telling me. Now *I'm* going it appears he will be too. Separately . . .'

She added the last part quickly, anxiously.

Falcone wondered why Michele would have rejected a social invitation from a man with whom he wished to conclude important business, at an event that was on his own doorstep, on property that was, technically, still their own. Then he checked himself. There were dangers in an excess of suspicion. The Arcangeli were pursuing the arrangement with Massiter out of financial necessity. It was, perhaps, only understandable if they found elements unpleasant.

'I have to ask something,' he declared abruptly. 'It's a personal matter, for which I apologize, but it can't be avoided. I need to know about Uriel's marriage. Is it true that it was more a family decision than his alone?'

There was a sudden, unexpected expression of anger on Raffaela Arcangelo's face. It made her look rather beautiful.

'Who told you that? It's nonsense.'

'Aldo Bracci told my officers. He said it was more than just a personal liaison. It was supposed to be some kind of alliance, that Bella brought knowledge with her, as part of the dowry perhaps. Knowledge that could help the business.'

She laughed. The anger disappeared in an instant. Falcone watched her sudden, flashing smile and wondered why a woman of Raffaela's looks had stayed single throughout her life.

'So we're accused of arranging marriages now, are we? And by him of all people? Let me tell you something. Murano may not care much for us. But it has even less time for the Braccis. They've a reputation that precedes us by a couple of centuries. Crooks and devils. Ask around yourself. So what else did he say?'

'That it was Michele who was interested in Bella initially. Not Uriel at all.'

She sat down on the bench by the window and gazed out onto the bright water.

'God, this place,' Raffaela Arcangelo murmured. 'Whispers in the dark. All this made-up rubbish.'

Falcone joined her.

'I don't mean to pry. You understand why I have to ask?'

'Of course.' She nodded, and turned her eyes away from the lagoon, staring him in the face. 'You don't like this kind of work, do you?'

'It's work,' he replied, a little offended. 'I don't get the luxury of choice. What do you mean, exactly?'

'In Rome, I imagine, you're dealing with different people – ones you know are guilty. You just have to find some way of proving it.'

'Sometimes it's like that,' he agreed. 'Not always.'

'We're not criminals here,' she insisted. 'You must understand that. I don't know what's gone wrong, but it's some personal matter, Leo. You can't use your normal rules to get to the bottom of this. Normal rules don't apply here. Not' – she added, smiling – 'that I'm in any position to give you advice.'

'It was Michele, then? In the first instance?'

She closed her eyes briefly.

'It happened after his marriage collapsed. He'd had his eyes on Bella. All the men did. She was very pretty. Very . . . accommodating too. I told you the Braccis had reputations. Sometimes that attracts men, in case you hadn't noticed. Were there others? Yes. Half the men of Murano, married men sometimes, or so they say. For Michele it was just a stupid infatuation. Nothing more. It came and then, when he realized how ridiculous the idea was, it passed. A few years later Uriel proposed to her. She was in her thirties by then. I imagine her options were running out. It never struck me as love, not even from the beginning. Simply a practical arrangement for both of them. Did we discuss it as a family? Of course. Uriel wanted to know Michele no longer had feelings, naturally. Not that any of us needed to ask. By then the business was in a bad way. Michele's been wedded to that ever since. He has no room for a real relationship.'

Those dark eyes flickered towards the lagoon again.

'You could say the same for all of us,' Raffaela added. 'And besides . . . to hear an accusation of that nature from a man like Aldo Bracci. I told you to look, Leo. Did you?'

Falcone thought about those old records and wondered how reliable they were. Michele Arcangelo's infatuation seemed much more recent, more real.

'More whispers in the dark, perhaps. He was simply cautioned, never charged. If there'd been real evidence—'

'There was evidence,' she interrupted. 'It was the talk of Murano. A scandal. No one could believe it. The two of them scarcely tried to hide what they were up to, though Bella was just a child, of course. She didn't know what she was doing. At least, I *believe* she didn't.'

'Such a long time ago.'

'Here? It's like yesterday. People have long memories. For good and bad. They don't bear a grudge. They nurture it. When Bella heard one of the neighbours had been whispering to the police, she walked straight into the Questura herself and told them everything. Everything she felt like, at least. He was lucky he didn't go to jail for what he did.'

He asked the question she was expecting.

'And afterwards? They made up?'

'They're the Braccis. A family. Of course the argument didn't last.'

'And you think the affair may have resumed? Even after she was married?'

She was suddenly circumspect.

'I don't know. He used to come here to see her from time to time. Ostensibly to speak with Michele about business. Bracci was always looking for extra work, not that we had much. I heard . . . sounds from time to time. Whether it was Aldo . . .'

Falcone waited.

'Oh, for God's sake, Leo,' Raffaela objected. 'I wasn't going to get into the habit of eavesdropping on my sister-in-law making love. What kind of person do you take me for? I simply couldn't avoid hearing things sometimes. It could have been her brother. It could have been someone else. Do you expect me to greet every single visitor at the door?'

'Did Aldo have . . .?'

'A key?' She was with him in an instant. 'Of course not. At least not that I'm aware of. Michele would have been livid if that had been the case. Though if Bella gave him one anyway – who's to know?'

Raffaela Arcangelo stared at her hands clasped over her knees, and frowned.

'I don't think Aldo ever really accepted the marriage. Funnily enough, in spite of his own background, I think he felt Uriel wasn't good enough for Bella. Perhaps if it had been Michele things would have been different. He resented us, though. We had money once. That's something he's never known. And perhaps . . .'

She glanced into his face, and there was doubt there, some plain, fresh concern.

'Perhaps that resentment amounted to hatred. I wondered about that sometimes. When he was here. Full of drink. With Bella. I heard shouting occasionally. I thought about intervening. He's a bitter, angry man. I wouldn't want to be on the end of that anger.'

Falcone stood up and stared out of the window down towards the small iron bridge. It wouldn't be difficult to get onto the island surreptitiously. A man could climb around the fence, or take a boat up to the jetty, perhaps an hour or two before Piero Scacchi arrived. Yet the question of the keys remained. Someone had locked the door on Uriel Arcangelo, leaving him with a key that could never work, fated to die.

'Tell me something outside your limits, Leo,' she pleaded. 'I've been as frank with you as I possibly can. Perhaps I can help more. I will, if you let me.'

Falcone mulled over the possibilities. There was nothing to lose.

'Bella was pregnant,' he said without emotion. 'She'd known for more than a week. Uriel wasn't the father. We've seen medical records. It's impossible. Nor do we have any way of establishing who the father was. Not in the circumstances.'

Raffaela Arcangelo screwed her eyes tight shut, moaned gently, then buried her head in her hands. The mane of long dark hair fell forward, covering her face.

Automatically, Leo Falcone reached down and placed a hand on her shoulder.

'I'm sorry,' he murmured and realized she was right: there was something too close, too personal about this case. He needed to think about the way he broached this kind of material. 'I thought perhaps . . .'

She raised her head. Raffaela's tear-stained eyes blazed at him.

'You thought I knew? This is insane, Leo. Three lives now. Gone. For what?'

Falcone blinked, feeling dizzy. The heat was different in Venice: humid and riddled with the stink of the lagoon. It leeched the energy out of him, made it difficult to think straight. He missed Verona where there were colleagues of his own age, and of similar experience. A line led through this investigation. He knew that, and knew he had to keep the search for it in his sight. Someone had killed both Bella and Uriel Arcangelo. Somehow Bella was implicated in her own death too, or so the evidence seemed to say.

'A child,' he murmured. 'She would have told someone, surely?'

'She would have told the father,' Raffaela said, her voice angry, determined. 'And . . .'

Her eyes flickered towards the window and the men below. Michele was the head of the family. Falcone wondered what that really meant. Was he supposed to be a party to everything?

'I need to speak to my brothers.'

Falcone followed her through the old, fading mansion, down the warren of dark corridors half lit by dusty chandeliers populated by dead bulbs, listening to the echoes of her hurried footsteps.

7

The Tosis were right about one thing: there was plenty of information on spontaneous combustion out there. Any number of lunatics, sceptics and pseudo-scientists were busy yelling at each other on the subject. Teresa Lupo had spent two hours sifting through the reams of material on the computer in Costa's apartment, saving the little she found useful, and examining the documents Anna Tosi had sent through the miracle medium of e-mail. After that, her head spinning with possibilities, she'd popped out to buy some pizza and water from the shop around the corner, returning to the computer immediately, spilling crumbs, Peroni-like, across the keyboard as she worked. All the same she was, she thought, none the wiser. No. She was a touch the wiser, just reluctant to admit it because there was something here which disturbed her greatly: a possibility that the Tosis had a point. This wasn't spontaneous combustion in some fantasy comic book kind of way, flames licking out from underneath Uriel Arcangelo's apron, sparked by some passing moonbeam. But people did die on occasion from an event which appeared, on the surface, inexplicable, a sudden, inner fire which seemed to consume them with a shocking rapidity.

'That doesn't mean there's no explanation,' Teresa reminded herself. 'You just have to find it, girl.'

Here. Stuck in a tiny police apartment in Venice, with nothing but a laptop computer for company. She thought about what she'd be doing if this had dropped on her desk back in Rome. Scouring the net for clues? Surely. But more than that, she'd be sharing the problem. And she knew with whom.

Teresa Lupo pulled out her mobile phone, reprimanded herself for a few brief milliseconds with the admonition that her absence was a holiday for her staff also, then dialled Silvio Di Capua's private number.

'*Pronto*,' yawned a bored voice on the other end, one which immediately jerked into alert suspicion once Silvio realized who was on the line.

'No,' he declared straight off. 'I won't do it. I'm ending this call now. You're supposed to be on holiday for God's sake. Go and fake a tan or something. Just leave me alone.'

'I haven't asked you to do a damn thing, Silvio! I'm just calling in to see how you are.'

'So I can't do the job, huh? Give me a break. Do you think I don't recognize that wheedling tone in your voice? I won't play. You can't make me.'

'Of course you can do the job! I wouldn't have gone away and left you in charge if I thought otherwise.'

'Then what? I'm not getting involved. It's bad enough you dumping me in the crap when you're here working. I'm not having it when you're supposed to be on vacation. Hear me, Teresa. The answer is no. No, no, no, no, no.'

There was an image of a charred corpse on the screen: Buffalo, New York, 1973. No obvious explanation. The man smoked. The man drank. So did millions of other people, all of whom managed to work their way to the grave without turning into life-sized spent matchsticks.

She smiled. Silvio was giving in already.

'You're not busy then?'

'Says who? I'm sorting out the paperwork you should have done months ago. I'm dealing with a couple of inter-departmental liaison meetings.'

'My,' she cooed. 'That sounds fun. Are there whiteboards and stuff? Have they given you one of those laser pens? Do you get to use big words and acronyms?'

'You will never understand management—'

'I *am* management,' she interrupted. 'So let me – what's the management word for it? – let me *cascade* something down to you, dear heart. When you want to say no, you say you're too busy. Not, screw you, I won't do it. Understood?'

There was a brief silence on the line. The roar of defeat.

'Just because I don't have much in the way of corpses doesn't mean I'm not occupied.'

'No corpses means no fun, Silvio. Admit it. I know when my little man is bored. You sounded bored when you picked up the phone. I've got a corpse. I've got a cure for that boredom, if you want to hear it.'

'No!' he insisted.

'Fine. In that case I'll hang up.'

'Do that! Go have a holiday!'

'Your word is my command. I am about to put down the phone. Or, more accurately, my finger is wandering towards the off button. Do you really want me to press it?'

'Yes!'

'Fine. It's done. I shall say just two words before doing so.'

A pause was required. Silvio always rose to histrionics.

'Spontaneous combustion.'

Teresa cut him dead, placed her mobile on the desk and began to count to ten. It rang on three. She let it chirrup five times before answering sweetly, 'Hello?'

'I detest you with every fibre in my body. You are evil. This is *so* unfair. You can't treat people like this.'

'Spontaneous combustion, Silvio. I have a corpse here, well, part of a corpse, and a Venetian pathologist, albeit one who's a couple of hundred years old himself, who's determined to write that finding on the death certificate. So what do you think?'

'I think it's a little early in the day to start drinking. Sober up, woman. See the sights. Catch a boat somewhere.'

'No kidding. It's all there. I have photos. I have reports. I have all manner of material I could send you if you'd like. Provided it doesn't interrupt your whiteboarding that is. I mean, I expect my people to have priorities.'

He hesitated, wary.

'Two points,' he responded. 'I will believe in spontaneous

combustion the day I come to accept the existence of werewolves. Second, you're in Venice where you are just another dumb tourist, Teresa, not someone with the authority to go investigating weird deaths, whatever the crazy locals believe. Most people tread in crap accidentally. You cross the street to do it. This is a habit I deplore.'

'I was asked to take a look! OK?'

'Who by?' he demanded.

'Falcone.'

'Oh shit. You're not telling me you're riding the range with the three musketeers again?'

'I ride the range with one of them a lot, in case you hadn't noticed.'

Peroni's presence still bugged Silvio somewhat. Her assistant hadn't lost the hots for her completely.

'I was using a metaphor. Let me put it plainly. Are you out of your mind?'

Maybe, she thought. If she really were considering the weird science stuff the Tosis were pushing her way.

'So what's your objection to spontaneous combustion?'

'The same objection I have to reincarnation. Or alchemy. It's nonsense.'

A tiny light went on in her head. There were times when she wanted to hug Silvio. His small accidental insights could be just what she needed to trigger her own imagination.

'Without alchemy there'd be no chemistry,' she remarked. 'You're a chemist yourself, along with all those other talents. You ought to know that.'

Silvio swore quietly down the phone. She was spot on. Alchemy may have begun with quacks, but it soon became science under another name. Glass makers like the Arcangeli were, surely, alchemists of a kind, too, sharing the same common bonds of secrets and substances, changing the shape of the natural world, bending it to their will.

'What I'm saying,' she continued, 'is that I'm beginning to believe this man really did die in a way that can be interpreted as spontaneous combustion. The question is: what does that actually mean? How could it happen?'

'Get their forensic people on it!' he objected. 'That's why they're there.'

She recalled how Falcone had slyly got her on side. It was a good trick.

'But they're not as good as you, Silvio. You've worked forensic *and* pathology. They're slow. They're unimaginative. This is Venice. They're wet behind the ears when it comes to real crime. It's just the tourist police out here,' she continued, steeling herself to what she understood to be a big lie. 'Trust me.'

'I know what's coming. You're gunning for resources. We get audited, remember? We have to assign work to cases. How am I supposed to hide all that from the managers here?'

She prodded at the keyboard, loading up the Tosis' documents and photos, adding in a few of her own, then she despatched the lot off to Silvio's private address.

'I'm sending you something to read,' she said. 'Go through it. Then get back to me with a way we can go forward with this. You've got till tomorrow.'

'Tomorrow! For fu . . .'

He was still cursing, with a florid ingenuity, when she hung up.

Alchemy. Chemistry. Analysis. There was a big, black hole in the Tosis' findings, one that hadn't been looked into closely enough because everything had to be signed off in a rush, and by another branch of the Tosi family who probably didn't bother to get too involved either. But without some scrupulous work Uriel Arcangelo's death would remain a mystery, would nag her with its unproven possibilities and hidden corners. People didn't just catch fire from the inside without a reason. Not in her world. It was important to make this clear.

It was also important to remember the medical details too. Bella's pregnancy was doubtless the news that would start punching Falcone's buttons. But it was Uriel who interested her. Uriel with his lousy sense of smell. If someone had soaked his apron in lighter fluid, would he have noticed?

There was a prerequisite and it was a lot to ask. If any other pathologist had made the same request of her she'd have sent them away with a sound ear-thrashing. All the same Alberto Tosi was a gentleman.

It took ten minutes to get through on his mobile. The man, to her amazement, was taking coffee and cake in a café, not poring over what little evidence he had, trying to wring some answers out of it.

'Professor!' Tosi said cheerfully.

'Please call me Teresa,' she replied. 'If I may call you Alberto.'

'Of course.'

It was best to be direct, to act as if this were a normal request, one that could scarcely be refused.

'I need a sample from Uriel's apron and clothing. And a piece of timber from the floor where he was found. The burned part. Nothing large. I need these sent overnight by courier to my lab in Rome.'

She recalled how technology impressed him.

'They have a new machine there,' she lied. 'Sort of a spectroscope on steroids. We borrowed the thing from the FBI to see if it's worth buying. I doubt we'll throw up anything you haven't uncovered yourself, of course, but it would be extremely useful if we could test some material from the fire.'

There was a pause on the line.

'You don't have a suitable case in Rome? This is most unusual. Surely—'

'Sadly not. We only have the machine until Wednesday, Alberto. You know what Americans are like. I'm probably breaking the law just telling you this. I'm not trying to interfere with your work, naturally. It's just the best opportunity I have to evaluate this particular toy.'

The decision hung in the balance.

'If I buy the thing you're welcome to come and play with it in the future,' she promised him.

Teresa heard the clink of a coffee cup, tried to imagine the glint of excitement in his eyes.

'This machine. What does it *do?*' Alberto Tosi asked, breathless.

'It's a kind of . . .'

Shit, she thought. Why did he have to ask a question like that, just when she least expected it?

'. . . magic,' she stuttered. 'You wait and see.'

8

It was infuriating. Every question he and Peroni threw at the Arcangeli brothers got bounced back with a short, curt unassailable reply. They weren't even surly enough to be evasive. Maybe the brothers really did have nothing new to tell. Costa finally got sick of Michele's cigarette smoke, excused himself, and decided to take another look around the foundry. The brothers and their workmen had been busy. He could see that they would, indeed, be back in production before long. New pipe work gleamed around the patched-up furnace.

He walked idly around the interior, thinking, doing what Falcone would have advised: trying to imagine himself into the scene. Uriel Arcangelo, alone with the fire and the molten crucible of glass which lay alongside his wife's blazing body, turning to dust in the flames.

Practical matters.

They counted, Falcone said.

He tried to work out what else they could have missed the previous day. It was impossible to tell. The floor had been clean. Any shred of unseen evidence that had lurked there before was now surely gone. The picture the island – perhaps the entire city – wanted to present to them, of a guilty Uriel trapped and dying by the side of his victim, still stood in place.

Costa wandered over to the carpenters and stared at the new doors. They didn't look good enough to last more than a couple of cold lagoon winters. The Arcangeli's workmen were on a different scale to those Massiter was employing on the palace along the quay; they were odd-job men, trying to come up with a quick fix. From what he'd seen of the previous doors, these simply followed the same design: a pair of thick wooden slabs, almost four metres high, joined in the middle by a heavy mortise lock, and attached to the original ancient hinges which were so solid they had remained when the firemen first entered, swinging their axes.

The new doors were ajar. Behind, on the quay, Costa could hear Michele and Gabriele Arcangelo talking to each other about when to restart the furnace, about glass, chemicals, times and temperatures, like two cooks trying to agree on some arcane recipe.

Peroni wandered over, grumbling, then smiled at the locals. They looked like father and son, both squat men, the elder with a beard. Murano seemed to run on families.

'Nice day,' Peroni said. 'You boys finished here?'

'Finished what we've been told to do,' the father said.

'So they're back in business?' Costa asked.

'They were in business before?' the son replied, extracting a brief chuckle from his old man.

They watched, idly smoking, as Costa walked up and pushed both doors, gently. Each went back on its hinges smoothly, and stayed open.

'You'd think there'd be springs,' Peroni commented. 'To make sure they'd stay closed. If that was my place, I'd have springs. Too many lazy bastards in this world leaving doors wide open. And all those secrets inside.'

'You'd think,' the father agreed curtly. 'We replace like for like, just as the insurance people say.'

'Is it really a secret?' Peroni wondered. 'Making glass, I mean?'

'We don't make glass.'

Costa tried each door lightly. The left one fell into place, as it should. The right stopped marginally short. A tiny amount, so little that most people wouldn't have noticed. Nevertheless, they hadn't been like this when Piero Scacchi had arrived. Someone had to have closed the right-hand door deliberately. It couldn't have shut by itself. Except . . .

The idea sparked in his head with a sudden clarity. Uriel couldn't have unlocked the door. His key didn't work. It must have either been open, slightly ajar as it was now, or someone had let him in.

He pulled the door shut. The lock was automatic, which meant that, had Uriel let himself in through the open door then closed it behind him, he was effectively trapped in the room. It seemed a neat ruse. Uriel would be bound to visit the furnace during the night. Once he was inside, there was no easy way out. Costa made a mental note to pass this on to Falcone. It could be useful information, and he wanted to make a point: that the door and the lock puzzled him too.

The old man was eyeing him with open, mute aggression.

'What's the big deal anyway?' he demanded. 'A man kills his wife. Doesn't happen much around here. Unless you know otherwise.'

'We're from Rome,' Peroni said pleasantly, then turned the key in the lock and pushed open the door to keep an eye on the Arcangeli brothers, who were still deep in discussion on the quay. 'We've got shit for brains in case you hadn't noticed. Do you know something? We don't have a damn clue about what happens around here. I don't even know why Uriel would *want* to kill his wife. Do you?'

The two of them shuffled awkwardly on their feet and said nothing.

'You're local,' Costa added, accusingly. 'Two people, your own people, are dead. Aren't you even interested?'

'He wasn't one of ours,' the elder grumbled. 'No one ever said that. People here mind their business. You should try it.'

'Does that make him less of a man?' Costa asked.

'You didn't know him. You don't know any of them. You wouldn't understand.'

'Bella was one of yours. The Braccis have been here for years.'

The son spat on the dry, dusty ground and said, simply, 'Braccis.'

Peroni gave Costa the look. It was clear they weren't liked either. And Nic Costa knew there was no point in trying to find out why. Talking to these two was as futile as throwing questions at the Arcangeli.

The men were looking behind him.

'Now *she*,' one of them said, a note of respect in his voice, 'is different.'

He turned and saw Raffaela Arcangelo marching towards her

brothers, striding across the narrow wharf at a determined pace, anger in her eyes, Falcone following behind.

'Michele!' the woman yelled. *'Michele!'*

It was one of those public events you couldn't not watch. The carpenters were all eyes, taking in everything.

'You should check those doors are done. They look a little flimsy to me,' Costa ordered.

'Stick to police work, sonny,' the old man bit back. 'We're taking a break.'

The pair ambled over towards the group by the water, just close enough to hear every word of the furious family confrontation developing under the burning sun. A noisy one, too, not without interest, though best played out, Costa judged, indoors.

He went up to Falcone and whispered in the inspector's ear.

'Sir, this shouldn't be happening. Not here. It's too public.'

'Let's see,' Falcone murmured.

Costa nodded towards the pair of eavesdropping carpenters.

'We've company.'

'Forget about the company.'

Costa glanced at Peroni and knew his partner was thinking the same thing. This was the old Falcone routine, the one they hadn't seen since they left Rome. The trick the inspector used from time to time of letting a situation come to a head, letting the emotions run out, then seeing where they led. Sometimes it worked for him, though Costa wondered if it wasn't like letting a couple of cars crash just to see who was the worst driver.

Something was different here. Falcone had an interest in this woman, one that went beyond the professional. It was implicit in the hungry way he watched her that she intrigued Leo Falcone.

What ensued was a bitter, full-on domestic fight among the Arcangeli, beneath the flickering flame of their iron namesake, an event that went, in some way, to the very heart of this peculiar family. It was as if Raffaela had been waiting for years to throw this kind of anger in the direction of her eldest brother, and with it all the accusations she'd been harbouring: of lies, of deceit, of a failure to protect the family's interests. The tide had burst and Costa wondered if either of them, Raffaela or Michele, understood how difficult it would be to return to their previous state of mutual acceptance once the storm had subsided.

Michele stood there, arms crossed, watching her, saying nothing, that frozen side of his face turned towards her anger, as if it were some kind of shield to protect him from the fiery stream of words that tumbled from Raffaela's mouth.

'You knew,' she said. 'You knew Bella was pregnant. She didn't tell Uriel. She didn't tell me. But she came to you and you did *nothing.*'

The dead eye glinted back at her like flawed glass, run through with some streak of impurity.

'Say something,' she spat at him. 'Speak, Michele! It's not like you to be lost for words.'

The dead side of his face turned away from her. He gazed at the hazy waterline, the little island of San Michele and the city in the distance, then returned to confront her again, good side visible, showing an unexpected degree of distress.

'Of course I knew!' he yelled. 'I'm supposed to know these things, aren't I? That's what I do around here. Take on all your problems and fix them. Because God knows you can't do that for yourselves. Not you. Not him.' Michele nodded towards Gabriele, who stood silent, watching the water. 'Not poor, dead Uriel most of all. What do you think he'd have done if I'd told him? Huh? If I'd said his wife had got herself knocked up? And who by? Her own stinking brother. What do you think he'd have made of that?'

Raffaela was staring at him, gasping for breath. Unable to speak.

'You're sure of that?' Falcone asked him. 'About the brother? She told you?'

'She didn't need to tell me,' Michele replied mournfully. 'We all knew what went on between them.'

'That was years ago,' Costa said. 'There's no evidence it happened recently.'

'Ask her!' Michele barked, pointing at his sister. 'She heard them. She knew. She never dared tell Uriel either.'

Raffaela shook her head. Tears were beginning to stream down her cheeks.

'I only said it was a possibility,' she murmured. 'It could all have been a mistake. Perhaps it wasn't Aldo.'

'Then whose brat was it?' Michele demanded. 'Not Uriel's, that's for sure. It wouldn't have mattered anyway. She'd still have come to me to sort out the whole damn thing. And I'd still have done it. I'd arranged for her to get rid of it. Today, in case you're interested. Paid in advance. I don't suppose I'll get that back from the clinic.'

'We had the right to know,' she insisted.

'She didn't seem to think so,' Michele declared, exasperated. Costa stared into his face. There could have been the making of tears in that single, living eye. 'I didn't want this, Raffaela. I didn't want *any* of this but it's what God gave me and I can't walk away. I'm sorry. I'm deeply, deeply—'

The old grey face went into his hands. Costa watched Michele's shoulders begin to heave, heard the choked sob come, just once, from his hidden mouth.

'Michele, Michele,' she murmured, then walked up and clutched her brother tightly, whispered some unheard words into his ear. The two of them stood locked together on the waterfront, watched avidly by three cops and a couple of Murano carpenters who had an expression on their smug faces Nic Costa didn't like at all, and Gabriele, who sat down on the kerb edge of the quay, eyes on the water still, looking like a lost child.

'I said this was a matter to be conducted indoors,' Costa reminded Falcone with undisguised bitterness.

To his surprise, Falcone nodded, looking repentant. He couldn't take his eyes off the distraught Raffaela, clutching her brother.

'I heard you, Nic. I'm sorry. I keep trying to apply the rules I use in Rome. It just doesn't work here, does it? Jesus . . .'

The carpenters were slinking towards the bridge, back to town. Father and son, for sure. They had that closeness seen on so many Murano faces, a tight, conspiratorial intimacy that formed a barrier to the world outside.

'No matter,' Falcone grumbled. 'It's out of the bag now. I want to see this Bracci character. I want to know what he looks like.'

Peroni nodded at the departing pair.

'We're going to have to hurry if we want to be first,' he observed.

Falcone sniffed. He looked tired. Unsettled. The heat was getting to them, Costa thought. This was all supposed to be so easy.

'Maybe we'll wait,' the inspector said, watching Raffaela Arcangelo detach herself from her brother, tears staining her cheeks. 'I owe someone an apology.'

Costa wondered about that. Falcone rarely said sorry. It wasn't in the nature of the man. Then the phone in his jacket began to vibrate. He took it out and heard Emily's excited voice on the line. He walked away, intent on keeping this conversation, at least, private.

'Nic?'

'Hi. How are things?'

'Fine. You sound down. Is everything OK?'

'Not so great to be honest.'

'I'm sorry to hear that. I have a favour to ask. Can you meet me at the party tonight? And bring my clothes? The evening dress and everything. I laid them out on the bed. No creases please.'

He couldn't get a grip on what she was saying.

'I don't understand.'

'You wanted me to get close to him,' she replied, a note of reproach in her voice. 'I've been working in the palazzo most of the day. I won't be finished in time to go back to the apartment. It's amazing here. Where are you?'

Automatically, his eyes went up to the vast glass palace next door. The sun was so bright all he saw was its fiery reflection. He was just a minute's walk away from her, as he watched the Arcangeli try to pick up the pieces of a bitter row, wondering what would happen to the Braccis now Bella's secret was about to go public.

'Outside the foundry but I don't think we'll be here long. Is there anything else you need?'

'Just you,' she said sweetly. 'And some time. I've news.'

Costa listened to her confident tones with unease. She had been supposed to talk to Massiter, nothing more. But it wasn't in her nature to hold back, not when some prize lay in her grasp.

'Good or bad?'

'Maybe neither. But it's instructive either way. Got to go now.'

The line went dead. Nic Costa glanced again at the gleaming palazzo along the quay. Emily was in there somewhere, out of reach.

9

Emily put down the phone and looked around the small storage room at the back of Hugo Massiter's apartment, built directly against the windowless brick wall that formed the entire rear of the palace, a supporting buttress of ugly clay that visitors were never meant to see. Nor was anyone meant to be witness to what lay before her now: bundles of letters tied together with string, piles of photo albums, document boxes all bearing the label of the same private detective agency based in New York, a name she knew, a solid, expensive firm that only worked for the most discerning of clients. Hugo had excused himself as soon as she'd issued orders for the new work. Lunch, he said, then a meeting, returning around four. Emily had borrowed overalls to work alongside the teams of carpenters, plasterers and painters turning the bare exhibition space into the location for a Venetian ball, had made sure they understood what they were doing, and had come to the conclusion that they were, under direction, good enough for the job. When she was satisfied Hugo wasn't about to return suddenly, she had gone upstairs to the apartment and tried to remember the lessons she'd received at the FBI academy, in what now seemed another lifetime. Searching homes without leaving a trace was an art she'd almost mastered because she possessed what it took: care, a good memory, and a feeling for the personality of the suspect into whose life she was intruding. Hugo Massiter was a careful, lonely, insular man, one capable of hard decisions without much regret, but marked by some event in his past.

The room beyond the large, elegant kitchen had been locked. She'd finally found the key in a small terracotta bowl next to the shiny new cooking range. In private homes there was always a key, the instructors had told her. Usually in an obvious place.

Behind the door lay a treasure trove of material on a single event in Hugo Massiter's life: the disproved allegations of murder she'd read about at Nic's that same morning. And two people: Daniel Forster and Laura Conti, in whom he had placed his trust.

Her hand fell automatically on the detective agency reports. These were of sightings of the fugitives after they had fled Venice. Or so the authors claimed. Emily was sufficiently familiar with intelligence reports to read between the lines. There was a grey area between rumour and fact in most of them. Hugo's money seemed to have bought much of the former and little of the latter. The reports talked of the couple's presence in various parts of the world – Africa, Asia and South America – but gave not a shred of hard supporting evidence. Photos, handwriting, phone conversations . . . all the artefacts that helped shore up vague suspicions were noticeably absent. The final letter from the agency was curt to the point of rudeness. Hugo's correspondence was absent but it was clear he had been questioning both the cost and the effectiveness of the operation. He'd tasked the agency with finding Daniel Forster and Laura Conti. They hadn't even managed to prove the pair still existed. The contract had come to an end some six months before, with the promise of litigation over unpaid fees.

Emily closed the file wondering what it told her. Hugo desperately needed to track down two people who had almost put him in jail. Why? He didn't need them for his own security. The authorities now accepted he'd been wrongly accused. What motive could there be apart from revenge? Except . . . Emily had formed a firm opinion of Hugo Massiter already: he was vain, ambitious, doubtless ruthless in business matters. But he had a firm sense of self-knowledge. He was aware of what kind of man he was. Revenge would surely have seemed petty to him, an unnecessary reminder of a pain still waiting to heal.

This impression was only confirmed by what she saw in the photo albums. They consisted of formal pictures from the series of music schools Hugo had sponsored in La Pietà over the years. Rows and rows of teenagers, all in smart black evening dress, some clutching fiddles and violas, smiling behind Hugo, who stood proudly to the front. And, in the final year, another figure. Someone who could only be the young, seemingly ingenuous Daniel Forster, next to his patron, a manuscript in hand, one he had claimed for his own.

Hugo had his arm around Forster. It was a paternal, affectionate gesture, though one which hinted, also, at ownership. I made you, he seemed to be saying. Which would render the final humiliation – being linked to the young man's misdeeds – doubly difficult to bear.

She skimmed through the posed photos of the years, scores of young people on the cusp of adulthood, smiling, happy, brought together by Hugo's generosity. The school seemed a joyous occasion. The city had lost something when the event came to an end.

Then she felt an extra sheet inside one of the plastic leaves, held up the album and shook the pages to release it.

The face of a woman in her late twenties – dark-haired, nervous, astonishingly beautiful – slipped out. The shot was from the waist up, snatched from a distance then greatly enlarged, judging by the grain. She was wearing what looked like a nylon housecoat, the kind of jacket a servant would choose. The picture was taken out of doors, in a garden somewhere, not in the city, with what appeared to be the sea shimmering in the distance. There was a genuine inflection of fear in her eyes. She didn't want to be seen. She didn't want to be recognized.

'Laura Conti,' Emily murmured to herself, then cursed her own stupidity. Be silent, the instructors had said. Always.

Laura Conti was lovely. She had the kind of face men couldn't stop staring at, with haunted, perfectly symmetrical features that would be difficult to hide. And she knew it too. In this illicit image she had the look of a wild creature fleeing something. The truth? Justice?

Emily recalled what Hugo had said to her earlier that day. In Venice it was the innocents who killed you. In this one photograph Laura Conti's features seemed to shine with innocence. Emily tried to recall the details of the case. Forster was the killer, not Laura. Was it possible she had been entrapped against her will? Nic's report suggested she'd hidden herself away on the Lido while Forster was in jail, never visiting him, never making herself known in public. Yet somehow he had, when released, found her again, re-establishing the relationship. Perhaps Laura hadn't been trying to hide from the police or Hugo Massiter's wrath at all, but from the man who regarded her as his own, Daniel Forster.

She slipped the photo back into the pocket where it belonged, not wanting to see any more. It was foolish to try to read so much into a single image.

Then she picked up the sheaf of letters and went through them, slowly, carefully. They were, in the beginning at least, short, intelligent, and articulate. Every one was from Daniel Forster, written in a sweeping, legible hand, the kind a student would use to get good marks in an essay. None of them ran to more than two pages. Most were confined to a single sheet. They spanned almost two years, the dates matching, as far as she recalled, the period in which Hugo had launched his legal campaign to clear his name, one that resulted in Forster and his mistress fleeing Venice like thieves.

'Dear Hugo,' Forster wrote in the first. 'Laura said you would re-emerge and, as usual, she was right. It may surprise you to know that I'm glad you're still alive. That said, it's important you understand the position we find ourselves in. It's impossible for you to return to Italy. If you do that, you surely know the consequences. I've made depositions to the authorities. I will testify in court if needs be. This is, as far as the locals are concerned, a closed case. Don't try to reopen it, please. Enjoy New York. Venice is behind you. Daniel.'

A benign though firm warning, then. Forster portrayed himself as a reasonable man, but one who would not demur at involving the Italian judicial system if necessary. And – this seemed important – no mention of where Laura stood on matters.

'"*I've* made depositions,"' Emily murmured. But surely, to be convincing, Forster would need her to back up his case.

Some eight months later, the tone was changing.

'American lawyers? Do you place your faith in them, Hugo? Surely not. I'd have thought that beneath you. Besides, we have lawyers too these days. Money to employ the best too, thanks to the book. You *have* seen the book, haven't you? If not, I'll send you a copy.

Inscribed. My version's down there now. Black and white and, as the old saw goes, read all over. Take a look and ask yourself: do I really want this to go on?'

Emily sifted through five more brief messages, noting the tone growing more bitter, more frightened perhaps. Then she flicked to the last, began to read, and felt ashamed to be engrossed by what she found.

Forster was now desperate. The handwriting was erratic. Words were scrawled in block capitals, the way a child wrote when he was anxious to make a point.

'Is this a VICTORY? Burning my book? Freezing our bank accounts? What did we do to deserve this, Hugo? Prick your vanity? Any more than that? Let me say it again. Let me SCREAM it till you understand. SHE'S NOT YOURS. She never was. She never will be. I'd die before I allowed that to happen. If you think about that – if you can remember who I am, what I'm like at all – you'll know that's true.

'You can't win. Not even if you bribe every last judge in Italy. If you insist on returning I will, I swear, do what I should have done all those years ago. Make an end to your miserable existence, once and for all. STAY OUT OF OUR LIVES. D.'

Emily Deacon drew a deep breath, placed the paper on her lap, and hated herself, loathed this prying into matters that were none of her business.

She's not yours. She never was. She never will be.

Was this really the true source of Hugo Massiter's grief? That Laura Conti, hiding away from the light of day like a frightened deer, was the woman he loved? Daniel Forster hadn't just stolen Hugo's reputation? The young Englishman had removed something much more precious, an item Hugo couldn't recover, not with all the money in the world?

Emily put away the album and the documents, ensuring they went back in the right places. Then she sat on the small stool she'd brought in from the apartment feeling miserable, wondering what she'd tell Falcone, wondering, too, what gave her the right to meddle in Massiter's affairs.

Two people had been murdered on Murano. Their relationship with Hugo Massiter was distant, financial only. Their deaths had caused him significant inconvenience.

'Poor—' she was about to say, when she felt a hand fall lightly on her shoulder.

Emily stifled a scream, recalled how she'd talked quietly to herself throughout, and knew at that moment what the miserable old bastard of an instructor in Langley would have said. Then she turned and looked Hugo Massiter in the face.

He didn't even seem angry.

'The palazzo looks wonderful, but I don't recall asking you to do anything to this room,' he said softly. 'Kind as it is of you to offer.'

She wrapped her arms around herself, hugging the paint-spattered sleeves of the overalls to her chest, ashamed.

'I'm sorry. I couldn't resist looking around. I wanted to . . . try to understand something.'

'You could have just asked. It's easier.'

'I wouldn't have known the right questions.'

'True.'

He took his hand away and cast his eyes around the room.

'Was this Falcone's idea?'

'No,' she lied, wishing she had the courage to be truthful. 'I was just being nosy. Really. There was something about you that didn't add up. I'm the curious type, unfortunately.'

'And you found . . .?'

'A photo of Laura Conti,' she answered straight away. 'She's very beautiful.'

'She *was* very beautiful,' he corrected her. 'I've no idea what she's like now. I haven't seen her in a very long time. I don't even know if she's alive. With' – his face grew old just saying the name – 'Daniel around, who knows?'

'I don't want to be in here,' she muttered, brushing past him to get out into the light, airy living room, striding to the balcony, bright in the lagoon sun, needing fresh air. The smell of paint and fresh plaster rose up from below. The main doors were open. The temporary stands, with some real pieces from Massiter's collection, would be in place. Soon the musicians would arrive, looking for their podium, which was probably still in pieces. At seven there would be guests. The palazzo would be ready for them by then. Even so, she didn't want to see it.

Emily took a deep breath, aware of his presence behind her.

'I can only apologize. I don't know what came over me.'

And all for Nic's boss, she thought, which was as good as saying for Nic himself, given how close the three men were these days.

'Well, it's out now. A burden shared, they say. I don't . . .' He was trying to convince himself of the right words. 'I don't miss her any more. It wasn't a sensible relationship. She was different. Not just beautiful, but perfectly untouched by the world somehow, in a way I never saw in anyone else. Which is why Daniel fooled her so easily, I imagine. I just wanted to know she was safe. That's all. I didn't – I *don't* – harbour any illusions about rekindling old fires.'

'Do you think she was guilty?' Emily asked. 'Of the deaths of those people?'

'No,' he replied with a shrug, as if the question was irrelevant now. 'Not for a minute. But she went with Daniel and that's what counts, in most people's eyes anyway. It's not what you do, it's appearances. That's all it was with me. If I'd stayed here and fought my corner instead of running away . . .'

'You could have lost everything.'

Massiter laughed.

'But I did, in a way! Don't you see? Oh, enough of this. I hate sounding maudlin. How are the builders doing? You look as if you got stuck in yourself.'

'I think the place will look fine for tonight. You should find yourself a good architect, Hugo. I'm not sure the structure here is as sound as you think. This is not a conventional building. There's more wood than I expected. Some of the ironwork . . .'

It was virtually rust. In some cities she doubted the palazzo would be approved for public use at all. But Massiter had sway with the authorities. Without it he wouldn't have got as far as he had.

'I can believe that,' he said, with a quick grimace. 'Hang on. I thought I'd found myself an architect.'

Hugo Massiter was very close to her at that moment, yet she didn't object to his presence. He regarded himself as damaged goods. Somehow that didn't daunt him though. He was a survivor, in spite of the odds.

'I don't think so.'

'Emily . . .'

It was so sudden. She couldn't move on the narrow balcony high above the island's cobblestones. Hugo was holding her forearms, his fingers lightly touching her skin, warm, affectionate.

'Please don't go,' he whispered. 'I know I'm only an old fool but I'd rather you stayed around a little longer. Work here, as much as you like. None of that' – he glanced at the storeroom door – 'means anything. It's history and history really is bunk.'

'Perhaps you could find her. I could help. I have friends.'

'I'm sure you do,' he said, smiling. 'But it doesn't matter. Not any more. I don't want Laura found. Wherever she is . . . whatever's happened, it's water under the bridge. It's time I started living my own life again.'

His head came forward. She moved, instinctively, wondering, all the same, what she would do if he attempted to kiss her.

Instead Hugo Massiter reached over her shoulder and peered down towards the lively grey water, looking past San Michele, past the busy vaporetto stops at Fondamente Nove, at Venice proper. A couple of racing skiffs were pulling across the lagoon, two lines of hooped backs in each straining for the lead. Approaching them were three large open boats making steady progress towards the island, each carrying a cargo of dark-suited figures.

'I see the musicians,' he said. 'They're early. Do you like music?'

'Some.'

'Good. You must never trust a person with no fondness for music, you know. It demonstrates a serious detachment from life. That young man of yours. Does he . . .?'

In one short instant, chastely, with the swift, easy grace of a relative, he brushed his lips against her cheek, was done, turning back to the apartment, beginning to whistle, something classical.

'Vivaldi,' she said.

He stopped, looked back at her, smiling, an expression of bliss.

'Perfect,' Hugo Massiter declared. 'You are, I swear, perfect. Apart from the outfit.'

The overalls were a mess. She wondered when Nic would arrive with fresh clothes.

'Never mind,' he said. 'I have an idea.'

10

The Braccis lived in a red-brick terraced hovel just a couple of hundred metres from their shabby little factory. The sunless street stank of cats, stale rubbish and gas from the nearby workshops. There was a small, restless crowd outside when the three cops arrived. The two carpenters were among them, sinister smirks on their faces. The bad-tempered, on-the-edge mood of the mob reminded Costa of his early days in the force when luck would occasionally push him into the uniformed squad working Roma–Lazio matches.

'You going to arrest him?' someone yelled as Costa led the way towards the door.

Peroni stopped and gave them the look. It got quiet, for a moment.

'Why would we want to do that?' he demanded.

'For messing around with his sister,' the heckler replied. 'And the rest.'

'You don't know what you're talking about,' Peroni barked back at him. 'Why don't you all just go home and let us do our jobs?'

The older carpenter butted in.

'If you'd been doing your jobs none of this would've happened. We don't like dirty bastards like Bracci around here. You take the sonofabitch away with you. Otherwise we deal with this ourselves.'

Falcone was on him in an instant.

'If anyone so much as sets a foot inside this house you will, I assure you, wake up in jail. Understand?'

'Call in uniform,' the inspector barked at Costa. 'I want a guard on this place, and anyone who so much as squeaks thrown in a cell for the night.'

Costa smiled at the carpenter, who was getting the full dressing-down treatment from Falcone, something no one in earshot was likely to forget. Then he walked away from the melee to get a little privacy. The duty man in Castello sounded sleepy, amazed by the request for assistance.

'You want *what?*' the bored voice on the other end of the line demanded.

'Uniform. All night if need be.'

'Would that be ten? Twenty? Any particular size or colour?'

'Just get some men here,' Costa retorted. 'We don't want a riot on our hands.'

There was a pause on the line.

'This is Venice, friend. We don't have riots. What have you people been *doing*?'

Asking the right questions, Costa thought. Which was, perhaps, not a local tradition.

'Three men minimum,' he snapped. 'Now. If this goes wrong, it's on your head.'

Then he walked to the door and kept his finger on the bell until a surly Enzo Bracci appeared in jeans and a tight grubby T-shirt. He was smoking a joint, eyes glazed, a familiar smell hanging round him. He looked ready for a fight.

'Get out of here,' Enzo muttered. 'You've done enough already, haven't you?'

Costa nodded back at the angry crowd.

'You want us to leave you with this?'

Enzo spat on the ground, not far short of Costa's feet, and glared at the approaching hulk of Gianni Peroni, followed by Falcone.

'Without you we wouldn't have had this. Is that what cops are for these days? Spreading shit.'

'We didn't mean for that to happen, Enzo,' Peroni said apologetically. 'And I'd advise you to put that thing you're smoking out of our sight too. Don't tempt me. We can't turn back the clock. We have to talk. Inspector Falcone here says so and you wouldn't want to go saying no to him now, would you?'

Enzo eyed Falcone up and down, flicked the smoke into the gutter with one bent finger, then opened the door mouthing a torrent of low curses.

Aldo Bracci was in the tiny, airless front room, a dark place, lit by just a single lamp. He was clutching a grappa bottle and swaying back and forth on a cheap wicker chair. Fredo was with him, his eyes full of anger and grief.

Falcone held out his hand.

'My name's Inspector Falcone. We need to talk.'

'Really,' Bracci mumbled, his voice thick and slurred.

Peroni pulled up three chairs. The cops sat down next to Bracci. Then Peroni gingerly removed the bottle from his hands.

'Not a good idea, Aldo. A man needs a clear head at times like these.'

Enzo Bracci was going crazy, shaking his head from side to side.

'Jesus,' he swore. 'How could you do this to him?'

'We didn't,' Costa said. 'It happened. We've got some men coming to deal with those jerks outside.'

'I can deal with them!' Enzo yelled. 'It's why they're here that pisses me off. We told you. He was with us all the time. We worked all through the night. You've got no right, no business, spreading all this crap around.'

'I can talk for myself,' Aldo muttered. 'Don't treat me like I'm a cripple.'

Falcone picked up the bottle and looked at it.

'Cheap stuff,' he said.

'We're cheap people,' Aldo replied. 'Didn't you work that out already?'

'So was it good?' Falcone continued. 'Having Bella marry into a family like the Arcangeli? Different class.'

'Hey!' Enzo bellowed. 'They're no different to us. We just don't bother hiding the fact.'

'Shut up!' his father screamed. 'They're here to talk to me. That's what they'll do.'

'So how did you feel about it, Aldo?' Peroni asked. 'Good? Bad? Indifferent?'

Aldo's eyes were watery with drink. He hadn't shaved in a while.

'I didn't feel anything! Bella was . . . hungry for a husband. She wanted someone she could control. Always the boss that woman.'

His dead, drunk face turned on them suddenly.

'*Always.* Not that anyone believed it once she turned on the charm.'

Falcone caught the hint immediately.

'You're saying she started what went on? You being what, four, five years older?'

Aldo's expression was unreadable under the dim lights.

'I'm saying nothing about that. Not a damn thing.'

'When did it end?' Costa asked.

'Maybe it never started.'

Peroni sighed, slapping his big hands on his knees.

'We're trying to help you here, Aldo. That's really difficult if you're just going to feed us bullshit. We've seen the reports. We know something was going on.'

'All you know is the crap morons like that' – he nodded towards the front door, and the crowd outside – 'spread around 'cos they've got nothing better to do with their lives.'

Costa wondered about this sad, embittered man. No money. No wife. No social life. The Braccis were outcasts in their own community. Just like the Arcangeli. Why? Because they were judged to be scum. Almost thirty years before Aldo and Bella had proved it by crossing the forbidden line.

'Was it her idea to let everyone know?' Costa asked. 'We don't want the details. We just need to try to understand.'

Aldo stifled a bitter laugh. He grabbed the bottle back from Falcone and took a long swig.

'Bella was Bella,' he muttered. 'She did what the hell she liked. She just loved being looked at. By anybody. Me? I was just one more fool on the list. It could have been anyone. She was . . .' he screwed his eyes shut, trying to force out the words '. . . older than the rest of us. Right from the start. I know that sounds like the self-serving crap you'd get from most men, but it's true. I was just a dumb, teenage kid. No girlfriend. Never was very good with girls. It was a game. We didn't do it more than three times. That wasn't the point. She wanted the excitement. The attention. It gave her a kick, having other people stare at us.'

'Dad,' Enzo interrupted, a bleak expression of shock on his face. This wasn't a conversation the Braccis had had before. 'You don't have to do this.'

'No?' Aldo stared at his sons. He looked almost relieved to get it off his chest finally. 'Listen to me. You're going to hear all about it anyway. Best you get the right version. *My* version. Bella was crazy. You never saw that because by the time you'd come along she was smart enough to hide it. But she had this ability to make you crazy too, to lock you in that little world of hers so tight you thought *that* was the place that was real – not what was out there, past the door. All the day-to-day shit. Chasing work. Trying to stay alive.'

'When did it end?' Costa asked.

'Years ago,' Aldo whispered, some fear and bitterness in his voice. 'It ended when the police came round and told my old man it wasn't a joke, a piece of stupid local gossip. She'd been careful to keep him in the dark. If anyone said something she just called them a liar, a mischief maker. It couldn't last forever. When the cops arrived, she turned the innocent. Blamed everything on me. Which was true maybe, in a way. I dunno. Not any more. I don't know a damn thing. Just that my old man took me out there.' He nodded at the back door. Through the grimy window lay a small terraced yard, full of old junk. 'And spent an hour or so beating me senseless.'

The two sons were seated by now, glassy-eyed, distraught. How many times had Aldo beaten them, Costa wondered? How often did the same old routine get passed down from generation to generation in places like this without anyone ever questioning it?

'When she died she was pregnant,' Falcone observed, getting straight to the point. 'Any idea who the father might be?'

Bracci looked genuinely surprised.

'Are you sure?'

'We've got the medical reports,' Falcone insisted. 'Six weeks pregnant. Was it you?'

'No!' Bracci looked astonished, offended too. 'I told you. Bella and I stopped that years ago. It never happened much anyway.'

'Then who?' Costa asked.

'How about her husband?' the man spat back.

Falcone shook his head.

'Physically impossible. We have medical records. Uriel couldn't father children.'

'Then I swear to God I don't know.'

'But you knew she had affairs?' the inspector continued, pushing all the time.

'I guessed,' he replied with a shrug. 'Bella liked men. She always did. Uriel was an OK guy. For an Arcangelo. But he wasn't . . .' Aldo made a gesture, a down-turned finger, unmistakable. 'At least,' he added, 'that's what she said.'

He glowered at the grubby carpet.

'Makes you wonder what she said about me.'

'You're sure she didn't tell you about the pregnancy?' Costa asked.

He laughed. A short, dry sound.

'Are you kidding? Bella didn't say a word. If it couldn't have been Uriel . . .' He shrugged. 'What would you expect? Guess she was planning to get rid of it.'

Just like that, Costa thought. Bella was a Bracci. And an Arcangelo too. Both equally practical. Deal with the child. Deal with the husband.

'It would really help,' Costa continued, 'if someone else could corroborate where you were during Wednesday morning. Families . . .'

'How many goddamn times do we have to tell you?' It was Enzo, furious again. 'He was with us. All the time. Go and find someone with a reason to do this.'

That was, Costa thought, an excellent suggestion, and was about to say as much when there was a resounding, violent crash. All six men recoiled in sudden shock. Following behind the brick that had shattered the window came a bottle, a wad of burning fabric stuttering flames at its neck.

'It's dealt with,' Peroni said instantly, and was on his feet in a flash, snatching out the crude fuse with his hands, uttering a quick curse, then extinguishing the rag with his big feet.

'Nice neighbours you've got,' he noted quietly, picking up the bottle by the neck, setting it upright on the table. 'We're supposed to have some people here to make sure things don't get out of hand.'

Costa walked to the door and opened it. The crowd looked bigger now. All men, all laughing, joking, looking as if they'd like to run up a little lynching party later on, when some more drink had been taken.

Three uniform cops stood in front of them, arms crossed, bored, unmoved.

Incandescent, Costa confronted the biggest, a man he half recognized from the Questura in Castello.

'You're here to stop that! Do your damn job.'

'Just came out of nowhere,' the cop mumbled with half a smile on his face.

'Don't let it happen again.'

'Sure,' the uniform said. He let loose a stupid, sarcastic smile, then wagged a finger at the mob. 'You hear that! The Romans got orders for you. No more throwing bottles at the pervert. OK?'

They stood there, sniggering.

'Not while I'm looking,' the cop added.

Nic Costa muttered a few choice insults under his breath and returned to the house. Aldo Bracci was back at the booze again, just as miserable, a little scared now too.

'Do you have some relatives?' Costa asked. 'Maybe this would be a good time to get out of town. Just make sure we know where to contact you.'

'This is my house!' Bracci screeched. 'You think I'm leaving? After all these years? Just because of those morons out there?'

Costa glanced at Falcone.

'We could take him into custody. I don't like the look of this place.'

'No,' Falcone replied. 'Not if he doesn't want it. If you change your mind, Bracci . . .'

The inspector hauled himself to his feet then marched outside and gave the three uniforms the A-grade Falcone bawl-out Costa and Peroni knew only too well.

'They won't bother you, Aldo,' Peroni said, once the volume beyond the door had died down a little. 'Not after that.'

Costa looked at the dejected, drunken shambles of a figure in front of them, shame and self-loathing written clearly on his face. The mob was the last of Aldo Bracci's problems.

11

Gianfranco Randazzo enjoyed his job, mostly. Castello was an easy station to run, with little more to do than police the tide of immigrants passing through the bars and restaurants, deal with a trickle of distraught ripped-off tourists and keep a lid on the local drugs trade. It was a place where routine ruled. In the narrow rambling warren of alleys that ran from the waterfront to the dead industrial land around the Arsenale basin lived a shifting, eager population that had to be reminded, from time to time, of its place. Randazzo was third-generation Venetian and understood from an early age that a little thievery was part of the native character. The city had been working its captive trawl of visitors for centuries. It was futile to pretend the place would ever change. What he'd come to appreciate in his twenty years as a cop, steadily working his way up the ranks, was the need for balance. The population was there to be controlled, to be kept in check, confined within accepted boundaries of behaviour, and pounced upon when some damn fool felt minded to overstep the mark. He could post a good set of statistics each month: few crimes, a clean-up rate well within acceptable levels, low staff turnover. Statistics mattered. They were the first thing the hierarchy looked at when they wanted to know if a commissario was doing his job. On paper, Castello's Questura was in a happy state until the Romans came, with their arrogance, their questions and their ever-present attitude. Randazzo lived by the idea that it was best to leave well alone, to keep a lid on things unless there was a very good reason to do otherwise. The Romans just couldn't buy that notion. From the moment they arrived they picked at every case that came their way until every last detail became apparent, however ugly, however unwanted. Despatching Falcone to Verona had made a difference. Then circumstances had changed. He'd hesitated over giving them the Arcangeli case, and would probably have baulked at the idea had there not been such overwhelming pressure from above for a clean result. The logic seemed incontrovertible. No one could argue with the findings of a team of outside police officers skilled in homicide.

All the same, if there was dirt to be uncovered on that closed, dusty island across the lagoon, the Romans would surely find it. They were fools, their own worst enemies, blind to the effects of their meddling. So now what should have been a simple, predictable investigation was growing more complex, more awkward by the minute, threatening to spread in ways that made Gianfranco Randazzo deeply uncomfortable. He'd listened in fury to the briefing Falcone had given him over the phone, explaining the request for a guard outside Aldo Bracci's home. Randazzo had said nothing at the time. Now he stood on the terrace of Hugo Massiter's apartment inside the Palazzo degli Arcangeli, wondering when the private boats of the party-goers would begin to arrive at the private jetty, and what he'd say to Falcone's face in an hour or so, when the reception began. Wondering, too, whether the Romans weren't the only fools hereabouts. Gianfranco Randazzo followed orders. His relationship with the wily, rich Englishman was not a matter of personal choice. Nevertheless, the commissario was aware of the delicacy of his position. Should the Arcangeli case fail to be closed on time, as his masters demanded, and the promised scandal ensued, there would be scapegoats. His head would, in all probability, be on the block, for no other reason than he'd done as he was told. It was difficult, at times, to strike the correct balance between duty and self-respect.

The young Roman's American girlfriend joined him. She was carrying a glass of spritz, well made, with an olive alongside the slice of lemon, just as a true Venetian would have demanded.

'Hugo said you'd appreciate this,' she said. 'Seems I'm the bartender around here as well as the architect. You'll have to excuse me, though. I've got workmen to yell at downstairs. The host will be along in a moment. Then I need to change.'

'You'll be ready in time?' Randazzo asked, enjoying being close to her. The quiet little Roman, who Randazzo suspected could well be the most awkward of the trio given half a chance, was a fortunate man. 'Massiter's got quite a guest list tonight. They'll want to be astonished. No one's been in this place, not properly, for years.'

'They'll be astonished,' she said, smiling. 'Wait and see.'

He let his eyes linger on her as she walked back into the room towards the door. Even in paint-stained overalls she was a sight to savour. Massiter passed her as she left, murmuring something Randazzo couldn't hear, patting her shoulder in a light, intimate gesture.

Then the Englishman joined him on the terrace. He looked content, smug. Massiter had no idea of the storm clouds gathering elsewhere.

'I can't believe a woman like that would be interested in some lowly Roman cop,' the commissario declared. 'Can you?'

'No accounting for taste,' Massiter agreed, raised his own glass, then took a sip. 'She makes a good spritz too.'

'Are you going to take her from him?' Randazzo asked.

The cold blue eyes shone like burnished stone.

'Free will, Gianfranco. There's no bucking it. I never take anything from anyone. I'm interested in presents not plunder. Unless something's freely offered, what's it worth? A little persuasion on the other hand . . .'

Randazzo stifled a laugh. The whole city knew what Hugo Massiter was. A man who couldn't resist women. A man who seized what he wanted, regardless of the cost, in money and human terms. His bank balance helped, but there was more to it than just cash and power. He had a certain kind of charm. Massiter understood what a person truly wanted, and was able to dangle the appropriate gift at the appropriate time. The commissario had spent some social time in the man's company. He had seen this skill in action, had wondered at the quiet, sly talent the Englishman had for understanding what was required to get his way. Hugo Massiter possessed a certain aptitude for persuading others to do his will, while at the same time convincing them he was merely going along with their own wishes, not pressing some kind of reward upon them. Randazzo knew all this for another reason too. High in the Dolomites, in a small, remote village, close to some good ski runs, was a compact, well-furnished chalet which now, through a front company based in Switzerland, was Randazzo's own – a tiny, to Massiter insignificant, bribe for some earlier services the commissario had performed.

'Take her after this business is done please, Hugo. It's complicated enough as it is. Let's just get the Romans to sign on the dotted line, as they will. Close that contract with the Arcangeli. Then let your *cazzo* have its fun.'

Massiter laughed.

'I'll never quite understand the Venetian love of coarseness, you know. Emily's a lovely thing. You shouldn't spoil my sense of anticipation with that kind of talk. Besides . . .'

The man could turn serious in an instant. Randazzo questioned whether, in truth, he had any other mood.

'They *will* sign on the dotted line, won't they? I'm not making any of this up. I must nail down that deal shortly or we're all in deep trouble. You do know that, don't you?'

Oh yes, Randazzo thought. He'd had that fact hammered home to him well enough by any number of city henchmen anxious to keep their reputations intact.

'They'll sign. If I have to hold the pen for them myself. It just seems a little more complicated than we first suspected. It's important they come up with something that sticks. Credibility is everything. There is it seems . . .'

Randazzo knew he couldn't avoid the point, awkward as it was.

'. . . the possibility that a third party was involved. A strong possibility.'

Massiter screwed up his face in a baffled grimace.

'The locked door. The evidence, man. Explain that.'

'Falcone can't,' Randazzo replied with a shrug. 'Not yet. But he's a persistent bastard. He will. One way or another. There's a problem with the woman's keys. They can't find them anywhere. I don't suppose . . .?'

Massiter gave him a withering look.

'I'm not some kind of burglar,' he growled.

'I know that,' Randazzo insisted nervously.

'Do what you're paid for, Randazzo. Sort this mess out. And quick.'

'Of course. They will come up with the goods. In time to save your skin, Hugo.'

'*Our* skin.'

'If you wish to put it that way. I'm still somewhat unclear about precisely what those goods will turn out to be, though.' He hesitated. Massiter was a man with powerful friends. All the same, the question had to be asked. 'I can't help but wonder. Do you have any idea?'

Massiter's bland face turned furious. He launched the half-full glass out over the balcony. It spun through the thin, hot air, despatching its contents, then tumbled down to the canal, falling just a metre short of a workman's boat manoeuvring for the jetty. The man at the wheel stared back up at them, furious, then saw Massiter's purple face at the terrace, and went back to the wheel, chastened.

'To hell with this,' Massiter cursed. 'You people have bled me dry over the years. Now, when I ask for a little in return . . .'

He didn't go on. Randazzo felt offended. He was doing his best. Risking much too.

'I think that's deeply unfair,' he noted. 'We've turned a blind eye to certain of your activities.'

'Not without reason,' Massiter pointed out. 'Or profit.'

'True. I . . . I know I shouldn't say this,' Randazzo stuttered. 'But it's time for some frankness between us. I want this matter closed just as much as you do. A little more disclosure on your part wouldn't go amiss. When I bury things I like them to stay buried. No new corpses, not when they can be avoided. It's best all round.'

'That little chalet of yours starting to feel somewhat small?' Massiter asked, icily composed now. 'What is it you're wanting this time? An apartment by the beach? Come on. You're a Venetian. You're not too shy to name the price.'

'It's not always about the price,' Randazzo said primly, feeling his temper beginning to fray. 'I need the truth. Everything. Particularly about your relationship with each of the Arcangeli.'

'That's simple,' Massiter snapped. 'I give. They take. It's the kind of relationship I have with most people in this godforsaken city.'

It was years since Randazzo had tried to think like a cop. Being commissario was admin and management. He had detectives to pursue the fine detail of crimes, their commission, their solution. All the same, he'd been one himself once upon a time. Not a bad one either. Not afraid to throw the odd hard, unexpected question into the conversation now and again, which was what he'd been paid for back then.

'And Bella?' Randazzo demanded, risking a guess, not caring if this went back to his bosses, because he wanted what they did: closure. A part of him resented Hugo Massiter too, detested the man's easy arrogance. 'She was a good-looking woman. Everyone says that. You like women. Was she, perhaps, part of the deal?'

Massiter turned on him, smiling, an amused, detached look on his face that made Randazzo regret he'd ever decided to walk down this path.

'My! You *are* uncharacteristically curious today. What on earth's prompting all this? Are you afraid those Romans will steal your thunder? Is your nose out of joint because there are finally some real police in Venice for a change?'

'That was uncalled for. I would like to know the truth,' the commissario repeated, unable to look Massiter directly in the eye. 'It would help all of us.'

'The truth?'

The blue eyes sparkled, holding his attention.

'The trouble with the truth is it's so damned hard to gauge. One man's truth's another man's lies. I'd have thought someone like you would know that better than most.'

Gianfranco Randazzo smoothed down the lapels of his fine-weave black cotton suit. Beneath he wore a well-pressed white shirt, and the red silk tie he'd bought on vacation in Osaka, the one marked with the pattern of his name in katakana script, the previous spring. He regarded himself as a dutiful man. Not perfect, but one who tried to do his job in difficult circumstances.

'Bella was having an affair,' he said sternly. 'It's possible she'd resurrected a relationship with her brother.'

Massiter's eyebrows rose.

'Strange habits they have out here.'

'Quite,' Randazzo replied. 'I merely said it was possible. She was pregnant. Her husband was not the father. So who was Bella's lover? I need to know. Falcone and his men are shockingly good at what they do, I'm afraid. It would be for the best if I were forewarned.'

Massiter stared silently out at the teeming channel of water.

'Paternity,' he said, looking glum. 'Now there's a thought.'

'I can't protect you from everything,' Randazzo snapped. 'There are limits beyond which . . .'

The Englishman was laughing. His shoulders heaved. A growing chuckle emerged from behind a set of bright, shiny teeth. He came close and touched the tie.

'Japanese?' he asked. 'How is your wife, by the way?'

'My wife has nothing to do with this.'

Randazzo had seen the way Massiter stared at Chieko whenever they met on social occasions. It wasn't the curious look she normally got when the locals discovered a woman from Tokyo had married a Venetian cop. Besides, Venice was an international city these days. Marrying a foreigner, a beautiful one, was nothing remarkable.

'This isn't funny,' the commissario complained, aware of the whine inside his own voice. 'Not at all.'

With swift, feline ease, Massiter was next to him, whispering in Randazzo's ear.

'On the contrary,' the Englishman murmured. 'It's delightful. Let's get straight to the point. Then I must go. There'll be locals down below soon, and I'll be damned if I'm leaving them alone with the valuables. So . . .'

Massiter pulled away, drew in a deep breath, certain of himself.

'The last time I saw Bella Arcangelo was two weeks ago. I never bed Venetian women for more than a month. It's a matter of principle. They cling, they paw, they grow tiresome. The bitches are best gone before the amusement begins to fade. I doubt I fathered a brat on her but you never know. No one ever will. I expect you to make sure of that.'

Randazzo swore, then asked quietly, 'You weren't here the night they died? You can prove it?'

'Oh . . . *that* night. Where were you for that matter?'

'I was working,' Randazzo snarled.

'Work. Play. For me the two tend to be much the same really.'

He knew something. He couldn't wait to say it either.

Massiter reached out and flicked some lint off the commissario's tie. The Englishman stared at Randazzo, his ageing film-star face devoid of feeling, a man who felt nothing whatsoever, about himself, about anyone. Commissario Gianfranco Randazzo knew he was idiotic for thinking he could tackle Massiter head on. It was uncharacteristically imprudent, a stupid mistake that would have to be rectified by some act of visible fealty.

'I was occupied until one in the morning. With company. After that, I slept alone.'

'Here?'

Massiter scowled.

'You're being very inquisitive, Randazzo. Is that wise? Besides, you surely know that's not possible. They don't allow me access at night. I had to beg for dispensation for this little party, even though it's in their interest as much as mine. No. I was in my apartment. First with a woman. Then alone.'

It wasn't so far from Massiter's vessel on the waterfront near the Arsenale. He could still have been on the island in time. Bella could have provided the key.

'Listen to me. You were busy until two, Hugo. No. Make that two thirty. This woman *must* confirm that.'

Massiter shrugged as if it were a matter of no consequence.

'This is important,' Randazzo objected.

'Very well,' he conceded.

'Stick to that story. Leave the rest to me.'

'I left the rest to you from the start,' he muttered. 'Look where it's got me.'

'I *will* sort this out this,' the commissario insisted. 'I assure you. This woman. We may need to know her name. She will vouch for you. You're sure of that?'

Massiter beamed back at him, amused.

'Given you're nothing but a possession of mine, one whose value appears to be rather less than the price I originally paid, you are, I must say, distinctly uppity tonight. I trust my tolerance of this impertinence will be rewarded. And . . .'

He hesitated before making this last point, a fierce, bright certainty burning in his eyes that chilled Gianfranco Randazzo's blood.

'. . . *soon*. Patience is not one of my virtues.'

'I cannot save you from yourself!' Randazzo answered, scared by his own impetuousness, aware that he had no idea how he could deliver what Massiter, and his own superiors, wanted. 'Will this woman say what she's told?'

Massiter was grinning again. The abrupt, scary chill was gone.

'I believe so. Perhaps you'd better ask her yourself. When you get home.'

12

It was almost seven. The three of them would be late for Massiter's party, but it was inevitable. Falcone wanted the men to write up everything in the Questura before leaving. It was important, the inspector said, to make sure all the facts, as much as they understood them, were set down for the record. He didn't want any room for mistakes, holes through which problems might slip. Teresa had been occupied too, in a way that hadn't proved entirely satisfactory if he read the troubled expression on her face correctly.

It was a gorgeous evening. Even on the vaporetto there was scarcely a hint of breeze. The city stood breathless, trapped inside its own archaic splendour.

'Was Leo right?' Costa asked. 'Did you get anything out of the morgue here?'

A disgruntled frown creased her face.

'Sort of. They're not exactly state-of-the-art. To be honest with you, it was a bit amateur hour there. All the serious stuff gets sent over to the mainland.'

The two men looked at each other. Costa knew they were thinking the same thing.

'And this isn't serious?' he asked. 'Two people dead? In very odd circumstances?'

Teresa was staring at the approaching island next to the vaporetto jetty, its trio of buildings misty in the heat haze. Costa followed the line of her gaze. Something about the Isola degli Arcangeli disturbed him. The place clung unsteadily onto the side of Murano proper by that single metal bridge, with its iconic angel, as if it were unsure whether to belong, or whether to cast itself off into the shallow waters of the lagoon.

'You'd think . . .' she murmured. 'I just don't know. I've persuaded Silvio to do a little work on the case. We'll see.'

'Oh wonderful,' Peroni groaned. 'How does Leo manage that? Getting everyone else in the shit alongside him?'

Teresa gave him a sharp glance.

'I rather thought we were invited because we're good at our jobs.'

'Yeah, yeah, yeah.' Peroni waved a big hand at her. 'I keep hearing that. But this isn't our place, remember. This belongs to the Venetians, and frankly they're welcome to it. We've got our orders from the commissario. A nice neat investigation. Wrap it up. Then go home.'

He put a huge arm around Teresa Lupo's hefty shoulders.

'Home,' Peroni emphasized. 'Just by doing what we're told for once. Is it that hard?'

Yes, Costa thought, but didn't say it. Something stank about the Arcangeli case and they all knew it. Spontaneous combustion. Damaged keys. Aldo Bracci too, locked inside his own house on Murano, an angry mob outside willing him to leave. Costa couldn't get the picture of Bracci out of his head. There was more than just misery inside the man. There was knowledge too, something he was, perhaps, wondering whether to share.

Teresa got back to the point.

'Silvio's got some ideas about this spontaneous combustion thing. He's more the chemist than I am. I've sent him some material to work on. Perhaps tomorrow, the day after, we'll know more.'

'What sort of material?' Costa asked.

'Fibres. From Uriel's clothes. People don't just catch fire, Nic. Not in this world. It was very hot in there. Very strange conditions. Uriel was partly deaf and had lost his sense of smell too. Someone who knew that could have doctored the apron. There's an explanation. Physical laws apply. It's just a question of understanding them. Maybe—'

She stopped. The two men looked at her. It wasn't like Teresa Lupo to be lost for words.

'Maybe what?' Peroni pressed.

'Maybe I was wrong. It's a kind of witchcraft. Or more accurately, a kind of alchemy. I've been reading up on the way they make glass. That *is* alchemy of a sort. They use chemicals and processes going back hundreds of years. If you wanted to set up a furnace like that now, somewhere else, the health and safety authorities would probably kick you out of town as soon as they saw the stuff you wanted to use. Glass is beautiful but what goes into it to make all those colours, all those features . . . I wouldn't want it round me day in and day out. Perhaps the suit or the apron picked up some substance. Accidentally. Or . . .'

She gave them that sly look, the one that said: you should be thinking this, boys.

'If anyone could come up with some way of faking spontaneous combustion, don't you think it would be a man who knew the inside of a glass foundry?'

Costa thought about the shattered furnace. Teresa was, as usual, on the ball. They should have done so much more.

'And Bella was pregnant,' Peroni added. 'You gave us that. Thanks. Though I don't imagine her brother's too grateful.'

'Oh yes,' she murmured. 'The brother.'

Peroni must have told her about what had happened that afternoon. Something didn't ring true.

'On the face of it,' Costa said, 'the brother's the best suspect we've got. The only suspect. We know he messed around with Bella once. He admitted it himself. His only alibi comes from his sons, neither of whom I'd trust for a moment. If Bella had told him about the pregnancy and the fact the child couldn't be Uriel's, he had a motive too – to keep her quiet. The Braccis have a reputation going back years. They've got form.'

She didn't look convinced.

'If I were Leo Falcone,' she said primly, 'I'd say you were trying to make your suspicions fit your facts. Bracci and Bella were playing those games thirty years ago, weren't they?'

'Something like that,' Costa confirmed.

'I'm no expert in incest or sexual abuse. But I am a woman. I've got to tell you, it doesn't fit. Why would they turn back the clock? Most people in that situation would want to put the past behind them; never remember for a moment all the stupid nonsense they got up to when they were kids. They wouldn't want to take those memories out of the box and bring them back to life. What are the stats for incest among people in their forties, outside the boondocks?'

'This *is* the boondocks,' Peroni grumbled.

'Is it?' Costa asked. 'It's a closed community. I don't think that's the same thing.'

'I agree,' Teresa said firmly. 'This place is too urban. Someone would surely have known if it had started again. Something would surely have happened.'

Peroni poked his head around the side of the boat. The familiar yellow sign of the Faro floating jetty was bobbing up and down on the water ahead. And something new: two bright blue neon signs had been erected on the little island next door. One, over the foundry, shone above the fresh glass and woodwork, announcing FOUNDRY. The second was five times its size and spanned the entire entrance of the palace in a large semi-circle.

'THE PALAZZO DEGLI ARCANGELI,' Peroni read, squinting at the sign in the distance. 'Something did happen, if you recall.'

'I know but . . .'

She wasn't going to start an argument. Costa understood her point all the same.

The vaporetto lurched to a sudden halt. Its klaxon sounded. Loud, angry voices issued from the cabin ahead. It was one of those rare incidents of a dispute on the lagoon. Two vessels cutting each other up, trying to fight for domination of the busy waves.

Nic Costa stuck out his head to see what was going on. Piero Scacchi's grubby motorboat was edging out from the jetty by the foundry, the black, taut shape of Xerxes seated amidships, in front of the figure of his master working the helm. The vessel carried no obvious cargo.

He could have made some kind of delivery, perhaps to help restart the furnace.

Scacchi fought his way past the stalled vaporetto, ignoring the curses coming from the cabin, then turned up the feeble motor, raising the vessel to what Costa guessed must have been its maximum speed. He looked glad to be leaving Murano, pointing the nose of his little craft straight for Sant' Erasmo.

'Hey!' Peroni yelled. 'Piero!'

His voice was lost in the roar of the vaporetto's engine. Probably just as well, Costa thought. Piero Scacchi was a player in the proceedings too. He lived in a place where the country habits Teresa ruled out in Murano were, perhaps, not entirely unknown. And he was privy, surely, to information on Hugo Massiter. Costa was unable to thrust from his head the story of Massiter's brush with the law, five years earlier, and those two disappeared characters in that episode, Daniel Forster and Laura Conti. He wondered what they would have to say in response to Massiter's version of those events. All the more so now, since Emily seemed destined to spend some time in the Englishman's presence.

A sound – distant, delightful – drifted across the still evening air. Just a short distance away, from the open doors of the palace, came the lilting notes of a small orchestra, the violins foremost, music that, to Costa's largely uneducated ear, sounded like Vivaldi. He strained to see beyond the boat stop, towards the private island. White banners festooned the iron bridge and the arms of the skeletal angel. Beyond, by the narrow jetty outside the palace, never used before when Costa had visited the island, a long line of private water taxis was queuing to unload its human cargo. People were in carnival costume: Renaissance, Baroque, English Elizabethan. The women stood waiting to disembark in bright, shining, full-length dresses of silk, damask and velvet, mantles around their shoulders, fans flickering, feathered hats pointing skywards. The men were equally varied: fake noblemen, pirates, soldiers, others dressed as commedia dell'arte figures, Harlequin in patchwork with his trademark stick, the plague doctor with his long, vicious beak, Pulcinella in sugar-loaf hat and white baggy costume.

'Oh my God,' Teresa murmured. 'It's Leo.'

Falcone's unmistakable lean erect figure was visible on the jetty. He was wearing a restrained dark uniform, like that of an old-fashioned military officer. Lines of gold braid stood on his shoulders. Colourful medals adorned his chest.

'The bastard,' Teresa complained. 'He knew all along.'

Raffaela Arcangelo stood next to him, in mourning still. Her medieval-style ankle-length dress was solid, dull black. At the high neckline an ornate lace collar, the colour of night, allowed only a glimpse of the pale flesh beneath. Her long hair was parted in the middle and tied back by a pearl-studded band.

'Now *that*,' Teresa added, 'looks like a couple.'

Peroni eyed the starry crowd mournfully then jerked his old, rather shiny tie tight to his neck, hoping, perhaps, the crooked knot would hide the missing button on his shirt.

'Thank you, Leo,' the big man moaned. 'Thanks a million.'

Teresa gave him a straight look.

'What's your beef? You're wearing a tie. For you that *is* fancy dress.'

'But . . .'

'But if you'd known,' she continued, 'you'd never have come. Would you?'

There was another figure on the jetty. She was walking out onto the bare stone in a long, piercingly bright white gown, a set of swan-feather wings on her back, the perfect, golden-haired angel, poised outside the shining glass palace, her outline dancing in the faintly malodorous heat like a figure from a dream.

Emily Deacon looked immensely happy, fulfilled and at home on the terrace of this palazzo, a place where Costa knew he could never feel at ease. Accompanying her was Hugo Massiter, wearing the costume of a key figure from the commedia dell'arte. Il Capitano, the boastful, violent soldier, a bundle of arrogance hidden inside a naval officer's blue uniform, a fake sword by his side, owner of a painted mask with a long phallic nose which now sat on Massiter's shoulder, its expression veering between covetousness and cowardice.

Something flickered inside Nic Costa's head: a memory from

school. Of all those old theatre stories, one in particular. About the Captain and how he kidnapped the lovely Isabella, the *innamorata*, the innocent and beautiful woman in love who never needed to hide behind a mask or, if Costa recalled correctly, saw much behind those of others either.

13

The dazzling interior of the Palazzo degli Arcangeli was breathtaking. Banks of orchids and roses stood in fragrant lines at the edges of the hall. Broad white ribbons festooned the wood and metal superstructure of the building, meeting to form a crown around the trunk of the fossilized palm tree at its centre. The three rising semicircles of glass glittered with the winking eyes of hundreds of tiny floodlights set in banks over the crowd below, a field of anonymous actors playing such old, old parts Costa had to delve deep into his childhood to remember their names. At the rear, on a low podium, the small orchestra was sawing away, still audible over the chatter of a good three hundred people, enough to make up several commedia dell'arte troupes.

Nic Costa thought he could detect Emily's swift and practical touch in places: vases of tall white lilies; skeins of fine gold wire, wrought in fluid, writhing shapes a good five metres above the crowd, like a near invisible skin between them and the fragile glass high above. Everything was muted yet purposeful too, and almost succeeded in hiding the haste in which it had been put together. Still, the event had the feeling of a party taking place in some newly reborn building waiting to find its purpose, a place that had woken from some long slumber only to find itself invaded by vandals.

They conversed briefly with Leo Falcone and Raffaela, who clung to the inspector's arm looking a little cowed by the glamour of the evening. Then they ploughed on, feeling awkward in such company, Costa searching for Emily again in the gaudy packed throng, Peroni and Teresa following in his wake.

It was soon apparent that the entire Arcangelo clan was there.

Most men wore the *bauta*, the tight powder-white traditional mask that fitted over the nose and cheeks, but left the mouth free for eating and drinking. Even so, these were modern times. After a little while in the baking, close room, the awkward fittings must have grown tiresome. Both Arcangelo brothers were out of theirs within minutes. Michele conversed with a woman Costa didn't recognize, looking animated, cheerful almost. A different creature to the surly individual they'd tried to pump for information earlier. Gabriele was less changed. Miserable in his plague-doctor costume, he stood alone, close to the drinks table, his long-nosed mask on his shoulder, gulping at a glass of spritz, unwilling or unable to strike up a conversation with anyone.

Costa excused himself as he pushed past a couple who were still masked, and dressed like neon peacocks, in a fashion that seemed more suited to a carnival in Brazil than a private party in Venice. Then he rounded a table of canapés, sighed as Peroni picked up a fistful and began munching, turned and found himself staring into the dry, dead face of Gianfranco Randazzo.

'Someone else in civilian dress,' he moaned, glancing at Peroni too. 'That's a relief. Are you wondering what the hell you're doing at this charade?'

'Eating,' Peroni declared, holding up a couple of delicate biscuits bearing bresaola, wind-dried beef, topped with sautéed porcini. The big man grimaced at his glass of *prosecco*. 'Don't suppose they've got any beer here?'

'Duty officers aren't supposed to drink,' Randazzo said curtly.

'We're aware of that, sir,' Costa replied, toasting the commissario for a moment. In spite of Peroni's protests it was good stuff, better than the weak fizz he usually found in the Veneto. 'Right now we're off duty. Right now we can do what the hell we like.'

Randazzo scowled. The man seemed tense, more unhappy than usual.

'So what's new? I suppose I ought to be grateful. At least I get a break from the complaints. You know we hardly ever need to send a man to Murano. It's that kind of place. Now I've got three out there. Doing nothing but push back the crowds. Why didn't you just take Bracci into custody?'

'On what grounds?' Peroni asked.

'That's for you to invent,' Randazzo snapped. 'Do I have to tell you everything?'

The commissario glanced at Teresa Lupo. Her presence made him uneasy somehow, a fact she wasn't likely to miss.

'I suppose you had a good day too,' he mumbled. 'Poking your nose in our business. I should have been told about that trip to Tosi. Before it happened.'

'Tosi phoned you?' she asked, surprised.

'Of course! He works for me.'

'Lucky man,' Teresa Lupo said pleasantly then turned her back on him and joined Peroni.

Randazzo prodded Costa in the chest.

'There are limits to what I will take from you three.'

Nic Costa wasn't interested in pursuing this conversation. Randazzo was a small man. Massiter's man, if Costa understood the situation correctly. He was here because he'd been told to be here. The grumpy, sour-faced commissario could entertain himself. Besides, he'd spotted Emily. She was over on the far side of the room, a dreamlike figure in white, free of Massiter, getting an energetic chat-up line from some idiot dressed up like an eighteenth-century French aristocrat.

Nic Costa nodded at Randazzo.

'I genuinely believe that to be true, sir. If you'll excuse me.'

Then, with a mild shoulder charge, a toned-down version of the play from his rugby days, Costa was through the costumed scrum, pushing them aside with a stream of muttered apologies, determined she wouldn't get away.

He picked up two fresh glasses of *prosecco* from a bewigged waiter in blue silk and pushed his way through the throng to her.

Emily laughed, a light, warm entrancing sound, and took her glass.

His eyes roved over the white, white, angel costume, the perfect feathered wings.

'I brought your clothes. You asked me. And this . . .'

He took the tiny bouquet of blood-red *peperoncini* from Piero Scacchi's smallholding out of his pocket.

'It's not much in these surroundings.'

Emily placed the waxy peppers carefully in the feathers of her right wing where they stood out like some strange, symmetrical wound.

'It's the loveliest thing I've seen all day,' she said.

There was a wicked radiance in her eyes. This was all a game. A tease, maybe. She revolved once, like an ethereal model, just for him.

'Don't you like it?'

'No.'

'Nic!'

He scowled.

'I like it. Where on earth did you get it?'

'Hugo has an account. He sent out to some costumier in the city. It was his idea.'

'I bet. Did he have any others?'

She blinked.

'I suspect so,' she answered frankly. 'I learnt quite a lot about Hugo Massiter today.'

'Does it help?'

'I don't know.'

She ducked behind one of the slender iron columns that ran in a line close to the edge of the hall, supporting the balcony above. There were crowds above them, scores of people, their feet clattering on the ironwork. The place seemed too delicate to be real. Her bright, sharp eyes scanned the mob to make sure no one was listening. The lively sound of the orchestra, working its way through the spring section of the *Four Seasons*, rang behind them.

'Probably not,' she said quietly. 'I learnt that he's obsessed with Laura Conti. The woman who almost ruined him, if you remember.'

Costa nodded. The story of Laura Conti and Daniel Forster wouldn't go away.

'He doesn't look the romantic type to me. He's rich. The kind of man who could have pretty much any woman he feels like.'

'I can't believe you said that!' she complained. 'Do you think it's just about money?'

'No! I meant – he's not married. He seems a solitary type, not someone to enter into a long-term relationship. I rather thought men like that attracted a certain kind of woman.'

'That's a retraction of a sort, I suppose. How about this as an explanation? The reason he's fixated with Laura Costa is precisely because she's *not* that kind of woman. She's someone who actually said no to him. Or perhaps said maybe, in the first instance, and then no, which would be even worse.'

'That would get to him?' he asked.

'It would get to most men, wouldn't it?'

There was something here he still didn't understand. It got in the way.

'As Falcone reminds me constantly,' Costa went on, 'Daniel Forster and Laura Conti aren't part of this case. What about the Arcangeli? What's his relationship with them.'

She shrugged.

'I don't know any more than you do. He likes women. Perhaps he was Bella's secret lover. It wouldn't surprise me. You have to appreciate something: women matter to him.'

'I'd gathered that.'

'No,' she said with a sigh. 'This isn't about me. It's . . . universal. Hugo's the kind of individual who sees women as a challenge. Scalps for his hunting belt. It's not about love. Or sex even. Or anything healthy like that. It's about possession. He's more charming than most, but that's what he's like, and he's very good at it too.'

Costa found the words slipped out, unbidden.

'Does he want you for a scalp?'

'Probably,' she answered without hesitation. 'But I don't feel flattered. Men like Hugo want women the way other men want cars. It's a question of ownership. I rather imagine that once he's sat in the driving seat, so to speak, the attraction wears off. It didn't with Laura Conti for some reason. That's what's bugging him still. It doesn't make sense to him. It doesn't fit in his neat, nicely ordered world which is a place where he's very much in control.' She took a sip of the *prosecco* and smiled, appreciating the taste. 'And it won't go away. Bella, on the other hand, did. That's as much as I know.'

'I guess that's a kind of definition of love,' he added. 'The not going away part.'

'I guess.'

Her blue eyes wouldn't leave him. When he saw her like this, lovely inside the stupid, radiant dress, with the stain of the *peperoncini* by her shoulder, he wondered why he ever doubted the bond between them.

'I think I've had enough of this masquerade, Nic. Shall we go?'

Costa's eyes swept the room, the silk and the satin, the wigs and the pale, powdered faces.

'You'd leave these people for a little police apartment in Castello?'

'No,' she said with a wry smile. 'I'd leave them for you, idiot.'

Nic Costa laughed. That was one more talent she possessed. Then he took one last glance around him. Leo Falcone was talking earnestly to Commissario Randazzo, free of the black-clad, shy form of Raffaela Arcangelo whose elder brother, next to Falcone, still held the unknown woman in conversation, an avaricious expression on his face. Close by, Peroni and Teresa were embroiled in an animated discussion by the side of an attendant whose food tray they pillaged between statements.

His eyes roved to the nodding waters, the moored boats, the stone jetty. There was someone there. The last person Nic Costa expected to see was walking into the Palazzo degli Arcangeli at that moment.

14

Gianni Peroni possessed an armoury of talents for infuriation. At that moment, surrounded by costumed buffoons, slightly giddy on three rapid glasses of good *prosecco* alongside untold canapés of lobster and bresaola, Teresa Lupo truly believed he was entering upon fresh ground in his ability to drive her crazy.

'Don't worry about it,' Peroni said again. 'It'll be OK. We'll see another doctor. There's a witch back home near Siena. Well, I say *witch*. It's more kind of folk remedies and stuff—'

'Gianni!' she barked, loud enough to send the harlequin next to her trotting off to find somewhere a little less noisy. 'Are you listening to a single word I say? This isn't a question of finding the right doctor. Or some country quack from one of your hick villages. It's human anatomy. Physics. Not some kind of magic.'

'That's what you said about spontaneous combustion,' Peroni reminded her. 'Until you started looking.'

Her head whirled. She felt like thumping his big chest with both fists.

'No. It's not like it at all. What I said was true. Spontaneous combustion, the way people think of it, *doesn't* exist. But maybe something we interpret as it does. That is *not* what I am talking about here.'

'Severe tubal occlusion.'

Notch up one more trick for the fury machine. Peroni's pronunciation was perfect, even if he didn't understand the first thing about what the condition was.

'Which means?' she demanded.

'Which means we look for some other solution. If that's what you want.'

'Christ! Let me put this in layman's terms. The wiring's burnt out. The plumbing's fucked. I am a freak—'

'If you were a freak they wouldn't have a name for it.'

'Shut up and listen, will you?'

He wasn't smiling. Or rather, he was, but in that wan, 'just tell me what to do' way that always made her feel helpless.

'I'm listening.'

She wished it were somewhere less noisy. Less public. It had been a mistake to bring up the subject now. But the *prosecco* had prompted her to get the thing over and done with. She had to get the news off her chest somehow. Keeping it tight inside herself did no good at all.

'I can't have children,' she said slowly. 'That will never change. You can fool yourself otherwise if you like, but I won't, Gianni. I can't. It just makes things . . . worse.'

Teresa Lupo was aware there were tears in her eyes. She wiped them away with the back of her hand, just in time for Peroni's arms to come round her frame in a strong, physical embrace.

'Does it matter?' she whispered into the side of his head, half wondering what all these people around them were making of the spectacle.

'Of course it matters,' he murmured.

She snivelled on his chest, then looked up into his battered face.

'I *want* children, Gianni.'

'And I want what you want. And we both don't get it, together.'

Together.

Just as Emily had said, on the waterfront, the day before, both of them dog tired, watching the dazzle on the water, picking at ice cream.

Together was what counted. Together was what would count for her and Nic too, one day. Teresa Lupo felt that in her bones. It was a fact, a solid, unmistakable piece of the future slowly emerging into the present, struggling to find form.

She glanced across the room. Emily was alone, a solitary white figure standing out against the pale old stonework of the hall, abandoned by Nic again for some reason, one Teresa wished she knew so she could beat him around the head with it and say: *'Look, for God's sake! People like this don't walk into your life – anyone's life – every day.'*

Cops and love, she thought. What a mixture. What a—

The room exploded with a deafening, deadly roar, a noise that rang off the fragile glass walls, echoing with an odd, resonant timbre, mocking, shaking them all.

This was a sound she was coming to recognize. One that people like Nic Costa and Gianni Peroni had introduced into her life. A single metallic scream, so loud she could feel her eardrums shrink under its violent volume.

'Gianni,' she murmured.

But the big man was gone already, punching his way through the overdressed mob, heading for an area of space that was opening up near the doorway, one that was getting larger by the second as all the costumed fools, the harlequins and the plague doctors, the medieval whores and the court ladies, suddenly got smart, remembered what century they were living in, and recognized the angry howl of a weapon.

'Get out of my damn way,' Teresa spat at some moron in black and white, flailing her arms, not wanting to think about what she'd see.

A man with a gun. There was always a man with a gun.

Both Nic and Leo Falcone were facing him down already, refusing to be cowed, standing to confront the madman who hid behind his hostage, a woman she recognized as the terrified Raffaela Arcangelo, shaking in her black widow's gown.

15

'Nic . . .'

He listened to the warning in the inspector's voice carefully, not taking his eyes off Aldo Bracci for a moment. The man was dead drunk, scarcely able to stand. A stupid, unwanted trick of the memory meant Costa recognized the weapon in his hand. It was an old Luigi Franchi RF-83 revolver, a .38 special with six cylinders, just under a kilo in weight, obsolete, unreliable, the kind of junk they took off small-time street hoods in Rome, people who couldn't shoot straight to save their lives. Not that it mattered. What was important was that this was a firearm, a small harbinger of death housed in ugly black metal.

'This is my call, Nic,' Falcone murmured. 'Go back. That's an order.'

They were just a couple of metres in front of Bracci and Raffaela, in the still bright yellow sun of the dying evening, beneath the wasted brilliance of a vast Murano chandelier suspended from the iron gallery above.

'He's drunk. He only knows you from this afternoon and that didn't go at all well,' Costa said quietly. 'Bracci just sees you as part of this problem. I came before. Give me a chance.'

'Nic . . .' There was a stern, desperate note in Falcone's voice.

'No, sir,' Costa declared, and stepped in front of the inspector, held his arms out wide, hands open, showing he had nothing with which to threaten the furious-looking Aldo Bracci, who cowered behind Raffaela shaking with fear and rage.

'Put the gun down, Aldo,' Costa said in a firm, even voice. 'Put it down, let the woman go. Then we can talk this through. No one gets hurt. Nothing goes any further. It's all going to be OK. I promise.'

Bracci's left arm was tight round her throat. Raffaela Arcangelo's hands hung loose by her side.

'Too damn late, you bastard!' Bracci's voice was a tortured howl. This man was not going to make sense. Costa tried to recall all the tricks a cop could use in these situations. And the golden rule: keep it calm.

'Talk to me, Aldo,' he said. 'Tell me what you want.'

'I want you off my back. I want . . .'

The man was close to tears, desperate, and Costa understood why. What had emerged on Murano that afternoon was irreversible.

'I want my fucking life back,' Bracci babbled, as miserable as hell.

Costa nodded, theatrically, making sure Bracci understood.

'I'm sorry about what happened. We just went round to talk to you because we had to. It's the job. We talk to everyone.'

Bracci's wild, drunken eyes rolled.

'You fuck up everyone? With these stories? You go round dredging up old dirt and scattering it round the streets like dog shit?'

'No. That shouldn't have happened. I apologize.'

'Some good that does me! So where am I supposed to go now, smart ass? Home?'

Aldo Bracci's life in that narrow malodorous street, with an angry face peeking out from every window, was finished. Costa understood that as well as he did. It was what made Bracci so dangerous.

'Tell me what you want.'

Bracci laughed. Spittle flew from his mouth, fell on Raffaela's black-clad shoulder. The laugh turned into a long choking cough. His shoulders heaved. He looked like a man who didn't care about anything, least of all himself.

Quietly, patiently, Costa persisted.

'You came here for a reason. If I knew what that was . . .'

The glassy, drunk eyes glared at him.

'If you knew what that was . . .'

The gun rose again. He was looking around, scanning the crowd, searching for someone, not finding the face.

Bracci jerked back his arm, fired again, straight into the chandelier above him, despatching a shower of tiny glass shards into the room. The crowd was screaming again, falling back even further, crushed against the temporary tables, sending the plates of delicate canapés and the glasses of sparkling wine crashing on the hard stone floor.

Costa didn't move. He looked at Bracci, resolute, determined to see this through. Two shots. Six chambers. If they were full when the man entered the room, there were just four left now. Not that any of them needed to be used.

'Put the gun down, Aldo,' Costa repeated. 'Let Raffaela go. Then we'll walk outside, talk this through. I'll take you anywhere you want – to the mainland – you name the place.'

The dead eyes blinked.

'Anywhere?'

'Anywhere you—'

Costa halted. A figure was scuttling through the crowd, quickly, something in its hand.

'No!' Costa bellowed.

It was Gianfranco Randazzo, striding into the space Bracci had made, black pistol in hand, firing straight at the pair, like a madman, almost random in his fury.

Costa leapt forward, tearing at Raffaela's gown, dragging her to the ground out of Bracci's grip. The unsteady figure above them didn't know where to turn, to his disappearing hostage, or to face the hot random rain spitting at him from Randazzo's weapon.

A red tear opened up in Bracci's shoulder. A sudden spurt of blood fell warm on Costa's face. Bracci shrieked. The old Franchi jerked in his hand, twice, firing nowhere in particular.

Screams came from all around them, hoarse, terrified voices uttered by a cast of fake actors forced suddenly into a cold and dangerous reality. Randazzo, in his fine black suit, casually walked up to the shattered stumbling figure of Bracci, took aim at the man's head like a back-street executioner and let loose one final shot into the man's scalp.

Bracci's torso jerked back under the force of the bullet. The

Franchi fell out of his dead hand, clattering to the hard marble floor, spent, its damage done.

Costa recoiled at the sharp, bitter smell of gunfire, then watched in disgust as Randazzo performed one final act, kicking the twitching corpse in the back, sending it rolling onto its side. Bracci's cheap, cotton work jacket, the same he'd worn in his tawdry little foundry, flapped open to reveal the man's bloodied chest.

Calm, unmoved by the continuing pandemonium around him, Randazzo stared down at his victim, seeing something. He crouched by the body, flicked the jacket closed.

The commissario reached into the side pocket then coolly removed a set of keys, joined together by a single ring, marked by a yellow sash.

He scanned the room.

'Was this what you were looking for?' Randazzo bellowed. 'Well, Falcone? *Falcone?*'

Costa was helping the weeping Raffaela Arcangelo to her feet. His arms shook. He fought to make sense of what he'd seen.

'*Are these her keys?*' Randazzo yelled, scrabbling through the dead man's pockets as the continuing commotion behind them grew.

Furious, Costa took two steps towards him, stared at the emotionless man in the black suit, now stained with Aldo Bracci's blood, then wrested the gun from his hand.

'Consider yourself under arrest. *Sir.* I'll see you in jail for this.'

Randazzo laughed in his face.

'What? Are you serious? You people are out of your depth here. You have been all along.'

A single long howl, louder than the rest and familiar in a way that made Costa's blood run cold, silenced him. Randazzo turned his attention to the back of the room, and was suddenly silent, the colour draining from his cheeks, an expression of unexpected dread frozen on his face.

Nic Costa had his back to the racket. All the same he could recognize that voice, that deep, furious bellow of despair. It was Teresa Lupo and somewhere inside the torrent of wordless anger streaming from her throat he heard his name.

Two stray bullets, screaming towards a room full of people, Aldo Bracci's final gifts to a world he felt had abandoned him.

Nic Costa knew what that meant. Knew too, somehow, what he'd see when he summoned enough courage to turn around and look for himself.

It could have been a painting. Something by Caravaggio, half deep shadow, half washed in the buttery rays of the dying sun. Peroni knelt on the ground, bent over the still figure there, rocking, silent, a lost, helpless expression set in his pained face. Teresa crouched next to him on her knees, fighting to do something, anything, with the rags in her hands, struggling to staunch the sea of red that grew like a flood tide from the figure on the hard, cold floor.

Leo Falcone lay motionless, his head in Emily Deacon's lap, his tan face staring back at them, eyes unfocussed, mouth gaping open, blood streaming gently from his lips, falling onto her white, white wings.

Part 4

THE INNOCENT

1

It was 1961, a cold summer in the Valle d'Aosta. Bone-chilling mountain mists hung around the family chalet outside Pré-Saint-Didier in the Little St Bernard Pass. A week had passed without sight of the rising bulk of Mont Blanc, separating this last wild piece of northern Italy from France and Switzerland, an aloof rocky giant, crowned with snow. The child, just turned seven, had felt lost without some view of the mountain. It was a consolation, during these long, lonely summer interludes, a kind of company. And that was the year – the very year, some odd external voice reminded him – when he needed company more than ever. The boy Leo was aware of himself, seated at the long, old wooden table, so roughly made it looked as if it had been shaped with an axe. Alone in the familiar living room. Yet not alone.

'You never did look,' the voice said. An old voice, familiar too.

'I never wanted to.'

It was, he somehow realized, himself speaking. Years older. Wiser too, perhaps. And sad. The child didn't believe in ghosts. His father, a practical, unemotional accountant who handled money for many of the larger northern corporations, would have no room for such nonsense. He'd thrown away some of the books Leo brought home from boarding school. They were too fanciful, he said, apt to give a child the wrong ideas. Arturo Falcone was, as he never failed to remind his son, a self-made man. He'd risen out of the misery and chaos of World War Two, putting himself through college by working as a barman and waiter at nights. Everything in little Leo Falcone's life came from this odd, unemotional man, a father on paper only, a distant figure, seen only in the holidays, when he'd retire to a chair on his own most times, with a newspaper and a glass, to bury himself deep in his own thoughts. Leo was an only child, which made the gratitude he felt he owed his father for any attention whatsoever both more deserved, and more difficult to deliver.

The room was freezing. His parents had left him there with nothing but this curious voice, a more desolate echo of his own, for company.

He looked at the clock, an old Black Forest cuckoo clock. Like something from a dream, the pendulum hung still, trapped artificially on the right side of the housing, which was a copy of a wooden mountain chalet, very like the one in which he now sat, stiffly upright on a hard uncomfortable chair, aware that the room was reverberating from some sound that had penetrated it from elsewhere, a booming, rolling, chiming noise, the metallic ring of bells followed by the lunatic chirrup of the cuckoo's bellows.

They talked of avalanches here, in the winter. The mountains were dangerous, solitary places. There were still bears, some said, and wild mountain men who would take a child just to enslave it, to put the stolen boy out into the fields to work the pastures, gone forever into a life of servitude, because someone had to work, always.

His father told him that last story. One night when he'd been bad. Or at least forgetful, leaving the key inside the glass front door, where any thief might smash the window, snatch it, put a hand through and enter. A stranger, an intruder, a man who could rip the fragile fabric of a family apart with his hands.

Keys are what stand between decent people and chaos, Arturo Falcone said, before he beat the boy Leo, not hard, but with a relentless, chill deliberation that was, in some way, more painful because of the mental hurt it inflicted. Forget the keys and your little world dies, you with it. Parents disappear. The lonely little boy from a cold, upper-middle-class family, becomes a dirty mountain goatherd, abandoned to a life of misery and shame.

Better off dead, his father said.

Dead.

He hated that word as a child, even before he fully understood what it meant. From an early age Leo Falcone found he was able to read the faces of others, see behind their expressions and guess at what they were truly thinking. It was a kind of magic, the very sort his father would have beaten out of him had he known it existed. But exist it did, and Leo knew what went through the minds of men and women, all adults, all better than him, when they said the dead-word.

Terror.

A long, slow uncontrollable sense of dread, one that wouldn't disappear until something – some other more immediate concern or, in his father's case, a bottle of mountain brandy – displaced it from their heads.

Dead.

The boy Leo found he was able to say the word himself, at this freezing, deserted table, and, for the first time, experience none of the sense of cold, inner foreboding he would have expected.

He drew the icy air into his lungs, two big, painful breaths, screwed up his face with an anger and force he would never have dared show had his father been present. Then he yelled, '*Dead, dead, dead – DEAD!*'

There was a sound from high on the wall. The frozen pendulum on the clock moved, making a single swing from right to left before standing still again, defying gravity, defying everything that Leo had come to believe was solid, safe and natural in the world. Then it spoke again, that twin chorus, half metallic bell, half thunderous cuckoo roar, the very noise that had awoken him in this place.

It wasn't just a cuckoo clock. He should have remembered.

The tiny wooden doors opened. From within, circling, circling, came two small, round wooden figures. Husband and wife, he in mountain dress, leather leggings, a colourful shirt with braces, and a small green hat with a minute visible feather in it. She . . .

Leo blinked. He remembered both figures now. The woman was large and bustling and funny, in a white dress with blue spots, a kindly, rosy face, set forever in a wooden smile.

This woman was gone. In her place was a naked figure, no higher than a finger, but made of flesh, real flesh, pink and white and flaccid in the way he'd noticed when his mother walked out of the bathroom wearing nothing, unaware he was there.

Real flesh with weals and wounds and blood, real blood, blood that spat and spurted out of her under the vicious, constant blows of the little man who circled, arms thrashing, blade flashing.

Little Leo blinked. The clock was changing, even as he watched.

Now the little man wore a surgeon's mask and a close-fitting surgical cap. His arm worked feverishly, slashing, slashing.

'Under the knife we go we go. . .' someone, the older Leo, half sadly laughing, said at the back of his head.

There was screaming too. Screaming from the little figures in the clock. Screaming from beyond this cold, cold room.

Little Leo's eyes fell on the door, the solid wooden barrier that led to his parents' bedroom, a place he feared, a place where he didn't belong. There was a huge carved wooden heart on the crossbeam, a sign of love, he imagined, though it somehow seemed out of place. And now this heart, old polished oak, was beating, slowly, weakly, pumping with a feeble resignation that was audible, moving in rhythm with his own frightened pulse, the two matched in unison deep within his ears.

Behind this palpitating wooden heart was his parents' sanctuary, their private place in which a child was never allowed, no matter how much he needed them, how frightened he felt. There was no glass panel here, no window, nothing to allow anyone to see what happened behind that solid, impassable wood. There was, too, no stupid, weak means to circumvent what was meant to be – safety, security, certainty – when you placed a key in the door and turned the lock.

It was there, on the table, taunting him. Old black metal, fancily worked so that it felt awkward in the hand, too large for the clumsy fingers of a child which grasped at the sharp angles of the handle and failed to find purchase. Even if he dared, their bedroom was forbidden territory. He'd known that all his short years. What happened there was for them alone, had no part in his life.

The bell and the roar of the cuckoo ripped through the air again. Leo watched the pendulum make a single crossing, from left to right, then stay stuck in time, spotted with blood from the little female figure who thrashed, and screamed and fought in her tiny, tightly defined circle of life on the porch of the chalet clock.

Nothing stops the flailing man, he thought. Not the pendulum. Not the ghostly voice in his head. Not God himself. Because the flailing man is part of God too, the part that always comes in the end.

But he couldn't say the words this time. The pendulum never moved. Some deep, primeval fear began to wake inside little Leo Falcone's head, turn his bowels to water, make him want to sit on this old seat and pee himself out of terror.

'The past is past,' the older voice said. 'Trust me.'

'So what do I do?' he asked, bitter, not minded to break down in tears because this always gave the adults some comfort, and would do even when those watching, older eyes were his own.

'What you'll always do. First and last. So much it will get in the way of everything else. *Think!*'

Leo waited and listened and tried to do as the voice said. He didn't want to be in this place. He didn't want to see behind the locked wooden door, with its crudely carved, dying heart, or use the big metal key on the table. More than anything, little Leo wished to sleep. To lay down his head on the table, close his eyes, think of nothing, embrace nothing but the dark which seemed, next to this crazed, inhospitable place, a warm and welcoming respite from the torments that were gathering around him.

'Please,' the old voice said, and it sounded scared.

2

Maggiore Luca Zecchini was a happy man. He was back in his beloved Verona after three days at a tedious conference in Milan. There would be a premiere of *Il Trovatore* in the Arena that evening, an event he would attend with a charming and beautiful tourist from San Diego he'd met on the train home the night before. And there was *pranzo* in Sergio's, the little restaurant around the corner from the office, a place where a man could gather his thoughts. Lunch, for Zecchini, was a staging post for the day, a time when one might reflect on a morning well spent, and look forward to a brisk afternoon of activity before shrugging off the dark, impeccable uniform of a major in the Carabinieri and re-entering civilian life. Few men enjoyed this small ceremony in the same way: as an ascetic exercise in self-detachment, not a quick opportunity for face-filling. Only one newcomer had, of late, entered the small circle of sympathetic friends invited to join him on occasion at Sergio's. Thinking about that unlikely individual now, Zecchini's mood became muted. Police work was never without its risks. He'd been with the Comando Carabinieri Tutela Patrimonio Culturale since its formation in 1992. The world of art theft and smuggling which he inhabited on a daily basis was not immune to violence. Two fellow officers from the south had lost their lives in the last six months mixing with gangsters trying to run some historic artefacts from Iraq through Italy on their way to Switzerland. All the same . . . some incidents seemed odd. Unnecessary. Inexplicable. And tragic, still, a week after the dreadful affair had appeared in the papers.

Zecchini stared at his plate of pork ribs with a portion of greens on the side and wondered whether they would really taste quite so good now. He should have asked Gina from San Diego to join him. Women loved the uniform. He used to joke with Falcone about their sartorial differences. The man from the state police always wore plain clothes, aware that the ugly blue wouldn't have suited him. Falcone wasn't an individual who fitted in easily sometimes.

Then his eyes wandered down the street and met a sight he found both puzzling and of singular interest. Two men were walking towards him. One, tall and bulky in an ill-fitting grey suit, had a very ugly, scarred face and the physique of a boxer gone to seed. The second was an unusual foil: slight, young, short, in shirt and jeans, rather innocent-looking, except, as Zecchini saw when they got closer, in the eyes, which were determined and a little bleak.

These were not, he thought, men to cross. And they were, somehow, recognizable too, if only he could place the memory.

Then the younger came over to his table, and asked, in a polite Roman accent, 'Maggiore Zecchini?'

'Yes?'

They looked at one another, uncertain, it seemed to him, how to proceed. Zecchini thought about their appearance, and what they might do for a living. Then the connection clicked.

'You're just as he described,' he said. 'Sit down. I'm in need of company.'

The bigger one was at the table in an instant, eyeing Zecchini's ribs. The younger man pulled up a chair, close to Zecchini. There was no one else on the pavement. He wanted to make sure they could talk in privacy.

'He mentioned us?' the elder, Peroni, he recalled the name now, asked, surprised.

'There were times when he talked about very little else. I only knew Leo for a few months. We talked a lot. We became friends, I think. In spite of the different uniforms. It's not impossible now, is it?'

Zecchini pushed away his plate.

'How is he?' he asked, a part of him not wanting to know the answer. 'I thought of visiting. But it seemed such a mess over there.

Such an imposition. Besides, I don't think an officer of the Carabinieri would be particularly welcome . . .'

Peroni shrugged.

'He wouldn't know. He's not recovered consciousness, not in a week. The doctors say it's touch and go. Whatever happens, I don't think Leo's going to be back in the job again.'

It was good news they even gave him some chance. From what Zecchini had heard they'd thought Falcone was little more than a breathing corpse at one point.

'That's hard to believe,' he said.

'I agree.'

It was the young one who spoke.

'Nic Costa. Gianni Peroni.'

Zecchini extended his hand.

'Please call me Luca. I asked that of Leo. I ask it of you. We're acquaintances. Not colleagues. That makes some things easier. And eat. It's been a while since I bought a state policeman a meal. Too long.'

He called over the waiter and listened to their orders: meat for the big man, some grilled vegetables for Costa. Zecchini was slightly disturbed to discover that, through his friendship with Leo Falcone, he felt he knew these men already.

'You're looking for work?' he asked, after the waiter had gone.

The papers had been full of the aftermath of the incident in Venice. A commissario had been suspended pending possible manslaughter charges. Costa and Peroni were on enforced leave, which was often the precursor to disciplinary action.

'We've got plenty of work,' Costa replied.

It was, Zecchini thought, just what he expected.

'That doesn't sound too good. I thought you were supposed to sit at home and twiddle your thumbs.'

Peroni laughed.

'The problem is, once you've been under that cunning old bastard for a while it gets decidedly difficult to do what you're supposed to sometimes. You mean you never noticed, Luca?'

Zecchini took a mouthful of his pork rib. It was cold. The meal was ruined, and he rather guessed it could only get worse.

'We came with a gift,' Costa said. 'Or rather a prize.'

'It's going to cost me?' Zecchini asked.

Costa watched the waiter come back with their food, then watched the man leave.

'Nothing comes for free,' he said. 'But, if we're right, if we get lucky . . . with your help. It's a prize I think you'd like very much.'

Luca Zecchini listened to the two of them. It only took a minute to realize the last thing he'd be doing that evening would be watching *Il Trovatore* in the company of the delightful Gina.

3

It had been more than a decade since Teresa Lupo abandoned medicine for what she saw as the more challenging world of working in a police morgue. Now she felt lost in a hospital, the Ospedale Civile of Venice more than most. The place seemed like an entire quarter of the city rather than a medical institution. It ran through a warren of historic buildings, modern accretions, and storeys of blocks that seemed like civil apartments, emerging on the bare lagoon waterfront between Fondamente Nove and Celestia. She couldn't help but notice the institution sat bang opposite another staging post on the journey of life, the cemetery island of San Michele, which blocked – happily, she thought – the view over to the Isola degli Arcangeli on Murano. The Venetians never did like to make more effort than was absolutely necessary.

Three things happened the night Leo Falcone had been hurried to the hospital in a speeding water ambulance, siren wailing, blue light flashing in the rapidly descending darkness.

First, she remembered how to yell at medics, good medics, people who were patently competent at their job, but just didn't understand the small matter of priorities. A man with a head wound as bad as the one Falcone had suffered wasn't in need of much analysis. He was a corpse in the making, screaming silently for someone to freeze the clock and keep him alive until a specialist could be got on the scene to work out if there was any way forward from this mess.

Second, she discovered she'd do anything to stop Leo Falcone dying. Theoretically, she didn't want *anyone* to die, ever, even if that put her out of a job. But this wasn't about theory. Whatever had happened between her and Falcone in the past, she now had some unexpected bond with this strange, distant, frequently arrogant man whose stricken body had been wheeled through the corridors of the Ospedale Civile at speed, navigating its spider's web of corridors on a journey, it seemed to her, to nowhere.

And third, she found out that she, and her Roman police pathologist's card, still carried clout. When they got Falcone into pre-op and found that Venice's one and only neurosurgeon was on holiday in the Maldives, Teresa just screeched at them to do what they could to staunch the bleeding, then wait for orders.

There was some luck in the world. Maybe a God even. Pino Ferrante had been at medical school with her all those years ago. On the way over in the racing ambulance dashing across the lagoon she had been remembering his hands, which were the most beautiful she'd ever seen on a man: long and fine and elegant, like something from a drawing by Dürer. Healing hands, that much was obvious by the time he'd completed his training and entered the outside world of medical practice. Pino was now a prosperous neurology consultant in his native Bologna, little more than sixty minutes away if he still drove a car the way he used to. And he was at home when she called, breathless, pleading.

Less than three hours later Falcone was in theatre, with Pino's gentle, firm fingers trying to perform wonders she could only guess at, while the four of them, two colleagues-cum-friends, two women who'd found themselves dragged unwittingly into this wounded man's life, waited on the terrace by the waterfront, swatting midges in the sticky night air, drinking endless plastic cups of bad coffee, asking themselves all manner of questions about the strange burst of violence that had torn through the Arcangeli's palazzo, and Hugo Massiter's party, that evening.

Then finally, reaching a decision, one found in anger and a mute, shared hunger for some semblance of justice. One that didn't require much effort, if they were honest with themselves. Or much discussion, because discussion just got in the way of what was needed.

There were facts before them, Nic said. Staring them in the face, taunting them. Gianfranco Randazzo worked for Hugo Massiter. That had been obvious all along. Randazzo had murdered Bracci to close the case and Massiter's deal, wounding Leo Falcone, possibly fatally, along the way.

It was meant to be a neat, tidy package, one that no one would try to untie, or attempt to see what might lie inside. Venice would, Nic predicted accurately, be determined to swallow the picture Randazzo gave them that night, even though there were so many unanswered questions. Why had the drunken Bracci gone to the palazzo in the first place? What exactly had he hoped to achieve by taking Raffaela hostage while searching among the masks and the commedia dell'arte costumes for the man he wanted, who was Massiter, Nic said, surely? And why the hell would he bring along a handy piece of evidence, the keys with their tell-tale ribbon, just to complete the story?

None of these issues would now be addressed. The tragedies of the deaths at the Isola degli Arcangeli were, for the city, closed the moment Randazzo's bullet shattered Aldo Bracci's skull. Leo Falcone had been what a certain kind of military man would call 'collateral damage', and all to crown Hugo Massiter king of the city.

They had looked at each other that night, listened to Nic carefully reeling his way through the known facts, feeling a certainty grow inside them, one that didn't need to be articulated to be understood. To the Venetians they were strangers, all of them. They'd be excluded from the swift tidying up of the facts that would now ensue. If Nic was right – and it soon turned out he was – they'd be squeezed out of the Questura too, kept away from any stray difficult facts.

Which was, if only the Venetians understood it, the stupidest thing the city could do. They didn't know Costa and Peroni. They didn't understand what kind of men they were. How the two would spend days, weeks, trying to peer beneath the wrapping of that carefully presented, utterly fictitious case Venice was giving to the world, picking at the seams until everything fell apart.

What were the facts? Nic asked at the time, acting out a fair impersonation of Falcone at his best.

Who benefited from what happened that night?

Hugo Massiter and his cronies in the council. And the Arcangeli, too, since they finally got the money they so desperately needed, even if it came with strings.

Who had a motive to kill Bella and Uriel?

There lay the lacunae. Uriel, from what they understood, was keen on the deal with Massiter. His death created difficult and expensive legal problems. But some motive existed. It needed to be found, and to do that, Nic said, they would follow Leo's rules. You mixed things a little. You piled on the pressure. You got nosy and difficult and kept on chasing down the lies.

And you imagined.

Bella was carrying Massiter's child, and trying to blackmail him into keeping her, something the Englishman couldn't allow, even if her death complicated his business matters. So Massiter, or one of his henchmen, killed her, doctored Uriel's apron in some way a man with no sense of smell could ever notice, sent him into the boiling-hot foundry with a key that couldn't work and which couldn't take him away from the scene of a crime that seemed, to the lazy, so obvious. Then fought to pin the blame for everything on Aldo Bracci, a man murdered in public, in a way that seemed to confirm his guilt.

Teresa Lupo mistrusted the imagination deeply, instinctively. She was a scientist, aware of how dangerous it was to produce a theory first, then search for the facts to support it. But watching Nic that night, seeing the fury and determination on his face, understanding for the first time how close he'd grown to Falcone since the death of his own father, Teresa knew she'd do anything in her power to help him. This wasn't the Nic Costa she'd first come to know and admire when he was a green detective in the Rome Questura, a little lost in the *centro storico*, the kind of peripheral figure who looked as if he might not last out the year. Events had changed him. Leo Falcone and Gianni Peroni had changed him, and been changed in return, too. And part of that change reflected on each of these three very different, now very close men. It was inconceivable that Nic and Gianni would walk away from this event. Inconceivable that she wouldn't throw in her lot with them.

And Emily . . .

*

After four days extracting every last scrap of information they could from the Questura, before they got sent on paid leave, Nic and Peroni left Venice, desperate to rustle up a few allies. Emily had gone on a different kind of mission, one that filled Teresa with deep misgivings because she understood how well a former FBI agent was trained for that kind of work, and the ruthless, selfless determination she was likely to adopt in pursuing it.

Teresa Lupo was left alone, clear about her own role. To find forensic, to nail down some facts that linked Hugo Massiter with Bella and Uriel Arcangelo, could, perhaps, place Massiter in the foundry that terrible night, and, more than anything, provide some sort of motive for why he would endanger his own business plans by murdering the pair of them in the first place.

She looked at the woman sitting by Falcone's bed, upright, alert, as if she truly expected Leo would wake up any second, smile, and ask for a coffee and a couple of *biscotti*. Teresa Lupo felt momentarily guilty. She wasn't alone at all. Raffaela Arcangelo had sat at Falcone's bedside for eighteen or more hours a day since he arrived, ever patient. And by the third day Teresa had, without asking Peroni or anyone else, plucked up the courage to bring her into their confidence, just a little, just enough so that a favour was hard to refuse. She was a good, straightforward woman. She admired Leo Falcone, clearly seeing in him something Teresa could only glimpse in the misty distance. She was also an Arcangelo, close to what had happened. She had access to the house and all the materials they needed to try to work some magic.

Teresa gazed down at the carrier bag of objects, each secure in a plastic envelope, which the two of them had assembled from the mansion and the foundry that morning while Michele and Gabriele were away, talking to the lawyers about Massiter's impending acquisition. Most important of all, some items from Bella and Uriel's bathroom that would provide DNA.

One of the devices attached to the unconscious Leo Falcone made a kind of beeping noise then went silent: wires and meters, CRT displays and drips; machines designed to keep a human being alive.

'There's no need to stay around,' Raffaela Arcangelo said in her calm, clear voice, shaking Teresa out of her reverie. 'I thought you had things you needed to do.'

'N-n-no . . .' she stuttered, surprised at being brought back to the real world like this.

The woman was in the position she'd come to adopt by the bed: stiff-backed in the hard hospital chair next to Falcone, a book in her hand. A woman's book, Teresa noticed. An intelligent romantic tale that all the papers had been writing about of late. It seemed to her that Raffaela Arcangelo had grown a little spinsterish before her time.

'Nor do you,' she observed quietly.

'I know. But I can comfort myself with the thought that it's just selfish. There's nothing left for me to do on the island today. Michele's locked in with the lawyers again. Gabriele too. Once that's over . . .'

She'd reached some kind of a decision, Teresa felt. One that had, perhaps, eased some long-felt burden.

'Once that's over I'm leaving. It's not' – she glanced at the prone Falcone – 'what happened. It's just a decision I should have made years ago. Now there'll be a little money. Perhaps I'll go back to Paris. I liked it there. I was a student, briefly. Unless I can be of some help to Leo.'

Teresa Lupo never looked over her shoulder. There was too much in the way of personal wreckage back there. And for Raffaela? Just a few dim memories. Faded, like old watercolours. It seemed a terrible time to start chasing them.

'This is an unusual thing for the likes of me to say,' Teresa observed, 'but I'd advise against making any rash decisions.'

Raffaela shook her head.

'It's not rash. I've wanted to leave for years. I just felt tied to that stupid island, to Michele's ridiculous dreams. He thinks he's some kind of a hero. Sticking to the old ways. Trying to keep some ancient craft alive when the rest of them turn out junk for the tourists. It's a delusion. I've lived here all my life and I can see what Venice is becoming. A graveyard, a beautiful one I'll admit, but a graveyard nevertheless. It drains the life out of you in the end. That's happened to Michele already, and he'll stay here ignoring that fact until it consumes him. I won't.'

Her bright eyes glittered with defiance.

'I *won't*. Once I've seen Leo back on his feet . . .'

There was a question there, one Teresa didn't feel able to answer at that moment.

'Once I've lost that burden from my conscience,' Raffaela continued, 'I'm gone.'

Teresa groaned, pulled up a chair by the bed, and took Raffalela's hands.

'Listen, please. What happened wasn't your fault. What—'

'I was the one Bracci was threatening! If I hadn't been stupid enough to let him get hold of me—'

'Then he would have grabbed hold of someone else. And Leo and Nic and Gianni would have done exactly the same thing. Don't fool yourself. They'd have done it for anyone.'

Raffaela stared at the still figure beneath the single white sheet.

'He will recover, won't he? That friend of yours seemed optimistic.'

She couldn't lie.

'There's a chance. There's a chance he won't. The brain's a curious organ. Pino knows more about it than anyone I've ever met. All the same . . .'

Raffaela Arcangelo leaned forward, earnest, suddenly intense, less in control of herself than at any time Teresa had witnessed.

'He *will* recover. I know it. And if there's any justice in this world someone will pay for all this bloodshed too.'

Teresa Lupo blinked, trying to take this in. She'd assumed Raffaela shared the opinion of the world at large: that Aldo Bracci, a man found with Bella's keys in his pocket, a man once accused of sleeping with his own sister, was responsible for the deaths in the *fornace*, and had met a deserved fate. There'd even been a letter in the local paper, *La Nuova*, suggesting Commissario Randazzo deserved a promotion, not suspension, for putting Bracci down like an animal that night.

Raffaela gently removed Teresa's hand from hers.

'I'm not a fool,' she said. 'I know why you asked for those things from the house. Leo confided in me. If he could speak now, he'd confirm that. I know why you're looking at Bella's belongings. You're not part of any official police investigation; you want the man who really did this to Leo. I want the man who did this to Leo *and* to my brother. And poor Bella.'

The dark, earnest eyes gazed at her, pleading.

'I tried to help Leo,' she continued, 'and I failed. I won't fail again. I promise. I owe him that.'

'This is not . . .' Teresa's thoughts were on Silvio Di Capua, who'd reported sick to the morgue in Rome, flown to Venice the night before, and was now organizing some private lab arrangements with a handful of specialist companies, places that could handle the material she wanted to throw at them. '. . . a conversation we should be having, Raffaela. There are risks.'

'What risks? They can fire you, and your police friends. What can they do to me?'

Teresa thought about some of the background material Nic and Gianni had managed to extract from the Questura's computers before getting thrown out. There were more than mere careers at stake. Hugo Massiter had all the makings of a big-time political animal. If he'd been Italian, he could have got himself a seat in parliament and looked very comfortable there. Massiter had connections, real criminal connections. And not with the old Italian guard either. He favoured the new mafia, men from the Balkans who rarely felt bound by any old-fashioned codes of honour.

'Tell me what you require,' Raffaela insisted. 'I don't need to know the details.'

It was, Teresa thought, worth a shot. It would drag Raffaela away from this quiet, bright room, where the air conditioning still didn't keep out the salty tang of the lagoon or the noise of the horns of the passing traffic. That would be a result in itself. The woman needed to remind herself there was a living world beyond these four white walls.

'Someone else was on the island that night,' Teresa said. 'Not Aldo

Bracci. Someone who had a reason to speak to Bella, we think. Someone . . .'

It was difficult to decide how far to go. She trusted this woman. She just didn't want to get her too deeply involved. It would be wrong to put ideas into her head, although they'd done that for themselves. Perhaps her objections were ridiculous.

'I can't say any more,' she admitted apologetically. 'If you could look again, that would help. Anything unusual. Anything at all.'

Raffaela nodded.

'Of course.'

Teresa glanced at the figure in the bed, wishing he'd do something. Cough. Snore. Any damn thing.

'He will recover,' Raffaela declared. 'I know it.'

'I'm sure you're right.'

A thought occurred to her.

'Did Bracci say anything that night? When he had hold of you?'

'Just drunken nonsense. I didn't understand any of it.'

Nonsense took on an importance of its own when it came from a man with a gun.

'What kind of thing?'

The dark eyes gazed at her, sad, resolute.

'I can't be sure but I thought he said, just once, "Where's the Englishman?" There were several Englishmen there that night. Massiter; some of his lawyers; some of the city's art people. It probably doesn't mean a thing.'

'Probably.'

How many Englishmen did Aldo Bracci know? Teresa wondered. He didn't move in art and legal circles. It had to be Massiter surely, not that a half-heard comment sounded much like evidence to her.

She took Raffaela's hands again and asked, 'This is just a wild guess, but do you think it's possible Hugo Massiter and Bella were having an affair?'

'No!' A sudden smile broke Raffaela's face. 'That's ridiculous!'

'Why? He looks like a ladies' man to me.'

'Bella! *Bella?*' She looked aghast at the idea. 'I mean this as no disrespect to her, but I think a man like him would set his sights a little higher. If the gossip's right he doesn't sleep with the poor. I don't think he needs to, does he?'

'You never saw any sign of it? He had an apartment next door.'

She waved away the notion with a firm hand.

'During the day only. Michele insisted on that. And Bella never went near the place. There were workmen around constantly. A man like Massiter would show some discretion, surely.'

It still wasn't good enough.

'Then somewhere else? He's got this boat, hasn't he?'

'So they say. I still – it feels *wrong*.'

Teresa glanced at the unconscious Leo Falcone.

'He always has some smart comment for these situations. Something that sends you back to look at what you had and try to see it in a new light. It rarely works. But then it doesn't need to that often.'

Raffaela was struggling to come up with something. This was, Teresa's instincts told her, a bad way to extract information from people.

'She left the island quite a lot during the day,' Raffaela suggested. 'I assumed she was visiting friends. Or shopping. Recently, Bella never seemed short of a little money.'

'Then she could have visited his boat?'

She looked doubtful.

'I suppose so. I'm sorry. This is all a little beyond me. Perhaps you're right. Is that what an affair would be like? Fitting in a few minutes in bed during the odd afternoon? It seems so feeble. So sad. But then I'm not an expert. Relationships . . .'

'Join the club,' Teresa agreed. 'Love is a mystery to me too.'

'But I thought you'd found it?'

She'd seen Teresa and Peroni several times in the hospital. Perhaps it showed.

'I think I have. I just don't know how I got there.'

Raffaela Arcangelo nodded. She liked this woman. A lot. That was all the more reason to get her away from Leo's bedside.

'*L'amore è cieco*,' Raffaela said softly, beautifully.

4

The idea that Leo Falcone had been seriously injured by anything more than bad luck offended Luca Zecchini's sense of fairness. To make matters both more complicated and more interesting, the state police inspector's two men had mentioned a name that pricked so many bad memories from the not-so-distant past it had ruined his appetite completely.

'You seem remarkably sure about the guilty party, if I may say so,' he observed when they'd finished. 'I heard Leo was the victim of an unfortunate accident. Sometimes these things are best left alone.'

'Until the next accident? And yes, we're sure.'

Costa looked tougher, more determined than Zecchini had expected from Falcone's description.

'I've followed this in the papers, Nic. They say the lunatic the commissario shot was responsible for those murders. That part of the case is closed. All they've got to do now is deal with their own. Are you telling me there's more? That Leo was shot deliberately somehow?'

'No,' Peroni conceded, and Zecchini found, to his shame, that a small part of him regretted the fact there would be no easy way to send them packing with their fantasies. 'It was an accident,' the big Roman cop continued. 'But killing Aldo Bracci wasn't. Randazzo was improvising there. Trying to do his paymaster a favour.'

They stared at Zecchini, expectantly.

'Even if you're correct, gentlemen,' Zecchini answered, 'what can I do? This is a case for the police. Not us. We don't intervene in each others' affairs. It would be unheard of. I couldn't contemplate that.'

'We're not asking you to cross any lines,' Costa said quickly. 'This falls squarely in your existing responsibilities. Art theft. Smuggling.'

Zecchini doubted that greatly.

'You know,' he said, 'perhaps you should be wondering what Leo would be doing in these circumstances? He's a practical man. He'd know when he was beaten. You're off duty for the time being. You don't have the right to question people, to investigate anyone, least of all someone of Massiter's standing. Also, I always found Leo to be reluctant, *meticulously* reluctant, to reach hard decisions in advance of hard evidence.'

Costa pushed away his plate. He'd hardly touched his food.

'We've asked ourselves that question. We'll have hard evidence. I don't want to mislead you, Luca. There are other lines of attack open to us. The Arcangeli case is far from closed. And the charges Massiter skipped away from five years ago.' He glanced at Peroni. 'Plus we may have some forensic too.'

Peroni didn't seem too happy with that last observation. Maybe the older man understood just how perilous it could be to play games like these. It was time, Zecchini realized, to come to the point.

'Then let me put it plainly. Hugo Massiter is a man of extreme influence and importance, and getting more so by the day from what I read in the papers. Once he becomes the owner of that island, he will be virtually untouchable. I live here. Everyone in the Veneto follows what happens in Venice because that's the place the money goes. Very large sums of money that bind the giver and the receiver in ways you people in Rome can't imagine. When that deal's done, Hugo Massiter will become something different: part of the establishment. You'd need written permission from the Quirinale Palace just to talk to him about a parking ticket after that. But now . . .'

'Now what?' Peroni asked.

'Now he's just a very powerful crook with some friends who ought to know better. If you screw around with him he will, surely, come looking for his revenge. I'm saying this from knowledge, not idle speculation. I've watched careers destroyed trying to take that man down. I'm not much inclined to invite the same fate.'

Costa's eyes, bright, alert, inquisitive, caught his.

'You know him personally?' he asked.

'No details. I'm just giving you the big picture. Massiter's a man who's wriggled out of our grasp so many times, then turned up smiling with not an *etto* of blame on him. You'd need a motive.'

'Got it,' Peroni interjected. 'This deal he had with the Arcangeli. He needed it closed down.'

'So why did he kill the brother and his wife?' Zecchini demanded. 'What's the point of that?'

'It's personal,' Costa said. 'He got Bella pregnant. She was putting pressure on him. He killed her, then set Uriel up for the blame.'

Zecchini was impressed.

'You can prove some of this?'

'We'll get there,' Costa insisted.

'You're going to have to do better than that! Suspicions fall off that man like dead skin. We've tried to screw Massiter for art smuggling in the past, many, many times. You people thought you had him for murder five years ago. Instead . . .'

It wasn't just about guilt. It was about proof, and the ability to see through the judicial process. They all knew that: police, Carabinieri, and the armies of lawyers who had, over the years, been assembled on both sides.

Costa was unmoved. Luca Zecchini tried hard to remember more of what Falcone had said about these two men: about their honesty, their disregard for their own persons when it came to a case that mattered. He was aware they were unlikely to be swayed by his opinion, but it was important to make his concerns known all the same.

'Leo's my friend as well,' he added. 'I don't think he'd want you to put your necks on the line for him. Not just on a hunch. Not like this.'

Costa peered at him. He seemed disappointed.

'Is that what you think this is? A hunch? Some personal vendetta on Leo's behalf?'

'It seems—'

'No! We've looked at our records, Maggiore. God knows what you've got on your side. Hugo Massiter is a cancer in Venice. He's everywhere: in the government; in the city; alongside all the organized crime that's coming in from across the Adriatic.'

They saw the expression on his face.

'You'd be amazed by the stuff we managed to dig up before they threw us out of the Questura. We called a friend in the DIA too,' Peroni said. 'We know about the Serbians and the Croats; how he plays them off against one another. And that's just the tip of the iceberg.'

Zecchini groaned. No one talked to the anti-Mafia people unless they were desperate.

'This isn't your field,' Zecchini warned them. 'Leave it alone.'

Costa gave him a sour glance.

'So you don't want him?'

Zecchini couldn't miss the taunting tone in his voice.

'I'd give my right arm to arraign that bastard on anything. But we've been there before and failed. That makes it harder to go back again, to get the lawyers to nod the case through unless it's more watertight than anything we've had before. And mark my words: what we've been able to throw at him in the past was good. He should have been in jail ten times over. Would have been too, if it weren't for his friends.'

'If the case is good enough,' Costa objected, 'even his friends will abandon him.'

'Really?' He couldn't believe they could be that naive. 'Well, here's something else I discovered. Every time we lose, he gets stronger. I'd need something special just to get my boss to read a file on Hugo Massiter right now. Once he's signed that contract, and all those millions of public money are behind him, all those grateful politicians in his debt . . .'

He looked at the wasted food. Zecchini had expected more of them. Maybe he'd be on the date with Gina after all that night. He wasn't going to stick his neck out over some amateur, unauthorized probe into someone who always managed to slip out of their grasp.

'And I regret to say I don't have a single piece of evidence to help you,' he added with a scowl. 'I wish I had. It's all spent. Useless.

There's nothing close that's fresh. If it was there, I'd be nailing this man tomorrow. Leo or no Leo.'

They had something to say, and it made them uncomfortable. A part of Luca Zecchini was beginning to wish he'd stayed in Milan.

Costa took a sip of his mineral water.

'You asked us what Leo would be doing in these circumstances. Let me tell you. He'd be turning on the heat. He'd be making moves that put Massiter in an uncomfortable position. A place where he was likely to make mistakes from which we could profit.'

Zecchini had seen enough of the police inspector's methods to understand this was probably an accurate interpretation. He still didn't see where it got them.

'Two lone cops on enforced vacation aren't going to be putting the heat on anyone,' he suggested.

Peroni smiled.

'No, Luca. But you could. You could pick up the phone, call the Questura in Venice and ask if they'd mind letting you talk to Commissario Randazzo for a while. Just to see if he knew anything about art theft.'

Zecchini snorted. It was ridiculous.

'I'm serious,' Peroni said, giving him a quick, icy look that Zecchini didn't like at all. 'We've taken a peek inside Randazzo's house in the Lido. It's empty. He's gone. The wife's gone. An expensive place for someone on his kind of salary. And all kinds of fancy stuff in there. Paintings. Ceramics. Silverware. We sort of found the door open—'

'No!' Zecchini waved his right hand in the big man's face, demanding silence. 'I don't want to hear this. Breaking into houses. Jesus . . . Are you insane?'

'You could just make a call,' Costa repeated. 'Ask for a simple interview. See how they respond. You could also get a search warrant for his place. You'll find something there. Look.'

Costa reached into his shoulder bag and took out a folder of photos. No more than ten. They showed antiques and paintings inside an airy, elegant house filled with pot plants and small palms, not the sort of place most police officers favoured.

'There are a couple of Serbian icons in there,' Costa observed. 'Good. Genuine, I think. Probably fifteenth century.'

'And this Randazzo would be stupid enough to keep illicit material around in his own home?' Zecchini asked.

Peroni let loose a low grunt of a laugh.

'Honest answer, Luca? Yes. As far as he's concerned they're just gifts. Trophies. From some rich and very influential Englishman. Maybe he didn't even know how deeply he was involved until it was too late. He saw shooting Bracci as a way out. A debt repaid. Massiter off the hook for the murders, and a clear way through for him to buy the island. Two birds with one stone. Neat, don't you think?'

Zecchini couldn't argue there. It was neat, if it was true.

'And maybe,' Costa added, 'Massiter liked to give him stolen objects just to cement the bond. So that, if Randazzo did turn awkward, he'd have some extra hold on him.'

These two were smart. Zecchini recalled a case where the Carabinieri had suspected Massiter of playing a very similar trick on a magistrate called in to investigate a minion of his caught bringing in contraband through Trieste.

'I could do these things,' he acknowledged. 'But why? What do I get in return?'

'Massiter,' Costa said quietly. 'We get you details of transactions, perhaps. Or storage locations. Routes. Vessels. An inventory of objects. We don't care who puts this man in jail. You. Us. The DIA if they like. He just has to go.'

'Like cancer,' Peroni echoed.

Zecchini laughed. They'd been trying to get that information for years. No one talked about Hugo Massiter. No one had the nerve.

'Now you're playing games with me,' he said, and looked at his cold food, wondering when he'd feel minded to sit at an outside table at Sergio's again. 'Let's just have a couple of beers, huh? Then say a few prayers for Leo. I don't think there's many doing that.'

They didn't budge. Luca Zecchini looked at this odd, stubborn pair and thought again about some of the stories Leo Falcone had told him. Stories he hadn't quite believed at the time. No one could be that unbending, that resolute about seeing an issue through to the bitter end.

Then it dawned on him.

'You've access from inside?' Zecchini murmured, amazed, and more than a little disconcerted.

Costa and Peroni glanced at each other and didn't say a word.

Luca Zecchini tried to think what that meant. Just the effort sent a shiver down his back. If the Carabinieri's meagre intelligence was right, Massiter now relied solely on the Balkans gangs for street-level muscle, men who were loyal to the end, did what they were told as long as the money kept coming, and never, to his knowledge, broke the code of loyalty and silence. It was inconceivable one of them would betray their *capo*. There was too much at stake. The punishment, if they were discovered, would be unimaginable. He'd seen the results of one gang punishment-killing in Florence. It would have turned the stomach of the toughest Italian mobster.

'You've put someone in?' he asked, incredulously, and got no pleasure at all in seeing the dismay on their faces.

'Jesus,' he murmured, then ordered three beers, a big one for himself. 'I hope to God you know what you're doing.'

Costa reached into his jeans pocket, pulled out a mobile phone, and said, 'We hope so too. Now will you make that call?'

5

The weather had lost its temper. It was a warm, bright evening, with a sweet salty breeze blowing in from the Adriatic. In Verona, Costa and Peroni were slowly working their way into the confidences of a small, specialist Carabinieri team, praying the scraps of information they owned would persuade Luca Zecchini and his colleagues to, first, order a search of Randazzo's house, and then pull in the man himself for questioning. In a small apartment in Castello, Teresa Lupo and her assistant Silvio Di Capua pored over the results of the first tests they'd run on the meagre material they possessed, scanning arcane reports and charts on Costa's computer, puzzled by the results coming in from the private labs they were using, both in Mestre and Rome, to try to extract some answers from the small amounts of debris and clothing they had. And in the Ospedale Civile the unconscious Leo Falcone, unaware of Raffaela Arcangelo by his bed, continued to dream, locked in a private world, part fantasy, part remembrance, a place he feared to leave, not knowing what would take its place.

'Leo,' said a voice from outside his world, a female voice, warm, attractive, one that possessed a name, though it escaped him at that moment, since he was the child-Leo, not his older self. 'Please.'

The mechanism on the wall whirred. The cuckoo's artificial bellows roared, the old chime tolled.

'I *need* you to live,' she pleaded. *'Leo . . .'*

As if it were a matter of choice. Both of them – the child and the man – knew nothing was quite that simple. In order to live he had to look, which was the last thing he wanted to do. Ever.

6

As Leo Falcone dreamed, some unconscious part of him listening to his inner voices and the caring tones of Raffaela Arcangelo penetrating from the world beyond, a sleek white speedboat crossed the wide canal between the hospital and San Michele, its varnished wooden prow aimed towards the open northern lagoon. The bright day was dying, the last of the sun turning the water into a lake of burnt gold. Hugo Massiter sat in the back of the vessel opening a bottle of vintage champagne with a familiar ease. Emily Deacon sat opposite on the soft calfskin seats, tired after a fruitless day spent on the private yacht moored by the Riva degli Schiavoni, trying to recall more details of her training back in Langley.

An Alitalia jet whined overhead, makings its descent to the airport that lurked at the distant water's edge, forever growing, eating away a little more of the wild marshland each year. She waited for the roar of its engines to subside then took the fluted glass, tasted the chill vintage Dom Perignon, telling herself that she would drink one glass and one glass only, then leaned back, letting her blonde hair reach into the slipstream created by the vessel's gathering speed, aware that Hugo couldn't take his eyes off her.

'Where are we going exactly? I'm used to getting directions.'

'You can leave the directions to me. We're going to the Locanda Cipriani. Torcello. You've never been?'

She'd heard of the place. Hemingway had written much of *Across the River and Into the Trees* there, in between duck hunts and drinking sessions. She'd read the book as a teenager, while going through the Hemingway phase. It was the unlikely story of a romance between a dying middle-aged American colonel, scarred by the war, and a young, beautiful Italian countess. A love that was returned. She hadn't needed to dip into a biography to understand that Hemingway had been telling his own story, recounting the growing fears and disappointments of age, trying to convince himself they could be balanced, if not countered entirely, by the presence of a teenager who was willing to have sex with him in a gondola at night. It was a lecherous old man's fantasy, and the tragedy was that Hemingway hoped in vain to conceal that fact from everyone, most of all himself.

'Tell me about Laura Conti,' she said. Massiter had spent the afternoon away from the yacht, locked in a series of seemingly endless meetings with lawyers, advisers and the Arcangeli brothers. This was the first real opportunity she'd had to start pushing some questions his way. 'I'm the curious type.'

Hugo raised his glass.

'And I'm the indiscreet one, as I told you. Except . . .' He glanced towards the low island in the distance and then at his watch. 'Dinner at the Locanda. It's been such a long time. And now there's so much to celebrate.'

'Except what?'

His smile fell for a second. He stared at her with a sudden, brutish frankness.

'Intimacies require intimacy. I'm no fool, Emily.'

She placed the glass, two-thirds full, on the polished walnut table that sat between them. Massiter's temporary home had been a place of some interest for her. The crew were mainly Croatian men, while the women who did the waiting and cleaning were Filipino. There was a small, locked office on the lowest floor, down a narrow set of stairs, beneath the eight cabins, the largest of which, Massiter's, occupied the prow. The vessel was, he said, rented, a necessary evil between selling his last apartment on the Grand Canal to raise funds for the Isola degli Arcangeli project and moving into his new home there. He wasn't happy in the yacht, though its opaque smoked windows kept out the curious glances of the tourists on the broad and busy waterfront leading from the Doge's Palace to the Arsenale. There had to be a reason he would have chosen a home like this, and that, surely, lay in the small office. She recalled the locked room in the apartment he had built for himself in the palace on the island. He had a fondness for small, dark places in which to hide things. It was simply a question of penetrating them.

'I never thought you were. I told you last night. Nic and I had a fight. I needed somewhere to stay, Hugo. Don't read more into it than that.'

She thought about Nic, who by now should have cleared out of his little apartment. He and Peroni had found some expensive temporary accommodation, two bedrooms, one little kitchen, not far away in one of the narrow streets in working-class Castello, squeezed between the Via Garibaldi and the Biennale gardens. There would be no free police apartment in Venice again. No secret moments in the tiny bed squeezed between the door and the window that gave out onto a pink-washed street criss-crossed with washing lines. And instead, what? She'd seen the expression on his face when he left. It had been grim and determined and single-minded. Nic needed to bring Massiter to justice, for Leo's sake. There was some debt lurking there, demanding repayment. Without that, she wondered, how he could ever be easy with himself?

'People who need somewhere to stay generally take their custom to hotels. You came to me. Why?'

She was uncertain how to handle him. Hugo Massiter was a mix of contradictions: wily in the ways of the world, yet almost innocent when it came to anything that touched his ego.

'I thought that was what you wanted. I was curious to see if I was right.'

He was watching her avidly, judging, avaricious too.

'Does he know you're with me?'

'No.'

She reached for the glass and drained it in two quick gulps, not even fighting the temptation. He was there with a refill the moment it left her lips. It was all a question of confidence. That was what the men in Langley said. A matter of building trust, of lies and skilled deceit.

'Is it important?' she asked. 'I knew I wasn't going to get the door slammed in my face. Or did you really think I could be your architect?'

This amused him.

'Why not? If it doesn't work, I'll find someone else. I've got the money now and money solves everything. Or at least I *will* have the money once I sign with the Arcangeli. After that . . . the island's perfect, just the thing I need to get me back on my feet.'

She wondered about the details of the deal. They could be important.

'Were you really that close to the edge?'

'Damn right,' he moaned. 'More than anyone knows. I still am until I have the Arcangeli's signature on the contract. Though I don't expect that to be a problem now. Tomorrow night. Six o'clock. It's done. A little ceremony in that beautiful dining room of theirs. Which will be *my* dining room afterwards.'

This puzzled her.

'I thought the Arcangeli were going to keep part of the house and you'd live in the apartment.'

He snorted.

'You didn't really believe that, did you? Does the master live in the servants' accommodation? I think not. There are a few changes to the contract that Michele has yet to comprehend. But he will. When I buy that island it's all mine. No strings. No caveats. I can do what I like. A hotel. An apartment block. Some retail.'

'And the Arcangeli?'

He looked at her, disappointed.

'They'll have capital. They need this deal badly. Their debts are now impossible to ignore.'

Nic had told her exactly what he'd come to see as the Arcangeli's real concern. They wanted a second chance to continue to make glass, a way to keep their art.

'But their livelihood. A working foundry, where they feel they belong. I thought that was important to them.'

'It's important to Michele. Uriel never gave a damn. Gabriele does as he's told. The sister's neither here nor there. They can take the cash. Open a bar. Dream their dreams. Do what the hell they like. Provided . . .'

He licked his lips. There were still some doubts here.

'Provided what?'

'Nothing you need worry about,' he replied curtly. 'There's a little . . . tidying necessary before tomorrow night. But I'm a tidy man. I can deal with that. No lawyer can throw a spanner in the works. It was messier than I'd expected, but there you go.'

'And then?'

He grinned, a broad, coarse gesture. This new expression changed his face, made his features become exaggerated, ugly.

'Then I prosper! More than ever. The auction business is as flat as this damn lagoon, but property . . . That island's worth ten times what I'm paying them. I can get any number of backers to redevelop it just by picking up the phone. So could the Arcangeli if they hadn't been so arrogant. There's only one industry in Venice now and that's cramming as many gullible tourists into the streets and fleecing them blind. No one wants glass. No one wants art, not real art anyway. The Arcangeli never learned that lesson. They tried to fool themselves it was different for them. It isn't.'

'They wanted to keep a little pride in themselves,' she objected.

'That's the first thing that goes out of the window,' he retorted. 'The leisure industry' – Massiter pulled a pained face as he pronounced the word in the American style . . . *lee*-sure – 'has no place for self-worth. It's money and money alone. Bring 'em in, send 'em home poorer, then get some more mugs to take their place.'

He waved a hand back at the city, then poured himself another glass of wine and relaxed back onto the leather seat, enjoying the lilting resonance of his own voice.

'That's all Venice has left these days. This isn't a real place any more. It's just a trickledown town, somewhere people are either dropping crumbs or picking them up. The young know it, which is why they're fleeing to the mainland. Can you blame them? Who wants to live in a museum? In twenty years there'll scarcely be a real Venetian left. The smart ones will have gone to earn good money elsewhere. The trash will be working in some vacuum-cleaner factory in Mestre, glad they own a car and can bring home the shopping in that instead of lugging it through the streets. Venice is just an old dead whore that manages to fetch a price on what's left of her looks. Anyone who forgets that is just an idiot romantic. And romantics lose perspective in the end. It can cost them everything.'

He called to the man in the white uniform working the wheel in the open cabin up front.

'No speeding, Dimitri. I think we'll make a leisurely time of it across the lagoon.'

The roar of the engine dimmed to a steady drone. Hugo flicked a switch by the side of the drinks cabinet. A spotless canvas roof began to unfurl itself from beneath the upper deck, stretching along the runners of the main cabin, hiding them from the burnished sky. After a second or two, all Emily could see was the grey line of the lagoon moving steadily past the narrow side windows, the occasional floating gull, and the nets of the few fishermen still working the waters.

He came over and sat next to her, then, in a swift, earnest gesture, kissed the naked skin of her shoulder. She thought of Hemingway's ghost, dreaming about finding an escape from the steady progression of the years with a young girl, locked together in a gondola rocking on the greasy lagoon waves.

'The question of intimacy will not go away,' Hugo murmured in her ear, his hand playing gently across her left breast.

The soft leather seats, the lapping of the lagoon against the hull – she fought to chase the images of what might be from her mind.

Emily shuffled herself away from his grasp, hung her head, trying to make sure she got this right, because Hugo Massiter was no fool.

'Not yet,' she murmured. 'I'm not ready, Hugo. I'm sorry.'

'When?' he asked, a brute flatness in his voice.

'What is this?' she snapped. 'Are we making appointments?'

'You came to me,' he said again.

'Perhaps you should turn the boat round. I need some space.'

'Space.'

He went back to the other side of the cabin, flicked the switch, waited for the canvas roof to draw back into the hull then barked at the boatman in a rattle of indecipherable Venetian dialect.

The boat picked up speed, the nose jerked skywards again.

'Of course,' he murmured.

A flicker of alarm sounded in her head. Something was wrong. Maybe she was a bad actor. Maybe . . .

His phone rang. Massiter went forward to the open wheelhouse, out of earshot.

Emily tried to picture herself in the training room at Langley. They'd had that all-important conversation just a couple of times, handled it briefly, professionally, not quite looking one another in the eye. Hoping, she understood, the question would never come to be asked in anger. How far would you go to get something vital, something you, or one close to you, desperately needed? Would you torture a man to stop a bomb blowing up in a school? Would you murder someone to keep a hostage from dying?

There were no easy answers, except when it came to personal matters. If it had a chance of success, would you hand over something that couldn't hurt, not physically, something most of us gave away for free anyway, sometimes to people we never loved, to strangers even?

They all said yes to that one. It seemed selfish, somehow, to countenance any other outcome.

She thought of Falcone, of Nic, Peroni and Teresa, and the conversation the four of them had had that night on the terrace of the hospital, when all their doubts began to solidify into something that promised to turn into hard fact. It seemed easy then to look each other in the eye and swear they'd not let the Venetians bury this particular case. Not when Leo Falcone lay somewhere between life and death in a bright white room overlooking the lagoon, in a place she could now see in the distance, rising and falling with the swell of the waves.

Massiter's low voice was indecipherable. In another lifetime she'd have owned the devices that could have penetrated the phone's electronic heart, recorded every whispered word he said. Now there was nothing but her own personal talents. Nothing beyond her fingertips.

He finished the call and came back to the cabin to sit across from her. She hadn't heard a word.

'You never stop, do you?' she commented.

'Never slow down, never grow old. You must allow me the odd fantasy.'

He looked grey and deadly serious at that moment.

'I was,' he added, 'doing a little of what our builder friends call "making good".'

The cold eyes roved over her.

'Tidiness is a virtue, Emily. And I like to think of myself as a virtuous man.'

7

They entered Randazzo's house at nine o'clock the following morning. It was in a quiet, shady residential street behind Gran Viale, the main shopping drag of the Lido, which ran from the vaporetto stop in a long straight line to the other side of the narrow island and the beaches, stretching out in front of the white whale-like colossus of the Grand Hotel des Bains. It was a weekday. Only a trickle of youngsters were heading for the sea, towels and swimming costumes in their hands. Overhead buzzed the occasional small plane, on the final approach to the little general aviation airport that sat at the northern tip of the Lido.

Luca Zecchini, a man with an eye for property, reckoned the place, a small mansion in what was known on the Lido as 'liberty style', all curlicues, outdoor steps and fancy windows, was worth a good million euros or more. Nic Costa didn't feel moved to argue. They needed some luck. It was now nine thirty in the morning. He'd heard nothing of moment from Teresa Lupo, nothing at all from Emily, and only received the briefest of messages from the hospital to say that Falcone's condition was unchanged. The one hard piece of news he had received came from Raffaela Arcangelo, via Teresa. The legal complications of the contract for the sale to Massiter had been resolved. There would be a brief signing ceremony that evening at six. Or so Hugo Massiter hoped.

The previous afternoon Zecchini and his men had worked hard to squeeze a warrant out of a Verona magistrate, one chosen for his discretion, since no one wanted details of the planned raid leaked. If they were lucky, the objects in Randazzo's home would prove interesting enough for Zecchini to demand an interview with the commissario, who was being kept discreetly out of view by the Venice Questura. From that point on they could, he hoped, begin to put the squeeze on Massiter. If Teresa came up with something, all the better. Costa's theory was that, once in custody on one charge, it would be easier to instigate a rolling set of investigations against Massiter – over the Arcangeli deaths and, if he could just find the right breakthrough, in connection with the stalled investigation involving Daniel Forster and Laura Conti too. Maybe they wouldn't get the personal pleasure of sending the man down, but once the momentum was there it would, surely, be impossible for Massiter to wriggle off the line.

If . . . they could assemble enough material to warrant an arrest before Massiter claimed ownership of the island. Once the Arcangeli's names were on that piece of paper, they would not simply be hunting one man, they'd be challenging the entire hierarchy of the city, men who'd staked their reputations on clinching a deal to secure the future of the Isola degli Arcangeli – and sweep its recent murky financial past under the carpet. That would make everything so much harder, perhaps too hard for a man like Luca Zecchini, who'd already stuck his neck out more than Costa had expected. Power mattered in Venice. Costa understood that, and so, too, did Zecchini. As the major said, every failed attempt to tackle Massiter seemed to leave the Englishman more in control than before. They had little time to start the ball rolling, and few clear ideas on where Massiter's weak point might emerge.

There were now eight Carabinieri officers in the grey, unmarked van, all armed, all good men, Costa thought. Zecchini had only assembled the people he trusted most. They'd committed themselves to Venice for the entire day, and they didn't intend to go home empty-handed.

Hunched on the seat opposite Costa and Peroni, Zecchini eyed them.

'Decision time, gentlemen,' he said. 'There's still room to get out of this. We could just walk away.'

'Leave us the warrant then,' Costa replied immediately. 'Whatever happens we're going in.'

Zecchini shrugged his shoulders.

'I hope Leo appreciates this one day.' He patted the man next to him on the shoulder. '*Avanti!*'

It was a brisk, professional operation. In the space of four minutes they ascertained the house was empty, removed the front door, and were inside, wandering through the big, airy rooms, admiring a residence that was surely beyond the scope of most senior police officers. Randazzo liked paintings. That surprised Nic Costa, though he couldn't help but wonder if it were really his wife's tastes they were seeing here in the selection of nineteenth and early twentieth century canvases, a handful of old religious icons, and set upon set of antique Japanese prints.

Zecchini walked around examining what was there with a professional eye, taking photos, referring from time to time to some visual database he kept on a little palmtop computer in his jacket pocket. He didn't say a thing. He didn't look happy. Peroni was shooting Costa concerned glances. This wasn't their only opening, but it was, the two men had assumed, their best.

'Luca,' Costa said when they'd been around every room on the ground floor, with the Carabinieri man shaking his head constantly. 'What have we got?'

'I don't know,' he muttered. 'Maybe something. Maybe not. If I'm going to pull this guy in today, I need something positive. I can't just do it on suspicion. Even if this is illegal, it's minor stuff, the kind of things you'd buy from an antique fair. Nothing terribly valuable. If we try to nail the bastard on this alone he'll just feign ignorance. Say he bought it at some sale somewhere. It's going to be hard to prove otherwise.'

Costa went over in his mind what he and Peroni had done when they'd let themselves into the house two days before. They'd looked at paintings mainly; they were what Costa knew.

'What about the icons?' he asked. 'Don't you think they're Serbian?'

'Sure. But what does that tell us? Without positive identification, without proof of provenance, all we've got are suspicions. There's nothing here that pushes any buttons. When I get back to Verona, maybe. But that's going to take time. Don't get me wrong. I can work on the paintings. I just . . .'

He was trying to soften the blow.

'I can't give you anything straight away. Sorry.'

Peroni was scratching his head.

'It wasn't just paintings,' he objected. 'That may be all you saw, Nic. But there was more. Weird stuff.'

Plenty of weird stuff, Costa thought, when he looked at the shelves: oriental ceramics, cloisonné vases, screens. Randazzo's home was a mishmash of styles, regions and eras that denoted a couple of uncertain tastes.

'The weirdest,' Peroni said, 'was in there.'

He was pointing to a small glass cabinet hidden in a corner near the fireplace, something Costa had never noticed.

Peroni walked over, opened the doors and returned with a small, very old statue. A squat, grinning figure in worn stone, seated cross-legged with a beaded necklace and an expression halfway between a Buddha and a satyr.

'It sort of stuck in my mind,' Peroni explained, pointing to the huge erection which rose between the creature's legs.

Luca Zecchini took the statue from him, turning it in his hands. He gave it back to Peroni, pulled the palmtop out of his pocket and began to punch the buttons. In just a couple of seconds he stopped, grinned at both of them, then turned the little screen round for them to see. It was a photo of something that looked very like Randazzo's carving.

'Babylonian,' he said, in a tone that brooked no arguments. 'Seen a few like this since Iraq fell.'

'It's the one in the picture?' Peroni asked.

'No. But it's close enough.'

'That's valuable?'

Zecchini nodded.

'In a roundabout way. These things are what passes for hard currency in the drugs trade. We're doing pretty well working on cross-border money laundering. It's not easy to move big amounts of cash around the world any more. You get asked awkward questions when you try to bank it.'

Costa had read about the system. 'So you ship valuable antiques instead,' he said. 'They're easier to smuggle. And when they get to the other end someone turns them into money and pays off the debt.'

'Exactly,' Zecchini agreed, impressed by Costa's knowledge. 'These things were household gods. Every worthwhile specimen was either in a private collection or Iraq's museums. There's so much stuff still leaking out of Baghdad, all of it through criminal channels, we're under strict instructions to report every last piece we come across.'

One of the little planes interrupted the conversation, buzzing low overhead. They had to wait for it to go away before anyone could speak.

'So it's good?' Peroni asked in the end.

Zecchini pulled out his mobile phone.

'It's a start. Commissario Randazzo and I need to meet. Are you coming along?'

Costa shook his head, and glanced at his partner.

'Gianni, you go. I've something to do.'

Peroni didn't look too pleased.

'Anyone I know? I don't like being kept in the dark.'

'Just a couple of ghosts,' Costa said, nodding towards the window and the blue sky beyond. 'And maybe not even that.'

8

While the Carabinieri were going through Commissario Randazzo's personal belongings, in a mansion too big for a policeman, Emily Deacon was sitting on the deck of Hugo Massiter's yacht across the water, picking at the remains of a late breakfast, shielded from the gaze of the tourists on the waterfront behind thick, smoked glass. She had waited for this opportunity. Massiter had left the vessel to visit his private banker in San Marco. From there he would go directly to an afternoon meeting with the Arcangeli at his lawyers in Dorsoduro. He had hinted, heavily, that she would be welcome at that final confrontation. Perhaps there were structural details to be negotiated. Perhaps he simply craved an audience. It was an invitation she had left open. There was work to do. The Croatian crew seemed to have departed en masse too. Now it was just her and the three Filipino women who cleaned and cooked and served, then retired to their quarters to await orders.

Evidence.

That was what Nic needed and needed desperately. In any form she could find.

She stood up, brushed the crumbs of the morning *cornetto* off her T-shirt, smoothed down her jeans, then rang for one of the Filipinos to come and clear up.

It was the youngest who arrived from the galley, dressed in white, dark hair tied back in a bun. A girl who looked no more than eighteen. Emily watched her with the unconcerned disdain she imagined was expected in the circumstances.

'What's your name?' she asked in Italian.

The girl's eyes flickered, fearful. Emily repeated the question in English.

'Flora,' she replied, still nervous.

'It doesn't matter that you don't speak Italian?'

'Supposed to.'

She didn't like talking. Massiter preferred his female servants to keep quiet.

'Says who?'

She glanced backwards, to where the men would normally be.

'Them.'

Emily wondered what the Croatians were like when they were on their own with these women. It wasn't hard to guess.

'I could teach you some words. If you like.'

'Not right.'

She knew her place. And this was, Emily realized, the wrong tack, not that she relished the only alternative.

'Mr Massiter's not happy with the state of his office,' she said severely.

The girl looked shocked.

'I cleaned it! Last night!'

'I don't care. He's not happy. If he fires you . . .'

Flora put down the plates. She was trembling so much she was close to dropping them.

'You won't get home, will you?' Emily continued. 'You'd just be destitute out there. No money. No friends. What happens to girls like that, do you think, Flora? Can you imagine?'

'I . . . keep trying.'

She was close to tears. Emily hated this.

'Come with me,' she ordered. 'Maybe we can get you a second chance.'

They went downstairs, three short flights, until they came to the secure metal door of Massiter's lair.

'Well?' she asked, crossly.

Flora fumbled with the bunch of keys on her belt, found the right one in the end, and opened the lock. Emily marched in, straight to the desk by the small porthole window, where a big notebook computer sat, then she swept a finger across the table, which was spotless, waved her hand in Flora's face and yelled, 'See this?'

'I see noth—'

'Not good enough. None of this is good enough. *You're* not good enough. I'm going to be in here for fifteen minutes. I'm going to make this place dirty in ways you couldn't even begin to guess. Then when I go, you come back in. You clean up. You do it properly. If I like what I see I say nothing to Mr Massiter. Nothing to the Croatians. It's forgotten. If not . . .'

Flora was in tears. Emily felt awful but knew she couldn't let go now. You did what you had to.

'Out!' she barked, and slammed the metal door behind the girl as she fled.

The computer was an expensive one with a wide screen, shut down, tethered to the desk with a security cable. She couldn't imagine Massiter letting anyone near it.

She took out the little plug-in memory pod she'd kept with her from her days in the FBI, pushed it into the slot, then turned on the machine, praying for an easy break. Smart people encrypted their entire PCs. Smart people were in the minority. The FBI pod was something any script kiddie hacker could run up himself for a few dollars of flash memory and a couple of downloads from the net. On a machine that hadn't been specifically set up to prevent its operation, the thing convinced the computer to boot from its operating system, not the normal one. Then it scanned every last directory on the hard drive and presented them naked to the intruder.

This was the kind of geek stuff they'd trained her in. There was nothing elegant involved, just command lines and obscure instructions, techspeak she'd committed to memory.

Massiter's notebook was just as she'd expected: secure as long as it remained in control, defenceless the moment she managed to boot it from her little device. Emily watched the familiar routine happen just as it should, watched her little pod take control. Then she scanned the directories, found the one Massiter had created for his personal account, copied the contents of the documents folder, before scouring the drive for his e-mail files, and copying them.

Finally she looked up the cache on his internet browser, caught all the temporary files, and captured them too. In under two minutes she had, she thought, recovered every possible piece of information relating to Massiter's documents, messages and the places he'd visited online. In the US she'd have committed several federal offences already, not that the FBI would have minded too much in the circumstances. In Italy . . . she didn't even want to think about the legal implications. There wasn't time. Nic needed help.

Reminding herself how that fact kept haunting her, she took the pod out of the notebook, pocketed it, shut the machine down, and spread a few stray documents around the place.

It was the perfect hack. Undetectable and comprehensive, a textbook piece of work.

Then she went back upstairs, found Flora and said, 'Clean it.'

She followed the trembling girl as she rushed into the office, watched her work feverishly clearing up the junk Emily had scattered around the place, tidy what she could in a room that was as clean as anyone could reasonably expect.

'Enough,' Emily declared when Flora had finished, wishing she could stop hating herself for this charade. 'Now lock this place up. Don't ever let me find it in this state again. Then we never say a word about this. Not to anyone. Understood?'

Flora nodded, scared witless, eyes glassy and damp.

'It's OK?'

'Yes. It's OK. Everything's OK. I'll tell him you've been extra good this morning. Don't worry about anything. Just—'

You couldn't let the act slip. They hammered that into your head at every last opportunity.

'Just keep this a secret between the two of us. Unless you want to be out on the street.'

When they went back upstairs the Croatians were still nowhere to be seen. Tidying up, Massiter had said. She could only guess at what he meant.

Evidence.

You collected what you could. You heaped it up in one big, big pile.

And you hoped to God some small piece would give you what you want.

She called Teresa and arranged to meet her for a coffee in the place they knew in the Ramo Pescaria, a little alley that led from this glossily artificial tourist world into a semblance of real Italy in the back streets of Castello. Then she walked into Massiter's private cabin: a long room, with a dining table and chairs, a TV set, an expensive hi-fi system and a drinks cabinet. His bedroom was next to it, occupying a good ten-metre length of the starboard side of the vessel. She walked in. Flora had been in here already. Fresh orchids stood in vases on each side of the king-size bed, which was now made up with clean white sheets, pressed perfectly, folded tightly to the divan.

Emily closed the door behind her, locked it, then tore off the sheets as quickly as she could, throwing them to the floor, fighting to get down to the mattress.

They were there, beneath the final slipcover, as she'd expected. It was standard training to look for them in any investigation of a personal nature. Dark, dried stains, rings and rings of them, halfway up the mattress, always a little to one side because something in the way human beings mated meant they happened this way.

She took a small penknife out of her pocket, knelt on the mattress, and, with great care, worked the blade around each dried puddle of human secretion. It wasn't just semen. They taught them that in Langley. There was, in most cases, vaginal fluid too, and with the magic of DNA that could be all the lucky breaks you needed rolled into one, a fixed, unshakable line that led back to the women who'd been here. Every rape case she'd worked on had examined this possibility. There was good reason to think it could help them now too.

There were sixteen in all, each a small circle of fabric which she stashed in a supermarket carrier bag. She left the fainter ones. It seemed inconceivable they'd have sufficient material left in their indistinct stains to make them usable in time. Then she took one last look at the mattress and heaved it over, so the 'wrong' side, which was clean and free of stains, was uppermost, put the slipcover back on, and lazily made the bed. That was another order she could bark at Flora on the way out. By the time Massiter discovered the damage – if he ever did – it would be unimportant anyway.

Ten minutes later, over a strong double macchiato, she passed the bag to Teresa Lupo, who looked at her, worried, short for words. Emily couldn't remember a time when the two of them had been like this, uneasy in one another's company, unable to make even a scrap of small talk.

She handed over the memory pod.

'Tell the Carabinieri I didn't have chance to look at them but I don't think Massiter's smart enough to have encrypted anything. He doesn't seem that sophisticated when it comes to computers. Also I suspect he feels he's inviolate when he's in that little room of his. I'll take another look around later.'

She checked herself. Over-confidence was a habitual mistake in the business she was trying to relearn. In truth, Hugo Massiter seemed to regard himself as inviolate most of the time.

'Will do.' Teresa nodded. 'Are you OK?'

'Fine. And you? Any news from Nic?'

'They're getting somewhere, I think. He sounded positive. He's leaving the Carabinieri to it for a while. Chasing something else.'

'That's good.' She glanced at the carrier bag. 'Some of that's old. Do you think we might have Bella there?'

'We've got good lab facilities. Silvio found them. Costing a fortune but this is the private sector. I can get results faster than I could back home. It's amazing what money can do.'

'It surely is.'

The thought had been nagging her all along.

'And you've DNA for Bella?'

Teresa nodded vigorously. 'From the house. It's unmistakable.'

'And anything else? If there were other women?'

She shrugged.

'It would be handy to have a database of every last woman of screwable age in Venice, of course. That would speed things up no end. But for now I guess we'll just have to try to factor them out. It would only tell us about his habits, of course. Bella's the only other sample we've got.'

Emily Deacon thought about this. Actions had consequences. None of them knew what they would be at that moment. She'd been taught to think ahead, to put markers in place that could be recovered later, used to prove who you were, what you'd done.

She took a clean tissue out of her pocket, put it to her mouth and carefully deposited a ball of saliva in it. Then she held the tissue out in front of her.

'Best give me an evidence bag. Then you can factor out that.'

9

The tourists rarely stumbled on San Francisco della Vigna. The church lay in a small campo close by the Celestia vaporetto stop, just a couple of minutes away from the hospital. But even Gianfranco Randazzo, who had never set foot in the place, and regarded this backwater of Castello as a *quartiere* well beneath his standing, had been surprised by what lay behind Palladio's severe white frontage. This was a Franciscan monastery still, more than five hundred years after its foundation. Beyond the gloomy interior, with its Lombardo sculpture cycle and canvases by Veronese and Bellini, lay a connected pair of quiet cloisters formed by two storeys of cells and offices. It was a community which seemed to come from another world, one untouched by the pressures of modern life. Doves flitted through the bars of shade made by the angular lines of columns. Flowers grew around the statue of St Francis that stood in the sun at the centre of the first cloister, opposite the cell they'd allocated him. Here, during the brief moments he was alone in the tiny bare room or seated in the shade of the colonnades, was a kind of peace, some guarantee of anonymity. The Questura had left him with no choice in the matter anyway. Someone had been pulling strings to keep him out of the way. He would remain in San Francisco della Vigna until the internal investigation, which he'd been promised would deliver nothing more than an admonition, was complete.

The worst part was the company. Two Questura jokers, Lavazzi and Malipiero, men he'd learned to despise over the years for their laziness and casual insolence, were deputed to be close by most of the time during the day, and were replaced by a changing cycle of equally dull drones each evening. Now he was unable to pull rank, their efforts at insubordination took new directions. Randazzo had grown tired of their vicious personal cracks after just a couple of hours. The prospect of a long stay in the monastery with these two was inconceivable. He would, before long, go over their heads and demand some new companions. But not just yet, because Gianfranco Randazzo had, in his days inside the monastery, failed to answer satisfactorily a question that had been haunting him since he'd been forced into this temporary exile. Were this duo there to keep him safe from the outside world? Or did the miserable pair really see themselves as jailers, ordered to keep close to him in case Randazzo felt like fleeing?

The last was ridiculous. Randazzo was aware of how many important men, Massiter above all, he had served that night in the palazzo. It was inconceivable they wouldn't repay the favour. Venice ran on rules, private, unwritten rules, but rigid ones nevertheless. Without them the place would simply descend into chaos. And one rule was inviolate. Debts were always repaid in the end.

Malipiero had just spent an hour or more complaining about the fact that the Franciscans didn't have a single TV set in the place.

Randazzo looked at him and asked, 'Why don't you try reading?'

'Huh!'

He sounded as if the idea was poisonous. Randazzo had managed to get through a couple of books in his time in the cell. Dry volumes on some arcane aspects of Italian law he'd made a note to read once they told him what was happening. The books made him feel better, containing some awkward truths he could throw back at a few city men should they need reminding of what he was owed. This entire episode was a necessary diversion in his career. He appreciated that. It didn't mean he couldn't profit from the experience.

'Books can help you get on,' he added.

'Helped you a lot,' Lavazzi sneered.

The two men looked remarkably alike, they could have been brothers. Both were around thirty-five, a little on the short side, running to fat, their corpulent frames squeezed inside cheap dark blue suits. They were the kind of men who ruined a decent commissario's statistics, until he turned on them and kicked them back out on the streets with the orders to get some work done. Then the petty crooks kept coming through the door, guilty and innocent, until Lavazzi and Malipiero got bored again and returned to drifting from bar to bar, bumming beers and panini.

'Why don't you two just go for a walk?' Randazzo suggested. 'It's stupid you being here all the time.'

'Those Bracci brothers are very pissed off,' Lavazzi replied. 'You blew away their old man in front of all those people. Can you blame them?'

Randazzo felt his temper begin to flare.

'I put down an animal who'd taken a woman hostage and was waving a weapon about. It was prudent. If I'd done nothing who knows what would have happened?'

Malipiero waved a sweaty palm at him.

'Don't want to hear. Don't want to know. This is not for us to judge. We've just been told to stick with you and that's what we do. I can't believe a man of your rank would suggest we disobey orders.'

'Incredible,' Lavazzi replied, shaking his head. 'Makes you wonder what the world's coming to. No discipline. That's the problem.'

'This is boring—' Randazzo began.

'*You're telling me!*' Lavazzi yelled.

The face of a monk, bald, tanned, friendly, with the cowl around his neck, appeared at the open window. The man put a single finger to his lips and went, 'Ssshhhh . . .'

Lavazzi waited for him to disappear then swore quietly, stared at Randazzo and said, 'We're all fucking bored. OK? Saying it just makes things worse. Besides . . .'

He looked at his watch. It was getting close to midday. Lunch-time. These two never missed the opportunity to stuff their faces, usually for free, Randazzo guessed. Their duty hadn't stopped them disappearing for an hour around this time every day, coming back with a rosy glow and some pasta sauce on their chops. All Gianfranco Randazzo had to eat was the plain, dull fare of the monks.

'We could go out for lunch,' the commissario suggested.

'You paying?' Malipiero asked immediately.

'If you like,' Randazzo replied. It would be worth it. Also, if he was picking up the bill he could order them to sit at another table and get some privacy for himself.

The two men glanced at each other. Randazzo's spirits rose. A good meal, a couple of glasses of wine . . . There was a little restaurant he knew in the Campo Arsenale, home cooking in the shadow of the great golden gateway, close to the four lions every Venetian knew had been looted from Athens in one of the republic's raiding adventures way back when. It was hard to walk anywhere in Venice without seeing something that had been purloined over the centuries. The city took what it wanted, when it wanted. Randazzo had learned that lesson as a boy.

He could see the greed glinting in the men's faces. A part of him wished he could persuade the pair to turn their backs on a visit from Chieko too, though he wondered what the rules of the monastery would be about allowing women into this bright little oasis nestling near the gasworks in Castello. That could be . . . entrancing if it worked.

Then he remembered Massiter crowing about her in that stupid apartment of his inside the glass palace and the way he'd ignored her ever since.

'Well?' he growled. 'I don't have all day.'

'Really?' Lavazzi laughed. 'Wait there. I'll make a call and check. Maybe' – he glanced at his partner, with an expression Randazzo didn't understand – 'it's not such a bad idea after all.'

Malipiero was quiet when his partner was gone. He was, Randazzo judged, the lesser of the pair.

'Who do you two keep calling all the time?' Randazzo demanded, cross for no real reason, wishing his temper would stay in place for once. 'Girlfriends? Boyfriends? Those are Questura phones. I get to see the bills when they come in. If you're running up private business on my account you'll get to know about it.'

Malipiero was staring at his fat, grubby hands and whistling some stupid pop tune that was on the radio all the time. That was, Randazzo thought, the closest he could get to entertainment.

He stopped whistling, glowered at Randazzo, and said, 'You know, I wish you'd make up your mind. Are you the upstanding honest guy here, or just like the rest of us? It gets confusing for simpletons like me.'

'Don't be so fucking impertinent!' Randazzo yelled.

The face came back to the window, offended this time, as close to cross as a monk could get.

'Gentlemen,' the man said, 'if you don't behave correctly here I shall have to ask you to leave. We are accommodating. We are, however, only human.'

'Yeah, yeah, yeah,' Malipiero grumbled, waving him down. 'Go say a prayer or something. We'll leave a little change in the box by the door.'

The monk disappeared, a worldly epithet echoing gently in his wake.

'You just leave one long line of satisfied customers everywhere you go,' Randazzo observed.

The whistling began again until a grinning Lavazzi returned, carrying something in a plastic bag.

'You're on,' he said. 'We're clear to go out for two hours. Then it's back in your cell, Commissario. Hope you brought plenty of money with you.'

'Enough,' Randazzo murmured, staring at the bag.

'Oh yeah,' Lavazzi added, still smirking like a teenager, 'there was a condition. You've got to go out in kind of a disguise.'

He reached into the bag and took out the contents. It was a brown monk's habit, complete with dressing-gown belt.

'With that bald head you're going look the part,' the cop declared.

Maybe it was another of the pair's jokes. Maybe someone back at the Questura really did think he ought be discreet. Randazzo decided he didn't care. He was going to have an hour in the outside world, with some real wine, not the piss the monks drank, some real food, in the dining room, at a quiet, shady table, while Lavazzi and Malipiero sat on the pavement in the sun, sweating.

Randazzo picked up the habit.

'Do I get some privacy?' he asked. 'To change?'

'There you go again, Commissario,' Malipiero went on. 'Asking us to break the rules. It's OK. Really. We'll just stay and watch.'

10

Teresa Lupo and Silvio Di Capua munched on cold pizza and looked at their workload: the e-mailed initial reports from the two labs they had chosen for their research in Mestre, one for chemical analysis, one for pathology, and the earliest results from the material sent via Alberto Tosi to Rome. It was now twelve thirty. From what Nic said they had no more than a few hours to come up with something the Carabinieri could throw at the Englishman. It wasn't looking good.

The most promising route should have been the data files Emily had – one way or another – got out of Massiter's computer. This was hard evidence, the kind detectives liked because you could pass it round the room and let everyone appreciate its worth without some geek there to translate. She'd passed the memory pod on to the plain-clothes detective who had come to collect it when she'd called, but not before everything it contained had been copied first.

Silvio, who knew computers so much better than she did, had tried to open the files in any number of ways she failed to comprehend. The best he'd got, while mumbling low curses and imprecations full of obscure acronyms, was a screen full of garbage and obscure characters. The files weren't just protected with a password. They'd been encrypted too, in a way Silvio recognized. When she asked, more out of desperation than hope, whether the encryption could be cracked he'd muttered something about months of work and vast amounts of some obscure thing called MIPS-years. Which, translated into everyday language, meant, as far as she understood it, someone could crack the files, but it would take a lot of time and more computers than someone like Alberto Tosi would believe existed on the entire planet. Months down the line, if a formal investigation into Massiter got under way, perhaps it could turn into something useful. For the moment it was worthless, which meant they were back at the beginning trying to read the runes of the scraps of material and human evidence they had.

After failing with the data files, they had turned to the reports on Uriel's apron and the wood samples. The more she looked at them, the more Teresa felt like screaming.

She glugged down some mineral water purloined from Nic's fridge.

'You're the chemist, Silvio. Ketone. What the hell *is* ketone? Refresh my memory.'

He gave her that 'I can't believe you don't know this' look that she was noticing more and more these days. Silvio had lost some weight recently and had refined his choice in clothes, which now ran to grey corded slacks and a pale lavender polo shirt. Not bad, she thought. If he kept on like this he'd finally get a girl some time soon.

'Industrial solvent. Labs use it all the time. *We* use it all the time.'

'You know I leave all that chemical stuff to you. Does it burn?'

'Er, yes,' he said sarcastically. 'Don't you read the warning labels on all those bottles in the lab?'

'Don't have the time. So his apron's been dipped in some inflammable industrial solvent. That's a start. At least we know we can rule out witchcraft now.'

Silvio was staring at her, a testy, disappointed expression on his face.

'Contamination,' he said.

'What?'

'The baboons from whatever passes as forensic around here had hold of this stuff before they let us get our hands on it, right? Behold. A classic case of lab contamination. You said yourself these people were amateurs.'

'I didn't say that at all! I said the man was old.'

'He's old. The lab's old. Their procedures are old. It's just shoddy work. These things are covered in the stuff. Did he say the original samples were affected by fire foam?'

'Yes. He said exactly that.'

'There you go. This is the sort of thing they teach junior lab technicians straight out of college. You never ever try to clean up crap with crap. Some moron's dumped solvent on this to get rid of the foam, and obliterated anything we might have found underneath.'

'For good?' She couldn't believe they were that stupid.

He pulled a sorry face.

'Well, no. But it makes it all a lot more difficult. A lot more time-consuming and expensive too. We could try sending the material away to some specialist labs. But with this degree of degradation, I don't know. And it would take weeks.'

'You mean Alberto Tosi or his creepy granddaughter, or whatever other of his relatives got in on the act, have screwed up this evidence completely?'

'Correct first time.'

'Oh great!'

'They could have done it deliberately,' he suggested, trying to cheer her up.

'Don't be ridiculous. Alberto's not the kind of man who'd play stupid games like that. If he was he wouldn't have let me have the stuff in the first place.'

'In that case they're just plain incompetent. Sorry. That's all you get.'

'Well isn't that just great?' she barked. 'So in that case where the hell are these DNA reports from our private people across the water? An hour ago they said an hour.'

'Don't take this out on me! I didn't spill all that junk on your precious evidence. Besides, an hour ago they said two hours, actually. By e-mail.'

'Screw e-mail,' she muttered, and phoned the company, got straight through to the head of the lab, then performed a brief impersonation of Leo Falcone on a bad day.

Five minutes later the report, still full of spelling mistakes and bad grammar, came through. Sixteen separate tests. A single specimen of male DNA in each.

'Thank God for the Y chromosome,' she murmured. 'The only

worthwhile thing to come out of the everyday penis since the dawn of man.'

Then she scrolled through the other results, conscious of Silvio leaning in very close to her shoulder.

'Eureka.' She felt triumphant for all of three seconds. The news about the apron and the floor had really got to her.

Bella was there in four of the vaginal secretions. The next twelve were unknown.

'One day . . .' Silvio murmured. She heard a familiar rant shuffling into earshot. About how the world would be a better and safer place if all of us just got tagged at birth, stored as profiles in some giant computer somewhere, files wheeled out every time a drop of blood or a trace of semen puzzled some slothful police officer who was too idle to engage his brain and go looking for evidence.

'I've told you before,' she interrupted, 'I'll tell you again. It's wrong. You have to leave people a little privacy, otherwise they don't stay human.'

She thought about the wad of tissue that still lay in her handbag, and would soon go where it belonged, into the bin in the street outside. She hadn't even considered mentioning it to Nic, though a part of her wondered if that was what Emily really wanted: to break the news through another. Even so, Nic had heard something wrong in her voice. She knew that. He didn't miss a thing.

'No one wants to know everything about everyone. It's unnatural. It's . . .'

Asking for trouble, she thought. You had to concentrate on what mattered and leave the trivial details to one side.

Something mattered deeply here. Bella had slept with Hugo Massiter. He was, perhaps, the father of her unborn child. In any normal police investigation these were starting points, pieces of information someone like Leo Falcone could pick up, mull over then use as a lever to extract other, more damning nuggets of evidence. And, in the end, with some luck, try to put together a picture of what had happened. But they hadn't the resources or the time.

'Try and think like a cop, Silvio,' she ordered. 'A woman's been incinerated in a furnace. What are the key facts you want to know?'

He shrugged. This wasn't his kind of game.

'Temperature. Can we get some more physical evidence from the remains?'

'No, *no. NO!*' she screamed, and wondered for a moment if it would be out of place to slap him on his pale and flabby cheeks. 'That's *us* thinking. Not them.'

'I've no idea in that case,' he confessed. 'How she got there maybe. They always ask that.'

No they didn't. Not always. With Falcone now out of action, the official version was that Uriel had put her in the furnace somehow, and since he was dead too, the whys and wherefores were unimportant, redundant.

Two violent deaths had occurred without the police ever seeking answers to one of the most fundamental aspects of any murder inquiry. How exactly?

She'd been around long enough to understand what, in the case of Bella, those answers were likely to be. No one could be forced into a searing furnace against their will. It was simply inconceivable, however strong the assailant, however feeble the victim. Bella would have had to be rendered unconscious first, and Teresa Lupo's instincts told her the most likely way that would happen. Not with alchemy but with the oldest killing tool in the book, raw violence that always, always left familiar stains in its wake.

'Jesus Christ,' she murmured. 'I must be losing my mind. We've two murders here and no one – not even old Alberto Tosi – has even seen so much as a blood stain. How often does *that* happen?'

She looked at her watch, phoned Raffaela Arcangelo's number and prayed the woman had abandoned the Ospedale Civile for a while. When she'd called that morning they'd been planning to wheel the unconscious Falcone into an MRI scanner for an hour or so, hoping all those deafening magnets whirring round his damaged head would see something that indicated he'd return to the living world some day soon. Teresa had dealt with MRI units when she was a doctor. She wasn't full of optimism. More often than not the best thing they told you was nothing, and the only news was bad.

'Have you heard something?' Raffaela asked immediately. 'They said they were doing some test. I couldn't be there all the time. I couldn't bear it.'

'It usually takes some hours, perhaps a day, for the results to reach the consultant. Nothing's changed. I'm sorry. It's not bad news though. I was wondering . . .'

She could almost feel the woman's tension down the line.

'Poor Leo . . .' she moaned quietly.

'I was wondering if you'd found anything.'

'Sorry, I forgot,' she confessed.

Teresa wasn't giving up.

'Is there anyone on the island now, apart from you?'

'No. My brothers are with the lawyers. I think they'll be there a long time. It seems Signor Massiter is changing the terms of the contract. Quite drastically too. Not that we're in a position to refuse any more.'

'Would you mind if we came and took a look around? I want to see Bella's bedroom. Perhaps take away some more samples.'

The bed trick had worked for Emily. It was worth trying again, though it still didn't put Massiter there on the night of the murder.

'Of course.'

'And one more thing. I need you to think hard about this, Raffaela. Did you see anything after they were killed – anything at all – that showed traces of blood. Marks on paintwork or the floor. Spots on a cloth. Something out of place – I don't know.'

Raffaela was silent. Teresa's heart skipped a beat.

'Raffaela?'

Teresa could picture the woman, her hand to her mouth, thinking, trying to work out what was wrong.

'You'd best come now,' she said eventually. 'I think I've been a fool.'

11

The thirty-year-old Cessna 180 performed a tight forty-degree right-hand turn low over the shining, mackerel-skin waters of the lagoon, an ungainly red and white bird with high wings and a couple of gigantic Edo amphibious floats jutting out where the undercarriage should have been. Andrea Correr, who owned a couple of hotels on the Lido, two restaurants in San Marco, and one of the biggest tour agencies in town, stuffed a cigarette in his mouth, then fought the wheel trying to remember the water-landing lessons he'd had nine years before on an alligator-infested lake a few miles outside Orlando. Correr liked to think of himself as a good pilot, an amateur, but one who'd built up almost a thousand hours in a decade of flying from the little airfield hidden away at the tip of the Lido. When some young cop had come out to the aircraft stand, waving his badge, demanding to be taken up on official business, and offering to pay for the gas, Correr didn't hesitate. He didn't have a professional licence, so he'd have to take the money as a contribution towards costs, and wouldn't, for a moment, dream of giving the man a receipt in return, not that he'd mentioned this small catch on the airfield pavement.

There was just one problem, and it was both the prize and the potential pitfall in the present proceedings. Costa seemed to think that if he found what he wanted Correr would simply land the plane on the water, taxi into the shore, leave him there, and then zoom back home. Given those big Edo floats visible to all, it was an understandable mistake. But his Cessna had been flown with the internal carriage wheels extended for as long as Correr could remember. He'd been talked into buying the expensive old floatplane by a flying-club regular who'd omitted to mention one salient point: the law forbade him to land it anywhere in the lagoon. Only sea use was allowed, and the choppy waters of the Adriatic were deemed too difficult for all but the most experienced of pilots. The only aircraft Correr had ever landed on water was a Piper Cub at the school in Florida, and that was a small, ancient, two-seater tandem contraption of canvas and wood, one that was started by standing on the float and hand-swinging the prop, more like a toy than a real aircraft, a plaything that flitted in and out of stretches of water rarely troubled by more than a passing breeze.

The 180 was a complex machine, with a variable pitch prop and more controls than he could handle sometimes, even after a decade of ownership, and an awkward retractable undercarriage that would have to be wound up into the floats before the plane so much as touched a single wave. And the lagoon was no still patch of Everglades lake, more the sea in miniature, with a dappled surface that was unreadable from above, riddled with invisible currents, under constant barrage from random blasts of gusting winds rolling all the way down from the Dolomites. A part of him told Andrea Correr he'd be insane to do as the young cop insisted. A part of him said he'd never get this opportunity again in his life, and he could always blame the police if it all went horribly wrong.

They'd been round and round most of the obscure islands of the lagoon, twice, all at the same barely legal height, all with the Cessna hanging in the air, bumping just above its stall speed, so that the young cop got the best view from the right-hand passenger seat in the turns. Andrea had lost count of how many cigarettes he'd smoked, despatching the butts through the open side window. Correr knew a few of these islands: San Francesco del Deserto, with its Franciscan monastery. Lazzaretto Nuovo, the former leper colony which now housed a scattering of disused military buildings. Santa Cristina with its tiny brick church. Others were just places on the cop's tourist map, a litany of unknown names: La Salina, La Cura, Campana, Sant' Ariano . . . just hunks of grassy rock deserted over the centuries, with, at best, a few derelict buildings to indicate people had once lived there.

Costa was starting to look desperate. Correr couldn't work out whether to feel disappointed or relieved. The thought of putting the bird's fat feet down on the lagoon still sent a tingle of anticipation and dread down his spine.

They were now over Mazzorbo, the long, barely inhabited island next to Burano, to which it was connected by a bridge. Correr hunted ducks hereabouts in winter, and liked to eat at the restaurant by the vaporetto stop where, in season, the local wildfowl regularly found their way onto the plate at prices that were a fraction of those in the city.

He glanced at the fuel gauge: good for another hour. Oil pressure and temperatures looked steady. The old Cessna was a reliable beast. Pretty soon though they'd run out of places to look. The lagoon wasn't so large from the air. They'd been low enough to see into people's gardens and swimming pools, low enough to get him a ticking-off once he got back to the Lido. No one liked intrusive flying. It just brought in complaints.

'So what exactly are you looking for?' Correr yelled over the noise of the engine.

The pair of them were wearing noise-cancelling headsets, but they couldn't quite keep out the racket from the hefty Lycoming engine up front.

'A man and a woman,' the cop barked back. 'Hiding.' Which didn't seem of much help.

'If I wanted to hide,' Correr suggested, 'I'd do it there.'

He popped the cigarette in his mouth once more and pointed to the island city on the horizon. From this height it seemed modest, a forest of brick spires rising from a tightly packed community of houses.

'They can't be there. People would recognize them.'

'Then maybe they're gone.'

The cop shook his head vigorously.

'Doesn't add up. They don't have the money. Besides, they've got ties. Strong ties. I just don't see them running.'

'So why are we looking in the lagoon?'

The little cop was gazing in the direction of Murano, towards the trio of weird, decrepit buildings Correr had been reading about in the papers. One day soon there could be a hotel there and a new gallery, thanks to the rich Englishman who was closer to men of influence in Venice than a middle-class local like Andrea Correr could ever hope for. Still, these developments were worth remembering. The travel agent in him knew there could be money to be had soon.

Costa squirmed in the passenger seat, then turned and looked at him.

'If I'm right, they had some help. From a farmer on Sant' Erasmo. Someone who knows the lagoon like the back of his hand. If he wanted to hide them somewhere I thought . . .'

He went quiet.

Correr wished he'd mentioned this idea before they took off.

'You're not local, are you? Most of the little lagoon islands are uninhabited. You couldn't just hide someone there. You'd need a roof over your head. Besides, those little ones get looked after by the conservationists and the archaeological people. They'd be screaming the roof down if they found so much as an empty Coke can. I don't think—'

'I know, I know.'

It was a stupid quest and Correr saw he didn't have to point that out.

'So where would you hide someone?'

Correr laughed. It was obvious.

'If I was a farmer on Sant' Erasmo? In my back garden. Or somewhere nearby. That place is bigger than Venice. No one goes there except the locals. I don't think they even have police.'

'They don't.'

'Then there you go. Search the island. You can't do it from the air. You're going to need a lot of men too because the *matti* wouldn't piss on you if flames were coming out of your ears.'

'Take me back there,' Costa ordered.

'Sure.' Correr wheeled the big tin bird round and set the nose on the low silhouette of Sant' Erasmo, black against the bright horizon. 'Anywhere in particular?'

'Southern tip. Away from the vaporetto stop. Away from everyone. You have a maritime map of the lagoon by any chance?'

'Four. They're known as charts by the way.'

Correr reached into the glove compartment, scrabbled behind several half-spent packets of cigarettes, and found the set he wanted. The cop stared at them, surprised.

'This is a floatplane,' Correr explained. 'Besides, I sail too. And I happen to like charts.'

'They've got buildings on them? Individual houses?'

'You'd be amazed what you can find on charts. Of course on Sant' Erasmo you'd need to double check everything.'

'Why?'

People from terra firma. They just didn't get it.

'Because the *matti* do what the hell they like. Throw up a little *baracca* for Grandmama, just so she doesn't have to annoy the hell out of you living in the same house. No one's going to tell the authorities. It happens all the time. And why not? Out here, who cares?'

It took less than three minutes. Then they went into another forty-degree roll, Correr feeding in some extra throttle and kicking the rudder hard so the G-force squeezed them into their seats a little. His passenger hadn't looked a good flyer when he came on board. Now Correr was changing his opinion. Just to check, he pumped in some more throttle and took the aircraft over to sixty degrees, nailing it into as steep a turn as he dared make at that kind of altitude, one that forced both of them hard into their seats and pitched the nose of the Cessna round in a vicious circle, as if it were tethered to a wire. At that angle even he could see down below: fields and shacks and mess. Just the usual.

A third of the way through the turn, he spotted something on his passenger's face. Correr went through three-sixty, levelled off, same height, same place on the horizon he'd entered the turn, gave himself ten out of ten for flying, then pointed the nose out to sea. The cop stopped looking out of the window and stared at him instead.

'There's a little shack down there. It's not on the map. I didn't notice it before.'

'Like I said. It's called a chart. There's a reason you didn't see it. You weren't looking. That's one thing you learn in a little plane. How to look.'

Costa nodded.

'When you made all that noise a woman came out and started staring up at us.'

'Was she pretty?'

'Couldn't see.'

'Maybe we should go back and take another look. A little lower this time.' He eyed the cop, expectantly. 'You *are* going to get me out of all the shit if it hits the fan, right?'

'Guaranteed,' Costa said, then strained backwards, looking towards the green tip of Sant' Erasmo.

Correr did the same. There was a tiny beach not far from the end. He had an idea what was coming next.

'I want you to put me down there,' Costa said, glancing at his watch. 'Now.'

'And then?'

He was thinking this through.

'Then you go back to the airfield. I won't need you any more.'

He sounded uncertain about that last point. Correr wondered whether to object.

'I can carry four people in this thing, you know. It's no problem. Really.'

He smiled, for the first time since they'd met, and, for no particular reason, Andrea Correr decided he liked this little man, in spite of the badge.

'Thanks, but no thanks. You've done enough. Just get us down please.'

Correr glanced back at the island. Someone was burning charcoal or something. The smoke was drawing straight off towards the open Adriatic, not too quickly, all in a straight line.

Land into a good, reliable wind. Taxi round and take off in the same direction.

His mouth was dry, in the way it used to be when he was first learning to fly on the Lido all those years ago, in a tiny fixed-gear

Cessna 150 that was a baby brother to this more complex bigger beast. He could still remember those lessons in Florida. They made it sound so easy after a while. In a way, making it easy was part of the secret.

Correr laughed to himself, took the half-smoked cigarette from his lips and flicked it out of the window. Then he worked the wirepull to withdraw the wheels back into the floats. The plane had been through its annual certificate of airworthiness only two months before. Everything, flaps, ailerons, throttle, gear, worked as smoothly as he'd ever known.

He pulled the 180 round into the wind, facing the island, and set up for a long, flat descent, nose up, holding the bulky Edos off the water at just the right angle, until he'd killed enough speed to make it safe to put them down on the waves. Hit it badly and you'd soon discover how hard an object water really was. Someone had written off a Cub while he was training, and that had been on a lake that looked like perfect glass, not the dappled random rippled mesh of wavelets that stood between them and the island.

The man in the next seat was bracing himself nervously. Correr knew why. He'd done the same the first time he'd landed on water. You never appreciated how much the surface would brake the aircraft. It wasn't like grass or asphalt. With a good landing the plane came in at around sixty knots, placed its feet on the surface, then got dragged to a halt in less than a hundred metres, which meant they looked perilously close to hard, stony land as they approached, too close, he guessed, and mentally began the countdown for a go-round if things got too near the margin.

Some story for the flying club, Correr thought to himself, then cut the power altogether, held up the nose, let the speed die, felt the yoke go weak and shaky in his hands as the wings began to lose their grip on the air . . . and, with a loud bang of wave against metal, landed the aircraft plum in front of the beach, coming to a rest no more than ten metres from the sand.

He undid his belt, opened the door and leaned out to look down over the side. He could see the bottom beneath the sea, rocks and pebbles and tiny fish.

'I can't go much further,' he said. 'Get down and walk out to the front of the float. You can guide me in until you see the sand getting so shallow I might hit it. These things don't do reverse.'

Costa was taking out his wallet, removing a wad of notes.

'Thanks,' he said, extending the money.

'No,' Correr replied with a smile, then grabbed the cash. 'Thank you.'

The cop had to wade through about a metre's depth of water to get on shore. Then Correr turned the plane around, taxied out into the open lagoon, turned once more and performed a take-off so perfect he wished the surly old instructor at the school in Florida could have seen him.

Wished, too, for the moment he could tell this tale in the flying-club bar. None of them had landed on the lagoon before. Chances were he'd never do it again.

The 180 roared over Sant' Erasmo. Andrea Correr leaned out of the window to wave goodbye. But there was no one to be seen.

12

The two of them had run into the broad, busy main street of the Via Garibaldi, threaded their way past the vegetable seller's boat, out into the back alleys of Castello and over the footbridge to the deserted island of San Pietro. Teresa had to scream at the Murano boat to stay at the jetty. Twenty minutes later they were in Raffaela Arcangelo's laundry room, looking at an old enamel bowl stained pink with bloodied water, a tangle of cotton just visible.

'I didn't think it was important. Everything's been so busy I never even got around to looking at the laundry baskets until yesterday. It seemed irrelevant somehow.'

'What seemed irrelevant? Don't worry about it, Raffaela. Calm down.'

She looked distraught at the idea she'd missed something. Raffaela had made that promise to Leo. From what Teresa could see, it still counted.

'Oh God. I'm so stupid! I-I-I . . .'

'Slowly, please. And calmly.'

She sighed.

'Uriel had an accident in the foundry five or six years ago. An awful accident. He was lucky he wasn't hurt more. All the same, it damaged his hearing. I felt so sorry for him. It also meant he had a bad sense of smell and nose bleeds from time to time. Terrible nose bleeds. There was nothing he could do but sit there with a cold wet cloth and wait for it stop. After a while, because it happened two or three times a week, I never thought about it any more. He was a man. It was just more washing. He just threw anything with blood on it straight into the laundry basket without thinking. He didn't know how hard it was to get those stains out. I told him. But . . .'

Teresa looked again at the bowl.

'You found a shirt with blood on it?'

'It was nothing unusual! It was just like I'd seen before!' Raffaela gazed at them with sad, apologetic eyes. 'I can't believe I could have been so stupid.'

'No problem,' Teresa said.

'But it's been soaking there since yesterday.'

Silvio Di Capua was eyeing the object in the water confidently.

'You could put that in a drawer for the next twenty-five years as it is and we'd still be able to get DNA out of it. And in twenty-five years . . .'

'Heel, boy,' Teresa cautioned.

Silvio couldn't stop babbling.

'More than that too. If this was part of the killing you can bet there's evidence on there we can't even see either. Sweat from his hands. Saliva. We can get them both.'

'Both?' Raffaela asked, blinking.

'Oh, you bet!' Silvio went on, eyeing the shirt greedily. 'If that doesn't ID the victim *and* the culprit it's going to be very unusual indeed.'

Teresa had to leap forward to stop Silvio snatching the wet shirt from the bowl, and got a grumpy glance for her pains.

'Let's deal with this one step at a time. Can you show me where you found this, please?'

They went up one flight of stairs and followed her down one of the mansion's dark dank corridors to a large bedroom that must once have been regal. Now the wallpaper was old and peeling, the bed still roughly made from the last time anyone had slept in it.

'I haven't been able to get round to doing anything in here,' Raffaela said. 'It didn't seem right somehow.'

'That makes it all the better for us,' Teresa replied, walking round, staring at the walls, checking the old raffia laundry basket that was now empty.

She stopped by the window, which looked out onto the rusting corrugated iron roof of one side of the foundry. She reached for the latch, threw up the glass, let some welcome air into the room, and leaned as far out over the windowsill as she dared.

With one hard push she got herself back inside and turned back to look at the adjoining wall. In an ordinary investigation this would have been the first place to start. But this case had been closed before anyone got round to opening it. She was amazed even Leo hadn't seen fit to take a closer look, but perhaps he had been distracted by other matters, personal and intellectual.

'Here . . .'

She pointed to a faint, tiny mark on the wall, something so indistinct Silvio and Raffaela had to come close and squint to see it.

Then Raffaela gasped and fell back onto the bed, hands to her mouth, eyes filling with tears and shock.

'Don't pass out on me, please,' Teresa pleaded. 'I need you. This is very standard minimal blood spray consistent, at this height, with a single blow to the head. Hard instrument, maybe a small hammer. My guess is . . .'

She moved Silvio in front of her, mimicking the position she believed Bella must have been in when attacked.

'Bella was here, standing, when he came for her. One powerful blow to the skull.'

She swung the imaginary weapon with her hand, landing it softly on the side of Silvio's head where fringe met bald scalp, just behind the ear.

'If he'd hit her repeatedly we'd have had much more blood than this. One blow would be enough to render her unconscious anyway. If he did it well, there'd be no noise either. Who else was in the house?'

Raffaela took her head out of her hands.

'I was here all that night. Michele and Gabriele too. It's not possible. We would have heard something. We would have woken up.'

'Everybody thinks that. You'd be amazed how often people in the next room sleep through murder. If there's no fighting, no gun . . .' This was a big, old cavern of a place. Dark, with plenty of places to hide. He could have waited for her in the bedroom, pounced with that one crashing blow then carried her downstairs without anyone knowing. It wouldn't have been hard. 'If he planned it, everything could have happened very quickly. Without a struggle, or there would have been signs. Then he moves on to Uriel and finds himself a scape-goat.'

'All the same . . .'

'Trust me,' Teresa insisted, then went back to the window. 'You need a ladder, Silvio. Out there, at the very end of the corrugated iron, you'll find some kind of tool. I can't work out what it is. Something from the furnace I guess, some kind of spike or maybe a hammer. He must have thrown it through the open window thinking it would reach the water. It was dark. No way of knowing it never got there. Now let's look at that shirt.'

They followed her back to the kitchen. Teresa Lupo felt she was on a roll just then. It couldn't get any better. She went to the sink and carefully poured off the liquid, leaving the fabric lying in a wet, wrinkled heap in the base of the bowl.

Then she looked at Silvio.

'I want you to take this and the hammer, or whatever it is, over to that private lab in Mestre straight away, tell them to drop everything else and run rapid DNA tests on anything they can find. Not just blood. Sweat. Saliva. Urine. Anything. You stay there breathing down their necks until there's an answer. I don't care what it costs. I don't care who you have to yell at.'

'The pleasure's all mine,' he said.

'It will be once you've been up on that roof. And after that,' she continued, glancing at Raffaela, 'you and I are going to visit Leo. He should be out of that machine by now. I can probably get a sneak look at the scans.'

She unravelled the wet material with a slow surgical care, then stopped.

Men were arrogant bastards sometimes. They were like dogs: they felt they had to leave their mark on everything.

On the pocket of the shirt, a fine cotton one, she now noted, were two initials, sewn into the fabric as a monogram: HM.

13

He wished he could scream. He wished he could move, and tried to will some life into his fingers, tried to believe something, a single nerve, the flicker of a muscle, answered in return.

Before him, the shifting, glassy door changed shape, became transparent, and Leo the boy was silent, recognizing the face that peered back at him.

It was his older self, the now familiar walnut tan, a sleek, shiny bald head, damaged, cracked, showing bloody fault lines, like those on Humpty Dumpty after the fall. The face of a man unaware of his status, unsure whether he was alive or dead, or simply somewhere between the two.

'Little Leo,' his elder self pleaded. 'Look and think, for pity's sake.'

The pained brown face faded. He could see beyond now, into the bedroom, the forbidden bedroom, the place where so many mysteries seemed to breed.

'You knew this happened all along,' the older Leo said. 'And, being a child, you did nothing. Yet you understand now, Little Leo. You can stop it in a way. Not in the past. But now. In your head. *Our* head. Just by seeing. Just by being there.'

'Afraid,' he whispered, hearing the same voice, noting the mutual frailty there.

'Leo.' The voice was so feeble, so ghostly, it terrified him more than anything. 'You *have* to.'

The thing hovered there in front of him, shaking manically with the racket beyond the door, and the clatter of the unseen machine outside this coffin of wood and glass.

'Afraid of the key.'

'Which exists in order that . . .?'

It was wrong to mock a child, even an unreal man-child.

He peered apprehensively through the transparent door and watched the kicking and the blows, watched how she rolled to lessen the pain, glancing back in desperation, staring straight at him, begging, asking why.

'To keep her in!' the child screeched. 'I told you, I told you, I told—'

He was there again, obscuring the view of his parents, for which he was thankful. Except his tanned head looked worse now, the cracks seemed to have multiplied, blood oozed through them, seeped down the walnut skin, ran into the bright, white eyes. They began to form all over this dying man's skull like a spider's web, ensnaring him, tightening, squeezing out what scraps of life remained.

'I hear your thoughts,' the fractured man whispered. 'I read the same fairy stories. Remember, Leo? Humpty Dumpty . . . "When I use a word," Humpty Dumpty said, in rather a scornful tone, "it means just what I choose it to mean – neither more nor less." "The question is," said Alice, "whether you can make words mean so many different things."' He was in agony, struggling for the strength to carry on. '"The question is," said Humpty Dumpty, "which is to be master – that's all."'

His eyes were changing, fading. These were the last moments.

'Facts are like words. We've learned that over all these years. They're open to interpretation. It is, in the end, simply a matter of who will be their master.'

The boy Leo looked at the figure before him and understood that, at this moment, he was seeing the saddest man in the universe, a man of bleak, worn-down emotions, though a being filled with knowledge too, possessed of an important secret the boy now understood implicitly, shared with his older self since it came, in the end, from both of them.

'The key . . .' said the fading face.

'. . . is there to keep me *out*!' the boy Leo roared. *'The key is there to keep me out! Out! Out! Out!'*

Somewhere beyond his imagination the metal beast screamed, a cacophony of gears, dying iron settling, its work finished.

The boy reached forward, held the key, turned it, saw in amazement the way the door became a real door, the wood that he remembered from his childhood, felt the old metal familiar in his hand.

It was the worst year. The one where his family had fallen apart, descended into divorce and hatred, a cold, hard place in which a small boy could do nothing except retreat into his shell, hardening that brittle armour that kept the harshness of the real world at bay. He remembered everything, everything his mind had blocked out over the years, about that dreadful holiday in the mountains, with the two of them locked in that distant, forbidden room, thinking their screams never found their way beyond the walls to reach a frightened lonely child lost for words, lost for action.

The wood disappeared. There was only light. And Leo – who was, he understood now, Leo both boy and man – found himself propelled forward, into the bedroom from which he was forever banished, forcing his way between them, pushing back the dead old dusty figure that, in some dark, damaged part of his head, represented what was left of the memory of his father.

He looked into the heartless face, enjoyed the surprise he saw, and said the word, the dread banned word, the boy Leo had never dared utter to him in his lifetime.

Leo Falcone opened his eyes – his real eyes, he noted – and found himself in a bright clinical room with the cloying harsh smell of a medical ward. He lay horizontal on a bed which was now being withdrawn from a large white, barrel-like object, one he faintly recognized from hospital scenes in the movies.

A pretty young nurse, with long black hair tied back in a bun and sparkling, happy eyes, peered at him, grinning.

'Welcome to the world, Inspector Falcone,' she said in a pleasant southern voice. 'It's been a long time.'

'How long?' he snapped. 'And where the hell are my men?'

14

An old monastery, hidden inside a church near the gasworks in Castello, no more than three minutes on foot from where Peroni and Costa had been staying for the last eight months. Neither of them had a clue it existed. For anyone trying to hunt down Gianfranco Randazzo, this was surely the last place to look. They would never have found it if Peroni hadn't called in one last favour from Cornaro, the one officer in the Castello Questura who hadn't treated the pair of them like lepers.

Gianni Peroni smiled at the pleasant monk in the brown habit who had greeted them, baffled and seemingly incapable of anything that might pass as assistance.

'We need to speak to Commissario Randazzo,' Zecchini said again, his face beginning to grow red with exasperation. 'Now, please.'

'This is a police matter. And a Carabinieri one too,' Peroni added.

The monk shrugged his shoulders and smiled.

'Then it must be very important indeed. But I was told Signor Randazzo was not to be disturbed. He is here, as I understood it, for the sake of his health. A man of a nervous disposition.'

That seemed to be pushing things a little far, even for an unworldly monk.

'He's on his own?' Peroni asked.

'No. Normally there are men with him.' The monk frowned and, for a moment, looked like someone who inhabited the world Peroni knew. 'Two ugly men in particular. Police officers, I believe. Not the kind of people we get in here very often. That part puzzles me, I admit. But we're here to do service. Not to ask questions.'

'Who's in charge in this place?' Zecchini demanded.

'No one at the moment. Administratively we are in what one might term an interregnum.'

As someone down at the Questura doubtless knew, Peroni thought.

'Father,' he said, and saw from the look on the man's face that he had somehow picked the wrong word, 'it's important we talk to Randazzo.'

'We have a *warrant*,' Zecchini added, brandishing a piece of paper.

The monk stared at the document.

'A warrant? What's that?'

'It's a piece of paper that says you'll damn well bring him to us whether you like it or not!' Zecchini yelled.

The curses he added rang around the bright, sunlit cloister, sending a flutter of doves scattering for the cloudless sky.

But nothing dented the monk's composure. He simply folded his arms and kept on smiling, silent. Peroni couldn't stop himself casting a sour glance at the Carabinieri major.

'We don't want to search a monastery,' he said calmly, 'and I'm sure you don't want that either. There would be so many officers. So much disruption. And noise.'

The monk didn't like noise. Peroni had watched the way his nose wrinkled when the volume of Zecchini's voice rose.

'No one wants noise,' he added.

The man laughed, and Gianni Peroni was surprised to realize he was laughing at them, and that there was precious little difference between a smile and sneer on his face.

'He's not here. They went out for lunch. No.'

The answer came before the question. 'I don't know where and I don't care. This is a small and quiet community, gentlemen. When we're asked to help the city, we do so without question. We trust our betters. Do you?'

Zecchini scowled at him then asked, 'Gone for good?'

The monk's arms opened, the hands raised in a gesture of futility.

'We're neither a prison nor a hotel. I can help you no more. I can . . .'

Gianni Peroni couldn't take his eyes off the doves. They'd assembled again around the foot of the statue of St Francis. It was a great place to hide a man. So good it seemed odd Randazzo had felt moved to leave, if only for a meal.

Then, as he watched, the birds began to lift, a whirling fury of grey and white feathers, rising, racing in every direction, mindless, terrified.

Four, maybe five, shots rang out from somewhere beyond the monastery's quiet walls, the sound bounced off its bright, clean terracotta and echoed around the small, perfect square, threading its way through the colonnades.

Luca Zecchini had his gun in his hand in an instant. The monk stared at the weapon, both shocked and angered by its visible presence.

'Where?' Zecchini yelled.

Gianni Peroni wasn't going to wait for this little charade to play itself out. Bawling out some scared, unworldly monk who'd never heard a gunshot in his small, protected life wasn't going to find them Gianfranco Randazzo. He marched his big frame back into the outside world, thought about what he knew of this area, and where a police commissario with a taste for good food might want to eat. There weren't many options. Then he began to run, aware, after just a few long strides, of Zecchini and his men playing catch-up in his wake.

15

Teresa Lupo had told Pino Ferrante a great deal about the patient whose life he'd saved during that long night when she had dragged him from his dinner table in Bologna. She'd told him how Leo Falcone was a man worth preserving, a fine, honest, conscientious *ispettore* in the Rome police, someone who deserved better than to be butchered by some naive Venetian surgical hack, even if they could find one.

Now Falcone lay back on his bed, eyes wide open and blazing at each of them in turn, spitting fury in all directions. Pino glanced at her and smiled, that self-deprecating smile she'd known from their college days, the one that couldn't offend a soul but still managed to say: 'Really?'

Even Raffaela Arcangelo seemed a little taken aback. Clearly this was one side of Leo she'd never witnessed.

Pino let Falcone exhaust himself with one final set of demands – all the latest case notes on Aldo Bracci and the Arcangeli case, what new forensic there was, and a recall of Costa and Peroni, from wherever they happened to be malingering, presumably to give him someone new to yell at – then sat down by the bed, folded his arms, and peered at the prone man there.

'Inspector Falcone,' he said mildly, 'you've been seriously wounded by a gunshot to the head. You have been unconscious now for more than a week. I would have hoped a man who has been through what you have would have asked me one or two questions about his condition. Otherwise . . .'

He now had a rather hard smile, it seemed to Teresa, one he'd learned since college.

'Perhaps I will be driven to the conclusion that you are not so sufficiently recovered as you seem to believe.'

Falcone, propped up on a couple of pillows, bandages round his scalp, his face lacking that full tan Teresa had come to take for granted, was silent for a moment.

Then, with all his customary bullishness, he replied, 'I am a police officer in the middle of a murder investigation. It's my duty to be kept fully informed. It's your duty not to get in my way. I would advise you to remember that.'

Pino waited. When it became clear Falcone didn't intend to utter another word, the surgeon said, 'Would you like to ask me anything now? Or would you like me to leave and allow you to continue bellowing at your colleagues until your strength runs out? Not that I think you have much energy left for that. The choice is yours.' He looked at his watch. 'I would like to be home in Bologna by eight, so please make your decision this instant.'

Falcone glanced at Teresa and Raffaela Arcangelo, as if they were somehow a part of this. Then, in a subdued tone, he asked, 'What the hell's wrong with me?'

'You were shot through the head,' Pino replied with a shrug. 'There was damage to the brain. It's a sensitive organ, even in an insensitive man. A mysterious organ too. I can go through the details later, but they won't tell you much. To be honest they don't tell me that much either. This is the way things are with neurological matters. What I see now is what I'd expected. Hoped for, to be honest with you. There is some paralysis below the waist. You should also expect to experience headaches. Blackouts maybe. And some side effects from the medication for sure. We will need to monitor all these things for a while.'

A purple blush of outrage began to suffuse Falcone's face.

'I have to work!'

'That's ridiculous,' Pino said bluntly. 'A man in your condition cannot work. Even if you were physically capable, your mental state is still fragile, however much you wish to believe otherwise. You need what any other man or woman needs in such circumstances. Convalescence. Constant care. Regular follow-ups. You will be reliant on others for some time. I trust you can teach your ego to accommodate this fact, *Ispettore*.'

'I . . .' The words died in Falcone's mouth. This was a situation he had clearly never encountered before, or begun to envisage for a moment.

'Leo,' Teresa interjected, 'you're no more or less human than the rest of us. Plus, you're lucky to be alive. Just take it easy. And then . . .'

She glanced at the consultant, who had just peeked at his watch.

'Oh, for God's sake, Pino! Since he won't ask, I will. How long will he be like this? What does it mean?'

'It means a wheelchair. For at least two, perhaps three months. Possibly longer. It is simply a matter of waiting. I have no crystal ball. It is possible . . .' He stared at Falcone to make sure this went home. 'If you're unlucky, you will be in a wheelchair forever. I don't think this is irreversible, but one can never be sure. You will need regular physiotherapy to work on that leg. I gather you are a bachelor. Perhaps there is a police home that could look after you.'

'A *home*?' Falcone roared.

'He will not go to a home,' Raffaela said quietly. 'Please, Leo. Listen to your surgeon. He surely knows what's best for you.'

'And what the hell am I supposed to do all day?'

'Relax,' Pino suggested. 'Read books. Listen to music. Take up a hobby. I recommend painting. It's a talent found in the most unlikely of men at times. Apart from the physio I don't expect you to experience much in the way of discomfort. Most men would appreciate the opportunity.'

'Most men!' Falcone spat back at him. He glared at Teresa. 'Get Costa and Peroni in here now.'

Pino shook his head.

'No. I absolutely forbid it. The stress of work is the last thing you need at this time.'

Falcone glowered at the surgeon.

'At least let them send me the files to read. A man's allowed to read, isn't he?'

'By all means,' Pino said, smiling. 'You can read to your heart's content.'

16

The food tasted better when Lavazzi and Malipiero had gone. Gianfranco Randazzo sat one table in from the window, alone in the room, eating and drinking slowly, enjoying the food and the solitude, trying to stretch out the meal for as long as possible. Escaping the monastery made him realize how he was beginning to hate the place. He was becoming sluggish and stupid. One more day. That was all he was prepared to wait. Then he'd get in touch with the right men in the Questura and in the city to remind them of a few salient facts and how it was impolite to have to call in favours by name.

It was now close to two forty-five. He'd worked his way through a larger meal than he'd normally have eaten: antipasti of soft-shell crab, calamari and mantis shrimp, *porcini* risotto, then lamb cutlets with a single *contorno* of spinach. All accompanied by the best bottle of heavy Barolo on the wine list. He felt a little drunk, a little angry too. All this was undeserved. Aldo Bracci was a lout and a criminal. The thug had got what was coming.

And Randazzo's reward? To be sent into some kind of exile, humiliated when he stepped outside for a brief respite, forced to wear the stupid, itching, sweaty robe of a monk, a disguise that fooled no one, he thought, not by the way the waiter had looked at him, stifling a laugh, when he arrived with the two idiots from the Questura, who'd spent the rest of the time filling their faces at his expense.

There were scores to be settled after treatment like this. Randazzo ran a few possibilities through his head. He wasn't going to be content with just a chalet in the mountains any more. Massiter would make millions out of the Isola degli Arcangeli. He wouldn't miss a few drops of that spilling over, trickling down to the man who removed the final obstacle to the deal.

He was going over a few more option when the waiter returned with another dish: tiny wild strawberries covered in cream and some kind of alcohol.

'I didn't order that,' Randazzo snarled.

'Keep your hair on. It's a gift!' the waiter remarked, grinning, mocking him. 'We don't get brothers in here so often. I'm hoping you'll be bringing along some *colleagues* in the future. If that's the right word. We always do good business with the Church. We can give you a little *sconto* off the bill if you like. How does ten per cent sound? Twenty for you?'

'You can start today.' He glanced at the tables outside. 'Make sure it comes off theirs too.'

He looked again. They weren't there. Lavazzi and Malipiero had, without his noticing, finished eating then somehow wandered off somewhere, maybe to bum a few drinks from some neighbourhood café.

Except. They were filling their faces for free anyway. It didn't make sense to Randazzo's befuddled mind. Sometimes, he thought, there were men who just had to bunk off work, even when there was no good reason. It was bred into their genes. Like a twist in the DNA that, if you could just unravel it, read, 'Lazy bastard, never going to change'.

Randazzo stared at the little piazza and wondered why he didn't eat here more often. It was Castello, true, but not like the down-at-heel working-class *quartiere* around the Via Garibaldi where the Questura kept some apartments. This was a good place to eat, a quiet and pretty location, one the tourists only found by accident. Classy. It deserved to be popular. The last time he looked every table outside had been occupied. Now there was just a single party left outdoors. Three men in business uniform, blue shirts, sunglasses, slicked-back hair, well-ironed slacks, sat at the opposite end of the terrace to the table the cops had occupied. Randazzo could understand why everyone else had left. It was hot. It was getting late.

The waiter had gone back to the counter, back to flicking at breadcrumbs and dust with his cloth. Randazzo got to his feet, a little unsteadily, and lifted the bottle of wine. It came up too easily from the table. He glowered at the Barolo, with its fancy yellow label and dark, dark glass. It was empty.

'Coffee,' he mumbled.

The waiter turned and grimaced at him, not even attempting to hear, not coming a step closer.

'What?'

'Coffee,' Randazzo barked angrily. 'And grappa. Good grappa. Not the shit you'd normally give out. Big one. I'll take it outside.'

On another occasion he'd have sat there anyway, looking at the Arsenale gates, thinking about those stolen lions. He liked his history, the good parts anyway. There was a time when entire naval fleets sailed out from the vast military boatyard hidden behind that castellated frontage. Big enough, powerful enough to browbeat the entire eastern Mediterranean into submission, to send emperors fleeing for safety, nations flocking to their treasuries to find some gold that could keep the Venetian pirates at bay.

Piracy and thieving. These were in the native blood. It was fruitless trying to pretend otherwise. He stumbled to the nearest table outside, fell into a chair, waited for the coffee and the drink to arrive, took one gulp of the latter, then poured some cane sugar into his cup and sipped at that.

He was next to the three businessmen, who were staring at him. They could go to hell, Randazzo thought. He'd heard them speaking. Small talk. In a language he half recognized because it was close to native Veneto.

The Croatians got everywhere these days: in the holiday business; in the smuggling rings. It was hard to draw the line between the legitimate ones and the crooks.

Randazzo gave them a sarcastic grin and mumbled, '*Salute.*'

The biggest raised his glass of beer and said the same back.

He considered mumbling some low insult under his breath then thought better of it.

'What do we call you?' one of the men asked. 'Father? Brother? What?'

Randazzo peered at them. In his view the Croatians were scum, mainly. Opportunists who'd just crawled their way to the other side of the Adriatic in the hope of screwing some money out of the first mug they encountered. He gave them one sour glance then got back to his grappa.

'Maybe he's supposed to be one of the silent ones,' the nearest suggested. 'You know. The kind of monk who never says a thing because he's too busy contemplating God or something.'

The weasel-like dark-eyed creature by his side laughed.

'Too busy contemplating his glass more like. And what's on his plate. You pay for that, Father, Brother, Sister, Uncle? Or whatever they call you?'

And they never had any respect. That was another thing that bugged him about the Croatians.

'I pay for everything,' Randazzo replied, trying not to sound drunk. 'Including scum like you.'

They were coming into focus now. One was older, bigger than the rest. Randazzo took a good look around the empty square.

'Lavazzi! Malipiero!' he yelled. 'Where the hell are you when you're wanted?'

'Language, language.' The big one tut-tutted under his breath.

'Where the fu—'

Randazzo cut short what he was about to say and looked inside the restaurant. There was no one there now. Not even the insolent little waiter. The piazza was silent and empty, not a face at any of the windows, not a hand pushing out ribbons of washing onto the ropes that were strung across the adjoining alleyways from one wall to the other. Nothing but him, the men and some old stone lions.

He sniffed the air. There was a stink here, rising up from the water lapping in the canal by the Arsenale gates, reaching him on the slightest of August breezes.

The big one got up, brushed crumbs off his trousers then took a final gulp of his beer.

'You know,' he said, 'I don't think there's anything worse than that. A man of the Church using profanities. Feeding his face with good, rich food when half the world's starving.'

He glared at Randazzo then nodded back at the restaurant.

'Back where we come from people dream about eating somewhere like this. Even the priests.'

But I'm not a priest, Randazzo wanted to object. Something, some note of alarm sounding in the Barolo-fuzz that filled his brain, stopped him.

The other two were up on their feet now, one of them with something to say.

'You know what's worse than a greedy priest?' he asked.

Randazzo yelled for Lavazzi and Malipiero again, swore he'd kick their asses when they finally dragged themselves out of whatever fleapit they'd found.

'What's worse,' the Croatian continued, coming close to him with a look on his face that was more disappointment than threat, 'is a crooked cop. One who takes what's on offer and still doesn't know his place.'

'A lack of gratitude,' said the big one, taking something out of his pocket, something black and dull and familiar, held loosely with a lazy disdain that made Gianfranco Randazzo start to shiver inside the hot, itchy Franciscan habit, 'is tantamount to a lack of respect.'

He stood in front of Randazzo now, the gun firm in his right hand.

'And that, Commissario,' he added, 'is why I've decided this doesn't happen easy.'

Randazzo's head cleared in an instant, every last confusing speck of the heavy blood-red booze fled somewhere deep inside him.

'I di-didn't talk to anyone,' he stuttered. 'I wouldn't talk to anyone. Tell him. Tell them all. I—'

They weren't even listening. They were just scanning the piazza, making sure they were alone.

'I'll pass that on,' the big one said, then stuck the pistol hard on Randazzo's right knee, just as the policeman was coming off the seat, trying to summon the strength and the courage to run. There was a compressed, powerful retort.

Gianfranco Randazzo lifted his shattered leg and, still convinced he was able to run, screamed when his foot hit the ground, felt himself falling, felt something stab through his chest and his gut – small, hot, metal devils whirling through him, cutting and slicing, fiery chunks of metal scorching through his flesh.

The paved piazza came up to meet him. His head banged hard on the cobbles, his teeth smashed on the hard, hard stone.

He looked up, trying to see them. Above him stood the stone lion, leering, a stolen object happy to watch something else being robbed from a man.

Then its worn features disappeared, replaced by the face of the big Croatian. An unseen object, hard, cold, metallic, came from nowhere and placed itself on a pulsing vein in Randazzo's right temple.

'*Ciao*,' the man murmured.

17

Scacchi's boat was still absent when they'd circled the island. Apart from the woman, anxiously scanning the sky, looking for the source of the noise, Costa knew he had nothing to go on. Nothing except an illicit little shack, somewhere at the back of Piero Scacchi's property, erected recently from what he'd seen from the passenger seat of Andrea Correr's plane. It was a shot in the dark. Just the kind of trick Leo Falcone would have pulled when things were getting difficult. He hoped a little of the old bastard's luck had rubbed off.

Costa walked up from the beach, climbed over a low rickety fence and found himself in a field. Immaculate rows of pepper plants, dotted with red fruit, ran in front of him, verdant on raised beds. Beyond a fence to the left lay similar ranks of purple artichokes, and to the right a field of equally proper spinach beet, a vivid sheet of green. Scacchi, or whoever tended these crops, was careful. Not a plant was out of place, not a leaf showed a sign of disease or insect damage. He recalled the way his own father had worked the vegetable garden outside the family house back in Rome, on the outskirts of the city, close to the old Appian Way. There had been the same peasant skill, the same monotonous, back-breaking care there, and it showed in the crops, in every shining leaf.

He looked ahead, towards the shack, no more than a hundred metres away. The woman was gone. Back inside perhaps. Or fleeing to find help, suspecting what was on the way. Costa thought about what he knew of the background of the case, took out his service pistol, looked at it, checked the magazine, then put it back in the holster hidden beneath his dark jacket.

Guns depressed him. They always had, and, he suspected, always would.

Then he took out his mobile phone and checked for messages. There were none. Not a word from Teresa or Peroni. Or Emily either, and he wondered why he'd thought of her last.

Casting these misgivings to one side, or trying to, he walked on to the little house, found the door open, went in, and said, quietly, calmly, with not a hint of threat in his voice, 'Signora Conti?'

The place wasn't what he expected. From the outside it seemed a rundown, rural hovel, plain white walls, poorly built, with a single small window giving out onto the tiny patch of garden, full of nasturtiums and roses, that sat in front of the cheap green single door. But from within it looked like a home, and not that of a peasant farmer either. There were paintings on the walls, only dimly visible in the poor light, a hi-fi system playing classical music at low volume, and shelves of books. The smell of food drifted in from an adjoining open door. The place was spotless, tidy and organized in a way which seemed, to him, more urban than rural.

'Signora Conti?' he called again. 'I wish to talk to you. There's nothing to fear.'

The woman came out of the kitchen, wiping her hands with a cloth, glowering at him. She had short light brown hair, an attractive, intelligent face, and eyes that kept darting around the room, in any direction but his.

'Who are you?' she demanded. 'What right do you have to walk in here? Flying your plane over my house.'

'Signora Conti—'

'Stop saying this name!' she insisted, voice rising. 'There's no such person here. Go please. Before I call the police.'

He took out the photo from his pocket. They had just one in the files in the Questura. It was old. She'd changed her appearance. Dyed her hair, cut it short.

He held it up in front of her.

'You're Laura Conti. I know why you're here. I know why you're hiding. Piero's done a good job keeping you safe. Getting someone at the airport to send him those postcards so everyone thought you'd fled, when all the time he'd provided you with the last place we or Hugo Massiter would look, close to him, close to the city. He's a clever man. A smart friend.'

'Piero?' she asked. 'Where is he? What have you done with him?'

'I haven't done anything with him. He's not here. I thought perhaps you knew—'

'He's the landlord. Nothing else. I don't understand what you're saying. It's nonsense.'

'Laura—'

'Not that name!'

He took one step towards her. She shivered at his closeness.

'I need your help,' he said. 'I need it desperately. And I can't allow this to go on. It's wrong. There's a time to run away, and a time to face up to your past. This is that time. You and Daniel—'

'Daniel, Daniel, Daniel . . .' she whispered, holding her head in her hands. 'What are you talking about? My name is Paola Soranzo. I live here with my husband, Carlo. We are simply farmers. Now leave us alone.'

Costa threw the photo on the table. She didn't even look at it.

'I can't do that,' he said. 'Not for your sake. Not for mine. I have to—'

He was reaching into his jacket, looking for his badge when the man crept up behind him, quiet as a church mouse, unseen until the moment the long, ugly double barrel of a shotgun emerged round Nic Costa's right shoulder and angled up towards his face.

A hand came round the left side of his chest, found the gun in its holster, removed it, threw the weapon to the floor. Then he came slowly into view. Daniel Forster could pass easily as a Sant' Erasmo farmer now. His hair was dyed almost black, long beneath a grubby beret. He wore a heavy moustache and stubble. And he had the farmer's hunch too, the bowed shoulders that came from working the fields. Costa was impressed. He raised his hands and kept them high.

'Signor Forster—' he began to say.

'*Shut up*!' the man yelled, then cracked the side of his head painfully with the barrel of the shotgun.

The woman was screaming, in fright or anger. Costa didn't know which. Then the hard wooden stock of the gun fell, and he tumbled to the floor, not caring.

18

The lawyers' offices were on the third floor of a block on the Zattere waterfront in Dorsoduro, with a view out to Guidecca, the low residential island opposite. Emily Deacon forced her mind off the conversation briefly and stared at the Molino Stucky, the old mill almost opposite. This was, like the Isola degli Arcangeli, a piece of Venetian obsolescence seeking a purpose in a new, changing world. Unused for decades since the company behind the towering, red-brick factory-like structure collapsed, it had been through any number of redevelopment schemes trying to revive the place for industrial or manufacturing purposes. Now it was being turned into a mix of hotels and apartments, a sign of the way Venice was headed. Massiter was right. There was only one form of commerce allowed in the city these days, the milking of ever-increasing numbers of visitors. Next to the Molino Stucky the Arcangeli's island was paradise, a unique mix of extraordinary architecture and location, not some ungainly refurbished mill block perched at the end of an island few would ever wish to visit. She could appreciate why Massiter didn't intend to be encumbered by the Arcangeli's futile aspirations to continue their glass-making trade regardless of its impact upon the project as a whole. He'd seen the main chance and was now intent on taking it.

She listened to the argument continuing to rattle from side to side, between Massiter's two surly attorneys, one English, one Milanese, and the single local lawyer representing the Arcangeli, a man who was both out of his depth and, it seemed to her, a little afraid of the Englishman. Michele sat by his lawyer's side, intent on stiffening his resolve every time some new demand from Massiter fell on the table, his one good eye staring at the sheaves of papers and plans that marked, as he surely knew, the end of the Arcangeli's tenure on their sad little island. Gabriele remained mute on the other side, looking as if he wished he were anywhere else in the world. This was all, she thought, Michele's game. He was driven by his ego, his desire to be seen as an equal to his father. Massiter's solution left him with nothing but money. Plenty of money. Several million euros to spare, even after the debts were cleared. All the same, it was apparent to her this was meaningless to him. Without some stake in the island's future, Michele Arcangelo would deem the deal worthless, unless the alternative was even more difficult to swallow.

The Arcangeli had conceded every point bar one. That last concerned the foundry. Michele was insistent that Massiter hold to his original offer, allowing them to work the place unhindered, and to set up a small shop to market their goods. It was a final sticking point, one Massiter was reluctant to let pass. On the yacht Emily had seen enough of the plans for the scheme to understand what he wanted for the building. It would be a restaurant and conference facility, sitting alongside the gallery in the palazzo, the premium hotel rooms of the mansion, and in front of a new hotel facility of cheaper rooms to be squeezed in at the rear of the property. The idea that he'd allow a working furnace, with its gas and smoke and industrial stink, to live alongside the rest of the island was unthinkable. Tourists demanded perfection, solitude, a promise of escape, not the Arcangeli clan's hot, noisy nights of glass-making on their doorstep. This doubtless explained why Massiter had concealed from the Arcangeli his greater plan for the island from the beginning, allowing them to believe his interest was merely personal, focused on the establishment of the exhibition facility.

There was a reason for Emily's presence in the room. She wanted to keep Hugo Massiter's trust, as much as possible, until it no longer mattered. Trust and usefulness were indivisible to him. So she looked at her watch and, quite deliberately, interrupted Michele in full flow as he embarked upon a bitter tirade about the swingeing changes being introduced into the contract at such a late stage.

'We've two hours to conclude this, gentlemen,' she said. 'Is it really worth pursuing these points? Or should we just call it a day?

Everyone from the mayor down is scheduled to see you people sign on the dotted line at six. If it's going to be cancelled, let's do it now.'

Michele's glassy eye glinted at her.

'The mistress speaks,' he snarled. 'Is this one more insult you hurl at me, Massiter? If so—'

'I'm his architect,' she interrupted. 'I'm here to try to ensure that, whatever contract Signor Massiter signs, it makes some kind of economic sense. He's too shrewd a man to wind up in the financial mess you did. I intend to keep it that way.'

The man's wrinkled hands stabbed at the papers on the table.

'So you *knew* all along that this was what was on his mind?'

Massiter was watching her, smiling. Impressed, she judged.

'Many people work on contracts of this scale,' she replied. 'None of this is one person's work alone.'

She felt emboldened by her position, enabled to play this charade.

'I apologize to both of you if this sounds rude, Signor Arcangelo. But an enterprise which is to survive must be based upon sound financial planning. Not daydreams.'

'Like ours?' Michele roared.

'Like yours,' she said calmly.

'We're artists! We're the kind of people who made Venice what it is!'

Massiter laughed, not unkindly.

'Oh, Michele. Please. Don't be so precious. You're a bunch of Chioggia boat-builders, one of whom happened to have an idea that worked for a little while. No one's interested in your art any more. It's passé. That's the problem with fashion. One day it's in. The next . . .' He held up his hands. 'You're too close to all this,' he continued. 'So am I in a way. Emily on the other hand has an admirable and cold indifference. We would both do well to listen.'

He glanced at her, a warm glance, one that almost made her feel guilty.

'Her advice is aimed at both of us. Whatever you may feel.'

'And that advice is *what* exactly?' Michele grumbled.

She knew the right reply instinctively.

'For Hugo? To walk away. To leave this room without even thinking about going through with this contract, even with the conditions sitting on the table right now. The survey of the island is incomplete and probably corrupt. I don't need access to the bank accounts of some of the people involved here to understand that most of the reports are down to bribery, not fact. The state of the foundations, of the construction, the iron, the wood, the entire fabric of the palazzo . . . Hugo's writing a blank cheque for everything and without at least two months spent on proper, independent surveys I can't begin to calculate what the possible cost of putting that place straight might be.'

'It's sound!' Michele yelled. 'Besides, he's squared the reconstruction costs with his friends in the regions. It's public money that gets spent, not his.'

'That's irrelevant. The place is a wreck,' she went on. 'Had the fire in the foundry gone on for another fifteen minutes we might not have a property to discuss. Which could have been for the better. You didn't start that yourself, did you?'

The man slammed his fist on the table.

'I didn't come here to be insulted.'

'Just a thought,' she continued. 'It could have made sense. Your island is a shell. Rotten, empty, just waiting to collapse. Without Hugo it will too. You need his money. You don't have time for alternatives.'

She looked at the brother.

'Tell him, Gabriele. You work in those buildings. He just sits in the house trying to cook the books. Tell him the truth. It's time someone did.'

The younger brother shuffled in his seat, refusing to look at anything but the papers on the table.

'Well?' Michele demanded.

'It's bad,' Gabriele said quietly. 'Worse than you know, Michele. The place is falling down. Sometimes I'd work and I'd wonder how long it would last. What might happen if we got another storm. It's . . .'

He stared at the images of the palazzo in front of him, the place restored to some kind of glory, the restaurant tables on the extended quayside, the boats bringing in the tourists to the hotel.

'It's time to put at end to this. We can't go on any more. Not without Uriel. Not without money.'

'I decide for the family,' Michele snapped. 'That was agreed. It's down on paper.'

'That's agreed,' Gabriele concurred.

'And if I don't decide,' the older brother continued, pointing an angry finger in Massiter's face, 'we all go down with this particular ship. You. Us. Those crooks in the city. Everyone.'

'Everyone?' Massiter echoed, laughing. 'I don't think so. I've a talent for walking away from train wrecks. Hadn't you noticed? Of course, if you really want to risk taking others with you . . .'

Massiter stared the man down. They both knew how unwise such a course of action would be.

Michele Arcangelo scowled and was silent.

Emily Deacon packed away her pen and notepad.

'I've got nothing else to add here, Hugo,' she declared. 'If you want to go ahead with this nonsense, then do so. Just don't wave the bill in my face when it all goes wrong.'

'Leave us some dignity,' Michele snarled. 'A place to work? A place to sell? Is that too much to ask?'

'Not at all,' Massiter answered. 'I've an industrial unit near Piazzale Roma. It's modern. Efficient. Take it. I've some retail outlets in the Strada Nuova too. Have one of those.'

Michele winced at the very name of the street. Emily knew the long drag from the station to San Marco, a parade of cheap tourist shops selling over-priced junk to gullible visitors.

'You can pass anything off as genuine there,' Massiter went on. 'Take them, Michele. Rent free for a decade. You can sell your little souvenirs.'

'The Strada Nuova . . .' Michele let loose a short string of Venetian curses. 'So I'm to be a shopkeeper?'

'There's a great future in shopkeeping hereabouts,' Massiter said. 'More so than in making glass trinkets no one wants to buy. These are luxurious times only for those who can afford it. None of us can pick and choose any more. I was content to live off an auction house once. Now I need to develop a little property, extend my range of friends. Only a fool thinks the world must change around him. We all have to find our own way. Listen to your own brother. Not me.'

Gabriele Arcangelo glowered at Massiter.

'I'd like some dignity too,' he remarked.

Massiter's face fell.

'Then take it,' he said severely. 'Don't test my generosity. A place to make your glass. A place to try to sell it. Free for ten years. Either that or ruin.'

He leaned forward, emphasizing the point.

'Utter ruin. Perhaps jail for you, Michele. Or worse.'

The older man shook his head, full of regret.

'I should never have allowed you through the door that day. I could have found others—'

'But you did!' Massiter replied with a sudden spirit. 'You *invited* me, if you recall. I only go where I'm welcome. I thought you understood that. And now . . .'

He withdrew a pen from his monogrammed shirt pocket. A large, gold Parker. Then he slid it across the table.

'You can use this in front of the mayor. Pretend it's yours. Keep it after. Just one thing.'

Michele glared at the shining pen.

'What?'

'Don't linger once the place is mine,' Hugo Massiter said with a deprecating smile.

19

By the time Gianni Peroni rounded the piazza by the Arsenale gates, uniformed state police officers were erecting tape barriers to keep out the curious, and stealing snatched glances at the corpse visible by the stone lion, still leaking blood onto the stones.

Shattered face uppermost, dead eyes staring at the blazing sun, Gianfranco Randazzo didn't look any more content with the world in death than he had in life. It hadn't been an easy departure either. Peroni was sufficiently familiar with gunshot wounds to recognize that this had been a particularly cruel killing. The commissario had been wounded several times in the legs and torso, then crawled from the overturned restaurant tables nearby, leaving a trail of gore, before suffering a final shot to the head, presumably while still on the ground.

Peroni knew a hit when he saw one. Randazzo had been taken out with a savage, single-minded deliberation, and it was clear from the way the uniforms and a couple of plain-clothes men were acting, more like disconcerted street cleaners than busy cops, that none of his killers had stayed around long enough to be apprehended.

Zecchini and his officers finally caught up with Peroni, breathless, wide-eyed at the carnage in front of them.

'I suppose I don't need to ask,' the Carabinieri major murmured, sweating hard, gasping to get some thin afternoon air into his lungs.

'Correct,' Peroni replied, eyeing a couple of plain clothes he recognized who were hanging around near the restaurant looking shifty, taking furtive sips at two small beers they'd secreted on the tables there.

'This is crazy,' Zecchini complained. 'Those shots weren't more than a few minutes ago. How'd they get here so fast?'

Peroni had thought about that one already.

'The local Questura's just round the corner. I imagine they would have heard the shots.'

All the same, it was pretty swift work.

He stared at the two men he recognized. The monk had pulled a disgusted face when he talked about the officers who'd been assigned to Randazzo. He'd felt the same way when he'd run into this pair in the Questura.

'Also, unless I'm mistaken, *they* were supposed to stop something like this from happening. Hey! Lavazzi!'

One of them turned. At least Peroni had remembered one name. The man looked scared.

'A word please.'

He didn't move, just stayed where he was, clutching at the beer, looking around for help.

The plain-clothes man who was placing a plastic sheet over the corpse swore malevolently, finished the job, then strode over to meet them. Peroni dimly recognized him: one of the faceless people inside the main Piazzale Roma Questura, a local commissario who had never so much as given him or Costa a second glance all the time they had worked in Venice.

He spoke with a flat, monotonous northern accent that wasn't local or welcoming.

'You people really should find better ways to spend your time.'

Zecchini reached into his jacket and flashed his badge.

'Carabinieri,' he said, nodding at the sheet on the ground. 'We've got a warrant to interview this man.'

'Sadly it seems you came a little late.' Some medics had turned up. They were running a gurney along the paving stones, looking as if they were ready to move the body. Peroni thought of what had happened on the Isola degli Arcangeli. Everything got taken care of so very, very quickly.

'You should wait until your pathologist arrives,' he said. 'At least look as if you're trying.'

The anonymous commissario came close and gave him an ugly look. He was a short man with a walrus moustache and black, lifeless eyes.

'Shut up, Peroni,' he replied. 'This is our business, not yours. And we *are* trying by the way. In ways we never had to until you and your Roman buddies turned up. What is it with you people? This kind of crap just follows you around?'

Peroni wondered how long he'd have to stay in Venice before he broke the habit of a lifetime and started punching people.

'Like you said, Commissario,' he replied calmly. 'This is your business. It was your business long before we happened to come along. I'm sure it will be that way long after we're gone. Look to your own rotten apples. Not us.'

'You're gone now!' the officer bellowed, livid. 'You're no longer attached to this Questura. If you start poking your ugly nose in where it doesn't belong I'll throw you in a cell. Understood?' He glanced at Zecchini. 'The same goes for you. This is a state-police case, nothing to worry the Carabinieri.'

'We have a warrant!' Zecchini said again, taking the papers out of his pocket.

'*You can't serve a warrant on a dead man*,' the commissario yelled.

'They can ask why the hell he's dead,' Peroni interjected. 'When you were supposed to have men protecting him. Or is that not a question anyone's supposed to raise outside your little circle of friends?'

Peroni felt a little guilty about that last crack. The Questura wasn't above a little petty corruption, he didn't doubt that, but some general collusion in the assassination of a colleague, even one as little-loved as Gianfranco Randazzo, was just a step too far.

'Look,' he continued, 'I'm sorry I lost my temper. I'm just saying, maybe we can help.'

'I don't want your help.'

This man was scared, Peroni realized. He probably didn't understand why. All he knew was that he had to keep everything tight and organized and secret until someone else made the decision about what to do next.

'I'm just saying this,' Peroni went on. 'You've got a dead colleague on your hands. A man who was under suspension. A man for whom the Carabinieri had a warrant on the grounds of art smuggling.'

This last information made the moustache twitch a little. A name came back to Gianni Peroni. He tried to sound amenable.

'Commissario Grassi, why are we arguing? I know your accent. You're Milanese. Not from here. They don't give a shit about you any more than they do about me. We're all expendable. Maggiore Zecchini here too. If the carpet turns out to be too small to sweep all this mess under who do you think gets the blame? The Venetians? Or the likes of us?'

Peroni watched the reaction on Grassi's face and reflected upon the plain fact that a craven man could be as little use as a crooked one.

'What the hell are you talking about, Peroni? They all said you people were crazy. This is a crime on my watch. It gets investigated by me, the way I say.'

'You've got a dead commissario. You've got two murders on that weird island out there. And some corpse in the morgue put there by this man . . .'

He nodded at the gurney. To his disbelief they really were lifting Zecchini's body and placing it on the stretcher.

'Do you honestly think no one outside Venice is going to be watching all this and wondering?'

Grassi thought it over.

'Wondering what?'

It was Zecchini who answered.

'Wondering whether it isn't time that someone from elsewhere came and took a look at what's been going on here. People are starting to talk, Commissario. It gets hard to stop after a while. Sometimes a man has to think of his own career. And let's face it . . .'

Zecchini shrugged. He looked a little more confident again, Peroni was glad to see. Some awkward grain of doubt had been bugging the Carabinieri man ever since Costa had pushed him into this game.

'We're here,' the major added. 'Doesn't that give you something to think about?'

Grassi nodded.

'Lots,' he agreed. 'But principally this. You're here to interview a dead man. Peroni's here because he's an idiot who can't keep his nose out of something that doesn't concern him. Neither of you have any right or reason to occupy my time. Furthermore, if you do that I will, I promise, become very, very pissed off indeed.'

The gurney wheels squeaked across the paving stones.

'So you've got some suspects for this, Commissario?' Peroni asked wryly.

'Good police officers make enemies all the time,' Grassi answered, then gave him a withering look. 'Lousy ones too, sometimes. Best you remember that.'

With that Grassi turned on his heels and went back to the gurney and the corpse, back to barking routine orders at the SOCOs who stood around lazily putting on their bunny suits like men wishing they could bunk off for the day.

Zecchini watched him go, shaking his head.

'I need a beer,' he moaned. 'Anyone care to join me?'

'I'm buying,' Peroni said.

The Carabinieri man turned and gave him some kind of look Peroni didn't quite understand. Furtive maybe. Or just filled with some impending guilt.

'No,' Zecchini added. 'This one's on me. Best find your partner too. We need to talk.'

20

When he came to, Daniel Forster was still there, gun by his side, barrel not quite in Costa's face. Near enough though. Costa felt the site of the blow. There was blood there. He winced.

'A little of the English comes back in your voice when you're angry,' he observed.

Daniel Forster glared at him.

'You deserved it.'

'You're making a lot of assumptions. Can I get up? Would it be too much to ask for some water?'

The woman spoke to him rapidly in English, something Costa couldn't catch, then she went to the kitchen and came back with a glass. Costa dragged himself off the floor and took the water, gulping at it gratefully.

'You won't do anything stupid, Daniel,' she said firmly. 'I mean that.'

Costa found himself shocked by the man's appearance. Daniel Forster was a cultivated man, now he looked lost, broken, damaged. It was Laura Conti who was protecting him, it seemed. Not the other way round.

'Hear me out . . .' Costa began to say.

The shotgun waved in front of him again.

'Shut up! We've planned, you know. We can be out of here in an hour. There are boats. There are people who'll help us. We'll be gone before they even find your corpse.'

The woman put her hand firmly on the weapon.

'No, Daniel. I won't permit it.'

Costa took this in.

'I'm not who you think,' he said, gingerly reaching into his jacket and offering the ID card there. 'I'm a police officer. I'm here to ask you to help us do what we should have done years ago – put Hugo Massiter in jail.'

Forster looked astonished. Then he laughed. It wasn't an encouraging sound.

'Listen to him, Daniel!' Laura Conti snapped. 'Give him a chance.'

'A chance for the police to put Hugo in jail?' Forster asked. 'How many do they want?'

'Just one good one,' Costa replied immediately. 'You can give it to us.'

It was the woman who answered. She fixed him with sad, resigned eyes and said, 'No, that's not possible. We can't help you in any way. I'm sorry.'

Costa didn't understand and said so.

'Do you just want to stay in hiding for the rest of your lives? Being people you're not? Keeping out of the way?'

'And staying alive,' Daniel Forster said glumly. He scanned the room, hating what he saw. 'Even like this.'

'I promise you won't be in danger,' Costa added quickly. 'We can provide protection. Whatever you need.'

Forster laughed again. There was a little less harshness in his voice this time. Nic Costa saw a glimpse of the man he must once have been.

'We had what we needed once before,' he said with a sigh. 'A home. Money. Our freedom. Most of all, each other. Massiter came back from the dead somehow and stole everything but the last.'

He put down the weapon, clutched the woman around the waist briefly, kissed her cheek, then looked across at Costa again, his face stony with determination.

'He won't take that away too,' he added.

'But this isn't who you are,' Costa objected, watching the way she closed her eyes when Forster embraced her, the shared pain there.

She looked at the ID card more closely.

'Hugo Massiter stole who we were years ago, Agente Costa,' she said. 'What kind of a life do you think we'd go back to?'

He didn't have an easy answer. Then his phone rang inside his jacket pocket, a noise so loud it made each of them jump.

Costa took the call, watched by them, closely. Peroni was on the line. He listened, said little in reply, then put the phone away. They must have seen the expression on his face.

'Bad news?' she wondered.

They both stared at him, interested but still unmoved, Costa thought.

'I thought we had another witness,' Costa said. 'One who could bring Massiter down if I failed to find you.'

'And . . .?' she asked hopefully.

There was no point in lying.

'He's dead. No witnesses. I can surmise – we've been able to do that a lot – but proof . . .'

She took the empty glass from him, came back with it full, looked at his head and wiped the blood there with a tissue.

'Are you beginning to understand?' Laura Conti asked.

'Not really,' Costa admitted. 'Tell me.'

'It's very simple,' she said. 'You can't win, and by the time you realize that it's too late, because he already has you. The moment you get close to Massiter you're lost.'

He thought of Emily, and the risk she'd undertaken, willingly, of her own volition, though he could have prevented it.

'Too late for that,' he muttered.

Laura Conti stared at him with sad, dark eyes.

'In that case I pity you,' she said.

He stood his ground.

'I won't back down from this man. Nor should you. He was responsible for the deaths of people you knew. Piero's cousin and his companion. He killed those police officers. He ruined you. I thought . . .'

Costa hesitated. He was getting nowhere.

'What?' Forster asked. 'That we'd want revenge? What good would that do us? We just want to survive.'

'Nothing more,' the woman added. 'You can't ask us to throw that away.'

'I wouldn't dream of it. As I said, we can protect you.'

'The way you protected your witness?' she demanded sharply. 'Please. We know this man better than you. Go now. Leave us alone. Tomorrow we'll be gone. You won't tell anyone we're here, will you? There are no secrets in Venice. Not for long.'

Forster was eyeing the gun again.

'You're sure of this?' Costa asked.

They both nodded. There was nothing left he could use, no coercion, no persuasion.

'We're sure,' she said.

He nodded.

'In that case it's important you listen to me. Massiter will sign a business contract in a few hours. A very large one. A contract which will seal his position in the city and beyond. Once that's done, no one will dare touch him. Not on a local level. Not a regional one. Not even the national authorities, I believe, because . . .'

Meeting this pair, seeing the fear in their eyes, brought home to him the scale of the step Massiter was taking.

'. . . he will have such power over so many people. It would be difficult, perhaps impossible to go against him.'

Daniel Forster swore bitterly under his breath.

'I won't tell anyone of your whereabouts,' Costa promised. 'All the same, it would, perhaps, be prudent to think of going as far away as possible, telling no one. Certainly not Piero. You'll just extend the risk to him further. If I can help in some way . . .'

Forster's eyes glinted in the gloom of the shack.

'I could have killed him, you know,' he said. 'Once before.'

'Why didn't you?' Costa asked.

The young Englishman stared at the gun, a look in his face that was both hatred and regret.

'Because I was a fool.'

21

There was chop beneath the boat. Piero Scacchi had spent half of his life on the water. Instinctively, without a moment's analysis, he knew what that lurching, shifting power slapping at the *Sophia*'s ancient, battered planking signified. Change was on the way. Another storm perhaps, or the return of the sirocco, sweeping its way up from the south, its belly gorged with dust. Summer never died easily in the lagoon. It fought and screamed in protest at the coming cold. September was now two days away. The heat would remain for a month or more. But the fire and anger in the season's belly would recede as *estate* turned to *autonno*, the cooling, dwindling days followed, finally, by winter's clear, icy calm. That was the time Scacchi loved more than anything, when the grapes sat working in the Slovenian oak barrels he'd owned for years, when duck and snipe were on the wing and Xerxes felt ready to enter any marshland, any amount of slush and ice and mud, to find the prey newly fallen from the same bright, cloudless sky that must have sat over the littoral islands a millennium before.

But change was everywhere, unavoidable, a fact that had to be accepted. Now money would be an issue again, and he had no idea how to rise to meet the challenge of finding it this time around. He had one final load of wood and seaweed ash, bought for a pittance from a farmer in Le Vignole, the islet just south-west of Sant' Erasmo, to be delivered to the Arcangeli as agreed, and then Piero Scacchi would work for the family no more. Whatever happened, an island owned by Hugo Massiter was a place he could not countenance entering. The memories of the past still burned, when he allowed them. Not out of some desire for revenge, that was an emotion Piero

Scacchi found utterly remote. What had happened five years before, the death of his cousin, the eventual exile of Daniel Forster and Laura Conti, belonged to a series of conjoined tragedies he had no intention of revisiting. For Scacchi, it was important to live in the present, a present he could feel comfortable with, if not control entirely.

The dog now lay in the front of the boat, its black head over the prow, enjoying the salt tang blowing into its nostrils. Scacchi couldn't see its sharp, dark eyes, but he knew where they'd be looking. In the flat margin between the land and the sky, the territory where the pair of them had hunted for years. Sometimes he envied the animal. In matters of importance it was wise, all-knowing. No creature escaped its eyes, ears or nose. No possibility for advancement – be it food, or pleasure or adoration – was ever missed on those rare occasions a visitor came to call. The dog was a being that lived within its own world, satisfied, unsullied by ambition, as unconcerned about tomorrow as the idiots in the city.

The future was somewhere Piero Scacchi couldn't help but confront from time to time, finding it to be a bleak and empty place, one with no easy decisions, no safe havens to hide.

They'd been in the shack he'd built for them for two years now and no one had noticed, no one beyond the island. This was longer than any of them had intended. They – and he included himself here – had to find the money for some kind of proper escape. Some way of fleeing Venice for good. Hugo Massiter was back forever now. Piero Scacchi saw it in the way people spoke his name; the awe and fear the sound of those very English vowels brought to their eyes.

His dead cousin had said many memorable things. He'd had a way with words Piero could never match. One snatch of conversation had struck Piero Scacchi in particular, though only afterwards, when Massiter was supposedly gone from Venice, Daniel in jail, and Laura safely hidden away in the Lido.

The conversation had taken place on the *Sophia* that fateful summer, before the storm clouds fell, the boat ambling across the lagoon from a picnic on Sant' Erasmo, Xerxes at the tiller, his delicate jaws steering them safe back to Venice with the leather leash Piero had made to allow the dog to navigate from time to time.

There were just a few sentences, ones that came back into Piero's head now with the kind of clarity that only came from a glass too many of his good, well-oaked red, gulped from the plastic lemonade bottle he kept in the tool compartment for emergencies.

In his mind's eye he could see still them, alive, ridiculously happy, so full of joy with each other. They thought these days would never end. Scacchi, poor dead Scacchi, was waving a withered finger in Daniel Forster's face for some reason, trying to close down an argument he thought no one else had heard.

'You cannot outrun the Devil,' the old man declared sternly. 'Never!'

'I know,' Daniel replied with a lazy, half-drunk smile. 'I've heard that one. You can't run from the Devil because he can always run more quickly than you can.'

'That is the kind of stupid, trite, predictable nonsense I would expect to hear from a television set, were I to own such a thing,' Scacchi announced. 'I am . . . *disappointed*.'

Scacchi had a way of making disappointment sound like a cardinal sin. Daniel had taken the tongue-lashing in his stride. He was no longer some naive young English student by then, but Scacchi's creation. A man of the world. The Venetian world.

'Then what?' Daniel demanded.

'You cannot outrun the Devil,' Scacchi said, raising his glass in time to the bobbing of the lagoon, 'because it is impossible to outrun oneself. He is both a part of you and part of something else too. But without that hold on your own soul, which you, Daniel, must offer up yourself, he's nothing. Merely a predator in the night. The boogie man, as the Americans would have it. A creature worthy of terrifying children, nothing more. Therefore . . .'

Piero recalled the way the old man drew himself up on the hard bench of the *Sophia*, determined to make this last point stick.

'. . . in order to conquer the Devil you must first conquer yourself. Which is the hardest, the bravest, encounter of them all.'

He was a cunning and pompous old bastard. Piero had known that all along, and had feared his cousin a little at times. But he'd had a certain insight into the way a man's mind worked too. That conversation had hung around Piero Scacchi's head for years now. What Scacchi was suggesting seemed both true and horrible. That those who dealt with a creature like Massiter in part brought their fates upon themselves. That there were no black and white certainties, good and bad, right and wrong. Only shades of grey, tipped one way or the other by the actions of those who, throughout, supposed themselves to be the innocent wronged parties in the proceedings.

Piero regarded himself as a simple, honest man. He never expected anything he didn't earn. He never looked for another to shoulder his private or public burdens. He sought a quiet life in a world he sometimes scarcely liked to think about. Though he was reluctant to admit it, this was, in part, a kind of cowardice, a craving for simplicity as a bulwark against the difficult, complex world beyond Sant' Erasmo. Elsewhere men and women moved to more intricate rhythms, feeding off one another out of laziness and greed, then going home, sleeping soundly at night, confident that their actions could be justified because that, from their perspective, was the way of things.

He fought no such battles. He hoped that helping Laura and Daniel hide was a kind of bravery. Sometimes, though, he wondered if he was merely disguising another act of cowardice – he couldn't in truth regard fleeing the Devil in any other way.

He glanced back at the low mass of his own island now emerging as he rounded the Le Vignole shoreline. The crooked, makeshift jetty of home sat there in the distance, calling to him, waiting for Scacchi and the dog to return and make the place whole. That was where he belonged. He and those like him. Not Daniel. Not Laura. They were victims in a drama that was partly of their own making. That didn't lessen his sympathy for them. In a way it made him more determined to help, since they seemed blind to their own culpability, outwardly at least. They had been robbed of their existences by Hugo Massiter, just as much as old Scacchi had. More, if he was honest with himself, since they continued to live and be haunted by the day they fell into his grasp. Scacchi had understood, from an early age, that, to a good man, the damaged deserved assistance from the whole. It was a duty he'd never questioned, not when his mother began to lose first her health, then her sanity. Life was such a brief, irreplaceable gift, and death so dark and empty and terrible, that he was happy to do whatever he could to improve affairs for those whom he pitied.

He kept looking at the jetty, thinking now of other visitors. The odd bunch of police officers, one short, young and enthusiastic, one old and ugly and wise. And the third, the inspector, who had a darkness in his bright, intelligent eyes that Piero Scacchi recognized the moment he saw it.

That man had danced with the Devil, though a part of him had yet to face up to the fact.

A little giddy from the wine, Piero found his gaze wandering, across the lagoon to the city waterfront and that long monotonous stretch of tall buildings running from Celestia to the Fondamente Nove. He read the papers avidly each day. It was important to be informed. They carried much about the rise of Hugo Massiter and how the Englishman had great plans for the Isola degli Arcangeli. They carried a little, though not too much, about the aftermath of the tragedy in the palazzo, an event he might have witnessed had he not delivered his cargo that evening, then made himself scarce as quickly as possible, anxious to get away from the peacocks and painted ladies pouring onto the island.

The troubled inspector now lay somewhere in that complex of buildings on the distant waterfront. Piero wondered whether the man had met his own personal demons in his sleep, and which of them would win if such a confrontation occurred.

'A man cannot outrun himself,' he said, aware of a slight slur in his voice, one that came from a plastic cup too many of the heady dark wine he'd extracted from the previous year's crop of Sangiovese, Oselata and Corvina vines that grew like tortured serpents in the dark earth by the sea.

Everything moves to meet its fate, he thought. All that changed was the pace, the speed at which one closed upon the final meeting.

His head swam. He wanted to give the dog another chance at the tiller, to point the vessel across the lagoon at the distant island, with its iron angel, for the last time, a burden he would never have to inflict upon Xerxes again.

Then something caught his attention. A water taxi, long, sleek and polished, rounding his corner of Sant' Erasmo, opening up its powerful engines, lifting its nose above the grey lagoon, speeding back towards the city.

No one ever used those boats on the island. They didn't have the money. They didn't have the need.

Puzzled, he thought about the *Sophia*'s decrepit, puny motor, so weak it could scarcely keep up with the trash boats that trundled garbage from the city to dump on some distant destination at the periphery of the lagoon.

He watched the water taxi's silhouette diminishing in the distance, and wished he could match a quarter of its speed. Piero Scacchi knew he had to see the Isola degli Arcangeli one more time, and then be done with the place for good.

22

Costa was still on the phone when they moored at the San Pietro vaporetto stop. The roar of the reversing diesel sent a flock of startled pigeons rising into the perfect sky. He gave the taxi owner a hefty wad of notes then stepped ashore, fixing his eyes on the crooked campanile ahead of him, wondering how to reach it through the warren of solitary alleyways spreading out from the waterside. Even here, on this deserted island only just attached to the main bulk of Venice, it was impossible to escape the city's drive for power. Until two centuries before, the sprawling hulk of San Pietro had been the city's cathedral, a symbol of the Church which the state had exiled, quite deliberately, to the distant periphery to make sure no one, not priest nor congregation, was in any doubt that the spiritual must always give way to the temporal. Today, what little power the area had once possessed had been entirely dissipated, blown away like pollen on the wind. Deserted save for a few pensioners enjoying the sun on the sparse green grass in front of the cathedral, it seemed an appropriate place to plan the final act of a conspiracy.

He'd called each of them as he made his way across the lagoon. Teresa Lupo had now given up watching Leo Falcone sleeping in the Ospedale Civile. She felt content about him. He wouldn't stir for a while. The surgeon she'd brought in to manage his case had assured her Falcone was out of danger, not that she'd needed his opinion. On the phone, her voice difficult to hear over the noise of the taxi battling across the lagoon, she'd told how she'd seen the fire in Falcone's eyes as the sedative fought and won the battle to put him to sleep. There might be difficult times ahead, but Leo would return to the fray, and keep on returning until something stopped him for good.

It was a quiet, pointed rebuke about Costa's own position, perhaps, but one he'd little time to consider at that moment.

Gianni Peroni would, he felt sure, still be furious after a brief and ill-tempered episode at the big Questura in Piazzale Roma. In desperation, and against Costa's advice, he'd made one last effort to persuade some individual above the head of Commissario Grassi that the murder of Randazzo could only be investigated properly if it were seen in the light of the Bracci case and, by implication, that of Uriel and Bella Arcangelo. It had been like screaming at the deaf. Peroni hadn't got beyond the pen-pusher at the desk, who'd made one call, to a name he didn't recognize, then told him the station was too busy to waste time on someone who no longer worked there.

It had taken a while for Costa to get through to Zecchini on his mobile. Zecchini was circumspect, unwilling to talk and had pleaded the need for some time to himself. The Carabinieri had an office not far from the Castello Questura, in the Campo San Zaccaria. It wasn't hard to guess what Luca would do next. Exactly what any safe, conventional officer would in the circumstances. Call back to base, explain the situation to a superior, await orders. Prepare to share the blame. A content, well-ordered man like Zecchini surely believed that only an idiot would put his neck on the block without good reason. The major had gone a long way already, all on the basis of a brief personal friendship with a man from a rival force. From the brief conversation they had, one in which Costa struggled to persuade him to come to the meeting on San Pietro, it was difficult to gauge how much more he, or his superiors, could accept.

And then, finally, Costa had phoned Emily, left a message, since she was on voicemail, and received a brief call a little while later, during which she promised to be at the cathedral as he asked.

There was no time to wonder about the hesitation in her voice, no time for anything but to try to devise a way ahead. It was now almost five p.m. The Isola degli Arcangeli would be signed away to its new fate in little over an hour.

Costa looked ahead and saw a slender figure in a dark silk suit standing half-hidden by the side of the crooked white marble campanile that leaned at an odd angle, set apart from the cathedral to which it belonged.

'Where have you been?' she asked directly when he joined her.

'Chasing ghosts.'

'Did you find them?'

This wasn't the conversation he wanted just then.

'Not exactly. It was a stupid idea, probably. I don't think Leo would have approved.'

Emily looked at the wound on his head. Laura Conti had given him a plaster. He could feel the sticky blood had oozed beyond the fabric.

'You're hurt, Nic.'

Her hand went to his hair, her eyes examined the site of the blow.

'Head wounds can be nasty. You should see a doctor.'

'Later. We don't have time.'

'Don't we?'

He hadn't seen her look like this before. Her eyes no longer shone. Her face had a flat, emotionless cast that made her seem older, sadder.

'And you?'

'I've been trying to get you what you want.'

'I know. Thanks.'

He touched her bare arm, then kissed the softness of her cheek, aware of the way she steeled herself against him.

'I mean it. Thanks.'

'I don't think it worked,' she murmured. 'I'm sorry . . .'

There was an expression in her face, a lost, desolate look he didn't recognize.

'Let's not pre-judge anything,' he said. 'We've more than one way to skin this particular cat.'

'Really? Are you sure he isn't skinning us? Along with everyone else?'

'Is that how it feels?'

'To me it does. Let's get started, shall we?' She nodded at the cathedral door. 'They're waiting for you. I want this out of my life forever after this evening. Understand this well: come tomorrow I'm gone from Venice.' Her blue eyes didn't leave him, looking for something she didn't seem to find. 'With you or without you.'

He didn't deserve any better. Costa had been pushing all of them ever since Falcone had gone into hospital. By force of circumstance, Emily had been close to Hugo Massiter. Costa had been blind to what that could mean. He had only really begun to consider the possible cost when he saw Laura Conti and Daniel Forster cowering in that little hovel on Sant' Erasmo, still terrified of a man they hadn't seen for years.

'Tomorrow we leave,' he said, taking her hands. 'Tuscany. Anywhere. Wherever you want. I promise.'

'People in your job make a lot of promises,' she replied, and strode through the door, into the dark lofty belly of the cathedral, empty save for a caretaker at the door and three figures seated on a wooden bench set in the shadows of the nave: Teresa, Peroni and, to Costa's surprise, Luca Zecchini, who sat between the two of them. He looked cheerier than at any time since the two of them had pounced as he sat eating a peaceful meal in Verona the day before.

Costa pulled up a couple of flimsy metal chairs, positioned them opposite this unlikely trio, and introduced Emily to the man from the Carabinieri.

'I wasn't sure you'd come, Luca. I wasn't sure I should have asked you, to be honest.'

'Hell,' Zecchini answered with a broad grin. 'Leo always said you people were good for keeping ennui away. I decided I was getting a little bored.'

'And your men?' Costa asked

'They're too young and too junior to risk being anything other than bored. I don't mind putting my own job on the line, but I don't extend that privilege to my officers. I imagine Leo's the same.'

Peroni emitted a loud guffaw.

'Sure,' the big man said, still laughing. 'That's why we're here.'

'If we can bring Massiter down, he's yours,' Costa offered. 'That should take care of any unpleasantness.'

'Mine. Yours.' The major shrugged nonchalantly. 'What does it matter? I've talked to my people, Nic. They've no ties here. Remember that. They've also got a lot of reasons to want Hugo Massiter in jail if there's a good chance of keeping him there.'

Costa nodded. He understood that last qualification well.

'On the other hand,' Zecchini added. 'If we screw up . . .' The way his pale, intelligent face turned suddenly glum said it all. 'He's going to be untouchable once he pushes this deal through,' he continued. 'Everyone knows it, everyone's basing their position on that understanding. He'll have people in his debt well beyond Venice: in the region; in Rome even. They're frightened of Massiter as it is. Once he's tied them up in all the loans and guarantees and whatever other backhanders go along with something like this—'

'We get the picture,' Peroni interrupted.

'I'm glad you do,' Zecchini said. 'This may be everyday stuff for you. For me . . .' Without thinking he pulled out a pack of cigarettes then, under Costa's steely gaze, took one look around the gloomy cathedral interior, laughed, and put it away. 'And in a church, too. So, people, what do we have? Can we charge this man with anything? Can we even put him under arrest?'

'I don't know,' Costa said frankly. 'What about the smuggling? You tell me.'

Zecchini scowled.

'Not a chance. Not with what we have.' He smiled at Emily Deacon. 'I don't want to disappoint you. I've no idea how you got that material. From what I know of Massiter it was a very brave thing to do. Our computer people are taking a look at it right now. They say that, without a password, it could take months to decode anything. Someone would have to sign off those resources too. I really don't see that happening. They're still looking. But . . .'

Peroni didn't look too happy with this.

'It's not just the computer files,' he objected. 'There's Randazzo. Massiter's relationship with him. That material in Randazzo's house.'

'Where's the proven link?' Zecchini demanded.

'It's got to be there! Bring Massiter in and ask him.'

'On what grounds? I've no evidence that says Randazzo got his illicit goods from Massiter. We've nothing that proves the relationship between them was anything other than proper, or to suggest Massiter was behind the shooting of this Bracci character.'

'We *know*,' Costa insisted.

Zecchini wasn't going to be moved.

'From what I've heard I don't doubt you're right. Otherwise why would I be here? All the same . . . in terms of hard fact, I can't see I've anything to help you. If we had a couple of weeks to run up an inventory of what's in Randazzo's house, check it off against a known list, perhaps then we'd have something, though a direct link to Massiter could still be hard to prove. But we're talking about lots of time and lots of manpower, and we don't have the luxury of either. If I'm wrong, just tell me. I can't see it any other way.'

'So that's my contribution out of the window,' Emily remarked. 'Is there anything left?'

'There's what we had to begin with,' Teresa suggested. 'Bella and Uriel Arcangelo. And now this.'

She reached into her large, black leather bag and took out the digital camera she always carried these days. On the bright screen was a photo of the monogrammed cotton shirt they'd found in Ca' degli Arcangeli. 'It's safe in a private lab in Mestre. Silvio's there working on it.'

'What does it tell us so far?' Costa asked.

'The blood's Bella's. And that piece of cloth belongs to Massiter, surely. Who we also know slept with her on more than one occasion on his yacht to get closer to the family. Incontrovertible proof, solid DNA. All the stuff you people love these days. Perhaps—'

She stopped, seeing the disappointment on their faces.

'What about the apron?' Peroni asked. 'I thought you'd got evidence it had been messed with somehow?'

'I was one step ahead of myself. It's been contaminated by Tosi's lab in Mestre. It could be weeks before we get a proper report.'

'We can't make an arrest out of that,' Zecchini said with a grimace.

'Why not?' she demanded. 'Think it through. Bella's pregnant. She's screaming at Massiter to own up to being the father. Perhaps she wants to ditch Uriel and move in with the Englishman. He could have set out to kill her in the house, then murdered Uriel and made it look as though he was responsible. Does anyone have a problem with that?'

'In principle, no,' Costa said. What they knew of the facts seemed to support the idea. Just as importantly, it seemed to fit with what Costa understood of Hugo Massiter's personality. Greed, sexual avarice, ruthlessness . . . and an agile facility for escaping the blame, pushing it on to others, as he'd done with Laura Conti and Daniel Forster. 'But it's supposition. There's not enough hard evidence.'

'*What?*' she screeched. 'To hell with deduction, let's rely on good old-fashioned chemistry. Bella's blood is on Massiter's shirt. If that's not evidence, I don't know what is.'

'It's a shirt that seems to have belonged to Massiter,' Emily pointed out. 'That's as far as we can push it. Bella could have taken it herself from his yacht. We know she went there. He keeps that apartment in the palazzo too. Even though he only uses it during the day at the moment, he must have clothes there. If you stood up in court and tried to use the shirt as evidence of Massiter's involvement you'd get torn to shreds. With good reason. It proves nothing.'

'It's going to prove everything!' Teresa yelled. 'Just wait.'

'What do you mean?' Costa asked.

'I didn't tell you this. I can't fit it into the timeframe you have, so it seemed irrelevant. But Silvio's found other evidence on the shirt too. We think there's DNA from the perpetrator. Sweat by the looks of it.'

Emily brightened suddenly. 'And it's Massiter's?'

Teresa didn't look any of them in the eye at that moment.

'Things aren't as simple as that. Blood's really easy to extract. This is a lot harder. Even so, I'm pushing to get some results.'

'When?' Peroni demanded.

She swore quietly then walked over into a dark corner leaving the four of them staring at each other in silence, listening to Teresa alternately bullying and wheedling down the phone.

When she came back she looked distinctly downcast.

'Even if Silvio pulls out all the stops the soonest we could get confirmation would be around seven this evening. Chemistry's like that. It doesn't lend itself to short cuts. Sorry.'

Zecchini stared at the two cops.

'Seven's too late. Massiter's safe by then.'

'Then perhaps we just have to accept he's won,' Emily said with marked reluctance. 'That this is as good as we're going to get. Leo will live. We can quietly pass this evidence to the right people at the right time. A few months down the line they could do something with it. Or hand the information on to the media and let them start working.'

'This is a job for us,' Costa said firmly. 'Or the Carabinieri. No one else. And either it happens now or it doesn't happen at all. We all know that.'

She smiled.

'There. You see. He's got you too. That's the way Hugo works. It's what makes him tick. Not the money. Not the property. It's the fact that he has a hold over people. He *owns* them. More people than ever. Us too now. And we'll get a call one day. A little favour from him. A little something in return.'

Peroni looked baffled.

'Why the hell would any of us go along with it?'

'Because he'd be offering something we wanted!' Emily insisted. 'For you two, maybe a lead. For me, some work. Who knows? That's how it begins. We mustn't let this man get any further into our lives, Nic. If he knew we were here trying to come up with some conspiracy to bring him down, and failing, do you know what he'd think? It would make him happy. He'd feel validated. He'd know he was inside us.'

Costa caught her eye then, wished there was more you could say with a glance. Hugo Massiter was inside her life already. Costa had invited him there.

'So he signs at six,' he said. 'And an hour later we get a report that puts him at the murder scene, one no one in their right mind will want to read. Teresa, there has to be a way—'

'No! No! No!' she screeched. 'I know what you're going to say and it's not possible. I can't change the laws of physics. Silvio's stretching everything to the limit as it is.'

They sat in silence, still. All apart from Luca Zecchini, who constantly rocked back and forth on the bench. He glowered at each of them in turn, half astonished, half furious and asked, 'So is that *it*?'

The rest stared at him.

'That's it,' Costa conceded eventually. 'We've nothing left.'

'*What?* Leo said something about how you never gave up,' he complained. 'Leo said you could always come up with something.'

'Leo's not around, in case you hadn't noticed,' Teresa objected bitterly.

'He told me he didn't need to be. Maybe I should go round to that hospital room of his, wake him up and tell him how wrong he was, if there's nothing better to do.'

It was Peroni who spoke next.

'There are only so many times we can bang our heads against this wall, Luca.'

Nic Costa's thoughts kept returning to the couple across the lagoon, and the promise he'd made. He remembered the terror in the woman's eyes when she thought he'd come from Massiter. Emily was right as usual, so perceptive, so sharp. Massiter's power was that he stayed with those he'd touched, like a virus in the blood. She'd been closer to Massiter than the rest of them. She'd felt that power, just as Laura Conti and Daniel Forster had. The damage it caused was deep, something to be resented and feared. But with that fear came some need for resolution too. This was the dilemma Laura and the Englishman faced, and had yet to conquer.

Running didn't work. It hadn't for Laura Conti and Daniel Forster. It wouldn't for Emily either. What he'd unwittingly made her do already threatened to destroy the remains of their relationship. He'd seen the dead look in Emily's face outside the cathedral, understood instinctively what it probably meant. She was an ex-FBI agent. When it came to getting the job done, nothing, not personal pride, not self-respect, would have stood in the way, and he should have known that all along.

Costa thought of that great glass hall where a stray bullet had changed all their lives, sent Leo Falcone spinning towards a brush with death, despatched the rest of them on a quest for justice that came at a cost he should have understood from the start.

The palazzo scared him a little. It was too full of memories. Emily in her lovely angel's guise, with the scarlet wound of the *peperoncini* on her feathered wing, falling under Hugo Massiter's sway. That lost moment at which the two of them could have escaped everything. And Leo Falcone stricken on the ground, blood seeping from his mouth as Teresa fought to staunch the flow.

He looked Zecchini in the eye, liked the sudden flash of interest he found there.

'We only need an hour, for God's sake. Surely we can stall him for that?'

'You'd think . . .' Zecchini replied. 'But how?'

Nic Costa smiled at the man in the dark suit.

'We don't need to arrest Massiter. We just have to keep him away from signing that contract until Silvio gets some results. Then you've got a prima facie case for taking him into custody on the spot.'

'But *how*?' Teresa wanted to know.

He didn't like the idea. He didn't enjoy breaking his word. There had been a time when Nic Costa would never have countenanced what he was considering next, but the more he thought about it, the more he realized he had no choice.

'By giving Hugo Massiter something he wants even more than the Isola degli Arcangeli.'

23

Alberto Tosi disliked public occasions. Especially one where the host had assembled an entire orchestra, placed it on a podium, and ordered it to play background music to the chink of glasses and the banter of idiots. Music deserved better than that. Had Anna not proved so enthusiastic – *insisted* was, perhaps a better word – he would have spent this hot high-summer evening on the terrace of his large apartment on Sant' Elena, the quiet, somewhat geriatric island beyond the Biennale Gardens and Castello, enjoying a spritz and the breeze off the lagoon.

Instead he was on the Isola degli Arcangeli watching a couple of hundred members of the city's finest prepare to feed their faces on dish after dish of rich delicacies supplied, doubtless at great expense, by the Cipriani, and all to mark . . . what? Tosi was unsure of the answer. To honour their own splendour in all probability. This was, he had soon come to judge, an unpleasantly narcissistic gathering.

Anna, to his disappointment, was part of the show. She was dressed in a rather short skirt and shiny red silk blouse, the skimpiest clothing her grandfather had ever seen her wear. The John Lennon spectacles had been replaced by contact lenses, which gave her a rather glassy-eyed look, Tosi thought, not that it stopped the men despatching inquisitive, admiring glances in her direction.

Had he cared, Tosi, in his old dark work suit, might have felt himself under-dressed. Everyone else seemed to be as fixated with their appearance as Anna was. Dinner jackets and evening dresses flitted around him in a constant swirl. Half the splendid, chattering dining rooms of Venice would be empty this night. Their owners had gathered on the Arcangeli's sad little island to raise their glasses to its supposed rebirth and, more importantly, Tosi felt, to the Englishman who had breathed new life back into the island. A man who was about to become a kind of modern Doge, honorary lord of the city, a grandee in all but title, elevated by his peers in a symbiotic process – one in which gratitude was both given and received. Tosi was coming to understand this only too well.

He'd watched the way Massiter strutted through his audience. A puffed-up peacock of a man, quite unlike most of the upper-class English Tosi had known over the years. At one point he'd wished for the courage to walk up to this newly crowned faux-aristocrat, and point out that sometimes the Venetians tore down the princes they had so warmly elected only a little while before. A screeching mob had cut the throat of Ipato Orso, the first Doge. Marino Faliero had been summarily beheaded by his fellow nobles, and at the age of seventy. Not that creatures like Massiter knew or cared about history. It was a subject for old men these days, though that was not the reason Tosi failed to make the point to his unwanted host. Respect and fear went hand in hand in circles such as these, a fact the old pathologist never let slip from his sharp and capacious memory.

Sometimes he wondered what Venice would be like fifty years hence. He was grateful he wouldn't be around to witness the transformation. The streets would echo to the gabbled tones of English and Russian and Chinese, anything but the gritty vowels of the Veneto Tosi still liked to speak at home on Sant' Elena. The place would be an international zone, run by foreigners for foreigners, with only dependent locals still around to hunt for crumbs.

Alberto Tosi believed he was a civilized man, one who had long understood that the world always changed. But sometimes, when he read the local newspaper and the latest plans to bring ever more hordes of tourists into an already over-choked city, he was unable to shake off the impression that progress was merely an illusion, a catchword designed to disguise the cruel trick being played upon the many by the few.

There was precious little space for self-respect in this new Venice, a quality Tosi regarded as essential, a badge of pride to be worn by everyone, from the man who made your coffee in the morning, carefully working the valves and pipes of his Gaggia machine, to an ageing city pathologist who was still more than a little disgruntled about being railroaded by the authorities when it suited them. Without self-respect, one was simply a wage slave for the faceless figures who seemed to own everything, control everything, pulling the city's strings from inside their banks and accountants' offices. Tosi had no problems with the idea of a society divided by class, provided each level had its own reason to survive. This new world unjustly divided its occupants into winners and losers, the few and the many, making a pretence of egalitarianism when, in truth, it was more closely, tightly and viciously elitist than the ancient regime it sought to supplant with its new cabal of rogues.

Massiter, a master rogue, as all knew and none dared say, played this game like a maestro. The Arcangeli had always been discerning about those they allowed beyond the outstretched arm of the iron angel and its torch, which now burned more brightly than ever. The Englishman had decreed that the gates to the island be open for the first time Alberto Tosi could remember. This evening anyone in Venice was welcome to walk through to admire the coronation.

Few, beyond Massiter's large and growing circle of hangers-on and succubi, seemed to have bothered. Tosi knew what the locals on Murano were like. They hated incomers. They'd loathed the Arcangeli for decades. Nothing, not money, not influence, would make them warm towards Hugo Massiter. This was an adventure beyond them, the arrival of the first speck of canker from across the water that would, one day, consume their impoverished little island and spit out in its place the same gaudy, transient hoopla found everywhere else in the city.

Tosi tasted his weak, badly made spritz and scowled. Then he saw a familiar figure approaching, one who generated both admiration and a little anxiety.

Anna followed the direction of his gaze. Teresa Lupo, the Roman pathologist, was striding towards them with a deliberate, determined gait.

'I'll see you later,' the girl muttered. He watched her depart in a flash of bright red silk, gone to where the young were gathered, next to the drinks table manned by serious, white-shirted waiters working beneath the fiery torch of the iron angel. This was only Alberto Tosi's second time on the Isola degli Arcangeli. The first had been almost fifty years before, at some grand gathering to which his own father had somehow managed to wangle an invitation. Those had been different days, with different people. It had been another two decades before the accident which closed the palazzo to the public for good. But even by then the island's fortunes had changed. Angelo Arcangelo was dead, and he took his dream with him to a temporary grave on San Michele across the water.

He was ruminating on this fact when his attention was drawn by Teresa Lupo's bright, cheery face.

'You're a little late for the crime scene, Alberto,' she declared with a brisk, sardonic smile.

He laughed and, for a moment, a rebel part of him wondered whether a lively Roman pathologist on the cusp of middle age could possibly be interested in an ancient widower with little to offer but the same shared interests.

'Which one?' he asked. 'This place has so many. Those poor people in the furnace. That Bracci character. Your own inspector. How is he by the way?'

'Much better,' she replied. 'But dreaming for now.'

'Dreaming is a talent to cultivate. Particularly tonight.' He finished the glass and took a second off one of the starchy waiters drifting by. Tosi scowled at the crowd. 'I wonder how many dreams these little lives encompass. They're all too busy counting their money or running through their wardrobes.'

There was a cunning glint in her eye, one he didn't quite trust.

'Perhaps they're here for the thrill,' she said with cryptic glee. 'To be so near the smell of blood.'

'In Rome they may play those childish games, perhaps. This is just Venice, Teresa. A small and simple city, where we lead small and simple lives.'

She scanned the glittering crowd.

'I don't think they'd like that description.'

'I don't think their opinion counts for much,' he answered, unable to suppress the bitterness in his voice. 'There's scarcely a real Venetian here.'

'What about him?'

She was pointing down to the quayside where an old, rather shabby boat, with an equally shabby man at the wheel, was docking near the warehouse. A small mountain of grey material occupied part of its meagre hold, alongside a pile of firewood, thin twigs, meagre kindling, the kind they used out in the little shacks of the lagoon. In the bows lay a small black dog, seemingly asleep.

The sight puzzled him. Then he saw the Sant' Erasmo marking on the stern.

'He's just a *matto* making a delivery. Wood and ash, by the looks of things. They use them in the furnace. Not for much longer from what I hear.'

She wasn't listening, which disappointed Tosi, a man not averse to gossip, of which there was plenty at the moment. Instead, Teresa Lupo was on the phone, anxious for some news, disappointed when she apparently did not receive it.

His gaze moved to the house. Some figures were walking towards the front door, watched by the shabby boatman. These were the type of men he recognized. Plain-clothes police officers, from elsewhere, not Venice, since Albert Tosi prided himself on the fact that he knew every last person on the city force by sight.

They had two people with them, a man and a woman, dressed in poor rural clothes, like the shabby boatman. Two people who were handcuffed, hands to the front, a cruel and unnecessary action, Tosi thought, since they showed no sign of resistance.

He turned away and stared at the foundry. It looked like new. The stonework had been cleaned. The long show windows were shiny and spotless. Soon the trinket-sellers would arrive, he guessed. Everyone knew what Massiter was like: he wouldn't allow glass-making on such valuable real estate for long.

'Did you really sign off Uriel's death as spontaneous combustion?' Teresa asked, apparently out of the blue.

'No,' he answered with a coy, sly reticence.

'Why not?'

'You made me think better of it. Sometimes we have a tendency to over-analyse. A man burns to death in a foundry consumed by fire. There are unexplained details, but in the end I remained unconvinced by Anna's efforts. She's a good girl. A little too enthusiastic at times. The young rely on their imagination too much. Age teaches one to rely on hard fact.'

She was regarding him closely, looking for some emotion, it seemed.

'It could have made things awkward, too,' she suggested. 'An unusual finding such as that would have attracted attention. Invited others to look, perhaps.'

'I agree,' he said, and raised his glass. 'To the unexplained!'

She was, he was coming to believe, a very attractive woman. Not physically, but in her personality. A difficult woman, though. One he would not wish to be around for long.

Teresa Lupo had an important point to make. He could see that from the sudden serious look in her face.

'I hope you don't mind me talking shop,' she went on.

'Not at all. Let me do the same. What about that material I gave you? Have you a report back from you magic machine in Rome?'

'No,' she replied grumpily.

'Ah.' He hoped there was some expression of sympathy on his face.

'Those samples you gave me were contaminated when we got them,' she complained. 'You should kick a few family backsides in that lab of yours in Mestre.'

He laughed, unsure of her point.

'Contaminated with what?'

She paused, as if she were hunting for the name, then said, 'Ketone.'

Alberto Tosi pulled a pained face. It was one of the chemicals they had to work with these days.

'Horrible stuff. Toxic. Highly flammable too, though very good at its job.'

He sighed. Sometimes you had to tell the truth. There really was no point in beating about the bush.

'I must confess something, Teresa. The samples I gave you were just that. Samples. The lab in Mestre did nothing to them. *Nothing*. As I endeavoured to explain when we first met, this was a closed case. There seemed no reason. What you had was what came straight from the foundry over there.'

She stared at him, astonished and, it seemed to Tosi, more than a little worried too.

'You did nothing to clean away the foam?' she asked.

'Not a thing. Why should we?'

Teresa Lupo was gazing at him with an expression of frank amazement. Alberto Tosi felt lost, unable to offer any comment which would make a difference.

'Then Uriel *was* murdered,' she said softly, almost to herself. 'And I know how,' she added, then excused herself and began to stride towards the house, pushing through the crowd, punching at her phone as she went.

24

Hugo Massiter stood in front of the *occhio*, the bulging glass eye, surveying the expanse of the lagoon. The three remaining Arcangeli sat in silence at the old family table, surrounded on both sides by lawyers. His. Theirs. Not that the difference mattered. Massiter knew the legal profession better than any fading Murano dynasty. There were, in his view, two kinds of lawyers: those seeking agreement and those seeking delay. In his time he'd used both. But only the former had been brought into the negotiations over the island, for him and, with a quiet, subtle stealth, for the Arcangeli too. In truth, a satisfactory conclusion – by which he meant a conclusion satisfactory to him – had never been in doubt.

He cast a cynical glance at the crowd below. Suits and evening dresses, caparisoned cattle come for the free food and drink, and the chance to touch the new emperor's robe. It seemed an age now since the evening of the carnival gala, and the death in the palazzo next door. People like these had short memories. As long as the Massiter name was on the way up, they'd be happy clinging to his coat-tails, hurrahing all the way. Nothing mattered but money and success. With those, a man could act as he liked. As his nature told him.

Then he caught a commotion in the crowd by the door, saw Emily Deacon fighting to push her way through, a fixed, anxious look on her attractive face, and recalled, briefly, the night before, trying to isolate what feelings he had from the practical issues uppermost in his mind. It had been a night of disappointment, if he were honest with himself. He enjoyed only two kinds of women: the averse and the enthusiastic. Either way you got a little fight, which was necessary to

Massiter's pleasure. Emily fulfilled neither requirement. She was a woman of duty, and duty always bored him.

Nevertheless, he'd hear her out. There'd be some interest there.

Beaming, he turned away from the shining window and its glorious view, turned his smile on the room, even on the miserable, mute Michele, with his dead eye and frozen cheek, and boomed, 'Oh my! Such long faces! Why? You all have your snouts deep in the Massiter trough now. You're prosperous. Millions, Michele. And – ' he walked round, behind the man, briefly placed a patronizing, magisterial hand on his shoulder, keeping it firmly there even as Michele flinched – 'that little lock-up in the city, a shop to sell your trinkets to the hoi polloi. What more could a Murano man ask?'

'Don't push me,' Michele muttered.

Massiter strode to the head of the table – the master's position – then sat in the high-backed chair there, surveying them, judging them. Miserable Michele. Lost Gabriele. And the woman, Raffaela, who seemed detached from everything, willing to go along with whatever humiliating solution Massiter could extract, provided the family survived, an intact bundle of visible misery.

'I'm only pushing you towards wealth,' Massiter said with half a yawn, 'which hereabouts equates with happiness, naturally. A small thank you wouldn't be out of place. And here's one more piece of generosity . . .'

He nodded at the huge portrait over the fireplace. Angelo Arcangelo, the dead patriarch, glowering at them all, his old, incisive eyes full of some harsh and bitter judgement.

'You can take that with you when you go,' the Englishman added. 'Bad art offends me. I don't want those hideous features staring down at my guests.'

There was a silence, broken only by the cough of one of Massiter's lawyers.

'Guests?' Raffaela asked finally.

'Guests.'

It was good to tell them now.

'Not that it's any business of yours any more. In a year I'll have a hotel here, and a restaurant that will put the Cipriani to shame. In two years a gallery to steal the glory from the Guggenheim. A modest, refined shopping mall for immodest, unrefined shoppers. Suites. Apartments. Facilities. That's what the modern world's about, Michele. A flash of transient joy for the masses before you move them on their way. Not' – he scowled, couldn't help it; Massiter hated to see lost opportunities, even those missed by men he could exploit – 'trying to squeeze a grubby living out of glass just because that's how it always was.'

Michele Arcangelo stared at his reflection in the old polished table, for the last time.

'Gloating is an unattractive trait, Signor Massiter,' the woman said with a quiet, firm certainty.

'I'm an unattractive man,' Massiter replied immediately. 'More people might notice if they weren't so blinded by their own avarice.'

There was a noise at the door.

'Visitors,' he said. 'Open the door, Gabriele. There's a good chap.'

The brother didn't demur for a moment, didn't notice Michele's vile, muttered aside. He let in Emily Deacon, by her side the young policeman, the one she had pretended she'd abandoned, an act that had never fooled Massiter for a moment. They looked uncertain of themselves. A little afraid, perhaps.

Massiter was on his feet in an instant, striding over to Emily, kissing her very quickly on the cheek, pumping the man's hand for a second.

'This won't be unpleasant, will it?' he asked meekly. 'Please don't spoil my day.'

'Why should it be unpleasant?' she replied.

He shrugged, looking at the little cop.

'I'm sorry this brief interlude between Emily and myself turned into a personal matter, Agente Costa. It was regrettable. And . . .' He smiled to ensure they understood. 'Pointless too. Those items she took from my yacht this morning . . .'

Massiter recalled the details the men had beaten out of the servant before throwing her out onto the street. It seemed a decidedly amateurish effort on Emily's part. She had disappointed him there too.

'They're of no use to you,' he went on. 'Even in Italy there are such things as rules of evidence. You can't try to obtain incriminating detail on a man by asking a pretty young woman to hunt for it in his bed.'

He watched the pain flicker on Costa's face, relishing the sight.

'Ah. I'm sorry. You didn't know. Or rather, you knew, but preferred not to acknowledge the fact. Self-delusion is a habit to avoid. Particularly in a police officer.'

He glanced at his watch, then back towards the party outside. The music had begun. Massiter had chosen the piece himself. It was the very concerto that had nearly put him in jail five years before, when he'd paid for its first production on the pretext that Daniel Forster was its original composer. He had no great fondness for the work, or any other music for that matter. There was no money in music, no fame either, not of the kind he needed. His choice was designed simply to make a point: that, if he wished, he could now do anything he liked.

'This is a social occasion,' he continued, noticing a new individual had now entered the room, one unknown to him, a senior-looking figure in a dark suit. 'Kindly have done with it. Why are you here?'

'We've brought you a gift, Hugo,' Emily said, eyes glittering. 'Something you've wanted for years.'

He laughed.

'Really?'

Massiter's right hand described a circle round the room, round the glass eye over the lagoon, the city beyond.

'What gift could the likes of you possibly have for me?'

Then he saw them and fell silent, mind racing, unable to believe his eyes.

They looked dirty. Peasant clothes. Peasant features. Too long in the sun, too much hard, physical work. For a few reflective seconds Hugo Massiter asked himself what kind of terror he must have instilled in Laura Conti and Daniel Forster to have made them inflict such an obvious punishment on themselves. Then his normal sense of composure returned, and with it a growing sense of triumph, of total triumph, a transcendental victory greater than any even he could have imagined on such a day.

'Who *are* these people?' he asked, amazed, stepping up to them, touching their grimy clothes, peering into their frightened faces. 'Daniel? Is it really you? Laura?'

The man retreated from Massiter's closeness, muttering some coarse words in Veneto. The older individual in the black suit came and stood between them, flashing a card with the familiar Carabinieri badge.

'Signor Massiter,' he said. 'I am Maggiore Zecchini. We believe we have apprehended the two individuals who slandered you all those years ago. We need to interview you about them. Now, please. I know you are busy. Nevertheless . . .'

Massiter found himself trying to catch the bright, sharp, terrified glint in Laura's eyes. She didn't look at him, only at the *occhio*, the great glass window to the lost world beyond.

'Why me?' he asked. 'Why now?'

The Carabinieri major shuffled on his feet, nervous.

'We have fingerprints for Forster. We know it's him. We have no identification records for the woman. It's important we know for sure. I understand you have business. This won't take long. But it's important we carry out a formal interview on Carabinieri premises. I have a launch waiting outside.'

Massiter laughed and, in a single swift movement, came close to her, took her shoulders, leaned down. She cringed, trying to pull away from his grip, but he was too powerful and had no intention of letting go, not for anything, the disapproval he could feel around him, Emily hissing at the young *agente*, furious, outraged.

The police were fools. Massiter knew this all along. In a way he had no need of his present position to defeat them.

He thrust his nose into Laura's hair, took a deep breath, hearing her begin to howl quietly to herself. She had the aroma of the fields and the sea, of animals and the soil. He listened to the music beyond the window and wondered how long he could bear to wait, how sweet the moment would be when he could trap her alone in a room somewhere, perhaps in a hidden corner of the apartment in the glass palazzo, where the music would still play in his head, and there would be no one, no interfering policeman, no do-gooder citizen, to prevent him taking, roughly or sweetly, the choice was hers, exactly what he wanted.

'Enough,' the young cop barked, and thrust himself roughly between their bodies, forcing her away. 'You must come with us now, Signor Massiter.'

'Why?' he asked. 'This is Daniel Forster. You know that as well as I. And this is Laura Conti, who worked for the late Scacchi, whom Forster murdered. You know that too.' He stared at her, hungrily. 'I have a little influence, Laura. I know this man Forster better than you do. Whatever you think, whatever nonsense he may have tried to instil in your head over the years, I can and will help.'

He turned to the Carabinieri major.

'She is a simple woman, Zecchini. Easily led. She's been through enough pain already. I won't allow any more.' And then, smiling at her, trying to see into those dark, frightened eyes. 'Laura. I know you had nothing to do with Scacchi's death, or that of those police officers. I will provide everything at my disposal to prove it. You will be free. I promise that. There is nothing to fear.'

He touched her cheap, faded shirt, until Costa, under the glaring eye of Forster, removed his hand.

'You need clothes,' Massiter said to her. 'A lawyer. Somewhere to stay. And some time in which we may become reacquainted.'

'You will come with us!' Costa ordered. 'Now. This is a criminal investigation, and you're a material witness.'

Massiter glanced at the Arcangeli. All of them too cowed, too miserable to say a word.

'Oh, please! I've a party to go to! And' – his face fell – 'many important people to see. People you would not wish me to disappoint.'

'You must join us now, sir!' Zecchini said. 'By nine o'clock at the latest you can return. Then have your party! Then sign your contract!'

They were so transparent. So idiotic.

'But gentlemen,' Massiter complained, 'there's no need! The

Arcangeli and I grew tired of dickering more than an hour ago. The contract's signed already. The deed's done. Several million euros are now on their way from the state and the city into my bank accounts, a few million on the way to theirs. All we're waiting for is the presence of the mayor and then I can break the good news to the parasites down below.'

He paused, allowing this to sink in.

'The Isola degli Arcangeli is mine. And everything that goes with it: every bureaucrat, every hack politician, every avaricious cop. You may take Forster to jail. You *will* take Laura to my lawyer, and then, when she's bailed on my surety, a place of my choosing. But for now . . .'

Still, they didn't give up. Two more were marching up the stairs.

25

There was a mob of dinner jackets and evening gowns all around her, a heavy brew of accents fighting for attention over the music. Teresa Lupo wanted to yell at them to shut their quacking mouths. Silvio had got through with a result, one that was early for some reason she couldn't hear over the din. What Alberto Tosi had said kept running round her head, not making any sense at all, not in the neatly aligned series of facts and suspicions they'd been chasing so hard these past few days.

She stood on the steps of Ca' degli Angeli, aware that Peroni and Nic had gone ahead with the rest of them, trying to separate Silvio's tinny squeaking in her ear from the racket all around her.

Then a waiter drifted into view, proffered a silver platter of canapés in her face. She gave him a desperate glance.

'Do me a favour. I just got a call to say my uncle died. I need a little quiet. Can you move these people along?'

The waiter's flat, unemotional face suddenly flickered with sympathy.

'Signora! I am so sorry. Of course.'

He was busy in a flash, shooing with a white-gloved hand, shushing them into a semblance of silence.

Finally, she could listen again to Silvio's babbling and hear what he was saying, making a mental note to herself as she did that it really was time to sit down with her assistant and teach him not to get over-excited at tense moments.

'Silvio, Silvio . . . Calm down.'

A heavy shoulder in grubby black brushed against hers. Instinctively she pulled back, aware this was the boatman, who didn't appear too clean from afar, or too bright from close up. He was covered in muck and ash, and holding a long bundle of kindling twigs tightly, both arms underneath the wood, striding into the entrance of the house, towards the broad marble stairs, intent on something, a fixed, hurt expression on his face.

Then she listened to Silvio one last time, relieved that he had finally managed to say what he meant.

Quick decisions. She both hated and adored them. She put the phone back in her pocket and followed in the wake of the boatman, trying to avoid the chunks of twig that marked his path, thinking, desperately trying to find some way through what she knew.

Teresa Lupo rounded the staircase and found the open door to the large, handsome room where they were all gathered. The warm, yellow light of the sun streamed through those curious windows she'd noticed from outside. Hugo Massiter, a man she'd only seen twice, once on a launch in the Grand Canal, once in the palazzo next door, stood in the centre of the room looking as if he owned everything around him already. The bricks, the mortar, but most of all the people.

'Nic . . .' she said, but no one was listening, no one was doing anything but look at the boatman, who shuffled stupidly, like an idiot, ahead of her, heaving the bundle of kindling in his arms.

It was the oldest Arcangelo who spoke first. Michele got out of his seat, one good eye flashing hatred and fury, emotions, she thought, that had been looking for somewhere to escape long before this poor, dumb native wandered into the room.

'What are you doing, you idiot?' Michele bellowed. 'What are you *doing*?'

There was a brief quiet lull. It felt like being in the eye of a storm.

'I thought you'd need firewood,' the boatman said in a dull, detached brogue as coarse as his clothing. 'They told me you'd still be working, Signor Michele. If you work, you need help.'

The couple she'd seen in handcuffs were there, trying to hold one another, trying to form some sort of bulwark against everything that surrounded them.

'Go, Piero,' the young man said, half choking on the words. 'There's nothing more you can do.'

'Do?' the boatman wondered.

The woman was sobbing, hating something about the sight of the boatman. Or fearing it perhaps.

'Piero,' she pleaded. 'Listen to me! *Go!*'

Michele Arcangelo walked up to the man, slapped him as hard as he could, twice across the face, front of hand, back of hand, screaming, with so much force Teresa could feel the hatred welling up from the man as he raged in front of them.

'*Matto! Matto! Matto!* Get out of here!'

But he didn't flinch. The firewood scarcely moved. He was looking at the Englishman. Massiter stood there, amused, arms folded, feet apart, the stance of a victor.

'Nic,' she whispered or simply thought, Teresa Lupo wasn't quite sure.

'Signor Massiter,' the boatman said in a calm, thoughtful voice, one that seemed more assured, and rather more intelligent, than she'd expected.

'You know my name?' The Englishman beamed. 'I'm flattered.'

'I know your name,' he said, nodding. Then he turned to look at the couple.

'Another Scacchi warned us about you, long ago. You cannot run from the Devil, he said. He finds you. Or you find him.'

'Piero, Piero!'

It was Gianni Peroni, working his way towards the boatman, with the kind of swift, certain intent she'd come to recognize. He could wrestle a man down in an instant if the sweet talk didn't work.

'No one moves,' the boatman said, and released the bundle of kindling, letting the twigs fall noisily onto the polished floor and the shining table, sending Michele Arcangelo into a paroxysm of screaming, foul-mouthed wrath once more. Until . . .

'Nic,' she said, and heard her own voice faintly over the sudden silence.

'No one moves.'

They froze. Not one of them, not Nic, not Peroni, or even Luca

Zecchini, felt like trying to steal a finger towards the pistols in their jackets. Something in the man's face told them this would be a very bad idea indeed.

In his hands, held with a lazy, knowing grace, was a long, old shotgun, double-barrelled, as worn and used as the man himself. A man who now punched the weapon into Hugo Massiter's chest, propelled him viciously to the great bowed window, sending him back so hard the Englishman's head cracked on the glass, breaking it with a sudden, piercing crash.

Hugo Massiter howled in pain and shock.

'No,' a female voice said, and Teresa was unsure where the sound came from, the handcuffed woman, Raffaela Arcangelo or her own dry throat.

'What do you want?' Massiter roared, raising a hand to his head, looking in astonishment and shock at the blood some hidden wound at the back of his scalp deposited on his fingers. 'What insanity is this?'

'I want nothing,' the boatman replied quietly, calm, unworried.

Massiter's face contorted with fury.

'Venetians! Venetians! Name your price and be done with it. A man like me has bought the likes of you all before. I'll buy you all again, twice over, if that's what it takes.'

Piero Scacchi didn't flinch, didn't take his eyes off the pompous Englishman trapped against the gleaming glass.

'You make two mistakes,' he said. 'I am not a Venetian. And you are not a man.'

He rolled off some catch on the weapon. The gun jerked, the room filled with its terrible roar. Hugo Massiter's torso rose in the air, flew back against the bull's-eye windows and was caught there by a second explosion, one that ripped his chest apart and sent him out of the room altogether, out into the open air where, for one short moment, he appeared suspended in a sea of whirling shards, a dying man flailing in a cloud of glass that reflected his agony as it tore his shattered body to blood and bone.

Then he was gone, and from the unseen quay below came a mounting communal murmur, more animal than human, a buzzing, humming storm cloud of fright, punctuated by the growing rattle of screams.

Teresa was half aware of one other event, too. Peroni had finally reached the boatman, held him at the fractured windows with just enough strength to stop him following his victim out into the golden evening before finally, more through the man's own lassitude than Peroni's considerable force, grappling him to the floor.

'It didn't match, Nic,' Teresa Lupo whispered, finally able to get the words out of her mouth though she knew no one else could hear. 'It didn't match at all.'

Meat and death. Opportunity and fear. Crouched low on the salty planks of the barque, trembling, unable to drag its keen eyes from the bloodshed on the quay, the animal's sharp, swift mind tried to make sense of the scene, failed and saw instead only the black dread, the final dread, the dark-not-knowingness. This was not the good death, a final sigh before the last sleep, a sudden storm of feathers dragged from breath to no-breath in an instant, then descending into the sharp cold littoral marches and a pair of soft, searching jaws. This was a wrong end, one that would change everything in the small, tight world the creature occupied. The dog watched the man, the much-loved man, stare out through the shattered glass eye of the window, some emptiness in his face the animal failed to recognise. It watched him look down to see his work, and as it did it felt, like a searing wound, his agony. Everywhere on the ground below bodies fought and jostled, screaming, fighting, trying to see, trying to be blind. And on the hard pavement, with a stink the dog knew well, lay some shattered heap of meat. Not human. Not animal. Not a part of this bright dying day. The animal waited, trembling. Instinct tightened his nostrils, more important than eyes or ears, open vessels into a consciousness that had to be guarded against the vile, dark city and the filthy liberating water. The animal sensed the finality of the act that had ensued from the loud, familiar roar of the gun, tight in the hands of the man, his master. Uncertain, aware only of the small knot of certainty in its gut that move it must, the creature found the side of the barque, stole swiftly, silently across the old familiar wood one last time, slid beneath the oily, noxious meniscus of greasy lagoon and began to swim through the chill back flow.

When the dog surfaced, the sound of their shrieking was scarcely diminished. Men possessed, the animal understood, a weaker, coarser form of consciousness. Puzzled, hurt, certain only of a single direction, it pulled hard in the black, greasy waves, then struck out, quickly, forcefully, towards the open waters of the lagoon.

Part 5

SOLITARY CEREMONIES

1

It was the second week of September, late afternoon under a sun losing its power. An unseasonable hint of chill, the coming death of summer, lurked within the breeze rising from the Adriatic. It chased across the grey waves, buffeting their faces as they waited on the edge of the graveyard on San Michele. Funerals always made Leo Falcone uncomfortable, though he'd been to many over the years. Now he was trapped inside a wheelchair, reliant on others in a way he found disturbing, a way that reminded him of a younger Nic Costa, once stricken in much the same fashion. There was no easy form of escape, no excuse to put work before personal matters. Nothing but the relentless internal reflection that had been dogging him for a week or more.

'Leo?' Raffaela asked. 'Are you ready? Michele was too mean to pay for private transport back. The boat service stops soon. We don't want to miss it.'

'A minute,' he said, recalling the coffin going into the fresh ochre earth beyond the line of cedars that separated them from the plots. 'I was thinking.'

There'd been so much time for that lately. Fresh thinking. Old thinking, the kind that had happened before he awoke and which still remained in his head, clear and unwilling to go away. The question, as Leo Falcone understood only too well, was what to do with those dark, unsettling reflections.

When Uriel Arcangelo went into the ground, a temporary sojourn, like every San Michele corpse, to be removed a decade hence to make way for more, his interment had been watched by just five personal mourners. The three Arcangeli, newly enriched by Hugo

Massiter's purchase of the island, Falcone, and the lawyer who had handled the family estate. The black-suited, quietly officious men of the funeral company outnumbered family. It seemed apposite somehow. The Arcangeli never ceased to be outsiders, even in death.

At least Uriel had received a more proper end than Massiter. The Englishman's power had vanished the moment his body shattered on the island's worn paving stones, scattering the crowds, sending them screaming.

When Massiter died some spell was broken. The city's burghers escaped discovery of their illicit financial transactions. The Arcangeli found their own money problems transformed, escaping from poverty to comparative riches overnight. The future of the island remained as much in doubt as before, but it was now someone else's problem, an architectural curio left in legal limbo, owned by the estate of a man with no known relatives, no apparent heirs. Already there were mutterings in the local press about a campaign to take it into public ownership. A hotel and an apartment block would one day rise on the Isola degli Arcangeli, Falcone felt certain of this. The way the family, even Michele, acquiesced to the notion after Massiter's demise indicated, surely, that its days as a struggling glass enterprise were past.

All the same, he found it remarkable how little the name of Hugo Massiter entered into any conversation or public discussion. After the initial flurry of publicity about the arrest of Piero Scacchi on a charge of murder, the story had quickly died away. The previous day there had been a brief paragraph on an inside page of one newspaper revealing that Massiter's body had been flown to England for a private burial paid for by his estate, an event that would, Falcone suspected, be watched by lawyers and accountants, if anyone at all. For Venice, at that point, in some final solitary ceremony, the issue of culpability would be closed, interred alongside the ravaged flesh and bone of Hugo Massiter. No one had been brought to account for the killing of Gianfranco Randazzo, which was, the papers now hinted, the result of a gangland row over an extortion racket in which the late commissario had been involved. No one, it seemed, much remembered the deaths of Aldo Bracci, or Uriel and Bella Arcangelo. Venice had a capacity for forgetfulness which Leo Falcone almost envied.

He forced himself to concentrate on the present, and gazed at Raffaela Arcangelo with that slow, selfish hunger allowed to a man confined to a wheelchair. She looked serene, complete somehow, in mourning. She wore a long black dress, expensively cut, and a thin woollen jacket against the chill breeze. Her hair had been styled by a professional, probably for the first time in years, he guessed, and now curved into her attractive, scarcely lined face. She had the appearance of an intelligent and elegant college professor, something, it occurred to Falcone, she could perhaps have been had her family not dragged her home from Paris out of financial necessity.

'What will you do now?' he asked.

She smiled, a little shyly.

'It's taken a long time for you to frame that question, Leo.'

There was no reproach in her soft voice, though perhaps he deserved some.

He glowered at the wheelchair, unintentionally.

'I'm sorry. My mind's been on other things.'

'Of course,' she said. 'I was being thoughtless. You deserve some indulgences.'

He didn't believe that to be true. His injuries *were* temporary, something to be overcome, not resented. Besides . . .

'Forget about me, Raffaela. I was interested in you. What will happen now?'

She glanced at Michele and Gabriele. They were already on the jetty, waiting for the next boat.

'They have their share of Massiter's money. I have mine. They have the property he wrote into the contract too. The offer of premises. A shop, not one in the best part of town but now they have the funds to change that. They'll try to make glass again. I don't think anything can stop them.'

Nothing short of bankruptcy, he thought.

'And you?'

She turned to face him, frank, wise, concerned.

'I don't know. What do you suggest?'

The question threw him.

'You can do what you want, surely?'

'I can,' she replied, nodding. 'For the first time in my life. And yet . . . I don't know. I've spent so long trying to hold the family together on that damned island. Now it's gone. I'm free. The trouble is freedom doesn't feel quite how I expected.'

The boat had arrived. Her brothers were getting ready to board, not even bothering to look back.

'Let's catch the next one, shall we?' she said, watching them. 'They don't need me any more. Or that's what they think.' A thought occurred to her. 'I could travel, I suppose.'

'Will you?'

She was staring at him again, a look that made Leo Falcone restless, unsure of himself.

'Probably not. I . . .'

This seemed difficult for her to say.

'I've been trying something new,' she confessed. 'Thinking about myself for a change. Not them. Not the island.'

'You make it sound a crime. It isn't.'

'I know that. But it still prompts awkward thoughts.'

Her dark eyes seemed torn between watching for his reactions and being afraid of what he might notice.

'I realize now that I've never been wanted. That's all. Never on the island. There was nothing there for any of us but duty. Not love. None of us ever had that, even in the beginning, I think. We were part of my father's dream, a dream that was about him alone. About making the Arcangeli name immortal somehow. He was a stupid, cruel old man. I know I shouldn't say that of my own father, but it's true. He was willing to sacrifice our lives for his, and look where it got us. Michele and Gabriele still chasing some phantom. Me an old maid.'

He had to laugh. It was such a ludicrous idea.

'I don't think anyone would describe you as that.'

'I wasn't talking about how people saw me,' she said immediately. 'I was talking about how I view myself.' She hesitated. 'I want to be wanted, Leo. I want to be loved. Just for me. Nothing else at all. Now *that's* selfish.'

He grimaced.

'I've never been much of an expert at love,' he confessed.

'That makes two of us,' she said.

There was a faint hue on her cheek. Make-up perhaps. Or the hint of a blush.

'You'll need help,' she pointed out. 'You may not like that idea but it's a fact. I've got nothing better to do. I've never seen much of Rome. I certainly don't want to stay here. We could just call it friendship. Nothing more. Unless . . . People change with time. Who knows?'

It was a temptation, more enticing than any Hugo Massiter could ever have thrown on the table.

But the child's screams rang around his head.

'You could go back to university,' he suggested. 'You said you loved Paris.'

'I did,' she answered, blushing openly now, worried, perhaps, she'd overstepped the mark. 'Not now. University is for the young, I think.'

'But what a person learns . . .' he mused. 'That stays with you. All your life.'

It was criminology in his case. Leo Falcone had never been in any doubt about his own future career.

'You studied chemistry, I believe?' he asked.

The question took her by surprise.

'Did I tell you that?'

He spoke to the child inside him, then waited, satisfied by its sudden silence.

'No,' Leo Falcone said. 'I checked. It's easy to discover facts about people. The difficulty lies in understanding what they mean.'

She gazed down at him, puzzled, a little annoyed by the way he'd turned the direction of the conversation perhaps.

'You have so much spare time at the moment, Leo. I'm flattered you should spend some of it on me.'

'Was it an easy choice? I can't quite see you as a chemist.'

'I was an Arcangelo,' she said. 'We were all supposed to be a part of my father's plan. I would have preferred to have studied literature. He was implacably opposed, naturally. What use are books or poetry when you're staring into a furnace?'

'You were a good student, I imagine. A conscientious one. A talented one too.'

She nodded, flattered.

'I'd like to think so. But I never completed my degree. Paris was expensive. The money wasn't there. Why are we discussing this? Is it relevant?'

'I think I know how your brother died,' he said. 'Would you like to hear?'

She stared at him, mournful, disappointed.

'Haven't we given the grave enough of our time today?'

'It won't take long.'

'Fine,' she snapped. 'But if we're to speak about the dead let's at least allow them to hear for themselves.'

Before he could protest, she took hold of the wheelchair handles and propelled him back toward the graveyard, beyond the line of cedars, rapidly reaching Uriel's plot, with its too-white marble headstone.

The place was deserted. There was not so much as a single gravedigger working on one of the neat brown plots. Falcone recalled what she had said about the vaporetti. The service stopped at the end of the afternoon. The cemetery island had no need of night visitors.

2

Teresa Lupo sat at the battered table feeling cold and stupid. They'd been all over the island. Hours of searching, calling, hoping. Now they were back where they always started: Piero Scacchi's deserted and depressing picnic area. And for what?

For a dog. An animal that thought it could swim the breadth of the lagoon to escape the madness on the Isola degli Arcangeli. Only, if it survived, to find its master missing, missing for a long time it seemed to her. There were, as far as the papers appeared to know, no extenuating circumstances, no mitigation Scacchi could plead. A *matto* from the lagoon had shot dead one of the city's leading lights at the moment of his apotheosis, with half of Venice's *prosecco*-swilling glitterati looking on. It was impudent. Downright bad taste. Scacchi, being a lunatic from the edge of the lagoon, would be lucky to see fresh air in less than ten years, however much the young couple, Daniel Forster and Laura Conti, pleaded on his behalf. At least they seemed to have escaped prosecution. She was glad about that. They looked like people who'd suffered, unjustly for the most part. From what she'd read they'd never recover what they'd lost. Massiter's lawyers had seen to that. But no one seemed much interested in activating the warrants that had been issued for their arrest. That would overturn too many old stones long settled into the dirt, with plenty of unwanted creatures lurking underneath. The pair were, at least, free to start their lives anew.

'Dog! *Dog!* Xerxes!'

Peroni was muddied up to his knees from wandering through the fields and the marshy land, bellowing for the animal. She wondered what he expected might happen. Would the creature suddenly march out of the lush grass wilderness at the lagoon's edge, wagging its tail?

He did some more yelling then came and sat down opposite, grim-faced, cross with himself.

She patted his big hand.

'Gianni. It's been more than a week. If he survived the water – and that's a big if – he could have starved to death here. We know the locals haven't been feeding him.'

They'd talked to plenty. Farmer and fisherman alike, none of whom looked as if they'd be much inclined to provide for anything that wasn't part of their own household. Nobody had even seen a small black spaniel, thin and hungry-looking, lost, puzzled why the little shack where it lived was deserted, day after day. Nobody, if she was honest with herself, much cared. Except for Gianni Peroni, who hoped to care enough to make up for everyone else.

'He's here,' Peroni insisted. 'I just know it.'

'Here we go. Instinct again. Be realistic, will you? The poor thing probably drowned.'

'No! You don't know dogs. Spaniels love the water. He could swim to the city and back if he wanted.'

'Now *that* I find hard to believe.'

'Believe it,' he said, then turned to the reedy little *rio* nearby and starting shouting again, bellowing the dog's name over and over.

She waited for him to pause for breath, then held his hand more tightly.

'Has it never occurred to you, dog person that you are, that the blasted things sometimes only come when called by someone they know?'

'That's not true! We had a dog when I was kid. He came for anyone who knew his name.'

She thought about this.

'What was he called?'

'Guido!'

'Fine. Listen to a little animal psychology. Dogs rely on syllables. Clearly differentiated chunks of language. Guido – GWEE-DOH – is an excellent name because it has two very identifiable syllables, the ideal number for something with a brain the size of a modest potato. Furthermore, these syllables are separated, and this is important, by a hard consonant, one pronounced when you move the middle of your tongue downwards, away from the roof of your mouth.'

He glared at her.

'I don't think dogs understand hard consonants.'

'You're wrong. Don't ask how I know this – it was a very long time ago – but they do. A dog with a good name like Guido knows when it's being called, even by a complete stranger. Whether the thing *obeys* is another matter, of course.'

'This is going somewhere?' he asked.

'Straight to the point. Guido is good. Xerxes – think about it when you say it, ZER-KE-SEES – is terrible. No hard consonant. Three messy syllables. The dog will have heard it over and over again from Piero and understood what it meant from the repetition and the intonation of his master's voice. From anyone else it just sounds like mush. Do I make myself clear?'

'Yes! So what do I do?'

'You come home with me. Then tomorrow we go back to Rome and attempt to resume lives which are as close to normality as our dysfunctional personalities will allow.'

'And the dog?'

She let go of his hand and wagged a finger in his face instead.

'You can't save everything, Gianni. It's just not possible. At some stage you – *and* Nic *and* Falcone – have to accept that there are casualties in this world. Besides, even if by some miracle you do find it, what the hell do you do next?'

She saw the guilty, furtive expression in his face and suddenly wished she'd never asked that question. A man who habitually rescued things always knew a place to put them afterwards.

'No. Don't tell me. It's the cousin in Tuscany again, isn't it?'

'Not quite,' he answered, and pulled some screwed-up papers out of his jacket, placed them on the table and smoothed them out. One was a faxed memo from the Questura in Rome. The second was a couple of sheets containing bad colour photos of a little farmhouse, not much bigger than Piero Scacchi's shack, the kind of papers you got from a property agency.

'I was meaning to bring this up in any case. They've offered us a career break. Me, Nic, Falcone. Career breaks are very much the in-thing in Rome just now. Refreshes the mind. Or something like that.'

She'd heard they'd been going the rounds, usually in the direction of people the boss class didn't know what to do with. The very idea filled her with suspicion.

'This would be the "we don't get to pay you any money but you piss off and stay out of our hair" kind of career break?'

'The job's still there if you want it. You just disappear. Six months. A year. More if you like.'

He paused, licking his lips.

'Maybe forever. My cousin Mauro's got this spare farm of his. Pigs. He can't sell it. I could get it for free for a while. See if I can make a go of things.'

She took a deep breath.

'You're leaving me? For pigs?'

'No!' he objected, shocked by the accusation. 'I'd only go if you could get a career break too. Wouldn't be hard. I know a few people . . .'

'Read my lips. I am not raising pigs.'

'They need doctors everywhere,' he said, shrugging. 'You could get a job at the surgery in town. They're nice people.'

'You checked this?'

'Kind of. But not in a committed sort of way. Not . . .'

He sighed and squeezed her fingers. Fat fingers. They were very alike in some ways.

'I thought perhaps it was time to try something different. Leo's going to be out of it for a few months. Nic's got ideas too.'

No bodies. No morgue. No budgets. She could rent out the apartment. She could go back to dealing with living people for a while. There were attractions. The trouble was it would take a kind of courage she was unsure she possessed.

'It was just a thought. I should have discussed it with you before I asked for these papers,' he admitted. 'I'm sorry. It was stupid.'

'If it worked, Gianni, you know what it would mean? We might never go back. No more Rome. No more Questura. No bodies. No fun.'

'This has been fun?'

'Sometimes. We got one another out of it, didn't we?'

'Well, yes, but . . .'

'But what? We're good at this. All of us. It's just that you three don't know when to stop. You just walk straight in and take it all head on. This habit must cease.'

He didn't like that.

'Maybe we don't know any other way.'

'Then perhaps it's time to learn!'

He didn't object. Peroni was always willing to consider alternatives. It was another of the unpredictable qualities that got to her.

'And if I do that we can both go on a career break?'

She looked into his battered face.

'Is that what you really want?'

'I don't know,' he answered honestly. 'What do you think?'

'I think we should find the dog.'

'You said he was dead!'

'He probably is. But try this thinking-round-problems idea. You haven't asked the right question. Even though you know it and, more to the point, *I* know it, since you've told me every last thing about the animal already.'

He sat there, mute, puzzled.

'Oh, for God's sake,' she sighed. 'Isn't it obvious?'

Teresa Lupo got up and set off for the little shack. She doubted it would be locked. She doubted Piero Scacchi, from what they knew, was a man who failed to keep a backup for anything that was important to him.

Gianni Peroni waited obediently at the table, watching her return, enlightenment dawning in his eyes.

When she came back, she placed the old, grubby shotgun in front of him, and kept the box of cartridges she'd found on her side of the table.

'Don't kill anything on my account,' she said.

3

'There was a substance on the apron,' Falcone explained. 'An industrial solvent. One used in laboratories everywhere, and in some manufacturing processes too. Sometimes in glass foundries. It's called ketone. Have you heard of it?'

She shook her head.

'It's been a long time since I dealt with chemicals.'

'There must be an inventory. We could look.'

Raffaela Arcangelo glowered at him.

'Why? Uriel and Bella are dead and buried. The world thinks it knows who killed them: Aldo Bracci. Nic has other ideas. He believes it was Hugo Massiter, and feels he knows Massiter's reasons too. Either way . . .' She shrugged. 'They're beyond us all now.'

'Undoubtedly,' he said, nodding in agreement. 'Nevertheless, think of those reasons. Bella was pregnant. Not by her brother. I don't believe that for a moment. It was Massiter. At least she thought so, and was probably causing trouble for the Englishman. Blackmail of a kind, I imagine. Threatening awkwardness over signing the contract. I have the impression Bella knew a man's weak points.'

She nodded.

'You're right, as usual.'

'Thank you. But it's the means that matter. Bella was killed, or at least rendered unconscious, in her own bedroom by simple force, then dragged to the furnace for disposal. Brutal, but scarcely unusual. Uriel on the other hand . . .'

He stared down at the grave. She folded her arms and looked at him.

'I don't understand the first thing you're talking about.'

'It's as if we have two different crimes by two different people. Uriel's death, that tainted apron, is tentative, half-hearted, almost as if it wasn't quite deliberate. From what I've read of Teresa's notes it had only a slim chance of succeeding in any case. Even with the burners to the furnace locked so that the temperature was unnaturally high, the chances of fabric impregnated with that substance actually igniting were slim. Uriel was deeply unlucky there. It's possible the presence of alcohol precipitated what happened. We'll never know. Nevertheless, it's as if whoever perpetrated that act was unsure whether he wanted to commit the crime in the first place. He was leaving it to chance, letting fate decide whether to ignite the apron and condemn the person locked inside the room to what could, from external appearances, be seen as an accidental death. Had that actually occurred and Bella not been killed also . . .'

'Then?'

'Then it would have gone down as an industrial fatality. No doubt about it. Which was why, in the beginning, I believed Bella must have been complicit in some way. All the same . . .'

He'd worked so hard to try to understand. Even now he was still struggling to grasp every last detail. Leo Falcone was aware that his mind no longer worked as efficiently, as ruthlessly, as it once had.

'I don't see the problem,' she said.

'The problem is that the contrast with Bella's actual death could scarcely be greater! That was swift, decisive and bloody. Deliberate, predictable. *Normal*, if such a word can be used of murder.'

She glanced back towards the exit.

'We don't want to be left here. Will this take long?'

'No.'

'Good. And your solution?'

'It was simple, once I thought about it. All those keys. All those ribbons. You're a family that misplaces items. People who pick up one thing when it belongs to another.'

'We're human,' she said pointedly.

'Quite. And, being human, Uriel took the apron meant for Bella that night, and she his. She wore it in the foundry, wondering why the place was so hot and the burners so difficult to control. Coming to no harm whatsoever, not until she returns to the house, puzzled, sensing, I imagine, that something's wrong.'

Raffaela signalled her tentative agreement with a raised forefinger.

'This could have happened, I suppose.'

'It did. And when she gets back, our reluctant killer, someone who wanted fate to make the decision over whether Bella lives or dies, is faced with a choice. To acquiesce or to act? To finish the job or pretend nothing has happened? It must have been difficult. There would have been a little planning in advance, of course. But the act . . . that had to be decided one way or another in a matter of moments, which is why, when violence was the course of action taken, it was so sudden. Her death had to be achieved quickly, before any doubts crept in. This was no longer a cerebral, detached event. It required strength, determination. Those blood stains on the bedroom wall . . .'

'From what I know,' she observed, 'Hugo Massiter was a strong and determined man.'

'Undoubtedly. But something unexpected has happened too. Before she's murdered, Bella has decided to call Uriel, who's half drunk, half sleeping in the office next door. She's told him there's something wrong with the furnace. It's overheating. Perhaps she wants to meet him there. So he goes in a little earlier than normal, finding the door ajar, since that was the way it habitually fell, and closing it behind him. The furnace is out of control now. The trap which was laid for Bella falls shut upon him, which was the last thing that was intended.'

He watched the way she glanced at the grave then turned away, a lost, sad cast in her eye.

'I said it was an accident all along,' she murmured.

'You did. As far as Uriel's concerned, I've no doubt you're right. I'm sorry that's no comfort to you. I wish there was some other interpretation I could place on events. I really do.'

To his surprise, she smiled.

'You were the only one with a kind word, you know. From the outset. It struck me from the start that you have a peculiar and rather touching interest in other human beings, Leo, yet very little in yourself.'

He gestured at the wheelchair.

'I've time to change. I'll try to think like everyone else. Not like a police inspector.'

'Is that what you do? I was rather under the impression you thought like a criminal.'

It was a perceptive observation, up to a point.

'If you look for explanations it's important to see events from both sides of the fence. The perpetrator's. The victim's. Criminals interest me. I admit it. I've never been much of a one for believing they're made at birth. Something happens. Something forms them. If I can understand what that something is, then . . .'

'Then you become a little like them.'

It was an observation, not a question. He wasn't minded to argue.

'This is the job I do. It would be surprising if something doesn't rub off along the way. But you're missing my point. Criminals are made, not born. Even a man like Aldo Bracci.'

Her face lit up with astonishment.

'Aldo Bracci was a brute and a thief! He slept with Bella all those years ago! You know that!'

'He was a Bracci,' Falcone declared. 'Wasn't he doing precisely what was expected of him?'

She was silent. Then Raffaela sat down on the bench next to the grave, glanced at her watch and said, 'We need to be going. The last boat leaves soon.'

'I'm nearly done. Aldo Bracci brings me almost to the close. Why do you think he came to Massiter's party that evening? Carrying a gun and Bella's keys?'

She shook her head, puzzled.

'Nic told me he believed Commissario Randazzo placed the keys in Bracci's pocket after he shot him. From what I recall that was certainly possible. Randazzo was in Massiter's pay. Isn't it obvious? The commissario was trying to make sure Bracci would be blamed for his sister's murder to get Massiter off the hook.'

Falcone scowled.

'Nic is young and clever but still has much to learn. I spoke to Randazzo that night. He barely had sufficient presence of mind to seize the opportunity to kill Bracci. Nothing more. Aldo had those keys. Someone, perhaps Massiter himself, perhaps someone else, gave them to him. In an anonymous letter, say. One suggesting they'd been found in Massiter's yacht, or that apartment on the island, proof that Bella, his own sister, was murdered by the Englishman because she was pregnant. Bracci was drunk already. It could have been enough to set him off.'

'The Braccis are a violent family. They always settle their scores in the end.'

Falcone concurred. 'Which everyone would know, of course. And if Aldo turned up at an event like that, dead drunk, the keys in his pocket, screaming nonsense, against Hugo Massiter of all people, who would have believed him? It would be one more piece of evidence against the brother, however much he'd try to protest. His class, his character, would convict him from the outset. It's a clever trick. To turn a man's own anger and reputation against himself.'

He caught her eye.

'It was unfortunate that he saw you first. That you were the one he chose.'

'I was by the door. The first person he met. You seemed preoccupied at the time. Inattentive, I might say.'

'I'm sorry. I wish I'd spent more time with you. I honestly do.'

She asked, 'Is that it? Can we go now?'

'Keys,' he murmured, seeing the image of the cabin in the mountains rising in his head again. 'Or more accurately, a single key. Uriel's for the foundry door. That was what puzzled me all along. That was what tricked me and I doubt I would ever have seen past it either, not without . . .'

A meeting with his younger self, in a place of their own joint imagination, returning to a pivotal event that had made Leo Falcone who he was.

'Keys are piece of metal,' she said. 'You're better with human beings.'

'Part of it was filed down,' he went on. 'Did I mention that?'

Raffaela looked hard at her watch and said, 'Leo. The boat.'

'The boat can wait. It was filed, and I couldn't understand why.

Or rather I saw only one reason, viewed everything from a single direction. Uriel was dead inside a locked room. The only key he owned had been tampered with to ensure it didn't work. It seemed so obvious. This was done to keep him in. There could be no other reason. Yet . . .'

'Leo!' she shouted, tapping her wrist.

'I was so stupid.'

He looked her full in the face, knowing now he couldn't be wrong, that in this deserted graveyard, with Uriel Arcangelo's corpse a metre deep in the earth beside him, there would be a resolution of a kind, though he was not sure whether it was one he wanted, or where, in the end, it might lead.

'The key was filed to keep him out, Raffaela,' he said, his voice rising unintentionally. 'It was Bella you wanted dead. Not Uriel. *Never* Uriel. You hoped to send her into the foundry, where the burners were fixed to rise and rise, with an apron that would catch fire if fate decided. You had to make sure Uriel couldn't get in if he tried. So you filed the key. Uriel, if he found his way there, would blame the lock or the drink. Then he'd look for Bella's keys, and fail to find them. Eventually he'd wake the person closest to him. His sister. You'd stall, I imagine. You'd an idea how long it would take for the furnace to do its job. And by the time you arrived to open the door, Bella would be dead. Victim of an unfortunate industrial accident no one would ever be able to explain entirely, but one that carried no suspicion of wrongdoing at all.'

She leaned back on the bench and closed her eyes, saying nothing.

'But Bella, or Uriel, picked the wrong apron. The furnace was in worse condition that you knew. From there, everything else followed. Bella's return to the house and your inevitable response. Your need to place the blame on Aldo Bracci, first. Then, when matters were beyond your control, Bracci's murder and that of Gianfranco Randazzo. Massiter's killing too, which happily occurred after the sale of the island you hate so much. So many deaths from such a simple mistake which no one, least of all you, could have foreseen.'

A trio of gulls screamed overhead, fighting over some scrap of food. Then there was silence. The two of them were, he knew, alone now in the cemetery, forgotten by any distant caretaker huddled in his watch house, charged to guard this island of the dead after the sun fell.

'Do they haunt you, Raffaela?' he asked.

4

It had been three days before the Questura had allowed Costa and Peroni out of their grip. Then they let go in an instant, rushing the pair of them out of the building with an admonition never to return. There would be no reprisals. Cases like Hugo Massiter's had to be buried in their entirety or not at all.

So Nic Costa bade farewell to Venice and, with a weary sense of acceptance, caught the first flight to Rome, one he chose because it landed at Ciampino, the small city airport, not far from the old Appian Way.

A place he both missed and feared, not knowing what would greet him at the old farmhouse that had, during their too-brief time together there, felt like home once more.

Emily was outside, working on the grapes that hung in black and green festoons over the terrace, when the cab deposited him in the drive. A wicker basket full of fruit stood by the door. She was dressed in jeans and an old cotton T-shirt, her blonde hair tied back to reveal her face, which was now a shade paler than it had been in Venice.

He dumped his bags on the old paving stones and thrust out the bouquet he'd picked up at the airport: roses and freesias and anything else that smelled sweet. She looked at them and laughed.

'That's the second bouquet I've had in a couple of weeks,' she said. 'Are you trying to spoil me?'

'I don't . . .'

He shook his head. She pointed to the timbered inner terrace. The bunch of *peperoncini* Gianni Peroni had bought from Piero Scacchi on Sant' Erasmo hung there, the flesh of the peppers slowly wrinkling, preparing for winter.

Emily nodded at the basket of fruit, then sat at the table where Costa joined her.

'I thought I'd better pick them. There are so many. Those vines need attention. You can't just leave things to grow the way they want, year after year. What do you do with all these grapes anyway?'

'My father used to make wine. Just *vino novello*. Simple farmer's wine. It's beautiful for three months and then it's vinegar. He never had time to show me how. Or I never had time to learn. One or the other. I can't remember which.'

'You've still got two weeks' leave. You could learn.'

No. He'd thought this through already.

'I promised you a vacation. Anywhere. Tuscany. I don't care. Just tell me.'

'Here,' she said immediately. 'Nowhere else. This is where we need to start, Nic. I need you to show me the places you knew when you grew up. I want a couple of bikes so you can take me cycling along the Appian Way. And now I want to learn to make wine. Is that OK with you?'

He wanted to hold her and didn't dare. He wanted to tell her what he was thinking and couldn't find the words.

'I didn't know if you'd still be here,' he said. 'I wouldn't have blamed you if you'd gone.'

Emily Deacon let her head roll back, untied her hair and shook it free.

'You obviously don't know me well enough yet,' she said. 'I am not, nor will I ever be, in the habit of leaving a man quietly. If I go you will hear screaming and language you have, previously, never associated with a woman of my upbringing. Do I make myself clear?'

He took her hands across the table.

'Good,' she added. 'Would you have hated me? If I'd left?'

'I'd have missed you. I'd have hated myself.' He peered into her sharp, inquisitive eyes. 'I'm so sorry. I never realized we were in so deep, or what I was asking. Can you ever forgive that?'

There was a faint, wry smile.

'Forgiving you was never going to be the problem. It's me. I don't know when or if I can forgive myself.'

Time, he thought. That was what they'd need. Time and each other.

'Tell me what to do.'

'Be yourself. Be here when I need you.'

Costa thought of his father and the turbulent period his life had entered in his thirties. A kind of peace had emerged in the end, but it hadn't been achieved without pain or sacrifice. That seemed to be part of human relationships, and it was only the child in him that tried to believe there was another, less arduous way.

'That I guarantee,' he said. 'None of this is easy, is it?'

'No. But I imagine it's better than the alternative.' She leaned forward and kissed him on the cheek. 'That's why I'm still here. As long as it feels this way, that's why I'll stay.'

'In that case I'm a lucky man.'

'Damned right you are,' she agreed. 'So how's Leo? Will he go back to the job?'

Costa had spent the previous morning with Falcone in hospital. It was good to see his progress, though the man was different somehow, as was their relationship.

'He's on the mend. Leo will be back in the Questura. In the end.' He picked up a bunch of grapes on the table. 'Before this turns to vinegar. We'll both be back.'

'Both?'

She leaned forward, in anticipation and some concern, waiting for the rest. It was good news. Costa had convinced himself of that.

'I have a small assignment along the way.'

'Where?' she asked quickly.

'Rome. Just Rome. With a little travel I think you could enjoy too.'

'Nic . . .'

He'd spent the previous afternoon discussing everything with Luca Zecchini over a long and enjoyable lunch in an expensive restaurant away from the tourist haunts by the Rialto. It was an unexpected offer, but the Carabinieri and the state police were supposed to liaise from time to time. It was a reward too, a deserved one.

'Zecchini's people cracked those files you gave them. Almost the first time they tried.'

'That's not possible.'

'They found the password. It was based on the phone number at Massiter's previous home in Venice. Apparently—'

'Apparently the Carabinieri have some very smart people,' she interrupted. 'What did they get?'

'Names. Bank accounts. Routes. Shipments. Everything. It's a gold mine. Read the papers over the next few weeks. Add up what you see there. It's the biggest breakthrough they've had in years.'

She laughed.

'Hugo always struck me as the kind of man who'd be lax about things. He felt invulnerable. He *knew* they'd never touch him.'

'They didn't. They just picked the lock. Without you . . .'

'Then . . .' Emily looked wistfully at the garden, with its rampant weeds and untended vegetables. 'I was going to say it was worth it. But it wasn't.'

Nic Costa looked at her, made sure she knew he felt the same way. He'd learned something in Venice. That there was a limit to the price he'd pay – and allow of anyone – from now on.

'No,' he agreed, 'it wasn't. There's an art exhibition planned for Rome in the spring. The biggest in years. Zecchini threw me a ticket to be part of security. It's a reward. I get to see such things. They're bringing a Caravaggio from London for the event. *Boy Bitten by a Lizard.* I'll have to make sure it gets here and back in one piece. Lots of others too. You've been to London. Do you know it?'

'It's wonderful,' Emily said, that familiar spirit of delight now back in her face. 'There's a young, innocent-looking boy, a flower in his hair, the kind Caravaggio liked. He's reaching into a bowl of fruit. All of a sudden a small lizard leaps out and bites his hand. Hard. You see his shock and his hurt, and it's all the more real because he was expecting pleasure. It's an allegory, I guess, about the sudden pain you can get when what you're really expecting is its opposite. You've never seen it?'

Paintings had left his life of late. He realized now how much he missed them.

'When you're unpacked you can help me with the fruit,' Emily Deacon declared. 'Caravaggio or no Caravaggio I'm not letting all those grapes go to waste.'

Nic Costa couldn't wait to witness the canvas close up, real, as alive as the day it was painted, with Emily at his side.

'Everyone gets bitten by the lizard some time,' he said. 'What matters is what happens after.'

5

'Why are you pursuing this, Leo?'

It seemed a curious question.

'Because it's what I do.'

'Without asking yourself the purpose? Or the price?'

She sat on the bench, still, confident. He heard the blast of the vaporetto's horn as it departed the quay on the far side of the island.

'It's what I do,' he said again.

'But why? The Venice Questura won't listen to you. No one will. Not even your own men, I think. Have you told them?'

'No,' he admitted. 'I wanted to discuss this with you first.'

'Always the gentleman,' she said with a brief smile.

'There *is* evidence,' he pointed out. 'You provided it yourself. The shirt with Massiter's monogram and Bella's blood on it. The second DNA sample there, which is primarily sweat, lacks the Y chromosome. Teresa found out shortly before Massiter was killed, too late to be of use unfortunately. It's female DNA. We don't have a sample of yours but I'd put good money on it being a match.'

'I washed everything in that house, some of it by hand,' she said, half-smiling. 'Would that be such a surprise?'

'Then . . .'

Leo Falcone had, to his dismay, never considered this. He was now abruptly aware that he had lost more of his sharpness in hospital than he'd appreciated. There was one plain fact outstanding, though.

'I asked Teresa to bring me the shirt. The monogram was hand-stitched, which would be unusual for a man who would buy his shirts in bulk, even from the best of tailors. Also the cut was poor. More the kind of thing Uriel would have worn than a wealthy Englishman.'

She continued to look at him, bemused, saying nothing.

'You stitched the letters on Uriel's bloodied shirt yourself when you saw the way Nic's mind was working. If the blame was to shift from Bracci, you wanted to ensure it went to Massiter, though not in time to ruin the contract, naturally. Forensic could clarify all this . . .'

'You're a man in a wheelchair, Leo. Not an inspector in charge of a murder inquiry. Badly cut shirts? Hand-stitched letters? Do you think anyone will listen to these ramblings except me?'

He wasn't sure he cared any more.

'I was pleased by this discovery,' Falcone went on. 'Had the shirt really been Massiter's it could only have meant you'd stolen it beforehand, with the idea of killing Bella directly in your mind; that what I was dealing with was a matter of forethought, not some desperate improvization after the fact. I was very glad not to be wrong on that matter.'

Raffaela Arcangelo waited, watching his discomfort at having to make such a personal confession.

'Men never consider these things, do they? Washing. Cleaning. Sewing. All the dreary work. All the drudgery. It just happens somewhere else, performed by unseen hands. None of my brothers noticed. Not even Uriel, who was the nearest to a true human being among them. I was simply one more element in the mechanism of that household. Like a machine or some menial from outside.'

'You sound as if you hated them,' he said, surprised.

She sighed and glanced at the line of cedars separating them from the pale brick perimeter wall and the lagoon. The trees rustled in the growing breeze stirred by the coming change in the season.

'Sometimes I did. Not often. Mostly I felt nothing. Nothing at all. I was the woman. I had to sit there listening to Michele dream up his ridiculous, hare-brained schemes to make us rich again. I had to watch Gabriele turn out glass that would never sell when, with a few changes, with an ear that listened to the outside world, we could have made a little money at least.'

'Michele thought that was the job of the *capo*.'

'Quite! And a woman's never going to fill those shoes, is she?'

'I'm sorry.' Falcone was genuinely shocked. 'I rather imagined there were simpler issues here.'

He hesitated to go on but the bafflement in her face made it impossible to remain silent.

'I wondered if Bella was Massiter's only conquest in the household. Whether perhaps jealousy was involved.'

She laughed out loud then let her face fall in her hands. When she returned to look at him there were tears in her eyes, tears of mirth and amazement, it seemed.

'You thought I would sleep with that creature, Leo? Oh my . . . How could you be so blind? And you're such an observant man in so many other matters! You really do astonish me sometimes.'

Yet it had been easy to be blind. There had been a small fire of jealousy sparking the condition. Leo Falcone understood that. Feelings complicated everything, and had done so throughout.

'I've never slept with anyone,' she said. 'I'm a forty-seven-year-old virgin who has spent her entire life chastely wed to a single belief: that the Arcangeli are the greatest glass-makers in the world, and we must simply wait, like insects trapped in amber, until the rest of you come around to acknowledging that fact. Which was never going to happen, and none of them realized it but me. Whatever Hugo Massiter offered us for the island' – her brown eyes suddenly blazed at him – '*we would take*. I wasn't going to see that last opportunity go to waste. Certainly not over a little slut like Bella who'd sleep with anyone then call back with her price afterwards.'

'She told you about the pregnancy?'

Raffaela shook her head in amazement.

'Of course she did! Are you listening to a single word I say? I was the menial. The servant who washed and cooked and cleaned, while Bella put in her hour or two in the foundry every other night and slept her way round Venice the rest of the time. She told me *because it didn't matter*. All that pressure she was putting on Massiter. Threatening to bring the sale down around his head. She believed Michele's dreams, that Massiter needed us more than we needed him. The woman was too stupid to understand that what she was really jeopardizing was our own future.'

'You could have convinced her.'

'You're still not listening,' she replied with a sudden unexpected bitterness. 'Servants convince no one. If Bella had died as she should, we would all have been better off. As it was . . . Yes! I sent Bracci that note and the keys. I expected he'd make a fool of himself in public, nothing more, and if he took the blame, so be it. Or it could be Massiter, if Nic wished to persist with his obsession. Provided we had his money first.'

She peered at the grave, with its fresh earth and the raw headstone with the newly carved name.

'When she came back to the house I killed her. Then I went to bed and slept. What else was there to do? Poor Uriel never could get anything right. He was always walking into the wrong room, picking up the wrong piece of equipment. I saved him so many times. I couldn't be there every minute of the day.'

She put out a slender hand to the white marble and traced his name with a long index finger.

'Do they haunt me?' she asked. 'Not any more. Life is a series of decisions. Some good. Some bad. Most irreversible. I'm not going to look back, Leo. There's nothing there to see. Uriel's death was a tragic accident. The rest of them were criminals of a kind, with no great fondness for humanity. My main regret' – her hand moved away from the headstone, and stretched out to touch his own – 'is what happened to you. It was so undeserved, and for such a selfless act. I regret that bitterly. When I saw the state Bracci was in, that he had the weapon, I tried to stop him. You saw what happened.'

Her fingers tightened on his hand, her eyes peered into his.

'And you tried to protect me. I told you how desperately sorry I was so many times in that hospital, when I looked at you and didn't know whether I'd ever see that spark in your face again. Now *that* could have broken me. Nothing else. I almost resented it, you know. I thought I was too old and too worn down to be touched by anything. You proved me wrong.'

He shook his head.

'And all the broken lives?' he asked.

'Which ones?' she replied quickly. 'Mine? My brothers'? Bracci's, for God's sake? Don't presume to judge there. What about the lives you and your stubbornness have broken? Young Nic, who put his relationship with that lovely American in jeopardy because he thought something you valued, some distant, hazy notion of justice, was more precious than a simple human emotion like love? And you? Doesn't it seem somewhat ironic that my only real regret in all this concerns what happened to you? And that is the very last thing on your own mind?'

'I do what I do!'

She stood up and pulled his jacket collar more tightly over his shirt. The wind was getting up. The evening was closing in. Cold nights were surely on the way, weeks before their time.

'So what happens now, Inspector Falcone?' she demanded. 'You have a woman here who is willing to look after you for a while, and God knows you're a man who needs caring for. Shouldn't we both be a little selfish for once?'

'This isn't about you or me. It's about the law—'

'Damn the law! What law stopped Hugo Massiter being what he was? What law do all those bent politicians and crooked policemen feel they're beholden to? Play the martyr if you must, but at least find a better cause than that.'

He felt lost for words. Tired, too. That happened a lot at the moment. He was an invalid, however much he fought the idea.

She took out her mobile phone.

'I'll have to call for one of those taxi thieves now. It's just as well I have a little money at last.'

'We haven't finished!' he objected.

Raffaela looked at him, her face full of sympathy and affection. Leo Falcone felt lost at that moment. Venice was, he realized, beyond him, and always had been. It was simply his own arrogance that had tried to persuade him otherwise.

'As far as this matter's concerned, we have, Leo,' she said firmly. 'I'm taking you back to the hospital now. Next week we will begin to make arrangements for moving you to Rome. I hope you'll want me to come, but that's entirely up to you.'

'Get me out of here sooner,' he said, almost without thinking. 'I've had enough of this place.'

She smiled, then, before he could object, leaned down and kissed his cheek. Leo Falcone felt her soft lips brush against his skin, damp, warm, inviting, and tried to remember how long it had been since he'd been embraced by a woman.

'You're not alone in that,' she said. 'But this *is* finished, Leo. What we've discussed here I will never talk about again. Never, do you understand? The world is for the living, not the dead.'

'But . . .'

A single slender finger came and fell upon his lips.

'But nothing. That is the arrangement. Should you break it . . . should you be so rash as to drag me into a police station some day and try to raise these matters again, I will, I swear, do something you'll come to regret.'

He waited.

'I'll confess, Leo,' she said sweetly, taking hold of the wheelchair, propelling him towards the exit. 'And that's a promise.'

6

Gianni Peroni stood by the little *rio*, saying the g-word over and over, pointing the empty weapon at the evening sky. Perhaps it was the gun, or the possibility of change. Whatever the cause, Teresa Lupo, watching him, felt her senses were preternaturally alert. She could hear every last mosquito whirring busily in the reeds, the croak of frogs, the discordant squawk of squabbling gulls, and, so soft they scarcely mattered, the occasional ghostly plaint of a far-off city vaporetto.

Then, nearby, something subtler. Crawling, squirming, hiding all the time, an animal that lurked in the undergrowth, watching, waiting, trying to decode what its senses revealed.

She sat at the picnic table, eyeing the papers with the little farm's photos uppermost, determined not to peek at the details since she knew they'd simply discourage her. It was a small, rundown place. A world away from the bustle of the *centro storico*. A possibility for them. She put it no higher than that.

Peroni barked the g-word again. Still the animal didn't come.

She considered the situation. The last boat back to the city went in half an hour. She'd no intention of staying in Piero Scacchi's shack for the night. There really was no alternative.

'I take it back,' she declared, throwing the box of shells, which he caught in one gigantic hand, grinning at her. 'Give the dog what it wants. If you can, that is.'

He cocked his head. A single glinting eye winked at her. She was surprised, and also a little dismayed, to see the way he was able to grab a couple of cartridges from the box, drop the rest, then rattle two into the gun without even having to look, snapping the weapon shut with a certain, loud clatter.

'If I can?' he asked. 'I'm a country boy. Born and bred. You should never forget that.'

'So, country boy—' she was about to say when what he did made everything unnecessary.

'*Dog!*' he barked with a fresh, commanding insistence.

Within the space of a few seconds a feathery shape emerged from the reeds, its lithe body rising like a bullet, chased on its way by what sounded like a rough, sharp bark. Peroni swung the gun. A single, now familiar, sound rent the peace of the lagoon. Teresa watched in shocked admiration, and a little wonder, as the bundle of feathers turned in on itself, rolled into a ball, then tumbled into some prickly thicket on the far side of the *rio*.

A black shape chased through the water after it, half swimming, half leaping, disappearing into the vegetation for a moment before emerging with a triumphant, energetic swagger, something soft held tight in its jaws.

Gianni Peroni broke the gun, dropped the two cartridges, one spent, one live, on the ground, held the weapon over his arm, then extended his open hand across the *rio*.

'Good dog,' he declared loudly. '*Good* dog. Now come.'

Piero Scacchi's spaniel emerged from the reeds carrying the dead bird, marching towards him, full of pride and expectation.

Fur matted and dishevelled, it looked as skinny as an abandoned orphan. The animal walked up to Peroni, dropped its prize at his feet, then sat, a tired black triangle wagging a short stumpy tail uncertainly, eyes never leaving his face, rapt in the man's approval.

Teresa Lupo watched the two of them admiring each other and said nothing.

Eventually Peroni looked up at her, patting that small black head, his face as serious as she'd ever known it.

'You don't want to go, do you?' he asked.

'No,' she said straight away. 'Not yet anyway.'

Not when the possibility became real. It wasn't cowardice either. Something told Teresa that dreams were meant to be hunted down on home territory, not chased in some never-land around an unknown corner.

It was a sweet dog all the same. Quite unsuited for the city, where it would be terrified by the noise and the traffic and the commotion.

'Laila would love him,' she added. The girl was another of Peroni's rescues, a bright, recovering teenager out on a farm in Tuscany, someone who'd adore the animal given half a chance.

'I know,' Peroni agreed, with a swiftness that made her realize this thought had been with him all along. He didn't look disappointed at all. He was good at hiding his feelings. She knew that.

Quietly, stealthily, Gianni Peroni slipped an old leather leash round the animal's neck then held it firmly, with affection.

'Let's go,' he said.